Making It Home

Christine Campbell was brought up in Gourock on the Firth of Clyde and now lives in a village near Edinburgh with her husband and youngest daughter. Christine also has four married children and ten grandchildren.

Also by Christine Campbell
Published by YouWriteOn and Legend press
2008

Family Matters

Making It Home

Christine Campbell

The characters and events in this book are entirely fictional.
No reference to any person, living or dead,
Is intended or should be inferred.

Published in 2009 by YouWriteOn.com

Published by YouWriteOn.com
And Legend Press
Printed by Lightning Source

Christine Campbell

My grateful thanks to all the friends and writing buddies
who have critiqued, advised and generally encouraged me in
my writing, to Sharlene for proofreading under pressure, to Tim
Pow for the cover photo for this novel, and my to son, Andrew,
for the cover photo for my last novel, *Family Matters.*
And, most of all, to my dear husband, who has always been
a tremendous source of help and encouragement.

Dan sat back on his heels, staring at the book in his hands. It was beautiful. It had been carefully wrapped in an old silk scarf and hidden deep in the space between some loose bricks. How long it had remained secreted there he could only guess, but it had the appearance of being very old. And it was beautiful.

His first instinct had been to call out to Kate. She loved old things, was always trailing round second hand shops, bringing home silly bric-a-brac, though he had to admit she found some bargains too. She had furnished this place with her 'finds'. He raised his head to call, then remembered.

Chapter 1

Kate was a 'floater'.

She didn't really need to work at all. Dan was earning well enough and the kids had long since grown up and left home. But Kate enjoyed the company, the routine, the life of the workplace. She was naturally a gregarious person and the house was too quiet now that Vicky and Paul were gone.

Dan was a reticent man and his long silences had become more noticeable as he got older. So she fed on the bustle of the few hours she spent at her work during the silent mealtimes and lonely evenings of her married life.

It hadn't always been so. When she was first married, just being with Dan, looking after their tiny flat, cooking for him; it had all been an adventure. She had been so young, so ready to love, so eager to live. She hadn't noticed the silence, it hadn't mattered. It was filled with the songs in her heart.

But the years had passed as they relentlessly do. The shiny newness of married life dulled like the copper pans that hung in her kitchen. Dreams of happy-ever-after seemed childish now.

So, when the children became independent, she sought paid employment for the first time in her life, her workplace of the past twelve years being a large department store in Edinburgh. Because she was only part-time, she was used wherever she was needed. She 'floated' from department to department, floor to floor, when someone else was sick or on holiday, or they were short-staffed for any other reason.

She was a 'floater'.

But that was at work. That was what she *did*. It wasn't what she *was*. It wasn't *who* she was.

She was steady, reliable, always there: someone you could depend on.

Perhaps that had been the trouble.

When she started in Harrison's, she didn't imagine she'd be there for long. She had other plans, other things she thought she'd try. But somehow time had passed and here she was, twelve years on, still 'floating'. But, some day…

Meantime, the bustle and life of the shop kept her going. Being a 'people person', a keen observer of life's passing pageant; she liked to imagine the lives of the customers she served. Sometimes, when the shop was quiet, she'd act out the different kinds of customer for the entertainment of her colleagues. Or she'd tell them the history she invented for them, complete with all the voices she needed to make the story live. Sometimes she'd have them laughing; sometimes they'd be enthralled by the drama she unfolded before them.

"You should be on the stage! You really should," Brenda, from Coats told her.

"Better than anything on the telly," Marie from Kitchens assured her.

Throughout the shop, she was invariably greeted with delight when sent to any department.

"You have a way of making the day pass quicker," Tom from Gents Shoes told her.

Who of them would guess the life she lived herself? The cheerful, helpful assistant and entertainer donned a sadder mantle when she walked through the shop door at home-time.

Since he always left his work at the office, she assumed Dan had no time for her stories and sketches of shop life, doubting he'd find them either amusing or interesting, if he even remembered where she worked: she mentioned it so rarely.

But, in the shop, she found an audience eager to share her observations.

There was the Careful Shopper, often a mother of an indeterminate brood, seeking good value, an occasional bargain, always examining the considered item carefully, minutely, testing for weaknesses, on the lookout for flaws. Unusual for her to purchase first time. More likely she would go off to make comparison elsewhere, returning in a day or two with new resolve to complete the transaction. Never a big spender, often handling the luxury items but never with any serious consideration.

Kate would smile as she served this lady, silently wishing her happiness, longing to assure her that the children would not always be young, she should enjoy them while she could. All too soon they'd move on from computer games to dating games and, all too soon, they'd be gone: building a life of their own.

By the time the woman walked to the escalator, Kate had a complete, potted history invented for her, including a hard-working, taciturn husband, suitable children, maybe a dog or cat, sometimes even a mother-in-law. After she'd disappeared from view, the domestic drama would play on in Kate's imagination for a while till the next customer required her attention or until one of the girls asked for the story.

"You should write these down," Hilda from Toys told her. "I hope you've been writing these down."

There were the Holiday Shoppers, often American or Japanese, festooned with cameras and the paraphernalia of tourism, talking loudly, leaving an untidy trail of discarded items in their wake. They would wander in from Princes Street, still in wonder that there could be a castle on one side and the busiest stretch of shopping on the other. Their imaginations making the transition from military memorabilia to cashmere sweaters with no more than a glorious expanse of grass and flowers in between, cushioning the impact of the traffic noise.

For them, it was the old-world charm of Harrison's that brought them through the door. The soft carpeting, the wooden counters and graceful balconies. They were seldom disappointed by the wholesome virtues of the things proffered on the elegant rails and sturdy shelves.

Much depended on the age and race in deciding their stories and acting them out. The life of young Japanese students, chattering gaily in their indecipherable tongue, must differ greatly from that of the stocky Texan oil-couple. Kate would study them all and always there was a clue, here or there, to their history. She would smile warmly when serving them, wishing them a happy visit, glad that they could pass her way.

Never cruel, Kate would play the parts with a sense of fun but never cynicism: her caricatures were gentle. Should the subjects of her studies ever happen upon the act, they'd surely smile to see their lives so well portrayed.

Occasionally, there was the Frenzied Shopper, the one who HAS to buy something. *Now. Today.* Perhaps a last minute present for the hostess of the dinner party tonight, or the mother-in-law arriving to visit, or a suddenly-remembered birthday present, hastily chosen, usually totally useless, probably seldom appreciated. Kate smiled kindly as she served them, helped them with their choices, tutted gently at their lack of foresight and delighted her colleagues with imagined scenarios.

The Serious Shopper, the one who bought all that took her fancy, was one rich in imagery. Not hard to concoct a fitting drama around this one; the rich, spoiled debutante or the bored, unhappy, wife of the wealthy businessman. Kate would watch as a squirrel-like hoard grew on the counter, all to be wrapped and bagged and carried home, to be forgotten till the winter. Always falsely breezy, this one had no need of Kate's smile, never saw it was there, but Kate smiled anyway, with sad acknowledgement that here was someone less well-off than herself. Pity hindered her performance and she rarely lingered long in their theatre.

Funny about Phyllis and Naomi. How they had formed a friendship, the three of them. How their stories intertwined and became one.

Naomi fell into none of those categories of shopper.

Neither did Phyllis. She was a very well-dressed, well-spoken, typically Well-Bred Lady; curly grey-haired perm, red lipstick and gloves. Kate guessed she was about late seventies, early eighties.

Nothing remarkable there.

Many of their customers fitted that profile. Harrison's was a classy, fairly conservative department store.

The fact that Phyllis shopped midweek was equally unsurprising. After all, why would a lady of her age and stage get embroiled in the busy Saturday stew unnecessarily?

Kate had been in Classic Suits and Coats for six weeks, an unusually long stint. She was covering for Mavis, the Westmorland saleslady, who had had a fairly serious operation. Poor Mavis was not doing so well and was not expected back for a few weeks yet, so Kate would have plenty time to settle in before being moved on.

She hated that.

Better not to get too settled, too comfortable. Before you knew it you were thinking of it as 'my department' and getting uptight about how it was run. Better to let the others, the permanents, the full-timers, worry about layouts and turnover.

On the plus side, after six weeks you could get to know the girls pretty well. And the regular customers. Having no wish to cause offence, Kate made it a rule never to deliberately impersonate individual customers, especially those who visited often.

Phyllis was certainly what you could term 'a regular customer'. She had been in, faithfully, every Wednesday afternoon of the six weeks Kate had been in Classic Suits and Coats. In itself that too was nothing remarkable. There were lots of 'regulars' in Harrison's; ladies of that certain age who liked to browse and linger among the homely suits and comfortable coats.

More surprising, however, was the fact that Phyllis bought something each time. These were expensive items. Not something you needed too many of.

"It's not for me," she confided in Kate as the pure wool, cashmere coat was carefully wrapped. "It's my daughter's birthday next week. She's about my size, a twelve, but a bit taller, so I'm hoping it will fit. Do you think she'll like it? I imagine she's about your age and height. What do you think?"

"I think she'll love it. I would. It's a beautiful coat. A lovely choice."

Phyllis smiled smugly. "You can hardly go wrong with a Westmorland coat."

"Exactly, Mrs Thaine. Now, would you like that delivered or are you going to carry it with you?"

"Delivered please."

"No trouble. If you'd just like to sign here." She indicated the dotted line on the sales slip, "I already have your address. Or would you rather have it delivered straight to your daughter?"

"No, no. My address. Thank you."

Nothing remarkable there.

But *every week*! Every week a coat, or a suit. For a daughter, for a sister, for herself.

"She must have plenty of money," Elaine, the 'permanent', concluded. She and Kate had often remarked on Phyllis's extravagance. "She's been a customer at Harrison's for years. Only buys the best. Last week, was it not one of the cashmere suits? The green one? Beautiful! For her niece, didn't she say?"

"She seems to be a very generous soul."

"And well-off!"

"I keep getting this feeling that I've met her before," Kate mused.

But Elaine was gliding over to assist her next customer, leaving Kate searching her imperfect memory for the where and when of it.

She had served Phyllis Thaine personally each of these past six weeks. But it wasn't that.

Her mind stole around the edges of the recollection while she tidied the counter. "Nearly hometime," she sighed, folding soft woollen jumpers, holding them to her, waltzing round the island unit, giving Elaine a dance as she passed.

"I don't know what I'll do for entertainment when Mavis comes back. She's not much of a one for dancing and storytelling," Elaine said, disentangling herself to straighten a rail of skirts.

It had been a quiet day, a long day. Of course, this was a quiet department, on the whole, both in marketing terms and literal: even normal sounds, footsteps, coughing, conversation, were muffled by the thick carpeting and the rails of wool garments. Mohair and cashmere, soft and warm to touch, discrete colours, gentle elegance.

A sheltered department.

Perhaps even a little dull.

Like having Sunday roast every day.

However, she sighed again, it looked like she was going to be here for some weeks more, so she would just have to get on with it.

Kate prided herself on her ability to 'get on with it'. She'd had to. Dan wasn't a man of action. Marriage to him, while not being particularly harsh, had been a little monotonous, a little dull too.

Well, a lot dull actually.

More mince and tatties than Sunday roast!

They never went anywhere, never holidayed. Unless you counted two weeks every second year down at her sister's in Dumfries. The other year, her sister came to them.

It had been better when Vicky and Paul were kids. At least she had been able to fill her life with all the ups and downs of raising children, all the comings and goings of teenagers, the passions and pains of young adult courtships.

She liked children. Felt alive with them. Probably why she liked working in Toys or Children's Shoes. The Food Hall was good too, nice and busy. And Kitchens. She liked working in Kitchens.

Of course! It had been when she was in Kitchens!

Mrs Thaine had been modernising her kitchen.

Every Wednesday afternoon, of the three Kate had worked in that department a few months earlier, Mrs Thaine had added to her set of pots and pans. Lovely pots they were too. Expensive. She had them delivered each time. Kate served her each time.

But Kate had forgotten. After all, it was hardly important.

That had been a few months ago, but since she had been in Classic Suits and Coats she had had that feeling of déjà vu, the address as well as the lady, whenever Phyllis Thaine came in.

Kitchens! That's where it had been.

Thinking of kitchens reminded Kate that she'd forgotten to take anything out of the freezer for tea. Oh well, she could always stop on the way home and buy something from M&S. Something easy, ready to cook. Her mouth watered at the prospect. 'Mmmm! Not just *any* ready meal! Mark's and Spencer's!' she crooned as she continued to tidy, her mind made up to go for the later bus and enjoy her browse in the M&S food department.

Nothing to rush home for anyway. Wednesday. Football on the box. Another lonely evening in the summerhouse.

When they had moved into their 'Attractive, Three-bedroomed, Semi-detached' twenty-eight years ago, she had asked Dan to knock down the old summerhouse in the back garden but he never had. Never had the time, she supposed. Or the energy.

She had wanted him to turf the back, give the kids more room to play.

The kids hadn't been bothered. There was plenty of room to play in the front garden or at the side. Besides, there was a swing-park just two blocks away, four houses, not too far, once they were a little older. She had no ally in her campaign to have the summerhouse removed.

The people who had the house before them had obviously not thought much of the summerhouse either. They'd neglected its upkeep and had used it to store garden tools and garden furniture. At first, once it became clear that Dan was not going to do anything about it, she used it for the same ignoble purpose, adding the children's bikes and scooters to its clutter.

Dan suggested she might use it as a greenhouse since it had a sturdy, wide shelf all round the inside, at about waist height, but until the glass could be scraped and polished, there was little light filtering through to nourish any plants she might like to grow. He made it clear that he had no intention of undertaking such a scraping and polishing work, that he didn't deem it worth the effort.

He preferred to sit in front of the telly than work in the garden. Well, she didn't suppose he was alone in that. If only he wouldn't simultaneously moan about the state of it. Oh, he kept the front tidy enough, mowing the grass fairly regularly and cutting the hedge. The shrubs and flowers had all been chosen by the previous owner for their hardiness and durability, needing scant attention, which was just as well, since that was all they got.

Every few years, he would use some of his holiday time to 'blitz' the house. At least two rooms would get a complete overhaul before he ran out of steam. She shouldn't really complain. He worked hard all week, deserved his evenings and weekends in front of the telly. Or so he told her when she did complain.

He never did get around to the summerhouse.

The first really big rows they had in that house were over it; the summerhouse. And it was there that she eventually went to sulk. There'd been nowhere else to go. She'd sat on a hard, plastic, garden chair, nursing her anger at his refusal to help her either pull it down or spruce it up. And she decided to do it herself.

She set about it with a will born of the rage inside her. It fuelled her, giving her the needed energy for the task on hand. She scrubbed and scraped, whitewashed and painted. She learned how to mastic windows and she bought sheets of hardboard for the floor.

Her original intention had just been to make it usable as a greenhouse, but as it emerged from the grime of generations of neglect, she grew to love the dilapidated old folly.

Each time she sank, exhausted, into that garden chair to survey her handiwork, the idea grew that here could be a special place.

She gradually cleaned it up, made it watertight and furnished it with a radio, a heater, some old, comfy chairs and rugs. All lovingly sought out and carted home one way or another from second-hand shops. It became her retreat.

When she and Dan argued or he was giving her the 'silent treatment', she sought the solitude of that leafy arbour, for she had filled it with plants of every shape and size, plants that flourished in its sun-filled warmth in the summer, plants that thrived in its shelter in the winter, their green, luscious smell mixing with the earthy smell of the compost, imparting a warm, fecund aroma of which she never tired, the smell of hedgerows in autumn, woodland undergrowth in spring.

When Dan was watching sport on the telly, something she had no love of, she withdrew to her gazebo of dreams. Because that is what she did there. She dreamed. She dreamed of a life very different from the one she lived, where she laughed and danced, surrounded by friends and family, seldom alone, never lonely: a life where she wandered those hedgerows and woods, exploring the hidden depths of the undergrowth, looking for treasure, wood anemones, columbine, ferns and mosses, sharing her finds with a loving companion, savouring the delights of each passing day.

Even when Vicky and Jonathan and their children stopped by, it was to the summerhouse she would come, bringing her grandchildren to share her garden room, telling them stories, spinning them dreams.

Just as she had when Vicky and Paul had been young:

As bedtime neared, she would entice her children from their outdoor games with promises of hot chocolate and stories in the summerhouse.

'Why do you call it a summerhouse, Mummy?'

'I don't know really. Perhaps because you could almost live out here in the summer, when it's warm.'

'But I like it best when it's winter and we have to have the heater on and the windows steam up and we can draw on them and the drips trickle down and we can play races with them and... it's our special place, isn't it Mummy?'

But it was never Vicky's special place as it had been Paul's.

Vicky was her father's favourite. She loved the things he loved, telly-sport, Coronation Street, the fireside with their slippers on.

It was Paul who helped Kate paint the summerhouse, inside and out.

When he was young, he lay along the old sofa reaching out to shake the dice, make his moves up the ladders, down the snakes. When he was older, it was here she taught him chess. They played games, told stories and whispered dreams and they built a bond as unshakable as she wished the old summerhouse was.

But it was getting old. The wood was rotting. The glass rattled. The wind found new gaps every winter. The old summerhouse needed more care and attention than Kate was capable of providing. Major repairs were becoming imperative and Dan was for knocking it down.

They'd had a blazing row about it and she had even slept out there one night. Hadn't returned to his bed ever since.

***

"Nice to see things never change." Vicky breezed into the kitchen the day after The Row. "You two not speaking again?"

"Hello to you too, dear," responded her mother. "Where are the children?"

"I dropped them off at Cub Scouts. So…" She waited, hands on hips. "What's it about this time? I could feel the atmosphere as soon as I opened the car door."

"The usual. Your father's being Bolshi."

"And you're being pig-headed, I suppose."

"That's right. You just take his side. On you go. Don't wait to find out the facts. Just make your judgement anyway."

Vicky shook her head. "I'm not taking sides."

"Of course you are. You always do." Kate threw the cloth she had been using into the sink.

"I don't!"

"Then why assume I'm being pig-headed?"

"Because you usually are."

"What would you know about how I usually am?" Kate questioned. "You never spend any time with me," she declared. "Straight into the damn telly with your dad, that's what a visit from you means."

"Good grief, Mother! Who rattled your cage?"

Kate picked up the kettle; banged it down again still empty. "I don't know why you bother to come at all!" She started to tidy the utensils that were gathered into a stone jar at the back of the worktop. "You could watch telly in your own house. You'd get more conversation out of your cat than you'll ever get from him," she said, nodding towards the living room.

Vicky's eyes went heavenward. "Guess it was 'him'," she muttered in response to her own question.

"Not that you're much better. For conversation," Kate continued. "I can't remember the last time you sat and talked."

"Come on, Mum. Give it a rest," Vicky sighed, picking up the paper from the table, turning to the television listings, checking her watch.

"There! See what I mean?"

Vicky gave her a patronising grin. "Have you finished your tantrum yet?" she asked. "Only it's time for Eastenders."

The gathering storm glowered in her mother's eyes.

"Are you going to offer me a cup of tea or do I have to make it myself?"

"Oh, make it yourself!" were the words hurled back as Kate slammed out the back door.

"You can make one for me too, Doll," Dan's voice floated through from the living room. "Your mother's on strike."

Chapter 2

"You look sad," Phyllis said softly as she came to the counter the following Wednesday.

"Oh sorry, Mrs Thaine. I was miles away."

"And sad."

"Yes, and sad."

"Nothing too awful, I hope?"

Kate shook her head and smiled. "No, just a touch of nostalgia for a decrepit old summerhouse. Now, how can I help you, Mrs Thaine?"

"Well. You *can* help me actually. You always do," she smiled. "You're most patient and kind."

"Why, thank you," Kate said, blushing with surprise and embarrassment.

"So today, I'm not going to buy anything, but I'd like you to accept this little gift." Phyllis handed her a parcel. "I think it will suit you. And I know it will fit you, because we're about the same size, wouldn't you say?"

"Well… yes. We are the same size."

"A 'ten'? I thought so. Well. Aren't you going to open it?"

"But, I can't… I mean, I can't accept this."

"Why ever not?"

"It's really most kind of you, but…"

"No 'buts'. If I choose to give someone a present, I don't expect them to refuse."

"But…"

"Open it!" Phyllis commanded.

Stunned into obedience, Kate opened the parcel. It contained a beautiful, soft, cashmere cardigan. She knew immediately that she would love to have it.

"But I can't keep it," she said.

"Why not? Don't you like it?"

"I love it."

"Then have it. It's yours."

Kate raised it to her face. It was so soft. And the colour: the colour was of sunset, that few moments when the sky is on fire.

"It suits you. I thought it would. Goes with your auburn hair. What colour are your eyes?" Phyllis Thaine peered into her face.

"Sort of a greeny-brown I think," Kate answered with surprise.

"Hazel, I think they call it. You're an 'autumn', you see."

"Autumn?"

"Your colouring. Auburn hair, ivory skin, hazel eyes. Autumn. You suit the soft, warm shades."

"But really, I can't keep it. It's too much. You're too generous."

"Of course you can keep it. I can afford it, and I want you to have it."

"Well…" Kate hesitated. "Thank you!" She leant forward and gently kissed the older lady's cheek. There were tears in her eyes as she looked at her wonderful gift. "I don't think I've ever owned a more beautiful garment."

"Good! I'm glad we've got that settled. Now, tell me, when do you get a teabreak or something?"

Kate looked at her watch. "Well, I finish in half an hour."

"I'll wait for you in the coffee shop. Or are you rushing home?"

"No."

Nothing to rush home for. Wednesday. Football on the box. Another lonely evening in the summerhouse.

"Good. I thought it would be nice to have a coffee together."

Kate laughed. "It would be lovely. And I would be delighted. But only if it's my treat!"

***

"So tell me about yourself," Phyllis demanded after they'd bought their coffee and cakes and were settled at a small round table in Harrison's Coffee Shop.

The surroundings suited Phyllis. Kate had never really paid much attention to the place before. It was just somewhere to have a break and refreshment. Now, she noticed that it was quite elegantly furnished: dark wooden tables, comfortably padded chairs. There were pictures on the pale cream walls: prints of paintings she recognised as famous, Monet mostly, as well as some she'd never seen before. The lower half of the walls, below a matching dado rail, was the same dark wood as the tables and chairs. It all had an air of old-fashioned elegance: the perfect setting for such a delightfully old-fashioned lady.

"You're married." Phyllis nodded in the direction of Kate's wedding ring. "Any children?"

"Two. A girl and a boy."

"Ages?"

"Vicky's thirty-four. Paul, thirty-two."

"You must have been a very young mum."

"I was." Kate blushed. "Sweet sixteen… and wish I'd only been kissed!"

"Pregnant when you married then?"

Kate was a little taken aback by the older woman's directness. Often that generation were a little bashful about such topics. Her own mum certainly was. In fact, she never quite recovered from the shame of Kate's disgrace. She had made a great point of telling everybody that Vicky was a honeymoon baby. 'Six weeks premature,' she'd said. Pretty hard to be convincing though, when Vicky was a bouncing seven-and-a-half pounder!

"'Fraid so," she admitted.

"And no help for it in those days?"

"Absolutely not. We 'Had To Get Married'. No other choice. My dad made that very clear. Anyway," Kate laughed a little wryly. "I wanted to get married. Thought it was really romantic. Getting married, having babies. It's what I'd always wanted. Or at least, I thought it was."

"The romance wore off then?"

"Quickly. Once I had two toddlers and a husband who didn't have a clue what to do with kids. I'm afraid Dan didn't have much time for them until they could watch the football. Although, to his credit, he was a good provider. Worked hard. 'Department of Trade and Industry'. He's quite high up in it now and very well respected, as far as I can tell. Not that he talks about his work. Just that my neighbour's husband works in the same department. Under Dan, actually. He seems to think the world of him. Says he's a great manager." She shrugged. "He's beginning to get tired though. I think they've worn him down. He'd love to get out."

"Any chance?"

"Oh heavens! I hope not. I couldn't be doing with him underfoot all the time."

"He'd surely get something else though?"

"Perhaps." Kate shuddered. "Anyway, what about you?"

"Oh you don't want to hear about me." Phyllis held out the delicate china plate of cakes. "Here! Why don't you try one of these strawberry tarts? They really are delicious."

It became a habit. Every Wednesday they would meet for coffee when Kate finished work. By the time she moved to Petites and then to Household Linen, weeks later, it had become an institution, their hour together in The Coffee Shop.

Kate would describe her working week: the customers she'd observed, the lives she'd envisioned for them.

"I really look forward to my Wednesdays, you know," Phyllis confided. "I love your company. You're very kind to indulge a silly old woman like me."

"I don't know a silly old woman like you," Kate replied. "I know a lady, a very interesting, encouraging lady. You encourage me to analyse my life in a way I've never done before. It's funny, you know," she said between mouthfuls of strawberries and cream. "My life seems... well... it seems to have amounted to something when you ask about it."

"Every life amounts to something."

"I know... but..."

"You brought up two children. That's a great achievement."

"It doesn't feel like an achievement. Just a lot of hard work... and for what? To watch them go off and make a life of their own, with very little room for me in it."

"But isn't that what it was all about? Training little ones to be responsible, independent adults, ready to start the process all over with their own children? A twenty year project?"

"Huh. Twenty years! I wonder if the project is ever finished."

"Well, you can't have it both ways. Either they've gone off and become independent, leaving you with an empty nest... or they're still your project!"

"But you can have both, in a way... and not necessarily a satisfying way. Yes, they go off, leaving you with that horrible, empty, useless feeling, as though they systematically emptied you over the years, leaving you feeling wrung out and useless. But you can't quite stamp the project finished. You still worry about them. They still expect you to be 'Mum'. There for them at the drop of a hat when they need you; on hold when they don't. They don't include you in their life but they still expect to *be* yours. Sometimes I wonder if they think my life goes onto the pause button when they stop watching."

"But isn't it up to you how your life runs? Isn't it you who presses the buttons?"

"Except they've got the remote control."

"Then you must take it back," Phyllis stated firmly.

They sat in thoughtful silence for a while, the idea shimmering in the air between them.

* * *

It was while she was in Ladies Dresses that Kate met Naomi.

Every Wednesday, for four weeks, Naomi was waiting at the counter when Kate got back from her lunchbreak.

"Hi!" She waited for Kate. Others had tried to serve her, but she had declined their assistance.

"Hello again," Kate said with a smile. "How can I help you?"

"I was wondering..." She looked around almost furtively. "Do you think, I mean, would it be alright if I changed this dress?"

27

"Of course, Madam. No problem." She took the proffered carrier bag and pulled out the shimmering blue evening dress, checking it over cursorily. She had to check that it had not been worn or damaged in any way. But really! She smiled at the poor, plain, obviously unhappy woman in front of her. She felt it highly unlikely that this poor soul went anywhere she would need such a glitzy, daring garment. "Now, have you chosen something else, or can I help you do that?"

"Thank you. I wondered if I could try on this one?" She held up the hanger to display her choice.

"Of course," Kate said warmly. "Let me take it to the fitting room for you. Now, is there another perhaps?"

"Oh, I don't know."

"What about the black?"

"Oh, yes, that is rather pretty. Yes, thank you."

They went through the same performance, with different dresses, each week: Naomi chose one each week... then brought it back, unworn, to exchange it the next.

The floor supervisor frowned at each transaction she witnessed.

"Why do you let her away with it?" she hissed at Kate when Naomi was out of earshot.

"Look at her," Kate said. "Does she look happy?"

"So?"

"Well, if trying on these glamorous gowns, even taking them home to play make-believe, gives her a boost, why should we spoil it? Anyway. Isn't it shop policy to exchange and refund where there is just cause?"

"Yeah, but what's her 'just cause'?"

"She doesn't want to keep them."

"Huh!" The supervisor couldn't quite find grounds for refusal to make the exchanges... but it was clear she would like to.

"Meanness of spirit, if you ask me," offered Phyllis when Kate recounted the exchanges, both material and verbal. "Some people don't like to see others get pleasure from something they don't."

"I think you're right. Ms Ferguson seems such an unhappy wee soul. I wish I could help."

"I guess you probably do. By helping her indulge her dreams."

"Perhaps. But I'd like to do more. She's a young woman. Can't be forty yet. I hate to see her so sad already. I hate to see anyone so sad, actually... at any age."

"No, you're right. Do you think she'd like to join us for coffee?"

Kate laughed. "Why on earth would she want to join us for coffee?"

Phyllis looked hurt. "Well, why not?"

"Phyllis, she doesn't know us."

"So?"

"Why would she want to have coffee with complete strangers?"

"If she's lonely, perhaps she'd be glad of the chance of some company. Besides, perhaps we could help her if she's as unhappy as you think."

Kate softened. "That's a kind idea. But she told me today that it was her lunch-hour. Presumably, she works."

"Ask her what time she finishes."

"You're quite the 'Good Samaritan', aren't you?" Kate teased... but not unkindly. She smiled ruefully at her friend. "Trouble is, I've only till the end of this week in that department."

"Oh dear. What shall we do then?"

"I don't know that there's anything that we *can* do."

"We shall have to wait and see."

They didn't have to wait too long.

The next week, Kate was in Ladies Shoes... and so was Naomi Ferguson. It was Wednesday, and once again, after Kate's lunchbreak, but a little later.

"Well, hello Ms Ferguson. How are you today?"

"Oh, how nice. You took me by surprise. Aren't you usually in the dress department?"

"Yes. Or at least, I was for a few weeks. But how can I help you?"

"Actually," Naomi went through the furtive-glance-round routine, familiar to Kate by now. "I was wondering if I might change these shoes? I haven't worn them or anything," she added hastily. "It's just that... it's just that... they aren't... they don't..."

"That's no problem, Ms Ferguson. Now, what had you in mind?"

Kate, with kindly patience, helped her customer to select another pair of shoes from the many she brought for her to try on. It took almost half an hour. The supervisor of this department, being from the same mould as the one from Dresses... Kate wondered if it was their training or perhaps a requirement of the promotion... was furious.

"Did you not see the queue?"

"I didn't want to rush my customer."

"She's not much of a customer! Let me tell you something about Ms Ferguson. She has been coming in here for weeks now. She bought a pair of shoes... *one* pair of shoes... weeks ago, and she has been exchanging shoes on the basis of that purchase, regularly, ever since."

"So? Is she not still a customer?"

"Only in the loosest sense of the word! Now, Mrs Morgan. While you are in *my* department..."

Kate cringed. That's exactly what she dreaded happening to her if she stayed too long in one place. You could easily come to put performance above people. She shuddered.

"While you are in *my* department," her supervisor was saying, "you give her a minimum of time and attention. Get her to choose quickly and get on with the paying customers. Is that clear?"

Kate felt it was only too clear. There was a lonely, unhappy woman, trying to take some comfort from the choosing and buying of items she could probably ill-afford... and here was an unfeeling, uncaring organisation and its servants. The two could not be happy partners. Sooner or later, someone was going to get hurt. Kate doubted it would be the department store.

She wanted to protect Naomi, but was not confident she could, even if it was her business, which she was confident it was not.

"Why did you not invite her for coffee?" queried Phyllis later.

"How could I? You can't just suddenly say, *'Here's your shoes. By the way, do you want to come for coffee?'*"

"I would."

"You probably would. But I can't. She'd think I was mad... or worse... propositioning her or something!"

"Don't be silly!" Phyllis tutted, "You didn't think that when I asked you to have coffee with me."

"The circumstances were different."

"So? Engineer suitable circumstances."

"Huh! I suppose that's this week's challenge?"

"If you like. An important one though. Because it's not for *you*, you'll be doing it."

As it happened, thinking about Naomi Ferguson was low on Kate's list that week.

Dan was talking again about early retirement. It seems there was a chance it could come off.

"So what would you do, if you do get the chance?" Kate asked.

"What do you mean, what would I do? I'd take it. Have you not been listening, Katie? I'm not being made redundant. I'm seeking early retirement. I've requested it."

"I know that."

"So what are you on about?"

"I mean, what will you *do*?"

"I've told you..."

"Oh, for heaven's sake, Dan. I mean what will you do all day? If you retire, you won't be going to the office every day..."

"That's certainly the plan."

"So, what will you *do*?" Kate repeated yet again.

"Grief! Change the record, Kate."

"I mean, will you get a part time job, will you take up voluntary work, will you...?"

Dan stared at her. "Why on earth would I want to do that? If I wanted to go out to work, I'd stay where I am."

"But what would you *do*?"

"Don't start again, Kate. You're always moaning that we don't do anything together... Maybe we could do things."

Kate looked at him doubtfully. "What kind of things?"

"Oh, I don't know... things."

"Like watch daytime telly as well as evening? Wonderful!"

"You could give your job up too and we could..."

"Why does everyone want me to give up my job? I like my job. I only work three days as it is. I've no intentions of giving up my job so that I can vegetate with you."

"Okay, okay! Calm down. No-one says you have to... "

"Good! And don't tell me to calm down!"

"I just thought..."

"Well you can just think again, Dan Morgan. If you think..."

"Look, it doesn't matter what I think. You're obviously not ready to discuss this reasonably."

"Reasonably? Why should I discuss it reasonably? Why should I look forward to having even more of you sitting around the house? When would I get the housework done?"

"I could help you."

Kate exploded. "Help? When have you ever helped me with the housework?"

"When have you ever let me?"

They stood across the kitchen table from one another, both glaring angrily.

At last, Dan broke the tense silence. "Anyway, there's nothing definite yet," he mumbled.

"Good," retorted Kate. "That'll give you time to think about your plans, because if you think I'm having you hanging around *my* house, under *my* feet all day, you have another think coming!"

"*Whose* house?" Dan stared incredulously at her. "*Whose* house? I paid every penny of the mortgage on this house with *my* hard-earned cash. I have worked for more than forty years. I think I'm entitled to stop now, if I choose... *and* I think I'm entitled to sit around my own house, if I choose. And, if you don't like it, then you know where the door is!"

Kate stood, shocked into silence at last.

Dan had never said anything like that to her before. In all the years of their marriage, through all their ups and downs, the silly rows and the serious arguments, he had never suggested she should go. That he even thought it, that he might want her to, had never occurred to her. Nor had she ever thought of going... before.

They didn't speak for days. They each had a lot of thinking to do, or at least, Kate did a lot of thinking... and she hoped Dan did too. There had to be give and take here, and she hoped he'd do some of the giving.

She couldn't bear it if he retired without something else in mind other than hanging around the house... even if, technically, it was his.

* * *

"I often wonder if any of them could describe Me... Dan and the kids, I mean," she complained to Phyllis. "As a person, I mean. What I'm like. What I think. What I want? And I bet they haven't noticed that I've got grey in my hair now, that I have to wear reading glasses sometimes."

Phyllis stroked her hand. "Do *you* know what you want?"

Kate shook her head. "No," she smiled. "In fact, I don't think *I* know Me either," she laughed.

"Then it's time you spent some time getting to know You. Time to give yourself some attention."

"I wouldn't know where to start!" The smile still lingered but it had become more wistful, touched by the longing of a half forgotten feeling.

'Time to give yourself some attention,' the words echoed in Kate's mind as she made the meal that evening.

She watched her hands as they peeled the vegetables: they were dry and chapped, the nails too short and uneven, the cuticles ragged. Rinsing the potatoes under the running tap, she watched as her fingers went red with the cold. Drying them roughly on the kitchen towel, she felt them tingle, watched the warmth flow back into them.

After their meal, while Dan settled himself in front of 'the box', Kate searched in the drawer of her dressing table, certain that there must be a nail-file buried there. And some hand cream, she hoped.

She knew Phyllis wasn't talking about her appearance. But it was somewhere to start.

So she sat in her summerhouse, the radio tuned to Classic FM, and gently manicured her nails, buffing them to a healthy shine; creaming her hands, nourishing them, softening them, caring for them as she had never taken the time to do.

It was somewhere to start.

And she would talk to Vicky tomorrow about her hair: getting a soft colour put through it to hide the grey. Vicky had often offered, but Kate had never felt it mattered. She didn't care about the gathering grey, didn't think there was any reason to preserve the glow of her natural colour, didn't suppose anyone would notice either way. But now she knew it *did* matter, she *should* care, *she* would notice. She should do it for herself.

She stared at her reflection in the dressing table mirror as she undressed for bed. She had let herself go. Her hair had outgrown its style a long time ago and bunching it up in a crocodile clip did not disguise the fact that it was straggly and out of control. Dry too, she noticed; probably in need of a good conditioning treatment. Vicky would have a field day, doing all the things she'd been recommending for months. She smiled at the pleasure it would give them both, wondering why she had resisted the offer so long, why she hadn't seen it for what it was: an opportunity to draw closer to her daughter as well as look after herself.

Still smiling, she massaged cream into her neck and face, with far more care and diligence than she had in a long time, pondering at the effect Phyllis was having on her. These were not momentous changes to her life. But they were a start to living that life instead of merely passing it.

She couldn't help wondering where it was going... this life she was going to start 'living'.

Chapter 3

Wednesdays became the highlight of her week. Kate always went home feeling good; more positive, more alive, after talking to Phyllis.

Every week she would determine to find out more about Phyllis and each week she would end up knowing more about herself.

They would talk about Kate's children and her grandchildren, how they were doing, what they were doing. But never about Phyllis's family. She neatly sidestepped any questions Kate posed and changed the subject so skilfully it wasn't till much later that Kate would realise she'd been outmanoeuvred.

Phyllis seemed happy to have her company, even claimed to enjoy it, though Kate sometimes wondered why, since she so often ended up moaning about her discontent. But it was Phyllis who drew that out of her, encouraged her to talk about how she felt, what she thought. Perhaps Phyllis just liked to be needed, to offer advice, pleased it would be accepted.

"I live on my own now," she confided one day: one of the few facts Kate gleaned from their meetings. "It's nice to have a friend to meet up with for coffee. Like the old days, when I used to meet my college girlfriends in the tearoom on George Street. Afternoon tea, with cream scones and buttered crumpets."

"Why did you stop?"

"The war. Just the war," Phyllis sighed, changing the subject back to Kate. "That's a good cut Vicky's given you this time. Really suits you," she said.

Under her tutelage, Kate had begun to care for her appearance: what she wore, how she did her hair, applied her makeup; every effort noted by her tutor.

"Thank you," Kate accepted the compliment graciously. "You are so good for me Phyllis."

Phyllis, in turn, smiled with pleasure. "Actually, I'm really an interfering old woman. But thank you for not saying so."

But Phyllis *was* good for her. It had been a long time since anyone had paid her a compliment. Or taken the time to ask what was worrying her. Or helped her take a long, close look at herself. Dan didn't seem interested.

Had he always been like that?

When had they stopped being interested in one another? Because she had to admit that the disinterest was mutual. It had been a long time since she had asked Dan what *he* was thinking or feeling.

She used to be interested: there was a time when she thought Dan was wonderful, fascinating.

She met him at a party. She shouldn't really have been there. It was in her friend's house: parents on holiday, brother having a party. He had allowed Kate and Susan to stay, on condition they helped clear up afterwards. It had seemed a small price to pay for the thrill of being at such a mature gathering.

Susan's brother was a good bit older than they were. Consequently, so were his friends. They seemed much more interesting to the two teenagers than their friends from school. These party-goers all *worked*. In offices or shops. Out there in that Exciting, Enticing, Big, Bad World.

Kate noticed Dan because he seemed different from the others. He was quite tall and not bad looking, nothing extraordinary, but not bad. Dark hair, a bit long at the back, but she didn't mind that; dark eyes, heavy eyebrows, quite lean, looked as if he took care of himself. Not bad looking at all. He stood apart, not moodily, but quietly, comfortably. He seemed to be totally at ease with himself. Not self-conscious as the boys at school were, and not swaggering as some of his friends were. Just comfortable in his own skin somehow.

It had been a pleasant surprise to find that he had noticed her too. Assumed she was older, of course.

By the time he realised she was still at school, it was too late. She was only sixteen and pregnant.

Dan didn't seem to mind that he *had* to marry her. When her father had fumed and roared at him, he had calmly apologised

37

and assured him that he was more than happy to take responsibility and could comfortably provide for his daughter.

Her father was mollified, her mother consoled and Kate delighted.

Looking back, she could never remember if Dan had ever actually declared his Undying Love. But she had kind of assumed that as read. And, to his credit, she was confident he had remained a faithful husband.

The initial fascination she had for him was overtaken by the wonders of pregnancy and childbirth. She stopped seeking to solve his mystery and contented herself with the secrets of motherhood.

But now the children had grown. The secrets were finished and she had forgotten the mystery. She and Dan had remained strangers in many ways.

"So, tell me," Phyllis asked one day. "Vicky is like her father, you said. So what about Paul? Is he like you, d'you think?"

"I don't know really. Perhaps," Kate said thoughtfully. "He isn't much like Dan. so I suppose he's more like me. We have a lot in common. But he's a lot more... a lot more..." she searched for the right word. "Oh, I don't know. He's just more *together* than I am, if you know what I mean?"

"I think I do."

"He knows what he wants and what he *doesn't* want. For instance, he isn't married. Says he doesn't believe in marriage. Says it's a piece of paper with the power of iron bars. Prison bars."

"Is that how you feel?"

"A bit. I mean, I believe in marriage. I think it's right and more... more *proper,* I suppose. And I'm glad I married Dan and everything," Kate hesitated. "At least, I *think* I am. I certainly could never have brought up a baby on my own. Not back then. Besides," her voice was stronger now. "If I hadn't married Dan, I wouldn't have Paul and Vicky, would I?"

"So Vicky's a hairdresser. What does Paul do?"

"He's a teacher. A P.E. teacher. I would have loved to do that."

"I thought you didn't like sport?"

"Not on the telly. I'm just not a spectator. I was good at sports at school. Loved it. But I hate sitting watching other people do something I can't do and would have loved the chance to try. You know?"

"Yes."

"It's the same with 'soaps'. You know, like 'Coronation Street' and 'Eastenders' and those. I can't be bothered watching other people living their lives. I'm afraid I'd forget to get on with living mine."

"So tell me about your dreams."

"Dreams?"

"You know." Phyllis leant forward, her elbows on the table, her hands one on top of the other under her chin. "Everybody dreams. When I was a little girl, I dreamed of being a vaudeville star. A dancer. My father would have been horrified to know I even knew what they were! But I had seen the posters outside the old Playhouse Theatre and I fell in love with the Exotic Dancers. 'Exotic' having a completely different meaning back then, I hasten to add. I grew out of the notion, of course, but it was replaced with other, more attainable dreams."

"Like?"

"Like being a doctor or a nurse. I think I fancied myself as another Florence Nightingale. But what about you? Was there never a dream?"

"Librarian. When I was a little girl I always wanted to be a librarian."

"You like to read?"

"Love it. But more than that. I just love books. I love handling them. The feel of them, the smell of them," she sniffed the imagined fragrance lovingly, her eyes closed, her hands held like an opened book. "Turning the pages, feeling their smoothness, the words almost like Braille under my fingers, I'd touched them so much. Sorting them: tall ones to the left, getting smaller, fatter too, lining up along the shelf. " Her hands scanned the length of the imaginary shelf.

"Old books?"

She opened her eyes. "Any books. Hardback, paperback. Books. Just books. I used to play libraries with my pals. I made library cards and I stuck little paper pocket kind of things in the inside cover of all my books." She leaned closer and lowered her voice. "And some of my sister's. Though she used to go mad when she found them."

"Did she not play with you?"

Kate shrugged. "Not really. She had her own friends. They were more interested in roller-skating, bikes, the outdoor stuff. And I liked that too. But I loved books."

"Did you read a lot?"

"Oh, all the time. Used to drive my mother crazy. Whenever she wanted me, called upstairs for me, my head would be 'stuck in a book' and I'd not hear her first time. Or second time. She'd end up having to come up… and then she'd be mad. But she didn't mind really. She thought reading was good for the mind. 'Broadens the horizons' and all that."

"Do you still read a lot?"

"Lost the habit a bit when the kids were young. You don't get the same time, do you? But I always have a book on the go now. Usually read in bed for a bit… and in the summerhouse of an evening."

"But you didn't become a librarian?"

"Left school without the necessary qualifications."

"To marry Dan?"

"To marry Dan," she nodded. "Then there were the kids. Then it was too late."

Phyllis shook her head. "It's never too late. You could still go to college, get qualified."

"Mmmm… Don't know if I'd want the hassle. You know. In with kids. Having to study. Starting a new job."

"But isn't a change just what would perk you up? Give you back a bit of sparkle in your life?"

"Mmmm… maybe." She shrugged. "Don't think I want it enough any more, to be a librarian, I mean."

"But you still have a passion for books."

"Passion?"

Phyllis smiled. "Yes. Passion."

"I've never thought of myself and passion in the same sentence."

"Well you should. You are a person more than capable of deep passion. You've just let me see a glimpse of it."

"Such an old fashioned word."

"Such a neglected quality in your life. You've let it dim with the years. You need to feel it more often. Give it rein. "

Kate raised her eyebrow.

"Oh, I'm not talking about sexual passion, as you well know. I'm talking about letting yourself get lost in the pleasure of the things you like to do. Feeling that pleasure deeply. Indulging yourself a little. Nothing harmful. Not overindulgence. Just remembering to 'stop and smell the roses' as the saying goes."

"You're a lady of some passion yourself," Kate grinned.

"Anything else? What else did you imagine you might do with your life?"

"When I was in my teens I fancied myself as a novelist. I had won a couple of essay prizes at school. Thought I was pretty nifty with the pen."

"And?"

Kate shook her head. "Oh I don't know. Dan, marriage, babies. There wasn't time for writing."

"Ever?"

"Oh, I dabbled. A few short stories. Nothing much."

"Do you have a typewriter?"

"No, nothing like that. Though I have thought, from time to time, of saving for a word processor. But it would take for ever on my wages."

"Would Dan not help you?"

"Goodness, no! I wouldn't ask him. He has no idea. He probably thinks I'm practically illiterate."

"So, do you still write?"

"Now and again. When I have time. Sometimes in the evenings when Dan's watching telly. I've got a stack of old notebooks in a box in the summerhouse."

"Is that where you write?"

"When the muse takes me," Kate nodded.

"Do you enjoy it?"

"Love it."

"Then you should do more of it."

"You're probably right."

"I'm certain I am," Phyllis declared. "You're a great storyteller. I imagine you'd put it well on paper."

"Thank you."

"It's important to do things you enjoy, you know. Things that give you pleasure. Life shouldn't be hum-drum," she added, warming to her theme. "It doesn't have to be sweeping changes like college, new job... You don't have to do great things. Make grand gestures. Often it's the little things that make life worth living. Like listening to music you enjoy, reading a good book, walking in the park. Taking time out for yourself."

"I used to love walking. Used to take Paul for long, long walks. Up the hill, round by the Loch. All over the place. Even got ourselves lost once. We had gone up the..."

"*Used to.* Don't you walk any more?"

"We used to go on a Saturday while Vicky and Dan watched the football on the telly. When Paul went off to college, I didn't have anyone to go with. Never much liked walking on my own."

"I don't know that it's safe these days anyway. A woman walking alone. Do you have a dog?"

"No, we never got into the pets thing much. Paul had a couple of gerbils once, but we were never a doggie family, I'm afraid. Vicky had a touch of asthma as a kid, perhaps that's why."

"You should join a walking club."

Kate looked at her friend in surprise. "A walking club? What a good idea! Do you know, I never thought of that. Oh. But, I couldn't possibly."

"Why not?"

"I wouldn't know anybody."

"You didn't know me a short while ago."

"But that's different."

"Not so very different. Once you met the other walkers, you'd soon get to know them."

"I suppose."

"You have something in common with them already. You know they like walking."

"Well, that's true."

"Just think. Fresh air, healthy exercise, companionship, nice views…"

"Alright, alright," Kate laughed. "You've sold it! But how on earth do I go about finding a walking club?"

"Well now, my dear. There's a challenge for you!"

Kate leant her elbow on the table and rested her chin on her hand. "Mmm… that is a challenge. I wonder if you can find them in the Yellow Pages?"

"I have a good pair of walking boots at home. Never wore them. What size do you take?"

"A five."

"I thought so. You can have them. I'll bring them next week. And a pair of those thick walking socks." Phyllis laughed. "I'm unlikely to use them now. I was eighty-eight last birthday."

In fact, Phyllis brought the boots and socks into the shop the next day, handing them over the counter with a delighted smile. "Thought I'd surprise you," she said. "Knew you wouldn't be expecting me today."

"No, I wasn't. This is great." She looked into the bag. "They look perfect. But you must tell me how much they were. I'd like to pay for them."

Phyllis just laughed and started to walk away.

"Please." Kate started after her.

"Not at all. I won't hear of it."

"But they look brand new. Obviously expensive…" She stopped and looked at Phyllis with a puzzled frown. "I can't imagine why on earth you would have bought them."

"At my age?" Phyllis supplied.

"Well…yes. Sorry."

"Oh," Phyllis said with a wave of the hand. "It was a whim. Ages ago. Kidding myself I was a young thing." She laughed. "I'm a silly old fool sometimes, you know."

"No, never that," Kate attested stoutly.

But Phyllis leaned across conspiratorially. "I can assure you I am," she grinned. "But I'm absolutely harmless."

"And far too generous."

Phyllis often brought her a present. Each time, Kate would demur, genuinely embarrassed by her new friend's generosity. Stunned by the scale of it this time, she tried to remonstrate with her when they next met for coffee.

"But why shouldn't I bring you a gift now and then? I'm an old lady. It gives me pleasure."

"But I can never repay you…"

"You have already. You give me your time. You treat me with courtesy and kindness. That goes a long way, you know. The days of 'the customer is always right', are long gone," She sniffed as she stirred her coffee. "Not many salespeople bother with the niceties these days."

"Well, in here, they are supposed to. The training… "

"The training gets forgotten as soon as most of them are on the shop floor!"

"Oh well… "

"Anyway. Enough of all that. Have you done anything about the walking club?"

"Oh yes!" Kate's face lit up. "I found one."

"Yellow Pages?"

"I tried them. Found a section headed 'Outdoor Pursuits', but there were no walking clubs listed. I tried a couple of the numbers but they couldn't help so I thought of the Youth Hostel… you know, the one down Leith Walk? I went in there on Friday. They had a lot of information booklets and things and when I asked the girl at the desk, she was really helpful and gave me the phone number of someone she knew who likes walking," she paused to catch her breath. "and *she* knew someone else who belongs to a club that meet every Saturday at the gates of the park, so she took my number and phoned her friend who phoned me and made an arrangement to meet me there. It was as easy as that."

Phyllis laughed.

"It's great," Kate continued. "There are several ladies my sort of age, as well as some very unfit folk trying to get fit. You know, on diets etc., needing some exercise along with it. So I'm not completely out of my depth. I met them all on Saturday. Some of us took a stroll... and I mean 'a stroll' round the park. The others went off for a more serious walk."

"And did you *enjoy* it?"

"Oh, absolutely! It was wonderful. It rained and I still loved it."

"I can tell. You're fairly glowing with it."

"You should have seen me by the time I got home! Bedraggled, wet hair, muddy shoes... but rosy cheeks, better posture, fresh-air smell. It was lovely."

"Marvellous."

"I didn't wear the boots though. It wasn't really that kind of walk. But Martin... he's the chap who leads us off... he says I should next time, even if it's a similar walk. He says it's good to break them in. Let my feet get used to them. So they'll get their first airing next Saturday. I think we're going round the Loch. It's not a hard trail, and you can walk on grass most of the way." Her face was radiant, her eyes dancing. "It's years since I did that walk. Oh, I'm so looking forward to it."

"I can see that," Phyllis laughed. "I've never seen you so alive."

"I can't thank you enough for the suggestion... and the boots... and the socks... and everything. Oh dear! Am I gushing now? I just feel...well, like a kid."

"You seem like a kid."

"Sorry."

"No," Phyllis smiled indulgently. "Don't be. It's lovely. Refreshing and lovely."

"Anyway," Kate took a deep breath to calm herself down. "Thank you. The boots are going to be perfect."

"My pleasure. As I say, I'm unlikely to be using them myself."

"Did you used to go walking then?"

"Do you know what I was meaning to ask you? How's it working out with your Paul and that girl? What is it they call them these days? His 'partner', is it?"

"Yes. Gillian."

"Yes, that's the one. You told me about her. How are they getting on? Any better?"

Kate shook her head. "Not really. I think it's almost over."

"Oh dear."

"They're always rowing. Paul thinks she should move out. It's his flat, you see. Says she spends so much time over at her pal's flat, she'd be as well moving in with her. I hope she does, you know. I don't much like her. She's a bit... oh, I don't know...flighty. She even flirts with my Dan! Not that he'd notice. He hardly looks away from the box while they're there. They always call when Coronation Street's on."

"And what's happening about Dan's job?"

"Oh that!" Kate toyed with her cream scone. "He's talking now about early retirement."

"Early retirement! How old is your husband?"

"He'll be sixty next month."

"Huh, *thought* he must be older than you. You're what? In your forties?"

Kate blushed at the compliment. "I reached 'the big five-0' three months ago," she confessed.

"They used to say 'life begins at forty'."

"They still do... and I'm ten years too late."

"Well, don't you believe it. It begins any time you're ready to take it on."

"Oh, I've been ready long enough. Life just doesn't seem to be ready for me."

"Nonsense. What about the walking club?"

"True. And it's great. And I know I'm going to love it. It certainly is the beginning of something. But it's only a Saturday. What about the rest of my life?"

"What would you like to do with the rest of your life?"

"Oh, just about anything... other than fade into the wallpaper in a pre-war semi-detached," Kate sighed.

"Get out and do it then!"

"But what? Get out and do what?"

"Librarian... writer... you'll think of something," Phyllis said with a knowing smile. "You'll know what to do when the time comes."

Chapter 4

She had another row with Dan that weekend. He had put in his application for early retirement and it was beginning to look like he'd get it. He wanted her to be pleased for him, couldn't understand why she was not.

"I told you," she said, facing him across the kitchen, the plate she was drying still in her hand. "It won't work, you being home more. It'll only give us more time to get on one another's nerves."

"Why, Kate? Why does it have to be like that?"

"Just because it is!"

"That's not a reason, Kate. It's not even an excuse. It's so typical of you."

"What's that supposed to mean?"

Dan shrugged and walked through to the living room. Within moments, she heard the sound of the television clicking on and the end of the conversation.

She hurled the plate at the door and took herself off to sulk in the summerhouse.

When she came through the kitchen later, on her way to bed, she noticed the broken crockery had been neatly swept up and disposed of, in much the same way she felt her viewpoint was.

She was so upset and angry that she didn't join the walking club on Saturday. She knew it was silly not to go, knew a walk in the country was just what she needed to put her in a better humour. But she wasn't ready to give up the heat of her anger yet. She didn't want soothed.

Nor did she want reasoned out of it. Wasn't in the mood for home-spun wisdom. So she begged off coffee with Phyllis on Wednesday.

So, it was two weeks later that Phyllis asked if she'd found a way to ask Naomi to join them yet.

"No, I haven't," she snapped... then immediately regretted it. "Sorry, Phyllis. I didn't mean to snap. It's just... I've had other things on my mind."

"Anything you want to talk about?"

"No, not really."

"Oh dear, that bad, is it?"

"Worse. I'm really miserable. Probably because I know I'm at least partly in the wrong, but..."

"Well, that's a brave admission to make."

"Thank you. But it's not so brave really. If I was going to be truly brave, I'd admit I'm totally in the wrong. But I'm not going to... because... well, because I'm not!"

"Why don't you tell me about it, dear?"

"Thank you, Phyllis, but no. I don't think I come out of it too well, and I'm not ready to face that yet."

"Okay, let's change the subject. What are we going to do about our Ms Ferguson?"

"Oh Phyllis, she's not *our* Ms Ferguson... and I really don't see that there's anything we can do about her."

"Does she still come in?"

"Yes."

"Still exchanging shoes?"

"I don't know. I'm in Household this week."

"So how do you know...?"

"One of the girls told me. Apparently, she asked for me. As far as I can gather, the supervisor is beginning to get quite unpleasant with her. She's told the girls they've only to serve her if there's no-one else waiting, and they've only to allow her five minutes."

"That's not going to help her, is it?"

"How do you mean?"

"Well, the poor girl obviously has a problem. She sounds like a compulsive shopper who can't afford to shop. She seems to be trying to cope by having the pleasure of shopping without the pain of paying."

"Quite the home-psychiatrist, aren't you?" Kate commented, but not without a little admiration for an explanation that seemed to fit poor Naomi's bizarre behaviour.

Phyllis chose to ignore the comment. "So, what are we going to do?"

"I told you…"

"I know, you don't think it's up to us to do anything."

"Right."

"But we must," asserted Phyllis. "Otherwise that poor girl is going to get herself into difficulty."

"But isn't that *her* responsibility?"

"But, don't you see? She's ill. She needs help."

"But we're not qualified to give it."

"Instead of 'butting' like two old goats, we need to think of something… qualified or not. Who else is going to help her?"

"I don't know. *We* don't know. We don't know anything about her. She could be getting therapy already for all we know."

"True… but a bit more help never goes wrong," Phyllis said firmly.

"You really are impossible," Kate sighed, shaking her head.

* * *

Saturday's walk was to be a longer one, starting at the foot of one of the beautiful Border hills.

"Not a difficult walk, a slow, gentle climb, grass all the way, picnic at the top, so bring a backpack." Martin, the walk 'leader' telephoned to give her the arrangements because she hadn't joined them the previous week.

Fortunately, he phoned on Friday afternoon while Dan was at work.

She and Dan were still a little cool with one another and Kate was glad she didn't have to explain the phone-call. She didn't feel ready yet to share her new Saturday treat with him… not that he'd want to join her, but he might make some disparaging remark and the atmosphere would deteriorate again.

However, when Paul popped in on Friday evening… alone for once, having finally finished with Gillian… she was delighted to share her excitement with him.

"Oh Mum," he said as he hugged her. "That's really cool. You should've joined a club like that years ago."

"I know. I just never thought of it till now."

"Well, I think it's a great idea. What does Dad say?"

Kate glanced at the closed door and lowered her voice. "He doesn't know, so please don't mention it when you go through the room."

"You mean you've been slipping out of the house, every Saturday for weeks, without telling him where you're going?"

Kate nodded. "Well, only one so far."

"Do you think that's wise, Mum? I mean… what if he thinks you've got a fancy man or something?"

She laughed. "Don't be ridiculous, Paul. Why on earth would he think that?"

"Well, isn't that what happened to his Dad when he was a wee boy? Did his Mum not run off with someone or something?"

"Yes, but his Mum was a floosie."

"A what?" Paul hooted.

"Shh! He'll come through to see what's keeping his cup of tea."

"Well, really Mum! A 'floosie'! Where on earth did you come up with that?"

"Oh, you know what I mean. I don't know what the current slang is for a loose woman."

Paul hooted again.

"She fell in love with all things American during the war, particularly, all 'things' in uniform. His father wasn't even sure that Dan was his kid. Then she upped and left him to bring him up on his own. I don't think they had much of a homelife."

"Probably why he's such a miserable sod now."

"Paul!"

"Well he is. And I do know what the current slang is for that. But, in deference to your feelings…"

"Thank you."

"So, where does he think you go every Saturday?"

"Shopping, I suppose. He doesn't ask, so I don't tell him."

Paul picked up the tea-tray and started towards the kitchen door. "Fair enough. If he's not interested enough to ask. It would serve him right if you did have a fancy man. Hey!" He spun round to look carefully at her. "You don't, do you?"

"Of course I don't! And watch that tea, you're going to spill it!"

The walk was superb. It wasn't a particularly warm day, but dry, perfect for walking. The countryside she had to drive through, to get to the starting point, was delightful, all rolling hills and green fields, not many villages or hamlets but plenty of cows and horses. She hadn't been down this way for years and had forgotten how pretty it was.

By the time she had found the lay-by where the others were gathering, she was already humming softly to herself and was more than a little eager to start.

As the walk progressed, she found that she was still able for the gentle climb. Martin had described it well, it was gentle. Gentle and soothing. Her mood became lighter than it had been for weeks and she continued to hum quietly.

One of the older gentlemen of the party attached himself to her on the way up the hill and sat by her while they picnicked. His conversation was inconsequential, but pleasant enough. She found herself smiling as she thought of her chat with Paul.

She looked at the gentleman sitting on the grass at her side. No, he held no fascination for her. He was probably a few years older than Dan and had worn well but she was not attracted to him.

She thought more fondly of Dan than she had for a long time, smiling again to herself as she compared his tall, slim build to this smaller, more rugged companion of the day.

Funny how Dan had stayed so slim, considering how little exercise he took. Perhaps the fifteen minutes or so of press-ups and whatever else it was he did every morning, was worthwhile... though she'd always laughed at him. She felt a little ashamed of her laughter suddenly. Why shouldn't Dan want to keep fit? He'd often defended himself by reminding her that he had an office job, a sedentary lifestyle.

She wished he had enjoyed walking. In fact, she didn't *know* that he didn't. With a spasm of guilt, she realised that she'd never actually asked him. It was something they didn't make time for when they were courting or while the children were young. She'd never invited him to walk with her and Paul, when they used to go off on a Saturday. And she hadn't invited him since.

How can you be married to someone all these years, thirty-four years, and not know something as basic as whether or not he enjoyed a walk?

The frown that accompanied these reflections was smoothed from her brow by the soft breeze that sprang up as they started out on the return leg of the walk. She allowed such troubling thoughts to be gently blown away to gather like the fallen leaves, where she could ruffle through them another time.

When she got back at the end of the day, instead of finding Dan sitting in front of the TV, as she'd expected, he was standing at the back door studying the garden.

"Where've you been?" he demanded.

"What're you doing?" she asked suspiciously.

"I had to forage for my own lunch."

"Oh, you poor soul!" she exclaimed sarcastically.

"Not that I minded," he said as he turned back into the kitchen. "But it would've been nice if you'd mentioned you'd not be in."

"And I suppose you're waiting now for me to get your tea?"

"No, thank you," he replied icily. "I've already made it. There's some soup left in that pot, if you want it."

"What, from a tin?"

"No, actually. It's home-made."

"You made it?"

Dan nodded. "You forget. I used to live on my own. I practically lived on home-made vegetable soup for years."

Kate lifted the lid of the pot. "Mmm. Smells good actually," she said grudgingly.

"Thank you." He shrugged. "Help yourself."

"What were you looking at so thoughtfully when I came home?"

"The garden. In particular... that." He waved his hand disparagingly at the summerhouse.

"Why?"

Dan walked through to the living room and came back with a letter in his hand.

"What's that?"

He held it out to her. "Read it. It's the acceptance of my request for early retirement."

She froze. "When?" she asked, taking the letter. "How soon?"

"That pleased for me, eh?" he said softly.

Kate tossed the letter onto the table without reading it. "And have you thought any more about getting a part time job?"

"I told you. I have no intention of getting a part time job."

"But..."

"And, just before you ask what I *am* going to do, I intend to enjoy my house and garden." He nodded towards the back door. "And the first thing I'm going to do is take down that old monstrosity."

"Oh no, you're not," Kate said. "That's my summerhouse."

"It's an eyesore, a wreck. It's coming down."

"But I told you, I don't want you to pull it down. I want you to mend it."

"And I told you it's not worth the effort... to say nothing of the cost."

"You can afford it."

"It's coming down," he said, shaking his head, raising his hand. "And that's all there is to it."

"No!" Kate said through gritted teeth.

Dan raised his eyebrows scornfully.

"If you touch that summerhouse, I walk out," she said.

But it was Dan who turned and walked away.

Kate spent another night in the summerhouse. She couldn't bear to stay under the same roof as Dan, let alone in the same room.

Being in the same room had not been a problem lately because she had moved into Paul's old one after the last big row. Dan had never asked her to return to his room or his bed, so, normally it was enough to go their separate ways at the top of the stairs.

But tonight, she wanted to be here. She wanted to protect her sanctuary. Surely Dan would not destroy it? He must know how much it meant to her. But perhaps he didn't care.

She gazed fondly around her. Every piece of furniture held a memory, told a story. She remembered vividly how she had hunted down each item. She would scour the second hand shops and the salerooms, week after week, until she found exactly the right piece. Some of them, she had managed to manhandle into their Ford Escort, many of them had to be delivered.

She would watch them being placed by the bemused van drivers and their helpers. She knew they wondered what kind of home this was for these lovely old relics... a funny-old-relic sort of place itself. She watched them look around it with curious expressions, but she didn't care.

This was her place: her sanctuary. She was making it special.

She stroked the sofa fondly, remembering how pleased she had been to find it. It had deep, soft cushions and was long and low: perfect for lying, thinking, dreaming; perfect for cuddling up with the children, telling stories, playing games. Its lovely russet colour had faded a bit, but it was still mellow and warm. The chairs, each one different, each with its own story, blended and contrasted and altogether made a pleasing picture.

She had spent far more care in their choosing than she had in choosing the furniture for the living room. That had been bought one Saturday, many years ago. One of the rare shopping trips she and Dan had embarked on together. She had nagged until Dan had agreed to the trip. It had been a disaster from start to finish.

She accused him of not being interested in their home.

He accused her of being too fussy.

She muttered and nagged.

He glowered and swore.

They couldn't agree on anything.

In the end Dan had made a disputed, but firm, decision about a three-piece suite, paid the bill, arranged for it to be delivered and shepherded her out of the shop. He had no desire to repeat the fiasco, so he went home, leaving Kate to choose the carpet and curtains, the bookcases and coffee tables. This she did with expediency, having lost any enthusiasm for the task.

Not surprisingly, their living room lacked the warmth a more harmonious equipping might have given it.

As the light faded into evening, Kate sat huddled on her sofa, enjoying how the last rays of the sun lit up the plants around her and filled the summerhouse with its glow. She was hungry now, but her pride would not allow her to taste Dan's soup. So she fell asleep, hungry and lonely but secure in the realisation that Dan was most unlikely to summon up the energy to do anything about the summerhouse. After all, he hadn't knocked it down when she had pleaded with him to do so… why would he do it now? She felt foolish that she'd got so upset about something that was never going to happen. He just wanted to rattle her, to get her back for not letting him know she'd be out all day.

Vicky brought the boys round on Sunday, so Kate and Dan tried hard to hide their coldness with one another. It was an unvoiced truce for the sake of the children. Vicky, of course was not fooled.

"What is it with you two? Every time I come, I feel as though I've walked past the open fridge door."

"Are you staying for tea? Will chicken be alright?" Kate asked. "And your Dad made some soup."

"Lovely. I like Dad's soup."

"Oh," Kate looked at her with surprise. "I didn't know you were familiar with it."

"Don't you remember? When you and Paul used to go walking on a Saturday, Dad used to have a pot of soup ready for you when you came back."

"I'd forgotten."

"He always felt you'd be tired by the time you got home and that was our best chance of getting fed," Vicky laughed. "D'you want me to peel some spuds if we're staying?"

"Fine. You can do some carrots too, if your father's left any. I'm just going to see if the boys want a drink."

So much she had forgotten.

When had these things become unimportant? When had she stopped seeing his kindness… or wanting it?

* * *

Kindness. Naomi Ferguson had thanked her for her kindness. All she had done was spend a little time with her, helping her try on some dresses.

Kate was back in Dresses this week, and sure enough, Naomi was wandering through the rails of clothes, looking sad and lost. Kate watched her for a while before she approached to offer assistance. She watched how Naomi touched the fabrics, obviously taking some pleasure in their richness. From time to time she would hold something against her to see the length, or take a dress to the mirror to check the colour. She seemed to have no idea of what suited her for she always picked out bright, almost gaudy clothes while Kate felt she needed softer, warmer colours… not necessarily autumn colours, as Phyllis had convinced her *she* needed… more the gentle shades of spring, perhaps. Phyllis would probably know if that's what would suit Naomi's fairish hair and sallow skin. She certainly needed something warmer than the dark grey suit she was wearing. It did nothing for her. She looked particularly grey herself in it.

"What about this lovely cornflower blue?" Kate suggested as she approached.

"Oh, hello. How nice. You startled me. I was away in a dream."

"Dreaming of somewhere nice to wear that lovely dress?" Kate smiled.

"Oh, no. I mean. Yes… sort of."

"I do think the blue, the soft cornflower, would suit you better than the red, you know. Why don't you try it on?"

"Do you think so? I always think... I'm sort of... sort of colourless myself. I thought the bright colours would cheer me up."

"Perhaps you're right. But sometimes they can be a bit overpowering, don't you think? The softer shades might bring out colour in *you* instead of it being their colour that dominates."

"Yes, I see what you mean."

"Why don't you try them both on. See which one looks better. I'll wait by the changing room and give you my opinion if you like."

"Why, thank you." Naomi's eyes shone with emotion. "That would be so kind. Thank you." And she bustled off with the dresses.

While she waited, Kate thought about the quality of kindness. Here she was, only doing her job, and it was perceived as kindness.

Phyllis was kind. Not just with her thoughtful gifts, but also the way she was *interested*. It wasn't just a passing of time, a curiosity satisfied. She made you feel she *cared* about your life. That it mattered how you felt, what you thought.

That was the sort of kindness this poor woman needed. She must find a way to do what Phyllis wanted and invite Naomi Ferguson for coffee. Phyllis would surely do her a power of good. But Kate was still undecided how it could tactfully and inoffensively be done.

"Oh, there you are!"

Kate jumped at the unexpected sound of Phyllis's voice. It had broken into her reverie as though her thoughts had found reply.

"Phyllis! How good to see you," she said a little breathlessly. "You're just the person I needed."

"Oh that's a lovely way to be greeted," beamed Phyllis.

"This is Ms Ferguson, a regular customer of mine." She indicated Naomi as she appeared from the changing cubicle.

"And this…" She introduced Phyllis. "…is a lady who really knows about colours. You're just the one to tell us what would suit Ms Ferguson best. She's trying on this red." Kate pointed to the dress Naomi had put on. "And the same in cornflower blue."

Phyllis looked kindly at Naomi. "Well, my dear, you look stunning in that one. Let me see." She took a step back.

Naomi stood shyly, unsure of this new turn of events. She looked anxiously to Kate.

"It's okay," she reassured. "Phyllis here is a very good friend of mine. You can trust her judgement completely. She tells me she has studied up a bit on colours."

"Well, I bought a book about it, anyway." Phyllis laughed modestly. "Let me see you in the cornflower," she ordered gently. "I've a feeling that might be even better. I think the red might be the wrong red for your soft colouring. Too harsh, I think."

Obediently, Naomi went back into the cubicle to change.

"Is this the one you told me about," Phyllis mouthed.

Kate nodded and received an answering wink from her co-conspirator.

If help is what Naomi needed… the Cavalry had arrived.

Somehow, by the end of the afternoon, Phyllis had managed to persuade Naomi to join them for coffee.

"How did you do it?" asked Kate as she sat down.

"Well, after she had exchanged last week's dress for the blue one, I suggested she come over to the mirror beside where the hats and scarves are, so that I could explain about her colours."

"Her colours?"

"Yes, you know, like I told you before. By and large people's colourings can often be seen as seasons."

Kate nodded.

"Well, anyway. I took her over and draped a few scarves around her to show her how some colours brought out her own colour, and how others make her look dull."

"And could she see the difference?"

"Of course. Surprised her how nice she could look with the right colours."

"So?"

"So she bought a scarf."

"No, I mean, how did you get from there to inviting her for coffee?"

"Oh, I just did. When she said she had to get back to work, I said that was a pity, because I'd enjoyed her company. So I asked her what time she finished and told her we'd be here."

"And she said she'd come?"

"Of course."

"Well done!" Kate patted her friend on the back. "So what time does she finish work?"

Phyllis looked at her watch. "Oh about five minutes ago. She should be here anytime. But look, I wanted to show you what I bought."

As usual, Phyllis had a variety of carrier bags at her feet. She always had something to show for her day out, usually gifts for friends or relatives, seldom something for herself. The heavier or larger items she had delivered, the rest she liked to carry home. Shopping was obviously something Phyllis thoroughly enjoyed.

Perhaps she is qualified to help Naomi after all, thought Kate... or at least to understand her.

"Where is Naomi?" she asked at last, after all the purchases had been examined and exclaimed over. "How long did she say it would take her to get here from her work?"

"Five minutes. She works in an office on Rose Street." Phyllis consulted her watch again. "I would have thought she'd be here by now. Perhaps she's been detained."

"Perhaps she's not going to come."

"Oh, I'm sure she'll come."

"Why ever not?" Kate laughed. "I mean, I'm sure she thought nothing odd about a perfect stranger inviting her for coffee!"

"I'm not a stranger!" Phyllis protested.

"Not to you, you're not!"

"And not to you."

Kate leant across the table and touched Phyllis's hand. "No, of course you're not. Not to me. You've become a very dear friend to me," she assured her. "But you are a stranger to her," she said gently. "And she does seem a very shy person."

"Oh dear!" Phyllis looked stricken. "You don't think I've frightened her off, do you?"

"Never mind, perhaps it's for the best. How could we have helped her really? She needs qual…"

"She needs warmth and friendship, that's what she needs. And we could offer her that," Phyllis said vehemently. "We shall just have to try another time!"

"You don't give up easily, do you?" Kate said with admiration.

"Not when I can scent a challenge," replied Phyllis.

"You and your challenges. At least this time it's not for me."

Chapter 5

She didn't see Naomi again for a few weeks, perhaps because of the department she was in. She couldn't imagine Naomi would have much to enjoy in Gents Shoes. On the other hand, she knew that Phyllis was scouting around various departments, various days, around lunchtime and she'd had no luck 'bumping into' her either. Perhaps they'd cured her after all… aversion therapy. Kate smiled to herself at the thought.

"Nice to see a woman happy at her work."

"Oh hello, Paul. What are you doing here?"

"Shoes, mother. I need new shoes."

"Oh!"

"You do sell shoes, don't you?" He indicated the displays around him, grinning.

She laughed. "You just took me by surprise, monster," she said affectionately. "Why are you not at your work, anyway?"

"School holiday, October week," he said as he examined a pair of black loafers.

"Oh, of course."

"Do you have these in a ten?"

She took the shoe from him and walked over to the store-room. "Don't go away," she smiled. "I'll be right back."

When she returned with the shoes, he was sitting comfortably with one ankle resting across the other knee. He looked so self-contained, so at ease in his own skin somehow. It was a little disconcerting sometimes to realise how much he was actually like his father… in looks and manner, anyway, the same dark hair and eyes, the same lean build.

He looked up at her. "This takes me back a bit," he said with a grin. "You fitting new shoes on me."

"You always were easily pleased with shoes. Just like today, even as a child, you would walk in, see a pair you liked, try them on, if they fitted, you would…"

"I'll take them," he finished the thought for her. "They're great."

"Don't you want to walk about a bit in them? Look in the mirror? Anything?"

"No, I know what they look like. They fit. They'll be fine."

"Too easily pleased," she decided. "You shop like your father. Minimum of fuss. Waste no time on it."

"Exactly. Talking of the old man," Paul said, as he handed her the new shoes and put his old ones back on. "When does he stop work now? Next Friday, isn't it?"

"I don't want to talk about it."

"Come on, Mum. Don't you think you're being a bit silly about this? I mean, Dad is going to retire now, whether you like it or not."

"I don't."

"I think we all know that. The thing is, Mum…"

"The thing is, Paul, that your father has been difficult enough to live with when he only came home for tea. He's going to be impossible if he's at home all the time."

"But why? You're not at home all the time. Unless, of course you gave up your job to spend more time with him," he said with a wicked laugh.

"Not you as well."

"No. I'm only teasing. Honest. Come on, Mum. It won't be that bad."

"You don't live with him."

"But I did. And it wasn't so bad. Dad's alright, just a bit on the quiet side."

"Dour."

"Introspective."

"Sullen."

"Come on, Mum. Just because he's not the chattiest."

"Come on yourself, Paul. Your Dad and I have very little in common. We've grown apart over the years. What we *don't* need is more time thrown together."

"Perhaps it is. Perhaps it's time you found some common interests."

"For instance?"

"Well I don't know. You'll have to work that one out for yourselves."

"No thank you."

"You know you're being ridiculous about this, don't you, Mum? And quite unfair. Dad's worked hard all these years."

"So he's already told me."

"He's entitled to stop now if he can."

"So he says."

"Well, it's true. Give him a break, Mum."

"Excuse me, Paul. Someone's waiting to be served."

He caught her arm. "Let him wait. Someone else can serve him."

"Paul!" She looked round helplessly and caught the eye of the supervisor. "Sorry, Mr Ellis."

"It's okay, Mrs Morgan. I'll serve this gentleman," said Mr. Ellis. He looked at his watch. "Perhaps you'd like to take your break now?"

"Thank you," said Paul. "She would."

Kate took the loafers to the counter and got Mrs Rennie to ring up the sale. "Here are your shoes," she said to Paul, thrusting them into his hands.

"Come on, let's get a cup of tea, Mum."

And his smile melted her angry heart.

"Oh, Paul," she said, when they were seated in the Coffee Shop. "Do you really think I'm being awful about your Dad's retirement?"

"Yes. I do," he replied sincerely. "Look, Mum. You know I love you. You and I have always been close. Much closer than Dad and I. But this time, I think you're in the wrong. I think you're behaving badly."

"Don't hold back, son. Say what you think!"

"Well I do. You've been giving Dad the cold shoulder for months now. And why? Just because you don't want him home more. That's sad, really sad. He's your husband for goodness sake. Have you no feelings left for the poor sod?"

"Paul!"

"Well, have you?"

"Of course I have!"

"Show him then. Be pleased for him."

They sat in silence for a while stirring their tea, letting the words brew.

"Are you going to his work's leaving 'do'?" Paul asked after a while.

She shrugged. "I hadn't thought."

"I think you should. You'll regret it if you don't. There'll not be another opportunity."

"Yes," she sighed. "You're probably right."

"I know I'm right."

"Okay," she agreed with a watery smile. "You're right. I should go."

"And you will go?"

Kate nodded.

Paul took her hand across the table. "That's my girl."

"I don't know what on earth I'll wear," she wailed. "What does one wear to a Civil Service, Upper Management, early retirement, leaving 'do'?"

Paul held his hands up. "Search me! I'm not the best one to ask. Why don't you ask Vicky? she goes with John to his 'work do' every Christmas, doesn't she?"

"I suppose so."

"Couldn't you get a new dress? A 'posh frock'? Something special?"

Kate looked at him scornfully. "You have to be joking, Paul. Have you any idea the kind of money a 'posh frock' costs these days?"

"So? This is a special occasion. It needs a special outfit."

"I can't afford to throw away that kind of money on a dress I'd likely only wear the once."

"I'll buy you one."

"Don't be daft!"

"No," he said earnestly. "I will. I'd like to buy you a 'posh frock'."

Kate smiled. "You are a dear boy, but no. Absolutely not. No-one is going to waste that kind of money on my account. I would take no pleasure in wearing what would amount to your next month's dinners."

"Up to you. Offer stands. If you're stuck, give me a shout."

"Thank you, but I'll find something, either in my wardrobe or Vicky's. Vicky's being the better bet."

Before she had the chance to ask Vicky about a dress, her problem was solved from an unexpected source... though by now she should have expected it.

As soon as Phyllis knew she needed a special dress, she offered Kate a choice of several.

"Of course you mustn't spend silly money on an evening dress."

"That's what I said to Paul."

"You'll have one though."

"No. That's the problem. I don't have one," Kate said carefully, thinking Phyllis had misunderstood.

"Yes... and I'm saying you *shall* have one."

"What do you mean?"

"You must come round to my house now and try some on. I have plenty evening dresses, most of them hardly worn. You shall have one."

"Oh, I couldn't do that."

"Why not? If you're afraid they won't do."

"Oh no, it's not that."

"Then what? Perhaps you don't like the thought of someone else's clothes?"

"No, no," she hastened to reassure her friend. "It's just that you've already been so kind to me. All the things you..."

"I insist," Phyllis said, already rising from the table, signalling that she wished the bill. "We'll go now and you can choose."

"But, Phyllis, I couldn't impose."

"You wouldn't be imposing. You'd be giving me pleasure. Come on now. Are you going to eat the last of that cake or do you want to take it with you?"

When they stepped outside the shop, Phyllis continued issuing orders.

"We'll take my car. I'll bring you back for yours later."

"It's okay. I come to work by bus."

"Even better. Let's go then. You can carry these bags for me. I'm just over there."

"But that space is for the disabled…"

"And I have a badge."

"Oh, I didn't know, Phyllis. What…"

"And don't go asking what's wrong with me, because I shan't tell you. Here we are. In you get, then."

The drive to Phyllis's house didn't take long… in fact it didn't take as long as it should have. Phyllis seemed to pay little heed to lights and signs. If she deemed it was safe and she wanted to go somewhere… then she went. Kate took a deep breath at the start of the journey and felt as though she didn't let it go till the end.

Making a mental note to get the bus home, she stepped out of the car in front of an imposing, old, three-storey, town house.

"Is this where you live?" Kate asked.

Phyllis nodded as she fitted the key to the lock. "Just the ground floor flat."

"Phew, it's… it's…"

"Posh?" supplied Phyllis, smiling as she held open the door for Kate. They entered a beautifully tiled entrance hall and Phyllis led the way to the door of her flat.

"Well, yes. It is posh. It's quite imposing. I had no idea…"

"I told you I was a foolish old lady with too much money and I am." She opened the door and ushered Kate inside. "Thank you, Mary," she said to the smartly-dressed, middle-aged lady who appeared to help her off with her coat. "Mary, this is my friend, Kate. She'll be having dinner with us." She turned to Kate. "You will, of course, won't you? You can phone Dan from here. I'm sure he won't mind, will he?"

"N-no… No, I'm sure he won't. But…but…"

"Kate 'buts' a lot," Phyllis said conspiratorially to Mary. "But I'm sure she's not after your job," she joked.

Mary gave a wide smile and held her hand out to Kate. "Hello there, I'm Mrs Thaine's 'lady butler'," she grinned. "Housekeeper, really."

"Oh, I see."

"Right, if you just go through there, Mary will show you where the phone is, and I'll look out one or two dresses for you to try on later."

"Thank you," said Kate automatically.

The flat was delightful. She had never been anywhere like it. The hallway was bigger than her living room at home… and better furnished. It was carpeted in rich, deep red, warm and welcoming, the dark wooden floorboards like a shiny frame round a rich canvas.

The richness of the carpet was echoed in the beautiful furniture; padded chairs and mahogany tables, stylish lamps presiding over posies of flowers, and doors… so many doors…

"This is gorgeous," she gasped out.

Phyllis turned to her. "Yes, it is rather lovely, isn't it? I'm glad you like it," she smiled. "I'm very happy with how it turned out. We just had it redecorated a year or two ago. It used to be rather dowdy, didn't it, Mary?"

"Yes, it's much nicer now. Brighter, more modern," Mary agreed.

"Anyway, on you go through to the sitting room. Make yourself at home. I'll be back in a minute or two."

The sitting room was even more impressive, tastefully decorated with white paintwork and again, dark, waxed floorboards, this time clothed with deep ivory rugs. Kate slipped out of her shoes, picking them up as she looked around herself, feeling the deep, softness and warmth of the carpet under her feet.

The walls of the room were ivory too and hung, not with dull, old portraits, as Kate expected, but with wonderful, colourful paintings… not Modern Art, but contemporary, stylish, original paintings.

"These are beautiful!" she breathed.

"Yes, aren't they?" Mary replied. "Mrs Thaine is quite a patron of the local art galleries, and I think she has excellent taste."

"Absolutely," Kate agreed. She was stunned by the originality of the works. They were hauntingly, evocatively beautiful.

"Mrs Thaine has a liking for the African theme."

"I see that."

"She has found one or two artists whose style particularly pleases the eye."

"Absolutely," Kate sighed again.

The furniture was tastefully sumptuous; the sofas, deep and soft, their colours reflecting the mellow sunshine in the African paintings; the scattered chairs catching the sunsets portrayed on the walls; tables and lamps of marble and gold, and everywhere, flowers. Huge vases and tiny posies placed and scattered around the room, giving it a feeling of happiness and life.

Kate took a long breath of the heady fragrance of summer.

"It's just exquisite," she said softly.

Mary smiled and indicated the telephone, a dainty gilt and marble affair sitting on an equally stunning little desk.

"It's like walking into a fairy-tale. I've never seen anything like it."

But Mary was no longer there to hear, having melted out of sight, gone from the room soundlessly, her footsteps silenced by the plush rugs that carpeted the floor.

Kate sat at the desk but didn't immediately make her phone call.

Her hand caressed the cool, smooth surface of the marble-inlaid desk, her fingers tracing the carved wooden edges, lifting the little gilt pens, feeling the thick, creamy paper, gently touching the petals of the roses in the inevitable vase placed carefully by the phone.

She was stunned. She needed time to take this all in. She had guessed that Phyllis was 'comfortable', perhaps even 'well-off'. She had to be, to afford the purchases Kate was aware of, never mind any others she presumably made. But this was more than that. This was wealth. Solid, reliable wealth... and class. There was nothing gaudy, nothing ostentatious. It was just class.

Yet Phyllis had seemed such an ordinary, down to earth, kindly soul. Apart from her love of and capacity for shopping, there had been nothing about her to suggest all this. Nothing ostentatious, nothing gaudy. She too was class.

The golden clock beside the phone reminded her that Dan would be getting home from work about now, probably wondering where she was, or rather, where his tea was.

But she couldn't leave the cosseting of all this gentle luxury… not yet.

High ceilings dressed with wide cornices, tall windows dressed with folds of voile and swathes of rich silky materials, lights suspended from ornate ceiling roses, not quite chandeliers, simpler but very stylish… a special room, it wrapped itself around her like a soft comforting blanket.

She sighed.

The cool feel of the marble desk under her hands told her of the task she was shirking.

She phoned Dan.

"Hi, it's me."

"You okay?"

"Yes… yes, I'm okay."

"You sure? You sound different? Are you still at work?"

"No…no, I'm not still at work. Look, something's come up, Dan. I'm sorry. I'm not going to make it in for tea. There's a lasagne in the freezer. You could microwave that, if you like, or there's…"

"The lasagne'll be fine. You sure you're okay?"

Kate sighed. "Yes, Dan, really. I'm fine. Look, can we talk later?"

"Sure."

"See you then."

"Right. See you."

Kate put the phone down and wandered over to one of the sofas. She sank down into its welcome, letting the tension that had built inside her so quickly, ebb away. When had she started tensing up as soon as she heard his voice? And why? He had never been a cruel man, quite the reverse, he tended to gentleness; but she didn't want it. Hadn't for a long time.

She looked around the room, feeling calmed by it. This was somewhere to be at peace, not somewhere for disquieting thoughts. Yet, somehow, it also invited reflection, meditation. The pictures... they all had a certain something... something that made you want to reflect on the quality of life, on its purpose. What had it all been about, the fifty years of her life? She had grown up too fast, had married too soon, been a mother too early: she didn't know who she was, what she wanted. There had never been time to find out, submerged as she'd been in the day-to-day routine of marriage and children. Now that the children were gone, it felt too late to find these things out. It didn't seem to matter any more. Or, it didn't use to...

Her heart screamed out that it does matter. It's not too late. There has to be more. There has to be more...

These implacable African figures in the paintings, bent resolutely to their tasks, what kind of life did they lead in that harsh land of sunshine? What did they feel? Had the scorching heat seared the feeling from their hearts? Did they bend to their tasks with resolution, or resignation? Were they happy?

"You look very pensive, my dear," said Phyllis, approaching silently across the room.

"Yes, sorry. A million miles away. In Africa, actually," she laughed, pointing to the paintings that had absorbed her so.

"Thought provoking, aren't they?"

"Yes, and very beautiful. This is a fabulous room."

"Thank you," Phyllis smiled her pleasure at the compliment.

"It's like walking into summer. A real summer room," Kate mused.

"That was my intention, to evoke the warmth and brightness of summer."

"Did you design it?"

"Yes. It was great fun planning it all, and I'm pleased with how it turned out. I wanted it to be comfortable, relaxing, but encourage..."

"Reflection?"

"Yes."

"It does. Very successfully. I love it. In fact, in a way, I suppose it reminds me of my summerhouse. That's what the summerhouse does for me." she looked around appreciatively. "If I lived here, I'd never want to leave this room. How do you manage to tear yourself away to go out as regularly as you do?"

"Well," Phyllis mused. "I suppose, the thing is that, although this room soothes and calms me, it energises me too. It makes me want to do something with my life. To be worthy of the pleasures the room bestows. Does that sound rather grand?"

"But I think I know what you mean."

"Do you? I've always had a very pleasant life, you see. I've been shielded from much of life's stresses and strains. Sometimes that can make one feel very unworthy, you know. Privileged, I suppose. And I have done nothing to earn the privileges, except be born into them." She sat down on one of the higher upholstered chairs.

"Is all this," Kate embraced the room, the house, the way of life in the grand gesture of her arms. "Is all this 'family money'?" she asked, adding quickly, "Sorry! A bit cheeky to ask."

Phyllis smiled. "It's alright, I don't mind you asking. Yes it is, or mostly it is. I suppose I have added my bit too. Shrewd investments, a good job," she shrugged. "I was a doctor, you know."

"No, I didn't know."

"I had a private practise later on. Retired years ago, of course. But the house was Mother's. She had independent wealth and she married money… so there was never a shortage, you see."

"I think I'm beginning to."

"But 'they', whoever 'they' are, would tell you, 'Money isn't everything. It can't bring happiness.' But it certainly helps," Phyllis said earnestly. "Having money has never made me *unhappy*. In fact, it has shielded me from a lot of unhappiness. But, then again, I don't suppose, in itself, it actually *brings* happiness. I don't know. I'm happy, but would I be happy if I hadn't had all the luxury and ease that I've had all my life. Who's to say?" she shrugged.

"I don't know really. I've never had all this." Kate looked around at the luxury that surrounded her. "But I've never lacked for anything I needed, either. Perhaps it's people like these..." She pointed to a group of African women, barefoot, waterjars balanced on their heads, their backs straight, their eyes impenetrable, walking back to their village in the early morning light. "Perhaps we should ask them what is needed for happiness. How would they count their blessings, do you think?"

"Yes indeed. My, but we are philosophical tonight."

"It's this room," Kate laughed. "It's cast its spell on me."

There was a soft knock at the door, followed by an announcement from Mary as she peeped round it, that dinner was ready.

"Perhaps you'd like to freshen up?" Phyllis asked.

"Thank you."

Phyllis led the way out of the sitting room and across the hall, opening one of its many doors. She reached inside and switched on a light. "There you are, my dear. I'll see you in a moment."

Even the toilet was adorned with flowers, their perfume giving the room a freshness that was very pleasing. The towels were thick, soft and Warmed. It reminded Kate of the only time she and Dan had been in a Very Posh Hotel. They hadn't been staying there, but had treated themselves to a special meal in celebration of something... she could no longer remember what... When she had visited the 'Ladies', she had been impressed by the flowers and the Warm Towels. A simple thing to accomplish, she supposed, but it had always meant luxury to her. Dan had laughed gently at her flush of pleasure when she told him afterwards. He had talked of installing a heated towel rail... but it was only talk. Dan rarely followed through on these promises. She shook away the irritation and went to join Phyllis for dinner.

* * *

"Let's see your 'posh frock', then," demanded Paul. "Who did you say loaned it to you?"

"A friend of mine from work... sort of," Kate added under her breath.

"Let's see it then."

Kate glanced at the kitchen clock. "Well... it'll have to be a quick look. Your father's due home soon. I don't want him to see it. I want it to be a surprise."

"Have you told him yet that you're going to his 'bash', next week?"

"Not yet," she replied as she made for the stairs.

"It will be a surprise then," Paul muttered.

"Don't worry, I will tell him. But not yet."

"You want him to stew for a while."

"No, of course I don't."

"But?"

"But I just haven't got round to..."

"To putting him out of his misery."

"Oh, I don't think he's miserable about it," Kate declared. "He'd probably rather I didn't go."

"Get real, Mum. Of course he wants you to go."

Kate shrugged. "Anyway, wait there a minute and I'll try the dress on for you." And she ran up the stairs happily, delighted to have the chance to show off her gorgeous new dress... because, of course, Phyllis had insisted on giving her the dress she chose.

It had been incredible. After a simple but delicious meal, they had gone to look at the dresses Phyllis had laid out on her bed. Half a dozen brand new, expensive evening gowns, each one more glamorous than the last.

"Oh, Phyllis," she had exclaimed. "They're beautiful. But they're far too posh for me."

"Nonsense!"

"I've never worn anything like these."

"Time you did then."

"But I could never carry it off. I'm not the sophisticated sort."

"Wait till you see yourself in them."

And Phyllis was right. As soon as she zipped up the first dress, Kate knew she wanted, more than anything, to glide into the hotel where the party was, dressed in one of these creations. She felt fabulous in them all. Phyllis knew which colours would suit Kate best; her taste was exceptional. It had been a difficult decision, but, in the end, Kate had chosen a long velvet sheath, the colour of burgundy wine, that draped softly from shoestring straps, skimmed flatteringly over her figure and fell gently to her ankles.

"Wow!" Paul said with genuine admiration as she floated down the stairs. "That is some Posh Frock!"

"Do you like it?"

"Mum, it's gorgeous. You look terrific."

"Do you think it'll be suitable?"

"I think you'll 'knock 'em dead'... to borrow a phrase."

"Thank you," she blushed. "I'd better go take it off now before your father sees it."

"Who did you say you borrowed it from?"

"Oh, just someone at work," she said, starting back up the stairs.

"I can't imagine anyone in your work owning anything as classy as that," he said. "It looks expensive."

Kate smiled as she turned away again. "Yes, it was a surprise for me too," she muttered to herself. "Be down in a minute. Put the kettle on, will you?"

Surprise. Yes, it had certainly been a surprise.

"But Phyllis, these dresses look brand new!"

"Yes, they are."

"Have you worn any of them?"

"I don't really go anywhere like that nowadays."

"Then why did you buy them?"

"I like them. I can afford them. Besides... I always knew I'd have a use for them one day!"

Chapter 6

Dan sat back on his heels, staring at the book in his hands. It was beautiful. It had been carefully wrapped in an old silk scarf and hidden deep in the space between some loose bricks. How long it had remained secreted there he could only guess, but it had the appearance of being very old. And it was beautiful.

His first instinct had been to call out to Kate. She loved old things, was always trailing round second hand shops, bringing home silly bric-a-brac, though he had to admit she found some bargains too. She had furnished this place with her 'finds'. He raised his head to call, then remembered.

She wasn't there.

He shook his head. How could he share this with Kate anyway, when they had shared so little in the past months? Months of rows and sulks, sharing strained silences and dark looks, but not mealtimes or the same bed.

Dan thought of it as the 'Battle of the Summerhouse'.

Kate had not wanted him to pull it down… latterly.

When they had first moved into this house, she had nagged constantly about it. But *then* she was nagging him to *do* it. She wanted it pulled down!

"It takes up too much room. There's hardly enough space left for me to hang a washing line," she'd moaned.

"Why don't you get one of those whirly things?"

"I don't want one of those whirly things."

"Oh well, that's up to you."

"We could turf that whole area, make room for the kids to play. They could have a swing and a slide," she'd reasoned.

"There's plenty of room for them to play round the side, or in the front."

"But I'd like them to play in the back. Where I could see them from the kitchen window."

"Anyway, there's a swing park not more than a stone's throw away," he'd pointed out.

"But I have to take them there. They're too little to go on their own."

"They won't be for long. I mean, Vicky's already six. She could probably take Paul, if you'd let her."

"But I won't let her, because she's far too young to be responsible for a four-year old."

"As I say, they won't always be too young."

"But they are just now."

"That's as may be, Kate. But it would be a heck of a lot of work to knock that old wreck down and clear it, and I don't have the time or the energy to do it just now. I'll maybe get around to it sometime, but not just now."

That had been... Dan counted it out in his mind... twenty-eight years ago!

Twenty-eight years, and this was him getting round to doing it at last.

Only now the silly woman didn't *want* it knocked down. Dan tutted, 'Talk about women being fickle!'

It had been a quite different 'conversation' they'd had a few months ago.

"But I don't want you to knock it down!" Kate had burst out.

"You're the one who said it was falling down."

"That isn't the same thing."

"Of course it is. Either it falls down or I take a sledge-hammer to it. What's the difference?"

"The difference is that you could mend it."

"Mend it? You want me to mend it? Look Kate, for years you moaned to me about it being an eyesore. Now you want me to patch it up? In your dreams!"

"There's no need to be like that. You could at least consider it."

"Absolutely not!"

"Come out and look at it. You haven't been inside it in years."

"And I don't intend to go inside it either. It's coming down, Kate. I'm not wasting time or energy on patching it up now. It's too far gone."

Kate opened her mouth to protest further but Dan raised his hand and turned away to switch on the TV. "I'll not hear any more about it. It's coming down!"

She closed her mouth and glared at him.

Dan shook his head. "I don't understand you, Kate. I really don't." He picked up the paper, terminating the conversation.

"No," she muttered through gritted teeth. "And you never have."

"What's that supposed to mean?" he demanded, looking up from the paper.

"Nothing!"

"Anyway, we need somewhere to keep the car, not all the neighbourhood mice," he muttered, resuming his scanning of the television listings.

"There are no mice," she protested. "And why the sudden urgency to have somewhere to keep the car?"

With a sigh, he lowered the paper again. "Because I'm fed up parking out in the street. In case you haven't noticed," he gestured towards the window. "Everyone and their granny has a car these days. Sometimes I can't get anywhere near my own house. I'm fed up walking the length of the street to get to my front door."

"You could make a drive up the side."

"I'm going to make a drive up the side. And a garage in the back to go with it."

"But I don't want a garage. I want to keep the summerhouse. I like sitting out there."

"We've got a sitting room."

"It's not the same."

"No, there's no mice to spoil the peace in here," he said as he turned up the sound on the television.

"I told you, there are no mice."

But Dan had stopped listening. He saw no point to the argument. He had made his mind up. The summerhouse was coming down just as soon as he got a chance to do it.

He couldn't understand her fixation with the place. It was a monstrosity, the ugliest outhouse he'd ever seen. How someone ever got planning permission for it!

It was far too close to the house for one thing. Different if it had been a proper conservatory, adjoining the house, but this wasn't. It was just the wrong distance away, too far to be considered part of the house, too close to be ignored as part of the garden. It was neither conservatory, greenhouse nor garden shed; neither use nor ornament. He could think of no reason on earth why anyone would build such a thing.

But someone had. Decades ago. Obviously before planning permission was needed.

Dan glowered at what was left of the strange structure; a mixture of old brick and stone walls, with long, wooden window frames holding long, thick panes of glass; the glass roof cracked and leaking, a flower-pot to catch the drips here and another over there; the smell of damp. Mildew. Like the smell of old football socks rotting in a neglected sports bag. Mixed with a hint of old garage floor. He shook his head. It really did have to come down.

If he hadn't hated it for its ugliness, he would certainly hate it for what it had become to Kate. He could see no reason why she preferred to sit out here rather than in the house with him. He kicked at the door. Rotten! Just as he'd thought. The wood was rotten right through. It had to go. The damn summerhouse had to go!

It really got to him. It reminded him of when she had been carrying the kids. How she'd sit hugging her pregnancy to herself, a secret smile on her face, in a world of her own, shutting him out. The summerhouse had become some kind of giant womb for her. He had no place in it or around it. He was shut out, he was lonely and he objected.

He grunted as he pulled the door from the hinges he'd unscrewed. Well, it wouldn't be shutting him... or anyone else... out any more.

The arguments this decrepit old place had caused.

But the more they argued about it, the more she haunted the place. When he came home late one evening, he found she'd been mooning around the summerhouse for hours instead of making him a meal. They'd had a spectacular row and she stayed out there all night while he fumed in the house. When he looked out after the late-night movie ended his evening's telly-viewing, he saw that she still had a light burning, so he went to bed, angry and more determined than ever that the monstrosity had to come down.

He thought she'd be frozen, with only her pride keeping her warm.

Now he realised she hadn't been cold. She had a proficient old oil heater. And she had a store of quilts and blankets in an old chest she must have dragged home from some second-hand shop. He expected them to be damp and fusty but they were fresh instead, smelling of lavender and roses, a musky rather than a musty perfume. He didn't want to soil them, but he was sure that, if he rummaged through them a little, he would find those little scented bags old ladies put in their underwear drawers. He closed the chest and smoothed his hand over the polished wood of its lid, ran his fingers along the scrolls engraved around it. Oak, he guessed, solid oak, heavy and strong; waxed and polished till it felt silky.

You have to hand it to Katie, he thought as he struggled to move the chest out of harm's way, *she knows a bargain when she sees one.* Amazing how she could see the potential in old things he'd think were rubbish, cart them home, do them up and they'd look pretty good. Stretching his back to ease out the strain, he studied the chest in its new surroundings. Perhaps the kitchen was not the best place for it, but there was no way he could get it upstairs on his own. Still, it would look pretty good anywhere: not a bad piece of furniture: she must have felt vindicated in her choice once she'd restored it.

But this time she's wrong, he told himself firmly, turning round. The summerhouse is rubbish. It has no potential. It's coming down!

* * *

Saturday, it rained and Kate nearly decided against the walk. However, she judged that, rain or not, the exercise was trimming her figure nicely and she wanted all the help she could get in that department before next Friday. The dress was gorgeous, but it needed her figure to be at its best.

So, she set off with a light step, glad she'd made the decision to come, looking forward to the rewards of the day... including a promised cuppa in the hotel where they parked their cars, when they returned from the nearby woodland walk.

It wasn't an arduous walk, but because of the inclement weather, they didn't dally to enjoy the views glimpsed from time to time through the trees. The party of walkers kept up a good pace and there wasn't much conversation, which suited Kate because it was the exercise she wanted rather than the company today. Her thoughts were company enough. She needed to get straight in her mind the whole idea of Dan's retirement.

Paul was right. She had been acting very badly and it was time she sorted her attitude out. Dan had worked hard all these years, and, if he could afford to retire, then why not? She would just have to adjust. True, she had her work... and her time with Phyllis... and her Saturday walks. It was just a matter of keeping busy, finding things to do that would occupy her enough not to mind Dan being around more.

Perhaps Paul was right about that too though: that she ought to try to spend *more* time with Dan, get to know him again. They had grown apart, were more like strangers. It would be good if they could draw close again.

She stopped walking for a moment as the thought suddenly struck her: Had they *ever* been close? Did they *ever* share much in common?

As the couple walking behind her overtook, she smiled absently and automatically fell into step behind them.

Perhaps it was time to get to know her husband... not *again*, but for the first time!

The rain never let up and they got truly soaked through, but Kate thoroughly enjoyed her day, nonetheless. She had done some serious thinking and had reached some positive decisions. She was humming as she parked the car and walked up the path, round to the back door.

She was halted in her tracks by the sight of her summerhouse furniture lying in the garden, soaking up the rain.

There was movement from inside the summerhouse itself, so she managed to make her legs propel her forward till she could lean against the doorway.

"What are you doing?" Her voice came out in a strangled croak. She tried again, louder. "Dan! What are you doing? My furniture…"

Dan looked up. There was sweat on his brow and his face was red with exertion.

"What does it look like?" he answered with irritation. "I'm clearing out this damn monstrosity so I can demolish it."

"But these are my things. I bought this furniture. You have no right." Her voice was shaking. She started vainly trying to pull the sofa back inside. "It's getting soaked. It'll be ruined."

Dan straightened up from the box he was loading with books and games. "Come on, love," he tried to placate her before the impending storm erupted. "It's only a load of old bits and pieces."

She glared at him. "That's all it may be to you, Dan Morgan, but it's mine." Her voice was rising. "Get it back inside," she said through gritted teeth. "Now!"

"Katie," Dan soothed. "The neighbours…"

"To hell with the neighbours," she shouted. "Get my furniture back in that summerhouse… now!"

Dan stood immobile, watching her pull and push fruitlessly. "I'm taking the summerhouse down, Katie. I told you. I'm not going to change my mind."

"No!" she screamed. "No, *I* told *you*… I don't want it pulled down."

"But it's finished. It's outlived its usefulness."

"To who? It was never useful to you. But it was to me. It *is* to me. This is *my* place, Dan. Don't you understand?"

"No, Katie, I don't understand. I never have. We have a perfectly good home, a comfortable living room. Why you should decide to cut yourself off out here…"

"You'll never understand."

"Right! I don't."

She looked again at the soaked furniture. "How long has this been out in the rain?"

"Not long."

"Oh, what does it matter?"

"Exactly."

"It's all ruined," she cried. "You've spoiled everything, Dan, everything."

"No, love. You'll see." He reached his hand out to her. "We'll redecorate the sitting room. You can choose the paper."

She looked at him in horror. "You *don't* understand, do you?" she said quietly. "You never have."

He shook his head. "I know you never liked that suite. We could…"

"Oh, it's not about paper and paint… or three piece suites. It's us, Dan! It's us!"

"What?"

"There's nothing there!"

"Where?"

"With us, Dan. There's nothing left." She looked around for the last time. "And now there's nothing left for me here, Dan. You've spoiled it." She trailed her hand along the arm of the sofa, watching the water run over her fingers. "Ruined," she said softly.

When she turned and walked down the path, she didn't know where she was going to go but, when she drove away, she didn't look back.

Chapter 7

He hadn't intended to start on the summerhouse till he'd finished at work, but he'd been hurt and angry that, yet again, Kate had gone out for the day without any indication of where she was going. He assumed that she wouldn't be home for tea…yet again… and didn't have the decency to let him know. He'd always thought of Saturday as a day of rest, but today, his anger gave him none. He couldn't settle to anything. Even the afternoon's sport on the box held no interest for him. *Where on earth did she go every Saturday? Who did she meet?*

He threw down the paper he'd been trying to read and strode out to the kitchen.

He hadn't intended to start on the summerhouse…

Who did she meet?

As he stood glaring angrily out of the window, not really seeing the rain, not really aware of the soup boiling on the cooker behind him… suddenly, he knew what would sooth his anger, suddenly he knew exactly how he wanted to spend this Saturday afternoon!

At first he made great headway. He pulled all the old furniture out into the garden. He rolled up the rugs and tossed them out too. Then he realised there were a lot of bits and pieces about the place, books and things as well as a load of plants.

Well… the plants would have to take their chances… he carried them all out to the garden, lining them up against the house and on the windowsill. They should be alright there… at least they'd get well watered. The thought passed across his mind that she must have been constantly out here with a watering can… there were so many of the damn things.

He went up into the loft, where he knew Kate had stored the boxes they had used when they moved into the house. He shook his head. Who in their right mind kept old boxes for twenty-eight years? He remembered the argument he'd nearly had with her about it at the time. He'd given in before things had got heated and put the stupid boxes up there, to keep the peace. It just didn't seem worth falling out over.

With a wry laugh, he hauled them down now, and carted them out to the summerhouse.

It was while he was filling one of them that Kate appeared, earlier than he'd expected, and lost the place.

Well, she'd probably be back in a while. He looked at the sodden furniture, the ransacked summerhouse. She'd not be sleeping out here tonight!

* * *

"Oh my goodness, you look frozen... and you're soaked! Come in, come in."

Phyllis drew her into the warmth of the hall. "Where on earth have you been? Oh, never mind, never mind. Let's get you out of these wet things." She helped her off with her coat. "Mary," she called. "Run a hot bath for Kate, please. Put some mustard in it. She's shivering."

"I'm sorry, Phyllis... I..."

"It's okay. We'll talk when you're warmed up. Into that bath first," Phyllis ordered. "Then Mary will make us a nice cup of cocoa. I'll go and look out something warm and dry for you to put on."

"I'm so sorry to descend on you like this." Kate shivered.

Phyllis looked at her kindly. "It's alright, my dear. Like I said, we can talk later." She stroked the tear stained face. "Then you can tell me what's wrong. Meantime, go and have a long soak in the hot tub. You'll see, everything will seem a lot better when you're warm and dry and wrapped round a mug of cocoa."

"So, what are you going to do?" Phyllis asked kindly.

Kate had told her all about coming home from her walk, soaked to the skin but happy, thinking about how pleased and surprised Dan was going to be when he saw her in the dress on

Friday. But it was she who got the surprise to find that he had started clearing the summerhouse.

"So what are you going to do?"

"I don't know," she shook her head sadly. "I suppose I'll have to find somewhere to live. A wee flat or something. I'm not going back to Dan, that's for sure. I'll pick up some stuff when he's out at work on Monday. I haven't even got my handbag with me." She looked at Phyllis helplessly. "I don't take it with me on the walks. Just a few pounds in my pocket… for emergencies… cups of tea and the likes." She managed a watery smile.

"Oh dear, " Phyllis murmured, buttoning her cardigan.

"I was wondering," Kate continued shyly.

"Oh dear," unbuttoning her cardigan.

"I was wondering if I might stay here. Just for tonight, I mean. Just till I think what to do."

"Oh, I don't think…" buttoning.

"I'm sorry, Phyllis," Kate said quickly. "Of course I can't put upon you like this." She started to rise. "It was wrong of me to trouble you with my problems. I'm so sorry."

"Sit down and finish your cocoa," Phyllis insisted, smoothing the front of the tightly buttoned cardigan with her hand. "Of course you were right to come to me. Who else would you go to. It's just that… It's just that…"

"I know, it's probably not convenient. No notice and everything."

Phyllis wrestled with her problem. "Of course I want you to stay. Where else would you go? But…"

"I could sleep on Vicky's couch… or Paul's. Yes. I could go to Paul's."

Phyllis made a decision. "No. This is silly," she said firmly, giving the buttons a final pat. "Of course you must stay here. After we've finished our supper, we'll… we'll sort something out."

Kate studied her friend's face. "Is everything alright with you, Phyllis?" she asked. "It's just that I've never seen you like this," she continued when Phyllis didn't reply. "You're usually so... well... so composed," she finished, indicating Phyllis' fluttering hands.

"Yes, of course everything's alright," Phyllis replied briskly. "Now drink up your cocoa and we'll see if Mary has any more in the pot."

But everything was not alright. Phyllis was unusually tense and fidgety. She couldn't sit still, kept getting up and straightening a cushion, or repositioning an ornament. Her face was pale and drawn, the furrows deeper in her worry.

Kate watched her as she sipped her soothing drink. When Phyllis eventually sat down again she leant across to touch her hand. "Phyllis. I'm sorry. I've been so wrapped up in my own troubles. I didn't think about it... that perhaps you were worried about something too." She stroked the old, wrinkled hand. "What is it? Do you want to talk about it?"

"It's nothing ... nothing at all. Just an old lady's foolishness. You drink up, dear, while I get Mary to look out some bedding for you." She rose, patting Kate's hand in return. "I should think one of these sofas would be quite comfortable, wouldn't you?"

"If you really don't mind?"

"Of course not," she smiled. "It'll be fun having you. I don't have many 'stop-over' guests. In fact I haven't had one in years. Yes, it will be fun. Everything will be just fine," she tried to convince her guest as she sought to convince herself.

* * *

On Sunday, Dan progressed well, hauling slates and timber off the roof with ease in his angry energy. He'd been right about the state of the place. The timbers were rotten, could have come crashing down at any time. He'd been right too about the mice. When he'd started hammering at the walls, the mice had scurried about frantically, not knowing where to go for safety.

Suddenly, he was sorry. Sorry for the homeless, frightened mice. Sorry for himself and Kate.

They had meant so much to each other once. They had wanted so much to be together. He had been delighted when she became pregnant and her dad had insisted he marry her. He'd wanted to anyway, but hadn't asked, assuming she'd turn him down. He was no great catch, nothing much to say for himself, too quiet, he was often told… while Kate, she was such a lively wee thing. Her energy had attracted him. The way she laughed, her animation as she talked, her enthusiasm for life: it had all been deliciously new to him. Like a first glass of champagne.

He smiled now as he remembered the way she scurried about when they were newly married, getting everything organized, building a home. Like these mice, searching for a new one. The difference was; they were frantic. Kate had been cool, cool but busy, always busy. She never seemed to stop. Everything had to be ready for the baby.

"Not now, Dan," she'd say when he put his arms round her swollen belly. "I'm busy."

"Not now, Dan," she'd say when he kissed the nape of her neck while she bent over the ironing. "I want to finish this before the baby wakes up."

Always busy.

Vicky had been a demanding baby, he supposed. Kate certainly was always occupied with her, feeding her, bathing her, cooing over her.

"Isn't she just perfect?" she'd say as he came in the back door at the end of the day. "Who's Mummy's perfect baby," she'd coo to her.

But Vicky was no 'perfect baby'. She took over the household from day one, claiming all of Kate's time and attention: a whining, grizzly baby. It wasn't till she was about four or five that she became something a bit more pleasing. But, by that time, Paul had taken over as Kate's pride and joy.

Paul was a lovely baby. Even Dan had to agree. He had a happy, smiling disposition and was very much Kate's favourite, so Dan tried to make it up to Vicky by giving her a bit more attention. She became his 'wee pal', and he was glad of the company.

He'd never been used to company, companionship. It hadn't been his, when he was growing up. Memories of his mother were hazy, but he remembered that she was never there... even when she was there, before she'd gone. She always had somewhere to go, someone to see. She never talked to him, never cooed over him, seemed to see him as an unwanted accessory that convention dictated she had to carry with her. When they went anywhere, his pram was parked outside and he was given what she called a pacifier... a dummy they called it now, he supposed... and left to amuse himself as best he could. He had been too young to know it was wrong, but too old to be in a pram, by the time it all stopped. Suddenly. She left, suddenly, when Dan was four years old.

One day she didn't take him with her. She just left him sitting in his high-chair, went out the back door and didn't come back. By the time his father had come home from work, Dan had cried himself to sleep, his head on the tray of the chair, his trousers wet and cold, his pacifier lying, lost, on the floor.

His father did his best to care for a child he doubted was his own, but there was no tenderness, no companionship. Dan grew up in virtual silence.

At school, he was a loner, untrained in social intercourse, unable to break into the camaraderie that seemed to exist in the playground. He stood alone and he learned to be self-contained, at home with himself.

It had seemed strange that he should find Kate, that she should have been attracted to him. They were so different. He had gone to the party at the insistence of one of his workmates, had no intention of staying, and there was Kate. Kate bustling about, filling bowls of nuts, handing round drinks. Kate busy, bustling, vibrant. She'd been a pretty wee thing.

Still was a very attractive woman: auburn hair, softened with a smattering of grey now, but still gorgeous; dark, greeny-brown eyes, not a bad figure.

He caught her looking at him, watching him. She blushed. He watched her. She blushed even more. He waited, helped her clear away the debris of the party, walked her home... and was lost.

89

It had seemed that here at last he would find companionship, someone to share his life with, his thoughts with. But he couldn't share his thoughts. He had no words to do that. He didn't know how to start, didn't know how it could be done. Kate hadn't seemed to mind. She talked enough for the two of them. He thought she was happy in their quiet home, busy, bustling as always. But he craved companionship. He longed to sit by the fireside, sharing secrets, getting inside each other's hearts. He never did work out how to start. And it was too late now. Kate wasn't here... and he didn't have a pacifier.

He sighed, shaking the thoughts from his mind as he had shaken the summerhouse.

But he found himself longing to see Kate. Longing to see her dark, laughing eyes, the way he remembered them that first time he saw her, when he caught her looking at him. She had blushed and looked away, but not before he had seen the smile in her eyes.

He longed to hear her squeal at the mice scampering about. He missed her. He'd been missing her for a long time now. Long before 'The Battle of the Summerhouse'.

She hadn't come home last night. He wondered where she'd been. Tried to think reasonably, rationally, without the nagging suspicion and fear that had tormented the sleepless hours of the night. With Vicky, perhaps? Or, more likely, Paul. No doubt she would turn up later.

He looked at his watch. It would be dark soon. He'd have to stop for today. Just as well, he was tired anyway. The unaccustomed exertions of the weekend had taken their toll. He would need a good hot bath before going to bed: hoped that would be enough to stave off the stiffness and pain he could feel gathering in his back and arms.

He straightened his aching spine, his anger gone, weariness settling in. He surveyed his handiwork.

A tall, straight man, he had always had to stoop to enter through the doorway, but that was no longer necessary. The wooden window and doorframes were broken, the long glass panes stacked against the wall of the house. The walls were half demolished: the doorway a gaping, topless hole in one of them. A good weekend's work.

Then he saw the book, or rather, its covering scarf. The golden brown colour caught his eye, contrasting with the grey of the surrounding stonework.

And he wanted to call out for Kate.

He unfolded the thin silk scarf, itself a lovely thing, autumnal and glowing, with a smoothness and softness that invited fingering. But his hands were dirty. It was a shame to spoil such a special thing, so he laid it aside in the kitchen, to look at later.

It gave Dan no pleasure to sit in the living room this weekend, so, after washing his hands, he made himself a cup of tea and sat at the kitchen table to examine his treasure.

Now he could see that the material of the scarf was fragile, thin with age and ready to tear if roughly handled. He folded it gently aside and lifted out the book.

How Kate would love such a book; bound in soft, brown leather with the pages yellowed, it smelled of rose petals and dust and years gone by. The edges of the pages had once been gold, but whether through time or usage, the gold had worn almost away, leaving merely a hint of its glory and a softness that was pleasing.

It had been a notebook, but had become a book of dreams. Some unknown hand had penned enchanting stories in immaculate copperplate. Presumably, the same hand that had decorated the pages with flowers and birds, illustrations that brought animals and people to life on the paper. There was even an illustration of a tiny mouse, scampering across the bottom of a page. He had not been the first to disturb them, then.

Some unknown person, a woman he felt sure, had sat and dreamed, out in the summerhouse, just as Kate often had. But this lady had recorded her dreams: she had left them as a legacy for him to find.

Unless, the thought struck him, unless Kate had found them already. But no, he was sure she could not have. She would have brought the book in to show him. She would have been too excited with her find to keep it to herself. He smiled as he remembered the many times she had burst into his peace with her enthusiasm for something she had spotted in some old shop, or a jumble sale somewhere. He wished now that he had shown more interest.

As the evening settled into night, Dan sat at the table reading the stories and poems. Some of them had obviously been written for children, but there was a depth in them, a layer that was not for the child, a longing, a searching for something more than a child would look for. They touched Dan in a way he had rarely been touched before. He felt drawn to the unknown author who wrote so eloquently of love and loneliness, feelings so cleverly hidden in tales of fairies and princes.

She sat by the child as he lay fretful, feverish, sponging his heated body, crooning softly to soothe him. She loved this child with a love that caught her breath. She tenderly wiped away his tears, though, in truth, they evaporated on his hot, flushed cheeks almost as quickly.

"Tell me a story," he pleaded hoarsely.

She smiled at her child. "What story shall I tell?" She gazed out of the window to the freedom beyond, the sadness in her heart bringing the story on its wings.

"Once upon a time, in a far off distant land...."

The child smiled. "You always start that way."

"Of course. Is that not how all good stories start?" She returned his smile and watched him settle, closing his eyes the better to wander in the valleys and mountains of her imagination.

"Once upon a time, long, long ago, in a far off distant land, there lived a prince.. A strong and handsome prince, wearing kindness as his girdle and..."

"What's a girdle?" The boy opened his eyes.

"Something you wrap around yourself tightly."

"Like a belt?"

"Like a belt... but better. It doesn't only keep things tucked in, it holds them together."

"Yes, I see." The child frowned a little as he closed his eyes again. "He wore kindness as his girdle…" he prompted gently.

"And loneliness as his cloak…"

"Why was he lonely?"

"Hush child," she soothed. "Hush and listen and I will tell you.

The prince was lonely because he lived alone. He had always lived alone… ever since his mother and father had placed him in his castle to care for those who lived on the land around it.

Because he was a kind man, the farmers and their wives and their children all loved him. The farmers would bow as he passed, their wives would bake for him and leave their breads and pies and cakes and pastries on the steps of the castle, wrapped carefully in their best tea towels. And the children were never afraid to climb in his apple trees or chase their ball through his orchard for they knew he would never shout at them or wave his fist if he caught them.

But he was lonely.

When the farmers bowed, he smiled and bowed in return but what he really longed to do was talk to them. Oh, he'd ask them about their crops or the animals in their care… or they'd exchange a word or two about the weather… but oh, how he longed to ask them instead about their thoughts, about life, about living, but most of all… about love.

He had never been in love.

The castle was strong and handsome too and around it there grew a beautiful brier hedge: wild roses of the deepest, prettiest pink, each one perfect, fragrant and blushing.

He had not planted the hedge. One day, it just started to grow, first one little bush, then another, and because it was so beautiful, he let it flourish undisturbed. He liked to look out from his castle and see it there, like a warm, safe protection from the cold, dangerous forest beyond.

Then one morning, as he stretched and yawned in front of his open window, he saw a wonderful sight.

A castle in the forest.

It rose majestically, the trees around it falling before it, giving way to its splendour. As he watched, he saw there were flowers growing in its garden, there were birds singing in the bushes and trees around it. It was a bright and happy place, he could see.

'I must go at once and introduce myself to my neighbour,' he thought. So he donned his best clothes, of finest silk, with golden buttons.

But when he reached his brier hedge, he was met by the most beautiful princess he had ever seen. He knew she was a princess because only a princess could ever be so beautiful, with such a lovely smile and besides, she had a tiny, dainty diamond tiara peeping out from among her curls.

They knew at once, of course, that they would fall in love. That was their destiny. So, every day, she would skip through the brier hedge to visit him. Or he would struggle through to visit her. But for him, it was a struggle. It was a struggle because the hedge had grown so thick and strong over the years. There were spaces here and there, spaces she seemed able to find and squeeze through, laughing, and they would talk of this and that and everything that mattered and they would hold hands and walk in the twilight not needing words to know their love.

But, just as their love was growing, they were unaware that the hedge was growing too. Every day, another thorn, another branch. Growing out of habit. Growing because it didn't know how to stop. No-one had told it it should. Soon, he could no longer go to her. Still, she was able to reach him... for a while.

But then, one day, an awful thing happened. She couldn't find a space in the hedge. Not the teeniest, tiniest gap. She called to him, "Cut down the hedge," she pleaded. "Chop it down. I can't reach you."

"I can't," he cried. "I've tried and tried. But I have no tools. I don't know how to break through."

They tried to touch: she stretching her hand as high as she could up, up to the top of the hedge; he wanting to grasp it, but the thickness, the thorns of the hedge held him back. Try as they might, they couldn't get through.

He withdrew into his castle to search for some tool that would break the branches, but he had none. He had never needed them before. The hedge had always served as a protection for him... until now, when suddenly... or had it really been so sudden? Hadn't it been getting more difficult over a long time?... until now, it had become a barrier, an impenetrable barrier between him and the one he loved.

He tried to cut his way through with his sword, but he had never used it much. It had become rusted and blunt and he had no skill with it.

He could hear his love weeping on the other side of the briers, he wanted so much to hold her again, to laugh with her as they used to, to dance in the garden, the grass soft under their feet, the flowers smiling on their happiness. But it was no use. He had no way to be free.

His beautiful princess waited faithfully for him every day. At first she felt sure that he would find the right tool, that he would sharpen and hone it till it cut down the hedge. But then she began to know that he couldn't, that she must try to reach him instead.

She tried to push her way through, but the thorns tore at her cruelly, ripping her fine silk gown and scratching her skin till it bled. Sometimes she thought she was getting there. She would see a tiny space, a chink in the thorny armour. She would gently ease her way as far as she could, holding back this branch, snipping off that flower, those thorns, but just as she stroked his beloved face, the brier would push her out, separating her from the one she loved, the branches springing back into place, the gap closing over again.

Gradually, she could find no tiny gap, not even the tiniest, teeniest one, it seemed. Her dresses were torn, her fingers red and sore from the thorns, her cheeks stinging with her own tears but what could she do? She had loved and lost. She must walk alone in her garden, tending her flowers, waiting, waiting..."

The mother looked at her sleeping child, touched his beloved cheek gently with her lips, relieved to feel his brow cooler, glad of the rhythm of his steady breathing. She was glad he slept for she knew not how her story ended.

When he rose stiffly from the unyielding kitchen chair to go to bed, he realised that his face was wet with tears; tears for something found, tears for something lost.

* * *

"Where's Mum," Vicky asked, looking round the living room door a few days later.

"I don't know," Dan looked up wearily from his paper. "I hoped you might know."

"Oh, like that, is it?"

"I started taking down the summerhouse."

"I can see that. The boys are out there now, crying over it."

Dan drew his hand across his brow. "Oh no, I never thought of that. They liked going in there with your mother didn't they?"

"Loved it."

"I should have warned you. You could have prepared them."

"Too late for that now, they're out there, picking through the rubble, checking whether you've thrown out their favourite games and books."

"I didn't. They're upstairs in your old room. I boxed them before I started."

"Well, that's something at least. But what on earth did Mum say?" She looked at her father's stricken face. "Oh dear. You thought she might be with me... because she's not here... because she's gone. Oh, Dad. What have you done?"

Dan walked to the back door.

"Callum, Josh," he called to the boys. "Be careful there. I don't want you hurting yourselves on that glass!"

"What have you done with Grandma's things, Gramps?"

"Where's my tractor book?"

"Where's the Monopoly?"

"Did Gamma keep my picture?"

He crouched down to take them in his arms, but, this time, they stood off from him, uncertainly. "Why are you knocking down Grandma's house?" Callum asked sadly.

"It was very old and it was getting dangerous," Dan replied carefully.

"Couldn't you have mended it?"

"Not really, it would have been too difficult."

"But Grandma will be sad."

Dan looked up at Vicky. He swallowed hard. "Yes, Callum. Yes, she is very sad. She's gone away a wee while… till it's all finished."

"Gone away?"

"Yes. For a wee holiday. Just till I can get it all cleared up so it doesn't make her sad anymore."

"Did you keep all the games?"

"Yes, and the books."

"But where will we play with them. Where will Grandma read to us?"

Dan reached out and Callum let himself be lifted in the air. "Right here," Dan crowed. "Right here in the house," he said, taking the child through to the living room. "You'll cuddle up right here on the sofa with Josh and Grandma, and…"

"I liked the summerhouse."

"I know Callum."

"So did I."

Dan set Callum down and crouched beside the two boys. "I know you did. And so did Grandma. But it was old and…"

"Did it die?" Josh asked.

Dan looked at him for a moment. He tousled his hair as he stood up. "Yes, I suppose in a sort of a way."

"Houses don't die, silly," Callum corrected his little brother.

Dan sighed. "But something has," he muttered to himself.

"Here Dad, I've made you a cup of tea," Vicky said as she handed it to him. "Right boys. Suppose you go up to the spare room. Grampa says your books and things are up there." She looked enquiringly at Dan.

He nodded. "They're in some boxes."

"You can look through the boxes and check they're all there."

The boys ran noisily up the stairs.

"They'll get over it, Dad. Once you've got the rubble and everything cleared, they'll forget it was ever there."

"I know," he sighed. "I've ordered a skip for next weekend. I'll not get much done before then."

"When did you start it?"

"Saturday."

"And Mum?"

"She's been away since Saturday."

"But it's Wednesday night now! Why didn't you phone?"

"I thought you would both be pretty angry with me."

"I can imagine Mum is furious, if you did this against her will?"

He nodded.

"But, why on earth would *I* be angry with you?"

"I assumed you'd agree with her."

"Why? It was an eyesore of a place. A wreck. I don't know why you didn't knock it down years ago!"

It should have been a comfort. To know that Vicky agreed with him, that she didn't think he'd been in the wrong. But somehow it was cold comfort. He wished he hadn't done it.

And where was Kate?

"Well, she isn't with me," Vicky assured him. "I'll give Paul a bell."

But she was not with Paul and he had no suggestions as to Kate's whereabouts.

So where was she?

With the same man she had been seeing every Saturday?

Chapter 8

They hadn't stopped for their usual coffee in the 'Coffee Shop'. Kate had been home to pick up some things on Monday, while Dan was at work. She'd left the car for him, since it was technically his, so Phyllis said she'd meet her after work on Wednesday.

"It's okay," Kate argued. "I can get the bus."

"But I'd like to collect you. It would give me pleasure."

So Kate had reluctantly agreed. Reluctant, not because she was ungrateful... but reluctant to be in the car with Phyllis driving.

"Look, Phyllis," she gathered her courage to say, "if we're to drive about together much, d'you think perhaps *I* could drive? I'm not a very good passenger," she added hastily.

"Oh, that's a good idea," Phyllis agreed readily. "I'll get you put on the insurance right away."

"Watch out!" yelled Kate.

"Oops, sorry." Phyllis stopped with a screech, just in time. "She shouldn't have been going down there anyway."

"She had right of way, Phyllis."

"Not really. I was here first."

"But she *did* have right of way."

"Oh, well, she's gone now anyway. No harm done."

"Not this time," Kate breathed to herself.

"Any sign of our Ms Ferguson in the shop?" Phyllis asked conversationally, seemingly unaware of the perspiration on Kate's forehead, or her white knuckles on the dashboard.

"Naomi Ferguson? No... no, I haven't seen her at all."

"Any news of her in the shoe department?"

"Not that I've heard."

"I wonder if she's alright."

* * *

"Are you alright, Naomi?" Bill asked.

"What?" She looked up, startled, like a frightened rabbit.

"Only you've been really distracted all day... longer... all week."

"I'm alright, thanks Bill."

"Only, if there's anything I can do..."

"Thank you. That's kind of you, but I'm alright. Really."

"Only, you haven't moved from this desk in days. You don't even go out to lunch anymore. And I haven't seen you eating here either."

"I'm okay. Really."

"And you haven't smiled in I don't know how long."

She smiled up at him now.

"Only I could take you out to lunch, if it would help. If you're worried about money or something," his voice tailed off.

"Oh, Bill. You really are kind, and it would be lovely to go for lunch with you sometime. But only if Rose is there too. I don't want to cause trouble for you."

Rose was Bill's wife. She was a possessive wee thing and regularly came into the office to stake her claim on 'her Bill'.

"Of course," he agreed readily. "It is money, then?"

"What is?"

"That's worrying you."

"Oh, that. No, well, not really. Only indirectly. I suppose it's part of the problem. But only, as I say, indirectly."

"Oh, I see," Bill said, obviously not 'seeing' at all.

"Look, don't worry Bill. I'll sort myself out. We could go to lunch with Rose some other time. I'll just grab a sandwich from 'Marks' today."

"If you're sure you're okay?"

"Sure."

"Right."

Bill eased quietly back to his own desk, obviously relieved to have done what he felt was his duty.

Naomi sighed. She would need to 'sort herself out'. If even Bill noticed that she was troubled, then she must look pretty glum.

"Could I see you a minute, Miss Ferguson?"

It was her boss, Peter Cartwright, the source of her troubles.

She rose slowly from her desk and reluctantly went to his office.

Closing the door behind her she leant against it and waited.

"Yes?" she enquired as icily as she could.

"Come on, Naomi. Cut the crap. Look, I'm sorry about last weekend. I've told you I'm sorry."

"You're always sorry," she sighed.

He came towards her. "Come on," he pleaded. "Stop the cold treatment." He put his arms round her and drew her to him. "I'll make it up to you. What about tonight?"

"Mary out, is she? Keep fit, is it? Line dancing?" She turned her face from his kiss, pushing his arms away.

"Come on. Don't be like this. You know you want me as much as I want you."

"I know you only want me when it suits you," she said coldly. "And that's not at weekends or holidays!"

"You know weekends and holidays are difficult for me."

"Then why tell me you'll come?"

"I thought I could. I wanted to." He tried to hold her against him again.

"No, Peter. Leave me alone," she said, forcing him away.

"Come on," he wheedled. "What did you expect, Naomi? You knew I was married."

"Not at first, I didn't."

He trailed his fingers down her arm. "You didn't ask," he shrugged. "I didn't think it mattered. You were determined to get me into your bed anyway."

She lifted her hand, tried to slap him, but he caught her wrist before the blow landed.

"You'll be sorry you did that, Naomi," he said as he held her arm down by her side.

"Oh, will I Peter? Why? What will you do? Punish me? Stop seeing me? Give me the cold shoulder? So, what's new?" She pulled away from him.

"You'd better say you're sorry," he warned.

"And while I'm at it, I suppose I should beg your forgiveness for being upset that you left me hanging about, yet another weekend, waiting for you to call, waiting with the table set, the meal ready. Should I beg your forgiveness, Peter?" Her voice had not risen, but it had become hard, bitter. She had had enough of this man. He had used her for long enough. She needed out of this relationship.

Peter sat down heavily at his desk. He put his hands over his face.

"Oh, Naomi," he said quietly. "I'm so sorry. I didn't mean to hurt you. Really, I didn't. I would have come if I could. I wanted to. Really, I did."

"Did you, Peter? What kept you then?" she hissed.

He looked up at her, pleadingly. "It just wasn't possible. Honestly. Mary had invited some friends. You know the kind of thing. Our kids are friendly with their kids. They were all there. There was nothing I could do."

She tried to harden herself, make herself immune to his smile, shut out those big brown eyes. "You didn't even phone."

He shook his head sadly, penitently. "I know. I wanted to. You've got to believe me. There just wasn't a chance." He smiled up at her, shrugging his shoulders ruefully. "I'm so sorry, Babe. Really I am."

She could feel the ice inside her melt. She wanted to believe him. He reached his hand out to her. She wanted to take it in hers, wanted to put it against her face, wanted to kiss it, to make everything better. His eyes were pleading with her. She knew he was going to win… again.

She went shopping at lunchtime. She had tried to stop herself. For two whole weeks she had made herself sit at her desk during her break, made herself think about other things. She knew it had become an addiction, one that she couldn't afford. She had to break it.

But here she was again. Shopping. And really Shopping. She had been so determined that she'd be strong that she didn't even have anything with her to exchange. She'd have to pay for her pleasure.

A hollow laugh escaped from her throat. Huh! If you could call it pleasure: this feeling of hopelessness that drove her to shop. This feeling that she was losing control, that she had to buy something, hold something, have something, something new, something different, anything, anything at all.

She hadn't meant to end up in 'Harrison's'. She got a fright in there not so long ago. Some old dear had chatted her up, asked her to coffee. Now why would anyone want to do that? She couldn't imagine the old lady really wanted her company. Let's face it: Naomi knew she was no great conversationalist. Never knew how to make small talk, never could make someone laugh, never did feel comfortable in company. So what did the old girl want? Perhaps she thought she had money? Perhaps she wanted a hand-out. She'd've taken her for coffee, spun some hard-luck story then asked for money. Just a loan, of course. Then disappear, never to be seen again.

What would she buy today? She'd limit herself to one good thing. Maybe two. But she was broke. Her Access account must be almost maxed out. It'd have to be one thing. Just a small thing. A scarf, perhaps. Or a blouse. She could maybe run to a blouse.

But it was the dresses that drew her. Dresses and shoes: these were her weaknesses. Perhaps just a very ordinary one would be alright. Not too expensive. Maybe she could ask Pete for a raise. He'd be in a good mood if she let him come to the flat tonight. At least at first, he would. If she asked before they fell onto her single bed, before he had what he wanted, before he was bored with her, had to rush home to Mary and the kids. If she asked then, when he was still playing his Seduction Game, when he said she could have anything she wanted.

But it was only a game. Later, if she reminded him about his promise of a raise, he'd laugh. He'd hold her cruelly by the hair, part of his Hard Man Game. He'd mock her for believing he meant it. Why should he give her a raise? What had she done to deserve it?

She had been leaning against one of the display rails, the familiar scene playing in her head, hurting her, immobilising her.

"Are you alright, Ms Ferguson? Can I get you something? Water? A seat?"

It was that kind sales assistant again. The one she used to look for.

"You don't look very well," she said. "Can I help you?"

Can she help me? Can anybody help me? *Can anybody help me?*

Naomi smiled, or at least she thought she smiled.

"Oh, dear," said the shop assistant. "Here. Please sit down." She had led her to a chair. Or had she brought the chair to her? How did she find it? Do they keep chairs handy for just such occasions? For when someone is lost. For when they've lost everything: their dignity, their youth, their love…

Years she'd been with Pete… waiting. Waiting for him to leave Mary. Like he'd always said he would. When the time was right. When Mary's health was better. When Mary got over the miscarriage. When the children were older. When… when… *when?*

"Drink this," the lady was putting a cup into her hand. Water. A cup of water. How was that going to help? How could that give her the courage to finish the Charade with Pete? To stop letting him force her to play his cruel games. A cup of water: an ocean of tears.

Obediently, she sipped the water.

"Is that better?" The assistant was smiling at her, crouched in front of her, genuine concern in her kind eyes. "Have you eaten? Have you had some lunch yet?"

Naomi shook her head. No, she hadn't had lunch yet. Hadn't been bothering with lunch lately. Or tea, really. It all seemed so pointless.

"Maybe we could go for some lunch together?" the assistant said. "I'm due for a break soon, anyway. Okay, Mrs Brown?" she checked with the snobby one, the woman who always frowned at you when you asked to exchange anything. The one who made you feel like scum, who put you right back in the gutter you were trying to climb out of. She'd probably step on your fingers if you were holding on to the edge. The edge sometimes feels so near, just there. One more step and, poof, you're gone. Over… over the edge.

"Come on, Ms Ferguson."

Lovely how she always remembers your name.

"Can you walk? Look, you can lean against me. That's right, lean on my arm."

How good to lean against someone, someone strong, someone you can trust.

"Good. Well done. One small step here. That's right. Good."

One small step for mankind: one giant leap for humanity. Or something like that. One small step, just one small step to the Edge. The edge of what? The edge of the world? The edge of the moon? They were walking on the moon. That's when they said that… about the one small step.

"Do you want me just to order something? Soup, I think. Soup's nourishing." She brought soup and a buttered roll. "Lentil soup today," she said. "Mmm… smells nice. There you are now. Do try it. It's lovely."

Obediently, Naomi dipped the spoon into the soup and brought it to her mouth.

Funny how automatic it all is. As if your body knows by itself what to do. Swallow now. Another spoonful. Swallow. A bite of the roll. Another spoonful. Mmm… yes, it is good.

"Mmm… it's good," Naomi murmured.

Kate beamed. "Yes, it is, isn't it? You're beginning to look better already. You've got a bit of colour back."

Naomi returned the smile. She did feel a bit better.

"How long is it since you ate?" Kate asked.

Naomi shrugged. She couldn't remember.

"I don't suppose you had breakfast."

Naomi shook her head.

"You really should have something, you know. Even if you only have a few pieces of fruit, it's important to have something in the morning. Gives you energy."

A nod. She knew it was true. It must be true. Hadn't Mum always told her that?

"Did you eat yesterday?"

Naomi shrugged. "I don't really remember," she said faintly.

"I thought as much. Going through a bad time are you?" Kate asked sympathetically.

Another nod. Afraid to speak, afraid that the sympathy would push her over the edge. The Edge. Never far away.

Kate leaned forward, reached across to touch her arm. Only a touch, only the slightest touch, but it was so good to be touched. Good to be touched in kindness. Bill was kind. Back at the office. Bill was kind. But mustn't touch. She wouldn't welcome his touch. Mustn't hurt his Rose. He was kind, but he had to be careful. He loved his Rose. Lucky Rose. To have someone love you, really love you. Care. Care enough not to touch another.

Help. This kind stranger was offering help. Naomi looked at her. Not really a stranger. Hadn't she been reaching out to her for a long time? Always asking, 'Can I help?' In the shop. 'Can I help?' Help to choose. Help to buy. Help to exchange.

"I wanted to buy a dress," Naomi responded.

"Well, if you're feeling better in a while, perhaps we can go back upstairs."

"Perhaps I'll buy some shoes to match."

"Let's see how fit you are in a bit."

"The soup's lovely. Thank you."

"Good. Would you like some more?"

"No, no, that was fine. Lovely," Naomi assured her.

"Good. Are you beginning to feel a bit more yourself?"

Myself? Feel more myself? What a funny thing to ask! Am I not always myself. Just me. The same 'me' I've always been. The same 'me' I'll always be? The 'me' on The Edge.

Kate looked at her watch. "I'm afraid I'm going to have to get back, now. Mrs Brown will…"

"What time is it?" Naomi jumped up suddenly.

"Two-fifteen."

"Oh, heck. Better get back. Late. Meeting quarter of an hour ago."

"Look. Do you think you're alright? Your colour's gone again." Kate leant across to support her.

"Got up too quick." Naomi sat down again with a bump.

"Take your time, this time," Kate said as Naomi started up again.

"Got to get back. Pete'll be going ballistic."

106

"Do you think you're well enough to be going back to work? Perhaps I should help you get home. Or to a doctor."

Naomi looked straight into Kate's eyes. "You'd do that, wouldn't you? You'd take me home. Me. A stranger. Nearly a stranger."

"Of course I will… if you need me to. I'll send word up to Mrs Brown."

"Incredibly kind!" Naomi said. "Why would you be so kind to me? I can't give you anything."

"I don't want anything," Kate laughed.

"You'd just do it out of kindness?"

"It's not such a big deal." Kate assured her. "We're trained to look after our customers."

"Doubt they meant taking them home."

"Probably not," Kate smiled. "But we can let that be our secret."

Naomi's flat was in the basement of an old tenement building. The entrance was at the back of the dark, dingy close. The sharp smell of cats was almost overpowering.

"Awful, isn't it?" Naomi said when she noticed Kate covering her nose and mouth as they neared her door. "Don't have to come any further. Be alright now."

"I'd like to see you safely in, if that's okay. You still seem a little unsteady."

"But…"

"It doesn't matter what state your flat's in," Kate smiled kindly. "I've brought up two children. I've seen untidiness before!"

"Let things go a bit," Naomi said as she unlocked the dark brown door.

"I don't think you've been well."

"No."

They entered the flat, unfortunately letting the awful smell in with them.

"That really is a dreadful smell out there. Is it your cat?"

"Don't have one." Naomi sank into a chair. "Pretty foul, isn't it? Keep telling the landlord. Doesn't care. Doesn't bother him. Doesn't live here."

"Do the other tenants complain?"

Naomi shrugged. "Don't know. Never see anyone."

But now that the smell of cats was receding, another smell became apparent.

"Oh dear," Kate said. "I think I can smell gas." She sniffed the air. "Can you smell it?"

"Probably," Naomi agreed. "Fire might leak a little. Not been using it."

"But it's cold in here... and damp, I should think."

"Yes."

"Is there nowhere else you can...?"

"No," Naomi said firmly. "Nowhere."

"But..."

"Don't need to stay." Her tone was becoming defensive. She tried to stand, but her knees were too weak. She fell back into the chair.

Kate was immediately penitent. "Oh, I'm so sorry. It's being a mother. I had no right to pass comment."

Naomi waved her apology aside.

"But, just before I go, can I get you something?"

"No. I'm okay," she sighed.

"You really don't look okay. Can't I phone the doctor for you?"

She shook her head.

"Sorry. I'll stop fussing. Once a mother..." Kate said apologetically. "But I really don't like leaving you here," she added, looking round at the dull, damp room, the cooker in the corner, the bed against the other wall, hardly a flat at all, just a room.

"I'll go to bed."

"But you must phone the gas company... that leak..."

"Yes. Tomorrow."

"Look, I don't like to be pushy or anything, but it really should be reported today... now. It might be dangerous."

108

"I'll do it now. Promise," Naomi reached for the phone book. "Look."

Kate waited while Naomi found the number and started to dial. "I'll let myself out then," she said sadly. "Perhaps I'll see you in the shop sometime... when you're better."

'Oh please God, no,' Naomi prayed silently, putting the phone down, as the door closed behind Kate.

But deep inside she knew that she would.

Chapter 9

Friday. Dan's last day at work.

"What are you going to do about his leaving party?" Phyllis asked.

"There's not a lot I can do, is there?" Kate replied sourly. "Since I've not seen or heard from him."

"Difficult … considering he doesn't know where you are. Must be worried sick, actually."

"Good."

"Don't you think it's time you let him know you're all right?"

"Not particularly."

"Well, I do. He'll have the police looking for you soon."

"He'll assume I'm at Vicky's… or Paul's."

"Do you not think they might have been in touch with one another by now? They might all be going frantic. Wondering where on earth you can be. They'll be dredging the river."

Kate laughed. "Can you imagine? What if they've reported me missing?"

"I don't actually think that's funny, Kate."

"Oh, I'm sure they're not that worried. I've not seen my face in the papers yet. Or on the telly."

"I suppose they could have checked whether you'd been in at your work."

"Exactly! That's what they'll have done. See?" she reassured Phyllis. "Nothing to worry about!"

"So that brings us back to the question of the party."

"What about the party?"

"I think you should go."

"How on earth can I go to Dan's leaving party, Phyllis, when it's *me* that's left, if you know what I mean."

"But you haven't really *left* Dan, have you? Not for good?"

"I don't know," Kate shrugged. "Maybe. I don't know yet what I want. I only know I'm still hurt. And angry. That he should care so little about me that he'd pull down my summerhouse."

"Why don't you see him tonight? Talk things over. Try to..."

"Try to what, Phyllis? Try to rebuild the summerhouse? Because that's what it'd take! I'll never forgive him."

"Don't say 'never', Kate. Never is a very long time."

"Well, that's how long it'll take."

"But you should talk it through with him. Find out why he did it."

"I know why he did it. He hates me having somewhere of my own. Somewhere I can be happy, somewhere I can breathe, somewhere I can sit and think, dream, make plans."

"You still have somewhere you can do these things. You can come here anytime you like, for as long as you like."

Kate stopped pacing round the sofa and came to sit beside Phyllis. "I know that, Phyllis. Thank you," she said softly. "Thank you so much. It is wonderful to know that. I love this room. I can imagine I'll grow to love it as much as my summerhouse. It's a summerhouse itself. But it's not *my* summerhouse. It's not *my own place.*"

"Oh Kate, I know it's not the same. I know this room, this house can't replace what you've lost. But it can help. It can help you not to become bitter. Not to let your loss destroy your marriage."

"Dan's already done that," Kate said bitterly.

"Not if you try to understand *why* he did it."

"I told you..."

"I know, you told me why *you* think he did it. But what about why *he* thinks he did it? You can only know that if you talk to him."

"Okay. So maybe I'll talk to him. But not yet... and certainly not tonight!"

"Why not tonight?"

"Are you joking, Phyllis? How can I turn up at his leaving 'do', in my 'posh frock'... which, just by the way, is in *his* house... to patch up my faltering marriage, when I haven't seen the man in a week? Quite apart from the cheek, the nerve it would take… what about the sheer practicalities?"

"Easy. You get all ready, showered and hair done, etc., here, then you get a taxi. Better a taxi than me driving you. No clues as to where you've been, in case you want to come back."

"In case? Of course I want… "

"You get a taxi to your own house…"

"*His* house, he reminded me."

"In time for Dan to take you to the party."

"Just like that?"

"Just like that."

"Why? Remind me," Kate said. "Why would I want to do that?"

"To save your marriage."

"I'm not so sure I want to save my marriage."

"Exactly! You're not sure."

"So?"

"If you're not sure you want to save it, then neither are you sure you *don't* want to save it."

"And?"

"If you should decide that you do…"

"Want to save it?"

"Then you won't have done something that you'll always regret," finished Phyllis.

"Which, of course is?"

"Not being there for a very important milestone in your husband's life. Not being there for him in front of all his friends and colleagues. Not being beside him when he closes a huge chapter of his life."

"Okay! Okay!"

"Am I getting through to you, Kate? I really think it's very important that you go tonight."

"I get the message," Kate sighed.

Phyllis sat back quietly.

"Just let me think for a bit," Kate said softly.

Phyllis patted her knee. "I'll go put the kettle on," she said.

She knew Phyllis was right. Just as Paul had been right when he'd talked her into going in the first instance. Of course they were right. But that didn't make it any easier to do it. She wasn't sure she was large-hearted enough to do it.

After all, Dan had not done the right thing. He had been mean and petty to her. But, then, two wrongs never did make a right, did they?

And she would regret it if she didn't go. If they ever sorted things out so that they could remain married. It would be a terrible gap in their joint history.

She looked around Phyllis's lovely sitting room. This was a beautiful place; one she knew would always hold a welcome for her. Perhaps it was time to let the summerhouse go. Perhaps.

But it had been wrenched from her, cruelly wrenched from her. She hadn't been allowed to 'let go'.

Phyllis came back into the room, followed by Mary, carrying the tea-tray.

"Well, what d'you think?" Phyllis asked as soon as Mary left the room.

"I think you're probably right," Kate sighed. "I ought to go. I will go. Now, tell me again how I've to accomplish the impossible?"

* * *

Dan was getting ready for the evening. He'd pressed his one good suit and bought a new shirt and tie. He had no heart for the whole business, but supposed it would have to be got through. He intended to tell everyone Kate was sick. He couldn't face any other explanation.

Paul had told him that Kate had intended coming... not that she'd dropped even a hint to him. But that was before. Before 'the demolition'. The demolition of his marriage, it had turned out to be, instead of only the demolition of a decrepit old summerhouse.

He sighed as he shaved. He sighed a lot these days.

He wished, with all his heart, he wished he'd not been so impulsive about it. He should have listened, reasoned with her, explained why it had to come down, got her to agree to it. He should never have just gone ahead like that. But, too late now. It was reduced to a heap of rubble… like his marriage.

He sighed again. Would it have made any difference? If she already has another man, does the summerhouse matter? Was she going anyway? Did he just push her to go sooner?

He heard the front door while he was in the shower, assumed it was Vicky come to cheer him on, maybe even to come with him, if she would. He had asked her, but she had felt it might make matters worse, make it more obvious that something was wrong. She was probably right, but he'd tried to coax her to come anyway.

The trouble was: he couldn't face it alone. Forty years he'd worked in the Civil Service. Forty years, many of them with the same people. Yet he had no friends to speak of. No real friends. The kind you could have a jar with in the pub. The kind you could share a good laugh with at the match. The kind who'd comfort you when your wife walked out when you needed her most.

At first, when they were married, at first he thought he wouldn't need other friends. There'd always be Kate to come home to, Kate to share a jar with, Kate to comfort him when things went wrong. But Kate wasn't there. Hadn't been there for a long time… for him.

"That you, Vicky?" he shouted downstairs as he came out of the bathroom.

"No, Dan," Kate said softly as he walked past her bedroom door. "It's me."

He stopped in his tracks, his hand caught in the towel he was using to dry his hair, his feet bathed in the drips that escaped the towel round his waist.

"Kate," he said, looking at her, taking in her new dress, her tasteful make up, her softly styled hair.

"Hello Dan," she said into the silence.

"Kate," he repeated.

"Yes?"

He cleared his throat. "You… you look lovely."

"You'd better get dressed or we'll be late."

"Late?"

"For the party. It is tonight, isn't it?"

"Party? Yes... oh, yes." he said as he looked at the towel he wore.

"Well?"

"Kate." He stumbled towards her. "I don't know what to..."

"Not now Dan," she said gently. "Just get dressed. We need to go soon."

"You... you're coming?"

She nodded.

"To the dinner?"

"Get dressed, Dan."

"Right." He finished drying his hair as he walked down the hall to his bedroom. The bedroom they used to share, where he still lay on the left side of the double bed, wondering if she was awake too, wishing the right hand side warmed by her body. He sat on the bed, momentarily bemused.

"Are you ready, Dan?" she called through, a few minutes later.

He shook off the towel and mechanically got himself dressed. An automaton, a robot, with no thoughts, no feelings.

When he appeared at the top of the stairs, she was there, waiting for him. Her coat on, her bag clutched to her like a shield.

"I don't want you to read too much into this," she said. "I'm coming with you tonight. To the party. But I want you to know I'm not coming home. Here. Afterwards."

"But why?"

"It doesn't matter why. I'm coming. Isn't that enough?"

He nodded. "For now," he said softly.

* * *

They travelled to the hotel in silence. There was so much to say.

As Dan opened the taxi door, he turned to her. "Thank you," he said huskily.

She smiled as he helped her out.

"You look fabulous," he said, helping her off with her coat.

Kate accepted the compliment with a blush. She felt good, really good, in the dress. She had lost weight in the week since she had last tried it on. It hung beautifully, skimming her curves, enhancing her figure, its mellow, autumnal colour giving her skin a warm glow. She had made up with care. Mary had helped her blow-dry her hair and had done a good job of it. She knew she was looking her best. She felt good.

She looked at Dan as he walked to the cloakroom. He didn't look so bad himself: tall, still slim, still straight; still kept most of his hair, the little bit of grey at the temples quite attractive. He was looking good.

"Hello, there, Kate. How are you?" It was Maggie Webster, their next-door neighbour. "Haven't seen you about much this last wee while. Been away, have you?"

"Just for a few days."

"Jim says they'll be sorry to lose Dan. A good boss, he says."

"Yes, you've said before," Kate smiled.

"How'll you manage? Having him under your feet all the time? Oh, I see he's making himself busy though, knocking down that old conservatory thing in your garden."

"Yes."

"That'll keep him out of mischief for a while."

"Yes. Oh, here's Dan. We'd best look for our table." She took Dan's arm. "See you later Maggie.

"Right, yes. Where *is* Jim? He's taking for ever to check in our coats." Maggie was already looking around for someone else to chat to while she waited.

"Sorry," Dan said. "Was she nosing? I was as quick as…"

"It's okay. Not your fault. She'd have cornered me at some point," Kate said wryly. "She'd noticed I'd not been home. How on earth do people know these things? She could have moved away a month ago and I wouldn't have noticed."

They found the function suite and were soon swept in with hearty congratulations for Dan and smiles and handshakes for Kate.

The evening went very well. Dan was presented with the obligatory gold carriage clock and a sizeable cheque. Kate was presented with a bouquet of flowers. Dan made a brief, but surprisingly funny speech. Kate smiled and mingled and smiled and chatted, playing the part of the dutiful wife. The buffet was plentiful and the wine flowed freely. Yes, the evening went very well.

She met an old friend she hadn't seen in a while, Liz Clarke, the wife of one of Dan's colleagues. She'd been telling Kate about her operation, a hysterectomy, and how much she wished she could get a break, a few days away, to gather her strength a little.

"As long as I'm at home," she said. "I find it very hard to rest as much as I should. Derek bought me a couple of books, but I just can't seem to get into them. I keep thinking of all the things I need to be doing around the place."

"I know what you mean," Kate sympathised.

"Before I can stop myself, I'm out of the chair and pottering about."

"But you can't just potter for long, can you?"

"Not when I know the kitchen cupboards haven't been cleaned out in months. And the hoovering's not being done as I like it."

"But you're not hoovering, are you? You really shouldn't."

Liz looked round furtively. "Don't let Derek hear you. He'd kill me if he knew I'd had the vacuum cleaner out."

"He'll not need to," Kate remonstrated. "You'll do that for yourself if you're not careful. Hoovering is a definite 'no-no' after a hysterectomy."

"I know, I know. But I can't stand seeing the house not right. It drives me crazy. I wish we could get away somewhere. Out of sight, out of mind and all that, you know?"

"Can you not get away?"

"Derek's too busy just now. The 'flu bug has decimated his department."

"Could you not get away somewhere yourself?"

"Where? Where does a middle-aged woman go for a few days on her own?"

"Your daughter? Could you not pay her a visit? She's only up in Dundee isn't she?"

"I thought of that," confided Liz. "But it really would not be much of a rest. She works all day and I'd end up doing her housework, I know I would. I couldn't bear to watch her come in from work, tired-out and then having to start cooking and cleaning. I'd want to have it done for her. It'd just be the same as at home… only worse, 'cause there's four of them to cook and clean for instead of just Derek and me."

"I see what you mean."

"And there's really nowhere else is there?"

"What about a health farm? They'd certainly look after you," suggested Kate.

"True. But who can afford a health farm? We're still trying to finish our conservatory."

Kate nodded thoughtfully. She looked around. How many of these women had a similar tale to tell? How many could benefit from a break such as Phyllis was providing for her? Somewhere to recharge the battery without discharging the bank balance too much. She sighed. Yes, it was good to be the beneficiary of Phyllis's kindness. But even Phyllis would not be able to offer a haven to all who needed it. She smiled as she thought of the glorious summery warmth of Phyllis's house.

Dan caught her eye. He smiled back at her, thinking perhaps that her smile was for him. She laughed. This time she would not blush. She was older and wiser now. She knew where these exchanges led.

When it was time to go home, Dan helped her into the taxi.

"Now what?" he asked. "Where do you want me to tell the driver…?"

"Home," Kate replied with a laugh.

Dan gave their address and settled back in the seat.

"You think you've won, don't you?" Kate said.

He spread his hands. "I didn't say a word."

"No, but I can see your silly grin."

"Sorry," he said, but he couldn't stop smiling. "I'm glad you came. Thank you."

"I'm glad too," she conceded. "But I'm not coming home, Dan."

"But…" he gestured towards the driver.

"Just to get changed."

"Oh."

They sat in silence.

As they stopped, another taxi drove up just behind them.

"There! I told Jim we could have shared a taxi!" Maggie shouted as she got out of it.

"Yes." Kate didn't shout. "Never mind. Next time."

"G'night." Maggie flowed up her path and poured herself into her house.

"She's had a bit too much," Jim whispered confidentially... and unnecessarily... across the dividing hedge. "Say, would you like to come in for a coffee?" he added enthusiastically.

"No.. Thanks all the same," Dan and Kate said in unison.

"'Night, then."

"'Night."

"Do you want a coffee?" Dan asked as they closed the front door.

"Certainly not with Jim and Maggie," Kate replied. "They're both sizzled."

Dan laughed. "Don't you mean 'sozzled'?"

"Whatever. They are."

"True. Anyway, I didn't mean with them. I meant with me." He coughed with embarrassment. "I feel like I'm asking you for a date."

Kate smiled. "That would be lovely, thank you. I'll just go and change first."

He caught her wrist, stopping her ascent of the stairs. "Please. Don't change... not yet. You look stunning. I like that dress. Please don't get changed yet," he pleaded huskily.

Halted in her purpose, Kate felt her resolve melt in the warmth of his entreaty. For a few moments more, they stood enveloped in the soft familiarity of their closeness, the enticing comfort of remembered intimacy but with a frisson of something new.

"Okay," she sighed, pleased with the compliment, touched by his sincerity.

He didn't release her wrist.

They stood, he in the hall looking up at her as she stood a few stairs above him, her hand resting on the banister, his hand on her wrist.

They stood, the clock in the living room behind them marking off the moments, heightening the suspense.

They stood, the air charged, neither one of them quite daring to speak, their eyes searching the depths of each other's very being… searching, wondering…

Suddenly, there was a loud banging on the front door.

They both jumped and Dan gently released her as he turned to open the door.

"Maggie says I should have insisted," Jim slurred.

"Tell Maggie, we still don't want to come over," Dan said firmly. "Thank you, but 'No Thank You'."

"Right. Right." He turned to go then turned back, swaying precariously. "Y'shure?"

Dan put out a hand to steady him. "Certain. Thank you."

"Right. Right." Jim stumbled back down the path, bumping into the hedge, almost falling over as he went.

"Are you going to be all right?" Dan asked. "Look," he turned to speak to Kate, but she wasn't there. "I'd better help you round," he mumbled to Jim.

He hoisted his neighbour's weight against him and delivered him safely home.

When he got back to his own house, Kate met him at the door. She had changed out of her dress and had her coat on, ready to go.

"Look, I'm sorry about the coffee and everything," she said. "But I'm not ready for this yet."

"For what?" Dan asked softly.

She gestured around her, between them, towards the kitchen, the bedroom.

"This. All this. To come back, I suppose. I've called for a taxi," she ended lamely.

"Oh, I see."

They still stood in the hall, at the foot of the stairs. The silence between them strained, stretched, crashing in their ears.

She didn't tell him where she would go. He didn't ask her.

Chapter 10

Saturday again. Saturday shopping. Everyone shops on a Saturday. What else was there to do?

Naomi wandered along Princes Street, trying to be content with window shopping... but it wasn't enough.

Perhaps, if she could just touch things. Not buy them. Just touch them.

She walked into Harrison's.

Dresses? No, too expensive. Shoes? Not much better. What then? A jumper, she could get a new jumper. She shivered. It was cold enough today. She really *needed* a jumper.

Ladies Knitwear, second floor. Not the lift. Get dizzy in lifts these days. The escalator would be better. Which way? Over there, beside the jewellery. A brooch would be nice on the jumper. Maybe best to wait till the jumper's chosen. But that's a pretty one.

"The gold heart, second row, on the end there. Yes that's the one. How much is it?" she asked the girl.

But she wasn't going to buy it, not really. Just pretend. Just looking.

"Access all right?" she asked.

Oh well, it's bought now. Can't be helped. Maybe be able to return it on Monday.

Up to Ladies Knitwear. Not to buy, just to touch. Can't afford the brooch *and* a jumper.

"Can I help you, Madam?"

Wish they wouldn't call you 'Madam'. Makes you think of a brothel. Prostitutes. Selling themselves for money. Does it count if it's for a job? Selling yourself to keep your job? Does that count as prostitution?

'A proper little madam', that's what Mum used to say when faced with a tantrum. 'A proper little madam'.

Is that what she is? Naomi Ferguson, 'Madam'?

"Are you all right, Madam?"

"Sorry, yes. 'Way in a dream." A nightmare, more like. "This one, how much, this one?"

The walk to the counter. Still time to decide against it. Plenty of jumpers at home. Too expensive.

"How would you like to pay, Madam?"

"Access, please."

Sweat it out. Don't run. Wait till the girl checks the account. There might be enough.

"There you are, Madam. If you'd just like to enter your PIN."

Naomi held her breath as she punched in the numbers, hand shaking, heart pounding.

"Thank you. That's fine," the assistant said as she handed her back her card and a carrier bag containing the all important jumper.

Got away with it this time. Best not risk any more. Stop now. Out of the shop.

No, downstairs. Not up to Dresses. Downstairs to the exit. Downstairs.

Naomi eased her way onto the Up escalator behind a couple.

Couples. What must it feel like, to be part of a couple? A real couple. Holding hands on the escalator, whispering about... about... whatever couples whisper about. What do couples whisper about?

Pete never whispers. Not unless its part of the 'hard-man' game and then it's more of a hiss than a whisper, so that doesn't count.

Anyway, being with Pete is not the same as being part of a couple. Couples can be seen together. Couples do things together, not just fall into bed, no talking, never mind whispering.

Dresses. Damn! Didn't mean to come to Dresses. Can't afford a dress. *Definitely* can't afford a dress. Not in here. One of the cheaper shops, maybe, but not in here. "Cheap and nasty," that's what mother called that first dress. The first ever purchase, bought with the jam-jar savings. All those twenty pence pieces. Amazing how they mount up. "Cheap and nasty!"

The red is glorious. Not really the right shade, according to that old dear the other week. Weird, that was. She was good though... with the colours. Red really is too bright... but it's glorious, absolutely glorious.

That first dress... that was red. Perhaps it *was* cheap. Jam-jar scrapings don't spread thickly. It wasn't nasty though.

It was bright, glorious red. It felt so good. To wear something new, something bought, not homemade, not handed down.

"Look at those seams," Mother said. "They'll not hold long!" And they didn't. "Cheap and nasty," she sneered, throwing the torn dress on the floor.

Naomi fingered the material gently. Expensive. Too expensive really. She took the hanger from the rail; walked to the changing room.

Just to try it on. Not to buy it. Certainly not to buy it.

Why doesn't it fit? Always bought a 'ten'. Perhaps it's bigger made. Some makes are. Bigger made, more generous.

"Do you have this one in a smaller size?"

"Sorry, Madam. That one only goes down to a 'ten'."

Walk away. Don't look at any more. Walk out the shop. Now. There's the escalator. Do it! Do it! Just walk out. Don't look at anything else. Sweating. Heart thumping. Keep breathing. Slower. Have to breath slower. Nearly there. Last department to walk through. Perfumes. Don't need perfume. Don't really like perfume much. Walk on out. Keep walking. Breathe, don't forget to breathe. Spinning. Everything, spinning. Get out. Get out now.

* * *

Saturday morning.

"Damn! Forgot to show her that book, last night," Dan berated himself, reaching across to take it from the drawer. Not that there was much chance. Surrounded by colleagues and their partners all evening, besieged by neighbours half the night. Perhaps if Jim hadn't come to the door just when he did...

He was sitting at the kitchen table, having finished his breakfast. He should have been starting on the summerhouse rubble. The skip had already been delivered. There was nothing to hold him back. Nothing except the nagging feeling that he wished he'd never started this particular project. It had already cost far more than he'd bargained for... and he wasn't thinking of finance.

The book, or more accurately, its covering, had caught his attention again, the way it had when he originally found it. This time a corner of the silk scarf was peeping out of the drawer where he'd put it for safekeeping. Once again, it stopped him in his tracks, redirected his thoughts. He found the stories haunting, the poems lyrical and wild, bursting from the pages as though freed from the captivity of many years. A lively tapestry embroidered by a loving pen.

He read again the written words, knowing they were simple; his intellect telling him they were untutored, his heart responding to their cry nonetheless.

> *I close my eyes that I may see that which my heart denies*
> *It whispers loud, I cannot hear, as into the night it cries.*
> *Where is the love you had for me?*
> *Where are the ties that bind?*
> *What will the cold morn bring to me,*
> *If the truth I cannot find?*
> *When we were young and blithe and free*
> *My heart caressed your soul.*
> *If 'twas for me you tarried here*
> *Why am I now alone?*
> *My love was true, my heart is broke.*
> *You care not this to know.*
> *The journey's done, the voyage o'er, so whither shall I go?*

He doubted they'd be considered literary masterpieces, but, in them, he recognised the echo of a kindred voice. Someone's pen heard the unarticulated whispers of his soul and wrote them down before he was born. Sighing, he let his hand rest on the yellowed vellum, feeling it warm to his touch, wondering, wishing…

Shaking off the unfamiliar, fanciful turn his thoughts had taken, he pushed his treasure away a little. Still caught in its melancholy, he sat unable to rouse himself for some time.

But he'd intended making an early start, getting the bulk of the clearing done over the weekend so that he could get the skip collected at the beginning of the week, getting the back garden into some kind of state that would be less off-putting for Kate when she came home… if she came home.

He wished she'd come home. He missed her. One of the things he'd been looking forward to about retiring, was getting the chance to spend more time with her. Perhaps if he'd told her.. Perhaps it was already too late.

Dan fingered the silk scarf, holding it around the opened book: a beautiful thing, something special… even *he* could see that. Kate was going to love it. Perhaps he should get it valued before he showed it to her? But probably not. She'll want to keep it. Something so special, she'll definitely want to keep no matter its monetary value, so no point bothering to take it anywhere. But maybe, just out of curiosity, he would.

With a sigh, he wrapped it in its soft cocoon as he walked through to the living room to put it on the sideboard, beside the few letters that were accumulating there. He hadn't remembered to give her those either. He sighed again, fingers lingering on the scarf as they had lingered on her arm last night, recalling the silk of her skin, still smooth and soft, her arms still young and firm, her shoulders beautiful, the dress wrapping her in a sensuous haze of colour. He ached for her.

The mantel clock ticked off the minutes.

He'd not leave the book there after all. Someone else might see it before her. He didn't want that. It was for her only. Something they would share together. He'd secrete it in the sideboard drawer.

Perhaps she'd already noticed there were letters for her. Perhaps she'd remember them, come by to pick them up. They could try again for that coffee…

Then he remembered.

He pushed the silken bundle into the drawer and slammed it roughly, scattering the letters across the sideboard. He stumbled back to the kitchen and sat down heavily, elbows on the table, hands covering his face, catching his pain.

It was Saturday, *their* day! She'd be off with *him*.

Last night he had thought for one brief moment that they could turn back the pages, flick through the album to the Old Days. When the photographs showed them smiling, holding hands, laughing together. Forget the empty pages, where time had washed over them without leaving much intimacy to record.

But the moment had died, its glow extinguished, stamped under his neighbour's heel.

And today was Saturday. She would be with *him*.

Dan pushed back his chair, the rising heat inside him warming him to action.

He rolled up his sleeves and set to. The summerhouse was down. Time to erase all trace of the damn place.

* * *

"Whew!" Paul whistled softly as he came in the back gate. He shook his head sadly. "It's like the blitz."

"What would you know about the blitz?" Dan grumbled. "If you're here to have a go at me you can just turn round and go back out that gate."

"You've got to admit it's a bit like… "

"A bomb site. Yeah, yeah… okay. You could always lend a hand, of course. Help me get it cleared up quicker."

Paul made no move.

"Well?"

"Yeah… yeah," he said quietly. "I will. I just need a minute."

Dan shook his head and got back to the task in hand. He was hoisting bits of timber and rubble into the skip, working his way methodically through the debris, erasing memories. Not only Kate's and Paul's… but his too. Memories of lonely afternoons watching football on the telly, wishing Kate would

126

sit beside him, reading or something. He knew she wasn't keen on the football, but it could have been pleasant just to be in the same room. Memories of lonely nights, wondering if she would come back inside before bedtime. Sometimes wondering if she would *ever* come to bed. Latterly wondering if she had already *gone* to bed. *Her* bed, the one in Paul's old room.

He wondered, what was the sequence? Did they row about the summerhouse, then she moved out of his room, *then* she got a boyfriend? Or, did she get a boyfriend, *then* have the row so she could move out?

He didn't suppose it mattered. She'd obviously lost interest in him a long time ago. When had *that* happened?

"We used to sit out here for hours," Paul reminisced.

"Tell me about it!" Dan growled.

"We'd play scrabble. Or chess. Or Mum would read to me. Or tell stories. Did you know…?"

"Look, are you going to help me or not?"

"Yeah, but listen. Did you know…?"

"I know I don't want to listen. I don't want to listen to you waxing lyrical about this place while I…"

"Why did you do it, Dad? It would have fallen down eventually anyway."

"Exactly! It was dangerous."

Paul pursed his lips. "Naw! It wasn't, Dad. It would've been all right."

"It was dangerous… and it was full of mice."

"They never bothered anybody though."

"Only a matter of time till they'd get into the house."

"Probably where they've gone now you've disturbed them."

Dan was silent.

"Unless you've…" Paul looked at his father in disgust. "You haven't, have you, Dad?"

"What else could I do? You're right. They'd've had to go somewhere. I didn't want them in the house."

Paul turned away, sickened. "Oh, Dad."

"Never mind, 'Oh, Dad'. I did what had to be done."

"Well, you'd just better not tell Mum."

"She claimed there were no mice."

"Yeah, well, she would, wouldn't she? And that's why. She'd not want you to... to do what you did."

Dan looked heavenward. "Lord, spare me from sentimentalists and animal lovers."

"Oh no," groaned Paul. "Look what you've done to the couch!" He knelt beside the dirty, soggy remains of his childhood bed of dreams. "It's ruined."

Dan shook his head and kept working.

"Could you not have saved the furniture?"

"And where do you suppose I could have put it?"

"Upstairs. In my old room. Or Vicky's. Anywhere. But you've left it out in the rain. It's been soaked," Paul said as he felt the cushions. "It's ruined." He sounded close to tears.

"It's furniture, son. Not a death in the family. Now, get real and give me a hand to get some of it into this skip."

"But it's awful. You've destroyed it."

"That was the general idea."

"But you don't know what you've done, Dad. You just don't know what you've done."

"Aye well, son," Dan sighed. "I've a fair idea... but it's too late now. So get your jacket off and gimme a hand."

* * *

Saturday, and Kate was going for a walk. She hadn't intended to go today, not after the late night, but Phyllis encouraged her to get ready and out.

"You look pale this morning. A bit of fresh air is what you need."

"A rest is what I need," Kate retorted.

"I doubt it. You look like you would just brood. Get out there and do your thinking in the fresh air. It'll be more positive."

"Who says I want to do any thinking?"

"Whether you want to or not, you will. Last night must have given you a lot more to think about than whether Liz what's'er name's going to recover from her hysterectomy," Phyllis stated wisely.

Kate had to agree.

She needed to think. She needed to work out where she was going, what she was doing.

"Hi there."

It was Martin, their walk leader.

"Hi," responded Kate.

"All right?" queried Martin.

"Great."

"Let's go then. Fifteen miles today. I hope you've brought your sandwiches." He looked around the assorted group. "All got rainwear? Let's get going then."

They very quickly sorted out into twos and threes and got under way. Kate found herself walking with Douglas, one of the older gentlemen of the group. She'd often found him alongside her on the walks… through no design on her part, but perhaps on his, she guessed. He was a widower, about the same age as Dan, she guessed again. His intentions, she didn't need to guess.

He had asked her out to dinner several times already and had been unperturbed by her refusals.

"You're a very attractive woman, Kate," he informed her.

"I'm also married," she replied.

"A bit of fun on the side does no harm."

"I'm really not interested in anything, on the side or anywhere else," she said clearly. "Really, Douglas. Having one man in my life is about as much as I want to cope with right now."

"And are you coping?" he asked.

"What do you mean?"

"Well… how's your marriage? I don't see your husband on the walks. Does he not mind you being out all day of a Saturday?"

"I don't really think that's any of your business," Kate snapped.

"Minds that much, does he?"

"I didn't say he minded at all."

"Bet he does though, doesn't he? Lovely wife like you. Off doing her own thing. I'd mind, I can tell you."

"Well, he doesn't," Kate retorted as she walked faster to catch up with Mr and Mrs Moffat, up ahead.

She could feel her neck hot and red, knowing he was behind, hearing him laugh. Damn cheek. Who did he think he was? What business was it of his whether Dan minded or not?

She'd said Dan didn't mind, not really considering it a lie. She assumed he wouldn't mind... if he knew... which he didn't. It all seemed pretty irrelevant right now. She needed to sort out whether she wanted him to mind... about walks or anything else in her life. And she needed space to sort it out, not some fool man to badger her and interfere with her thoughts.

Mr and Mrs Moffat were not the chatty sort. They smiled warmly enough as she joined them, but they wouldn't intrude on her thoughts with inane conversation. They plodded on companionably, happy to share the path with her but not looking to share her life.

'One man in her life enough to cope with'. Too much to cope with? Not necessarily... but certainly enough. There were a lot of things that she wasn't sure of right now, but that wasn't one of them. She knew absolutely that the last thing on earth she wanted was involvement with another man. She was past the 'bloom of youth'. It was unlikely that she could be swept off her feet by some ageing Romeo.

She laughed at herself for the realisation that, if anyone was to woo her and win her, she wanted it to be Dan.

* * *

"You need to woo her, Dad," Paul told his father as they loaded the wheelbarrow with bricks.

"Woo her? And how does one go about wooing these days? Always supposing that one wanted to."

"The same old things... you know, chocolates, flowers..."

"Your mother doesn't eat chocolates."

"Perfume then."

"I'm not that sure that she likes..."

"Dad!" Paul straightened up, hands on hips. "Are you being deliberately obtuse? You know what I mean. You need to go a-courting again."

"Courting?"

"Whatever worked the first time. I don't know. I wasn't there. But that's what you need to do again." Paul resumed throwing bricks and stones into the barrow.

"I don't think so, son."

"Well I do."

"That's because you don't know…"

"I know how to get myself a woman."

"No, I mean, you don't know how I got your mother. I didn't woo her. Or court her. I don't think I even won her. It just sort of happened."

"Well, can't you make it 'just sort of happen' again?"

"I wouldn't know how, son. Anyway, it's too late."

Paul stopped working again to study his father. "Well, I never knew you were a quitter. All these years. I thought you were the strong, silent type."

Dan shrugged.

"And here, you're not so silent. We've been chattin' on great style this afternoon. And you're not so strong. You're givin' up without a fight."

"No point, son. I think your Mum's got someone else wooin' her."

"Rubbish!"

Dan shrugged again and took the handles of the barrow. "I think that's about all, this run," he said as he wheeled it to the skip. "Here. Give me a hand to get this up the ramp."

They both put all their energy into the task of emptying the barrow, conversation giving way to grunts and groans as they tipped the heavy load.

"What on earth makes you think Mum's got a man?" Paul asked at last.

"Saturdays," Dan replied.

"What d'you mean, 'Saturdays'?"

"She goes out with him every Saturday… give or take…"

Paul sat down heavily on the remains of what used to be the wall of the summerhouse. "How d'you know?" he asked weakly. "Are you sure?"

Dan shrugged, his most familiar form of communication.

"Did she say she had someone else?"

"Where's she gone, son? Answer me that?"

Paul thought for a time. He shook his head. "I don't know, Dad. But I sure as hell am going to find out!" He threw down his work gloves and marched to the kitchen to grab his car keys.

"Where are you going? We're not finished here?" Dan called after him.

"*You* might not be… but, for now, I am." Paul called back as he shut the gate behind him.

He wasn't sure whether they always ended up at their starting point, but it was the only place he knew that was of any significance to the walking club. Kate had told him they often assembled at the gates of the park, so he hoped that they might return there at the end of the walks. They'd have to leave their cars somewhere, he reasoned, so it might be here. He parked alongside a rather sporty BMW, which he looked over covetously before searching the carpark for any sign of walkers.

He didn't really know how he would recognise if someone belonged to a walking club, or not, but he couldn't think what else to do.

She had told him she went walking every Saturday… but she hadn't told Dad. Why hadn't she told Dad? Was there some man in the walking club? She had laughed when he'd suggested Dad would think she had a fancy-man, but was she laughing to cover up? Would she tell if she had? Would she lie to save embarrassment? She wasn't staying at Vicky's and she wasn't staying with him… so where the heck was she staying?

He paced the length of the deserted carpark and back again.

Perhaps she thinks it's no one else's business. Paul felt strongly that it was *his*. She's… well, she's… she's *Mum*!

Mum goes with Dad. Mum and Dad. That's the way it has always been. That's just the way it *is*. Mum and Dad.

He thought of himself as a man of the world, suave even, sophisticated. He knew how to handle himself, knew how and when to begin and end relationships. No ties, no commitment. But that's him... not Mum and Dad.

Suddenly he was a wee boy again. Needing the security of knowing that Mum would be at home whenever he needed her. It was knowing *that* that allowed him to be free, allowed him to be big and brave: to take risks, to be independent, to be confident.

She couldn't leave home permanently. He couldn't let it happen.

If some fast-talking, sweet-walking macho-man... no, sweet-talking, fast-walking... whatever. If some man had hit on his mother... well... he'd have something to say about it. And it wouldn't be sweet... might be fast though!

By the time dusk fell, Paul was frozen and furious. He'd worked himself into a right state. But there was no sign of Kate, or anybody else who looked as though they might have been 'seriously' walking. The few strollers there had been, had long since hauled their cold limbs into their warm cars and were off. The car park was almost empty. Even the sporty BMW had gone, driven off by some fancy boy wearing a fancy leather jacket. Stupid berk! Didn't deserve a decent car.

Finally, Paul had to admit defeat. They obviously hadn't left their cars here. Wherever the walk was today, they hadn't set out from the park.

Now what?

He got into his car and turned the heater up full. He supposed he'd have to think of something else.

Chapter 11

On Monday morning, he was waiting outside the shop when she arrived for work.

"Hello, Paul. What are you doing here?" She reached up to kiss his cheek but he turned away. "Shouldn't you be at work?" A worried frown settled on her face. "There's nothing wrong, is there? Vicky? Your Dad?"

"No," he replied coldly. "They're fine."

"The boys?" Her face had gone pale.

"No. They're fine too."

"Thank goodness. But what is it, Paul? You should be at work."

"I've got a couple of free periods first thing. I needed to see you."

She looked anxiously at her watch. "But I'm due to start in ten minutes."

"It needn't take longer than that."

"Oh, Paul," she said softly, her face relaxing into gentler lines. "Something is wrong. What is it, pet?" She reached out to touch him. "What's happened?"

He drew away from her touch. "I think we need to talk, Mum."

"Hello, Agnes. Yes, I'll be in shortly. See you in a minute," she said in answer to her workmate's inquiring look. "Oh this is hopeless. Look. Why don't you wait for me in the coffee shop. I'll check in at the office and clear myself for a break. I'll explain it's family business... important family business. Okay?"

Paul nodded and they entered the shop.

When Kate rejoined him a little later, she looked much better. The colour had returned to her face and she had tidied her windswept hair.

"I gather you've been to the house then?" she asked as she sat down.

"Yes."

"And seen your Dad?"

"Yes."

"And he's sent you to talk me into going home?"

Paul leaned forward, his elbows pressed onto the table. "No. He doesn't know I'm here. I've come to tell you myself that you should go home."

"But you must have seen what he's done?"

"Yes."

"So how can you expect me to go back home?" Kate poured herself a coffee. "He obviously doesn't care tuppence for my feelings. He knew I didn't want him to pull down the summerhouse. I begged him not to."

"He says it was rotten. Dangerous."

"It could have been repaired."

"I don't think so, Mum. He showed me the timbers."

"He showed you what he wanted you to see."

"They were rotten through. The window frames on the roof were practically non-existent."

"They could have been replaced."

"It would have cost a fortune."

"Whose side are you on here, Paul?"

"It isn't about sides. It's done now. Dad shouldn't have gone ahead without your agreement."

"Which he'd never have got."

"But it's done now."

"Did you see what he did to my furniture, Paul? He had no right."

Paul's face softened a little. He put his hand on hers. "I know. I'm sorry, Mum. I think he regrets it."

She pulled her hand away. "You bet he regrets it! It cost him more than he thought it would." She stirred the coffee angrily. "I tried to warn him. I told him I'd walk out if he touched it."

"I don't think he believed you really would."

"Yes... well, I have. And I'm not going back."

"Where are you staying?"

"With a friend."

"A man?"

Kate laughed. "Don't be ridiculous, Paul."

Paul took a mouthful of coffee. "Dad thinks you've got a boyfriend."

"That's ridiculous."

"Why?"

"Your Dad knows I've never been unfaithful to him."

"But he thinks you are now."

"But why? Why on earth would he think that?"

He carefully placed his cup back in the saucer. "Because you're out every Saturday and you won't tell him where you go."

"He never asked."

"And you've left him."

"This is ludicrous. What on earth would I want with another man? They're more trouble than they're worth."

"He thinks you've left him for someone else."

Kate pushed her coffee cup away. "Oh, this is crazy! He pushes me into leaving then tries to make out it's my fault. That I've got a boyfriend. I don't believe this!"

Paul sat back, his legs reaching out under the table, his feet under her chair. He toyed with the pot of coffee that neither of them really wanted, watching her.

"*You* don't believe it, do you?" she asked incredulously. "You don't really think that I'd go off with someone else?"

"Well, you have. Haven't you?"

"I told you. I've gone to stay with a friend... a *woman* friend."

"Who?"

"You don't know her."

Paul looked around as though expecting to see the friend in question sitting at another table. "Introduce me."

"She doesn't work in the shop."

"Where does she work?"

"She's retired."

"So where did you meet her?" Paul persisted.

"That's a long story," Kate sighed.

"I like long stories."

Kate leaned forward to touch his hand. "You always did," she smiled at him. "We used to sit out in the summerhouse for hours…" Her voice died away, already thickening with tears. She shook her head. "He shouldn't have done it, Paul."

Paul softened. He held her hand. "I know, Mum. And I think he knows that."

"Too late."

"Yes," he sighed. "Too late for the summerhouse."

She nodded, hardly able to speak. "It sure is," she whispered. She blew her nose. "He shouldn't have done it," she repeated, her voice stronger.

"But he has."

"Yeah."

"But it's not too late for you and Dad. You haven't really left him, have you, Mum? Not for good?"

"I don't know." she shook her head. "I just don't know." She swallowed, fighting back tears again. "I need time, Paul. I need some time."

"But there's no-one else?"

"Of course not," she said with a sigh.

"That's okay then. You'll go back soon, won't you, Mum?"

Kate shrugged. "We'll see," she said non-committally.

Paul leaned back in his chair, his ankle resting on his other knee. "So," he said, after a while. "Can I get to meet this mysterious friend of yours?"

"If you want to. I think she'd like that."

"Good. Then I can see that you're being well cared for."

"And in female company," Kate added, giving him a knowing look.

He grinned back at her.

"You don't believe me, do you?"

"Of course I do, Mother. After work today be all right?"

She nodded, laughing. "Pick me up at five then."

Phyllis was delighted to meet Paul.

"I've heard so much about you," she said, shaking his hand.

"And I've heard nothing about you," was his riposte.

Kate hung her head. "Phyllis was my little secret," she said a little ruefully.

Paul looked around the hall. "This is a beautiful house."

"Thank you."

"Georgian?"

"Yes, it is. It was built in 1801."

"Adams?"

"Certainly his style, isn't it?"

"Lovely," Paul said approvingly. "I see you've kept the original cornice and mouldings. Beautiful. I like the way you've decorated it though, brought it up to date without losing its character."

"Thank you."

Mary appeared by his side to take his coat. She blushed at his smile of thanks.

Another conquest, Kate thought. She was proud of this charming man who was her son. She quietly awaited his reaction to the glory of the sitting room and was not disappointed.

"Oh, this is beautiful," he exclaimed. "Beautiful. Originally the ballroom?"

Phyllis nodded.

"Ah!" Kate understood now: the size, the shape of the room, the long sweep of it, the chandeliers. It had never occurred to her, but, of course, a house like this would have a history. A room like this would not always have been a sitting room. If she closed her eyes she could imagine the room: beneath the soft carpets there was a gleaming, polished floor, where dancers waltzed beneath the chandeliers, their chaperones sitting over there in the bays of the windows, their fans fluttering, hiding their gossiping mouths and sideways glances. The gentlemen gathered around the blazing fire, discussing the politics of the day.

"Adam fireplace?" Paul smiled his approval. "Untouched... beautiful."

Phyllis nodded again, pleased by his recognition of the pedigree of her home.

He walked further into the room and gazed around him. "Ah," he sighed, a smile of delight lighting his face. "But now you've chosen to change the ambience. Lynch?" he asked, pointing to one of the African paintings.

"Yes! You know her work?" Phyllis was surprised.

"Love it!"

"It's very special, isn't it?" agreed Kate.

"This is a very special room, a room where architectural elegance is mixed with the rawness of the African landscape." His hands tested the soft depth of one of the armchairs. "With a bit of luxury thrown in."

"A bit of a 'mish-mash', isn't it?" Phyllis apologised.

"A crazy mixture of styles: unconventional and brave, yet conventional and comfortable at the same time. You've taken what you like from the past and what you like of today and you've succeeded in turning the austere Edinburgh winter into such a sumptuous, joyous warmth. I wouldn't have imagined it could, but it actually does work!" he softly applauded her daring.

"You like it then?" Kate asked, unsure of the unsuspected knowledge and eloquence of her son.

"I love it! Very unusual, and very special. And I suspect..." he turned to Phyllis, who had seated herself on one of her more upright, upholstered chairs, "I suspect that you are a very special lady."

"Oh, she is," declared Kate warmly.

"You must be. To have taken my mother in."

Kate gave him a dig in the ribs. "Don't spoil it," she said. "You were doing great for a bit there."

"How long have you been hiding here, Mother?"

"I've not been hiding."

"No?"

"No. Phyllis was kind enough to let me stay for a while, after..."

"After you had a blow up with Dad?"

"After your father blew up my summerhouse... *my* summerhouse."

Paul walked over to gaze at another of Phyllis's African paintings. He took a deep breath of the room's ambiance. "But you don't need a dilapidated old summerhouse when you can come here."

"But it was *my* summerhouse. My special place."

"Mine too," he replied softly. He turned to Phyllis. "Were you ever there with Mum?" he asked her.

"No," she smiled. "I never had that privilege."

"Oh, it was nothing very special really," Kate dissembled. "It was just an old dilapidated summerhouse, as Paul said. But it was a place to dream in, a place to…"

"To cosy up and tell stories."

"A place to get away from the telly."

"A place to get away from Dad?"

"I didn't say that, Paul."

"No, you didn't have to. But it was, wasn't it? Like this is." He looked around. "You don't need the summerhouse anymore, Mum. Why don't you let it go? Let Dad off the hook?"

"You know you can come here anytime you want to… or need to," Phyllis supplied quietly.

Kate walked over to the marble desk. She ran her hand along the familiar smooth surface, caressed the petals of the roses in the familiar vase sitting beside the familiar phone.

"I know. Thank you, Phyllis," she sighed. "And I love it here. I wish I never had to leave it, but this is *your* home, not mine. This is not where I *belong*. I know that. I need to have somewhere of my own."

"You have…" Paul started to say.

Kate raised her hand. "I know, Paul. I know what you're going to say. But that's not *my* house either. It's your father's. He made that very clear."

"Come on Mum," Paul walked towards her. "You know he didn't mean that."

"Oh yes, I think he did, Paul."

"He probably said it in the heat of the moment. He didn't mean it literally. It's your home… both of you… it's …well… it's Home. It's where you and Dad live. It's where I come from.

It's Homebase. You've got to go home, Mum. You've just got to."

"*Got* to. Paul? I've not *got* to do anything. I'm a free agent... or so your generation have been telling me for years now." She was pacing, her gestures strong and defiant. "Telling me in every modern woman's magazine, on every trendy chat show. I'm my Own Woman. I've to be Myself. Independent. Answerable To No-One." She stood in front of Paul. "Or does that just apply to the under thirty woman? Oh, and of course... to men. Men can play free and easy, men can do their own thing. But not women. Not forty something..." She corrected herself. "*Fiftyish* women. Is that what you mean, Paul?"

"I wasn't saying that."

"But you said I've *got* to go home, and I don't *want* to go home. I don't even know where home is right now." She stopped pacing and sat down on one of the deep, yielding sofas.

Paul shook his head. "I don't know what to say, Mum." He too sat down, not beside her, but on one of the other sofas, where he could study her face, search for understanding in her eyes.

"You've already said it, Paul. I've *got* to go home."

"It's just that... I need you to go home."

"*You* need me to? But what about *my* needs, Paul? What if I need *not* to go home right now?"

Paul's face brightened. "Do you mean you will go home... but not right now?"

Kate laughed. "Look at you. Thirty-two years old, and you need Mummy to be at home... even when you're not!"

Paul blushed.

"You were always the same," Kate continued. "When you were at school, I wasn't supposed to go anywhere."

"I just liked to know you'd be there if I... if I was ill, or hurt myself or anything," he defended himself.

She got up and moved round behind him. Leaning over the sofa, she ruffled his hair. "What a cheek you've got, my son," she laughed. "You're the one who talks about marriage as some kind of prison sentence and here you are, chaining me to the kitchen sink."

"It's not the same."

"So where's the difference?" She walked away across the room, causing him to have to twist round to see her.

"It just is different."

"How? It still takes away my freedom, my rights."

"Oh come off it, Mum. It's not as bad as that."

"How would you know how bad it is? You left home years ago. You come and go as you please. You'll never let yourself be tied down, will you, my boy? No. But you want to make sure I'm well and truly in my place," she said as she fell back into the seat. "Well, hard luck, son. I've broken free. And I'm not ready to get back in the cage."

"Mum…"

"Forget it, Paul. I'm not going back. Get used to it. I'm here for as long as Phyllis'll have me. Till I find somewhere of my own. If that's okay with you, Phyllis?"

But Phyllis had fallen asleep, her soft snores having gone unnoticed during the scene that played out like an unheeded television drama before her.

They laughed softly, and Paul crossed to sit beside Kate.

"Okay, Mum," he said quietly. "Have it your way. I'll let you do your own thing."

She smiled at him. "I know you will, son. Because you can't actually stop me."

"I know." He spread his hands. "And I'm not going to try any more."

"Good. Then we can be friends."

"Had we stopped?"

"Not really," she conceded. "But you took a chance."

"Not really," he mimicked. "I knew you couldn't fall out with your favourite son."

"My only son."

Phyllis awoke with a start. "Mmm… pardon? Sorry, I seemed to have dozed off there for a moment. Sorry. It's the prerogative of age, you know. Did I miss anything of import?"

"Not really, Phyllis. Not unless you count the fact that Mary just put her head round the door to announce dinner's ready."

Paul stood up. "I'd better be going then."

"Not at all," Phyllis insisted. "You'll stay for dinner. Unless of course you have some young lady waiting for you, slaving over a hot stove?"

* * *

When it became apparent that Kate was going to be staying for a while, Phyllis decided that sleeping on the sofa was not a long-term solution. Comfortable as Kate assured her it was, it just wouldn't 'do' any longer. So she had had Mary and her husband, Joe, busy preparing a guest room for her.

Meeting her at the door when she came home from work one evening, Phyllis led her across the hall.

"It's okay, Mary," she said as Mary appeared at the door. "I'm just going to settle Kate into the guest room."

"Oh, but Mrs Thaine…"

"It's all right," Phyllis reassured her. "I'll show her."

"But…"

Phyllis waved Mary away and, with a deep sigh, she ushered Kate towards one of the doors leading off the hall. "This is the guest room," she said quietly. "It's newly decorated, so I hope the smell of paint will not be off-putting."

"You didn't decorate it for me, I hope?"

"Well… It needed doing anyway. I'd been using it for storage. High time I cleared it. I hope it's to your taste." She opened the door and switched on the light.

"Oh, but it's a charming room. Thank you," Kate said.

Phyllis sniffed the air. "I don't think the smell's too bad, do you? I've had the window open all day."

"It's fine," Kate assured her. "But I can't believe you did all this for me. You've been so kind to me Phyllis. Thank you." She gave her a hug.

"I had Mary bring your few bits and bobs through," Phyllis said, indicating the tidy bundle of clothes on the chair and the few things on the chest of drawers and dressing table.

"I'm sorry I've disrupted your lounge for all this time."

"That's not been a problem. You've been a tidy guest, but it's time you had somewhere more private to settle yourself and your few things than the sitting room. I'm just sorry that it's taken so long for me to organise. You see..." She hesitated, seemed about to say something, then changed her mind. "Anyway," she said breezily. "This room is yours for as long as you want it."

Kate looked around the room. Sunshine. Once again, a summer room, bright and uplifting. "It's beautiful, Phyllis, absolutely perfect. " She shook her head. "I don't know what to say." And raised her hands. "Thank you, Phyllis. Thank you so much," she whispered as she kissed her cheek. "But what's this?" she asked, noticing a dainty, antique bureau placed carefully in the bay of the window, a computer set up on the open top.

"For your writing."

"But I've never used a computer."

"Then it's time you learned."

"But I... "

Phyllis drew back the curtain a little to reveal a matching table to the side of the bureau. "There's a handbook, a printer, paper: everything you need, I think."

"But I don't understand."

"Don't understand what? It's quite simple. You like to write. I have a computer I don't use. You could learn to use it as a word processor. In fact, I could help you."

"You could?" Kate asked, her eyes wide. "Yes," she laughed. "I bet you could. Really, Phyllis, why does that not surprise me?"

"I took a few courses, but I haven't kept it up. It's not difficult, you know. You'll soon catch on."

"Yes... but..."

"Oh, do stop butting, Kate. It really is an irritating habit."

"But..."

"There! You're at it again! Just say 'Thank you, Phyllis,' and let's be done with it!"

"Thank you, Phyllis," she said obediently.

"Right! Dinner in half an hour okay?"

"Fine," she replied weakly.

"I'll leave you to settle in then."

"I don't know how to thank you."

"You already have."

"But it's so much: the computer, the room. It's beautiful, the room. Exquisite. Thank you." and she could say no more. Tears of gratitude and affection were not far away.

Phyllis smiled and closed the door softly behind her, leaving Kate to 'settle in'.

She sat on the bed and looked around again. It's true the room was beautiful: the high ceiling painted a delicate primrose, framed by a crisp white cornice; the walls a deeper shade of sunshine... clean, soft colours... with the freshness of new paint; pictures on the walls, echoing the ones downstairs; the ubiquitous, dark mahogany flooring practically hidden under deep, new rugs, their softness and depth verified as she padded across the room, touching things, her hand lingering here and there on soft fabrics, smooth polished wood. The ivory curtains and bedding were obviously new, as were the towels in the en-suite bathroom. Such luxury: thick, soft, Warm, new towels. She held them to her face, breathing in their delicious freshness, luxuriating in their softness. Everything so new. Kate wondered when Phyllis had bought them. For her? She hoped not.

And the computer... what joy, to be able to learn to type, to try her hand at writing on this new medium. She thrilled at the adventure of it. She sat on the chair in front of it, chuckling softly. Even the chair was carefully chosen... for comfort and for practicality; the perfect height, the perfect angle but soft and yielding too. She opened the drawer where Phyllis had indicated there was paper for the printer and, with the longing of the compulsive writer, her fingers caressed the milky-white vellum, eager to cover it with the ciphers of her busy mind.

And the room: quiet, relaxing, light and airy. Feel-good colours to lift the lowest mood, to stimulate the most torpid mind. Perfect for writing in. If she couldn't find the muse here, then she wouldn't find it anywhere. She wandered back to the huge bed, big enough for three at least: plump pillows encased in frilly slips scattered over it. She gazed about with wonder. What a room! She shook her head. What a fairy tale. What a woman! Phyllis wanted her to write. But why? What did it matter to Phyllis that Kate had a chance to do something she derived such satisfaction from? But it did seem to matter to Phyllis. What a woman. What a friend!

But how long ought she to impose on Phyllis's kindness? She had thought she would look for a flat, but Phyllis had been vigorous in her opposition to that idea, claiming that it was too soon for such a decisive step. 'Give yourself time,' she'd reasoned. 'You might yet decide to go back home.' Home. Back to Dan. She thought not. Yet Phyllis had reasoned that she was still angry, and she was; that 'one should never make momentous decisions in anger', so she hadn't. She was letting Phyllis spoil her with the gentle luxury of *her* home, shelving the reality of her actual homelessness if she should decide not to forgive Dan the unforgivable.

She lay back on the soft bed. Was he missing her? He'd seemed so pleased to see her. She had felt him reach out to her, wanting her... needing her, perhaps?

Was he cooking for himself, keeping the house clean, doing his own washing? If he missed her at all, would it only be for the absence of these services? The things she had always done for him, things she had never felt a burden, had never grudged but had never felt appreciated for. Or was that just her anger talking? In the early years of their marriage, he had often told her how much he enjoyed the meals she cooked, liked the way they were always ready for him when he came home. She smiled as she remembered how often he would put his arms round her waist as she tried to dish out their food. But she pushed him away, pleased at his affection, but aware that the food would cool. Did it matter? Did it matter so much to eat the food while it was hot? Had she cooled his affection instead?

These were disturbing thoughts, unwelcome because she needed still to be angry with him, wanted to punish him. She pulled herself to her feet, shaking the thoughts from her as she shook out her crumpled skirt. Enough of all this. There was food waiting for *her* for a change. Warm food, carefully prepared by Mary. Why shouldn't she enjoy the spoiling. She deserved it.

Chapter 12

Naomi went back to work on Wednesday after having a few days off. She didn't feel any better, but at least there were people in the office. Her tiny bedsit had begun to close in around her, the smell of gas mixed with cat's pee making her nauseous, the cold and damp seeping into her bones. She knew she should look for somewhere else to live, but lacked the energy to try. Probably couldn't afford much better anyway, on the pittance Pete paid... the pittance Pete paid...the alliteration gave her the only smile in days.

She avoided being alone with Pete, but knew it was only a matter of time till he exercised his right as her boss, and called her into his office. She shivered at the thought. It had been another long, lonely weekend, so her defences were down. She longed for company... even Pete's.

By lunchtime, she had managed to keep him at arm's length but was weakening. She went shopping.

"Can I help you? Oh hello, Ms Ferguson. How are you today?"

It was that nice sales lady again. Naomi smiled. "I'm sorry," she said. "I'm afraid I've forgotten your name."

"Kate. Kate Morgan."

"Yes, sorry. Mrs Morgan. I remember now."

"Are you feeling better?"

"Better? Oh..." Naomi remembered. "Oh yes... you took me home. Thank you, yes. I'm much better."

"Did you report that gas leak?"

"Yes," Naomi lied.

"Good. I'm sure that wouldn't have helped," Kate smiled.

"No, I don't suppose so."

"So... can I help you?"

"I... I'm not sure." Naomi was hesitant. It was the same old story. She hadn't intended shopping today, hadn't brought anything to exchange, couldn't afford to buy.

"Would you like just to browse for a while?"

"Yes... yes. That would be fine."

"You can let me know if you need any help."

"Thank you."

Help. Naomi knew she needed help. She had been to the doctor, had told him she was depressed, but couldn't bring herself to talk about the shopping thing. He didn't seem interested to hear how she felt, just wrote out a prescription and smiled sympathetically. She hadn't bothered to get the pills yet. But she knew she should. She needed help.

"This one," she decided, taking a shimmering evening creation to the counter.

"Would you like to try it on?"

Naomi sighed. She knew she should. If nothing else, it would give her time to change her mind, to stop herself spending money she knew she didn't have.

Kate was showing her towards the changing rooms.

"No. Thank you," Naomi stopped her as she came round the counter. "No. It's okay. I'll just take it. I'm sure it'll fit."

"But it's a size twelve, Madam. Is that not rather large for you? Would you like me to find the same dress in an eight..." Kate looked at the frail figure. "Or even a six?"

"No. No... just give it to me. It'll be fine. Please." She was shaking now. She needed to get out of the shop. Needed to get some fresh air. Needed the dress... something to have... something... anything... something to carry home...

"It's very expensive..." The shop assistant... Kate, didn't she call herself?... looked concerned.

Naomi smiled reassuringly. "That's okay. Access all right?" She held out the card. Her hand was shaking. She quickly placed the card on the counter.

This would be the last one. Just this one more time. She would get the prescription this afternoon. Then it would be okay. But, for now, she just needed this one last purchase. If the card was accepted. *Please God, let it be accepted.* This will be the last. No more. Getting out of control. Dresses she would never wear, shoes that had never felt the cold pavement… she didn't need more.

But she needed this One More. Just Something bright and heavy to carry. Something to carry into work. 'Been shopping?' they'd ask. Normal. Just like Normal People did. They went shopping in their lunch hour. You saw them all the time. Office girls, shop girls. Boys too. In the record shops, in the stores… spending their wages in their lunch hour. You could see them any day, walking along the street together, laughing, talking, peeping into each other's bags. Normal. It was Normal.

It was taking too long.

Kate was frowning, looking worried.

Sweat ran down Naomi's back.

Kate approached holding the Access card… no receipt… just the card.

"I'm sorry."

"Give me the dress," Naomi cried. "Just give me the dress."

"I'm sorry. There seems to be a problem with your card."

"Please." Her voice was weak… like her knees. Everything was spinning. Where was the chair? Last time, there was a chair. "Please, I need the dress."

"I'm so sorry. Have you another means of paying?"

This couldn't be happening. Last month it had been her Visa card. In the shoe department. She was ashamed to go back. The bank had already bounced her cheques and withdrawn her Switch card and her cheque book. She had no cash. But she had to have the dress.

"Please," she sobbed, her hand stretching out to take the precious carrier bag. The carrier bag she could carry as her badge of Normality.

Gently, Kate drew it away from her reach. "I'm sorry," she said quietly.

So tired. Naomi felt so tired.

Miraculously, the chair appeared. Kate had summoned it up from somewhere and gently lowered her onto it. "You really don't look so well, Ms Ferguson."

"Naomi."

"Pardon?"

"Naomi. You can call me Naomi."

"Oh. Yes. I see. Naomi, then. Anyway. You really are rather pale. Are you sure you really need the dress? Perhaps another day?"

"Dress?" Naomi had forgotten the dress. How could she have forgotten the dress? It mattered so much a few moments ago... but now... now she didn't care about the dress. She was too tired... too tired...

Someone appeared with a glass of water. "Should I call a doctor?"

"No. It's okay," Kate said. "I know the lady. I'll take her home. Explain to the office for me, will you Agnes?"

Naomi sipped the water. "So tired."

"I know," Kate soothed. "It's all right. As soon as you feel able, I'll help you out to my car."

"Should be back at work."

Kate shook her head. "Oh, I don't think so, do you? Really? You're obviously not at all well. I'm going to take you home."

Tears welled up in Naomi's eyes.

"Not yours," Kate smiled. "Mine... sort of," she added under her breath.

Naomi slept in the car.

"Poor soul," Kate whispered to Phyllis when she opened the door. "I think she's exhausted and I doubt if she's eaten in days."

"Mary can help you bring her in, while I put the kettle on." Phyllis didn't hesitate when she learned of her new guest. "Do you suppose she likes cocoa?"

Kate smiled. She knew she'd been right to bring Naomi home here. Phyllis would soon nurture her back to health. Hot cocoa: Phyllis's favourite comforter. Hot cocoa. Sitting wrapped in a soft rug, in that beautiful room, sipping hot cocoa... who could fail to be warmed and comforted? As for the shopping problem... that may take something more.

Mary helped Kate as they half carried Naomi into the sitting room and laid her gently on one of the sofas, having helped her off with her shoes and coat. Phyllis placed a soft, clean duvet over the shivering woman and sat on a chair beside her.

"I… I'm sorry," Naomi sobbed.

"No need for apologies… or anything else just now," Phyllis stated matter of factly. "Just rest. We'll work things out. Whatever is causing all this distress… we'll sort it out, my dear. But first, you need some sleep. Can you sit up to take this warm drink? It'll help you."

Naomi dutifully sat up for long enough to sip the hot, soothing drink that Mary had brought for her. She tried again to stammer out her apologies and thanks but Phyllis shushed her.

"Later," Phyllis insisted. "We'll talk later."

Then, for the first time in a long while, Naomi slept deeply and well, soothed as much by Phyllis's gentle reassurances as the sedative she had added to the warm drink.

When she woke and looked at her watch, she was surprised to see that it was still only early evening. She felt so much better, as though she'd had a good night's sleep. Cautiously, she slipped her feet into the fluffy slippers that were set out ready for her and her arms into the incredibly soft, cashmere robe laid out on the sofa.

When had she been undressed? She had no memory of it, yet here she was… wearing brand new satiny-soft pyjamas.

She padded over to the door. The smell of dinner cooking was enticing, and surprisingly, Naomi felt quite hungry. Not usual for her. She rarely felt hungry and seldom ate much.

"Well hello, sleepy-head! How are you feeling?" Kate must have been listening for the door opening. She laughed. "No use looking at your watch like that. You've slept round the clock and then some. Here, let me show you where the bathroom is. We can talk over dinner when you've freshened up and feel more comfortable."

Naomi smiled nervously as she followed Kate. She hugged the soft robe around her. "I don't remember the last time I felt so comfortable."

"Good. Then there's no need to dress for dinner. It's only me and Phyllis," Kate smiled back. "It suits you," she said, indicating the gentle, rose-coloured dressing gown. "As usual, Phyllis has chosen well."

"Why did you bring me here?" Naomi asked later. "What do you want from me?"

"Want? Why should we want anything from you?"

Naomi shrugged. "So why did you bring me here?"

"Don't you like it here?" Phyllis asked.

"Of course I do." She looked around the luxurious sitting room. "It's fabulous. Too good to be true. So why have you brought me here?"

Kate and Phyllis exchanged a look.

Naomi sat up. "Ah! Let me guess. Is it a high-class brothel? Are you," she looked at Phyllis. "Are you the 'Madam'? And you," she turned to Kate. "You must be the ... now, what would you call a female pimp?"

"I don't know," laughed Kate. "But whatever it is, I'm certainly not!"

Naomi lay back against the cushions, feigning disappointment. "You mean I'm not here to live a life of luxury, entertaining well-off gentlemen?"

Phyllis laughed. "That's a good idea, Kate. Perhaps we should..."

Kate wrinkled her nose. "Mmm... no... I don't think so somehow."

"So you haven't kidnapped me for my voluptuous body and dazzling good looks?" Naomi slipped the cashmere robe from her bony shoulders and pouted her colourless lips. "So why am I here?" she asked again.

"Because... because we felt... well, we felt sorry for you. Look, I'm sorry. It's not really any of our business. You just seemed so unhappy. And sick. And Phyllis is so kind and I just knew she'd make you welcome. And I couldn't bear to take you back to that awful place." Kate stopped. She put her hand to her mouth. "I'm sorry. That must have sounded patronising and I didn't mean..."

Naomi smiled. "It's okay. You're right, it is an awful place…and…" Her voice became husky with tears. "And I am unhappy… desperately, desperately unhappy."

"We want to help."

Naomi was fighting for control, willing herself not to cry, not to let go.

"Why? Why should you want to help? What's in it for you?"

"Nothing," Phyllis assured her. "Is it so unbelievable that we might just want to help because we just want to?"

"Frankly? In this day and age? Yes. I find it impossible to believe. I know nothing about you… either of you."

"Perhaps it would help if we…"

"And you know nothing about me. How do you know I'm not going to steal your silver while you sleep?"

"You're not, are you, dear?" Phyllis smiled.

"No. But that could be my intention for all you know."

"True… true. But I don't think so. Besides," Kate reasoned. "I brought you here. You didn't come with *any* intentions."

"Which brings us back to my question. Why did you bring me here?"

"You look exhausted, my dear," Phyllis remarked. "Why don't we sort all this out in the morning?"

"I am exhausted. But I want it sorted out now!"

"Very well, dear. Kate, why don't you ask Mary to make us some cocoa?"

* * *

It took Naomi quite a few days to recover strength, helped by a lot of sleep and a little food. 'Little and often' was Phyllis's maxim regarding food for an invalid, especially one who hadn't been eating properly for some time. She was also helped by the comfort and security of her surroundings. Not that her distrust and suspicions had been dispelled… more that she had consciously decided to ignore them, enjoy the pampering now and face any price that had to be paid when she felt stronger.

Phyllis insisted that Naomi's own doctor be called to check her over, rightly being concerned that they didn't overlook any underlying illness that needed treatment.

"Mental and physical exhaustion!" had been his curt diagnosis. "She'll be all right with rest and the medication she has already. Are you looking after her here?" He looked around approvingly.

"Yes," Phyllis nodded. "For as long as she wishes to stay."

"Fine. I'll not need to see her again unless anything else arises. Good day Mrs…"

"*Doctor* Thaine," Phyllis informed him haughtily, not really approving of what she deemed his uncaring 'care' of his patient.

He shrugged into his coat and into his car and was gone.

"And good riddance," muttered Phyllis as she closed the door behind him. "Now young lady," she said as she walked back into the sitting room. "You said nothing about medication. Perhaps we should have been administering it already."

"Oh, it's nothing. I hadn't even got round to picking up the prescription."

"What was it for?"

"Anti-depressants," Naomi admitted reluctantly.

"And was he offering any counsel along with them?"

Naomi shook her head.

"Didn't think so," Phyllis sniffed. "Well, if you'd like, I'll get Mary to get the prescription filled but I must say that, if there's enough of a problem to need anti-depressants, there's enough of a problem to need help, counselling or something. When I was in practice…"

"Were you really a doctor, then?"

"Of course I was. Did you think I was just trying to impress your GP?"

"I don't know," Naomi said thoughtfully, snuggling into the duvet like a contented kitten. "But I rather like the thought of being looked after by my own private doctor… even a retired one. Hey!" She sat up, suddenly resembling a street cat spoiling for a fight, the kitten look instantly banished. "You know I can't pay for all this, don't you?"

Phyllis laughed. "I don't want you to pay."

"And there's no-one else to pay."

"I don't want paid."

"Then what *do* you want?" Distrust was not so deeply buried after all, suspicion still prowling. "There's nothing I can do."

Phyllis sat on the edge of the sofa. "Relax, my dear. There's nothing I want."

"I'm not a lesbian, you know."

"Why on earth would I think you were?" Phyllis gasped. "You surely didn't think…"

"I don't know what to think. First of all you appear in a shop, giving advice about dresses, next thing you're asking me to have coffee with you and before I know what's going on, here I am, dressed in your pyjamas, lying in the lap of luxury, in your house. I don't know what to think. I'm scared to begin to work it out."

"Has no-one ever done anything for you before just out of common kindness, compassion?"

"Kindness! I can cope with a bit of kindness. Mrs Morgan, Kate, she's kind. In the shop. She's always been kind when I was in the shop. But that's her job. Not that any of the rest of them were ever kind. But this…" She waved her hand about vaguely indicating the room, the house, everything. "I don't know what this is. But I know it's not 'common kindness'!" She was up now, off the sofa, the duvet discarded, looking round for her clothes.

"But I assure you, that's all it is. You were ill. You seemed unhappy. Kate and I, we want to help."

"Why?"

"I don't really know. You just seemed to need help." Phyllis shrugged.

"Where are my clothes? Am I some kind of prisoner here?"

"Of course you're not. You're free to go anytime you wish." Phyllis rose quietly and walked to the door. "I'll ask Mary. She'll bring your clothes. They were soiled. Mary washed them."

"She didn't need to do that." The strength was leaving Naomi's body now, her fear and anger had subsided and the adrenalin rush was over, leaving her exhausted.

"Why don't you lie down again… just till Mary brings your things," Phyllis added hastily.

Tears welled up in Naomi's eyes. Gratefully she sank down into the comfort of the large settee. "I'm sorry. You've been so kind. It's just… it's just…"

"You're frightened," Phyllis supplied. "I know. I wish there were some way to reassure you. Perhaps when Kate comes home, we could talk. Try to work something out. Do you think you could wait till then?"

Naomi nodded, all resistance gone, washed away in the terrible tide of her weariness.

Phyllis quietly left her to rest, leaving the bundle of laundered clothes just inside the door.

Later, when the others rejoined her in the comfort of Phyllis's glorious living room, Naomi asked yet again what it was they wanted from her.

"You're like a dog with a bone," Phyllis remarked. "Worry, worry, worry! The only thing we want for you, is for you to get better."

"And then what?"

"Then whatever you wish. You can go home, back to work, get on with your life… or," Kate added, seeing the uncertainty in Naomi's face. "Or, you could hang out here for a while longer till you know if there's some other way to live your life. A way that could make you happier."

"Who says I'm not happy?" Naomi defended herself.

Kate raised her eyebrows.

"Well… no. Obviously I'm not," Naomi acceded. "Otherwise I don't suppose I'd be needing anti-depressants."

"Or starving yourself."

"Or shopping for things you don't need when you can't afford it!"

Naomi stared at Phyllis as though she had slapped her. "What? How did you? Who says I can't? What do you mean?

Are you saying I'm not happy and that's why I shop? What makes you think I have a problem with shopping?"

"What do you think? Do *you* think it's a problem?"

"Of course it's not a problem," she laughed nervously. "How could shopping possibly be a problem?"

"It is for some people," Phyllis said softly.

"Well, it isn't for me!"

Phyllis and Kate exchanged a look.

"You two aren't real," Naomi sneered. "I'm going to wake up soon out of this nightmare. Good Lord! You think *I've* got problems! You two are freaky! I want out of here."

"You're free to go whenever you want," said Phyllis quietly.

"Yeah…and I'm going," she said, grabbing the small bundle that was her clothes.

When Naomi closed the bathroom door behind her she leant against it for a moment or two. She was shaking, partly with fear, partly with the weakness that still lingered in her body.

What on earth had she stumbled into?

She crossed to the toilet and sat down. True, they were very kind. They had looked after her for days now, nearly a week. But they were crazy. Both of them. They were fruit-cakes. What was she doing here?

She started to dress.

She had to get away from this lunatic asylum.

Money! No money. Problem. How to get home? She didn't even know where she was. In Edinburgh, she supposed. Well, she knew Edinburgh pretty well. Once she found out the street name, she'd soon find her way. She was stronger now than she'd felt for a long time, thanks to their care. She'd be able to walk even if it were quite a distance. If not, she could always hitch a lift.

But when she was ready to leave, she suddenly became uncertain. They had been kind. More than kind. She couldn't leave without saying 'Thank you'. But that meant she couldn't just slip out, as she'd like to do.

In the end, it didn't matter what she'd planned. When she opened the door, Kate was waiting with her coat on, ready to run her home in Phyllis's car.

"I'm hardly likely to let you walk, am I? Not considering it was me who brought you here in the first place," Kate countered her protests. "Anyway, say 'Goodbye' to Phyllis while I bring the car to the door. It's down the street a bit."

It was a strained, awkward 'Goodbye' she said in the end... not knowing how to play the scene, not knowing whether to be grateful or horrified at the events of the last week.

But Phyllis was having none of that. She drew Naomi to her and gently kissed her cheek. "You know now where I live," she said kindly. "There will always be a welcome here for you. A warm meal and a warm bed if you need it."

Naomi stared at her benefactress with disbelief. "Are you for real?" she asked.

"I mean it, dear. You'll always be welcome."

"Right. Yes. Thank you," Naomi muttered. She turned as she went down the steps. "For everything," she added sincerely, the lump in her throat softening her voice.

The journey to her flat didn't take long, no more than fifteen minutes, but the silence made it feel longer.

"Thank you," she managed to mumble again as she got out of the car.

"No problem," Kate said brightly. "Take better care of yourself now... and make sure you get that gas leak seen to," she added.

Kate didn't look back as she drove off. This was the plan she and Phyllis had hastily agreed upon. Give Naomi space, let her think things over, let the gentle luxury of the house lure her back. They guessed that it would all seem less frightening in retrospect. Perhaps the contrast going back to her own bed-sit, lonely, hungry, cold, damp. The list of miseries would be endless, Kate felt sure, having seen... and smelled Naomi's place. Perhaps the contrast would break down her resistance to their help.

It was more of a contrast than even Kate could have imagined.

When Naomi put her key in the lock, she knew straight away something was wrong. The door swung open without the need to turn the key. Had she left it unlocked? It would be the first time. She was strangely security-conscious for someone who has so little worth stealing.

But robbery had not been the reason for entry. The door had not been forced. Pete had his own key.

The room had been 'turned over', not in search of valuables but in anger.

The cupboards and drawers all lay open. Their contents strewn about the floor: the glorious rainbow of never-worn evening dresses mingled with washed-out-grey underwear, a kaleidoscope of textures and colours, stabbed here and there with long-forgotten, out-of-date packets and tins of food.

The bed had been angrily stripped and the mattress pulled off in temper. Even her few dishes were smashed on the floor. Nothing had been spared the tempest.

It had obviously been an act of deliberate, savage vandalism and she was appalled by it, violated by it.

He had left his calling card. Printed across the wall, a lipstick message: "WHERE THE HELL HAVE YOU BEEN?"

Naomi hadn't moved from the doorway. She slowly slumped onto the floor and sat staring at the horror of the scene before her.

The phone started to ring but she was only dimly aware of its insistence, had no idea where it was or how to stop it.

After a while, the cat responsible for the noxious smell in the close, sniffed round her legs, sensing there was no resistance to its invasion of the flat. It picked its way across the floor, instinctively avoiding the shards of crockery and finding the scattered contents of the fridge, and lapped greedily at the remains of the rancid, week-old milk.

"What on earth?" Kate stood in the doorway, staring in shock at the scene before her. "Naomi. Are you all right?" She bent to help her up, but Naomi stared back vacantly without making any effort to move. "I brought you milk and bread. Couldn't let you come home to an empty fridge…" Her voice trailed off as she saw the contents spilling from its open door along with the results of its 'defrost' process.

"Oh Naomi! Oh you poor, poor thing. Let me help you up. Here hold on to my arm. Come on," she coaxed. "You can't stay here. Let's gather anything that's important to you and get you out of this. Who on earth could have done this?" She pointed to the message on the wall. "Someone was looking for you. Do you know who? Shall I call the police?"

"No." Naomi shook her head. "No, it doesn't matter," she said softly.

Kate put down the bread and milk she had been carrying and gently eased Naomi to her feet. "Is there anything you need from here? Valuables, papers? I'll gather up your clothes while you get anything else you want to take. Have you a case or a bag?"

Slowly, oh so slowly, Naomi picked up a few bits and pieces, turning them over in her hands, staring dry-eyed at the devastation that surrounded her.

Hatred, surely only hatred could have fuelled such anger, such malice. She stared at the bed, stripped, exposed, violated… as she had been so many times upon it. There had never been love. Only a cruel lust, a malevolent spitefulness, a satisfying of his basest desires. She shivered.

"Come, Naomi. You're in shock. I need to get you somewhere warm."

From under the bed, she pulled out a hold-all and pushed it towards Kate, then, while Kate folded clothes into it, Naomi emptied the few things remaining in her chest of drawers into a carrier bag. They gathered up anything else she might need and left the flat as it was.

"This can be dealt with another day," Kate told her and Naomi let herself be led to the car and driven back to the house she had left less than an hour before.

Chapter 13

When Dan walked into the office of 'P. Cartwright, Auctioneer & Valuator', there was obviously a problem. The reception desk was unmanned, the door to one office was open, revealing chaos but no personnel, and there was the sound of raised voices from behind the closed door of another.

He looked around for a means of announcing his presence but was spared the necessity by the sudden opening of the closed door.

"Oh, hi! Didn't hear anyone come in." The young woman looked harassed. She clutched a sheaf of papers retrieved from some untidy heap. She stepped back, reached behind her and carefully closed the door on the sound of still-raised voices. "Can I help you?"

Dan smiled. "This doesn't sound the best time to call." He turned to go. "Shall I come back later?"

"No." She shook her head. "We're just in the middle of a crisis. Nothing to worry about," she said with a sigh. Having divested herself of her bundle, she reopened the door without knocking. "Pete," she smirked from the doorway. "You have a customer."

A half-formed curse hung in the air like a bird of prey, its aborted swoop becoming a flutter. Dan waited in the silence that followed, amused by the unprofessional conduct of 'Mr P Cartwright, Auctioneer and Valuer'.

The receptionist busied herself tidying the pile of papers, trying to conceal the mixture of embarrassment and scorn that coloured her face.

"Mr Cartwright will be with you in a moment," Dan was assured by a red-faced man, also clutching an unruly bundle, who emerged from the war zone and hurried into the other office.

Dan took a seat and waited patiently. He was in no rush. Retirement suited him. Though never prone to angry outbursts, he remembered the frustrations of managing an office, so sympathised with the boss while disagreeing with his methods.

Peter Cartwright appeared composed and charming as he ushered Dan into his office, making no apology, affecting nonchalance. The past ten minutes might never have happened.

When Dan showed him the book he had found, Peter Cartwright examined it carefully. "Difficult to say, really, what it would fetch on the open market. No claimed authorship. Could be anyone. Probably no-one. Seems old," he decided, turning it over in his hands. "From the binding, I'd say, possibly as old as eighty, ninety years. Might be able to find a private buyer…"

"I'm not interested in selling," Dan assured him quickly. "Not just now, anyway. Just thought it'd be interesting to get it valued."

"You could take a chance at auction, but, if you don't want to sell… Probably better to take it to a book dealer. Furniture, ornaments, clocks… they're more my line… and property, of course." Peter Cartwright rose and offered his hand. "If you change your mind, Mr Morgan, let me know. We could put it into auction any time. See what it would fetch. You could set your minimum."

Dan wrapped the book in its silk scarf and took it home, not really disappointed by the lack of a valuation. In many ways it was more fitting not to try to put a price on it. How much, the warmth of understanding? What price the pain of love?

He put it away carefully. At an appropriate time, it would be a gift for Kate. He could wait. Patience was one of his 'virtues'.

* * *

Paul sat on the bench watching the world go by. He arrived early so that he could do just that. It was Saturday, so there was plenty of 'world' to watch. Edinburgh was good for that. Especially in summer, of course, but even now, this late in the year, when the leaves had dropped and the wind had tidied them away, there were still the stragglers to watch. The intrepid, the 'budget tourists', looking for off-season bargains and finding off-season scenery. The castle looked dark and forbidding in the rain. Any colour left in the gardens was washed out by the grey drizzle. But Paul loved it.

A couple walked by, huddled under their umbrella, their guide book, limp and smudged. What did they make of Scotland in the winter? Had they expected snow perhaps? Like on the calendars? Princes Street looked impressive in the snow; the Scott monument rising like a giant stalagmite, deposited by the dripping clouds; the gardens spread like a fresh, white cotton duvet over the flower beds. But how often did it snow in Scotland? Really snow? Enough to make this grey winter pretty?

Paul laughed out loud. The joke of it all was that he loved it. He loved this wet, grey drizzle. He loved the feel of it, the smell of it, the cloak of it. He became an unobserved observer. No-one expected to be studied as they scurried about keeping dry… or trying to. The ones who didn't care about the rain looked out from under their hoods and brollies and saw only the things they had planned to see. He could watch and draft his pictures, weave his stories around their imagined lives.

"Why on earth did we have to meet here?" Vicky demanded crossly.

"Oh hi, Sis!" Paul swung round on the bench. "Didn't see you coming. Expected you through the other gate."

"Could we not have met inside somewhere? I'm soaked already. And look at you! You've not even got a hat or a brolly or anything. You really are the limit, Paul."

"D'you want a seat?" Paul asked gallantly, wiping a cascade of water off the bench beside him.

"No, I do not! Or not here anyway. You can buy me a coffee."

"Harrison's?"

"Don't be thick, Paul. We can hardly sit in Mum's shop discussing what on earth we're going to do about her."

"Why not? She doesn't work on a Saturday."

"Because we just can't. Come on! Let's go to that wee coffee shop on Rose Street."

Paul laughed. "Any one in particular, Sis? I mean there only are the odd half-dozen or so."

"The nearest. Anywhere to get out of this rain."

Paul placed the coffee cups on the table. "Okay!" he declared. "Family conference called to order. Item one on agenda: What are we going to do about Mum?"

"Can you never be serious?"

"Sorry," he frowned. "Serious face." The frown deepened. "Very serious face." The frown became a grimace.

Vicky sighed. "I don't know why I bother."

"Frankly, my dear… neither do I."

"Mum?"

"Mum's fine."

"You've seen her?"

"I've seen her, and she's fine." Paul settled at the table, leaning back in the chair, his legs sprawled wide in front of him. "Happy, I'd say."

"Great!"

"Look, Sis. What *is* your problem?"

"I don't know what you mean. It's not me that's got the problem."

"Your tone: the way you speak of Mum. What's your issue? Did she not buy you a Barbie doll when you were six or something?"

"Ha! Ha! Very funny."

"What then?" Paul asked. "Mum's okay, you know."

"So you said."

"No. I mean, Mum's *okay*, as in, Mum's cool. She's not so bad."

"Wonderful even!" Vicky muttered.

"What *is* your problem?" Paul repeated.

"I said, 'I don't have a problem'!"

"Yeah, but you obviously do."

"I just don't think it's so 'cool' to go off, leave your husband and family with no explanation, no reason."

"Maybe she had a reason."

"Like?" Vicky demanded.

"Like, maybe she was unhappy?"

"How could she not be happy?"

"I don't know," Paul shrugged. "You're the woman. You're the one who should be having the girly chats with her." He waved his hand about. "Has she never said anything to you?"

"Me?" Vicky laughed. "Mum talk to me? Yeah, that'll be the day! I'm still waiting for the birds and bees conversation!"

"You seem to have managed... kids and all that..."

"No thanks to Mum! I'd still think babies grew under the rhubarb, if I was waiting for her to tell me the facts of life."

"Really? Are you serious?" Paul drew his legs in and sat forward to lean his arms on the table. "Do you mean Mum never told you about the gooseberry bush?"

Vicky chose to ignore his ridicule. "She never was one for 'girly chats'. Can't remember her ever sitting on the end of my bed, asking about my boyfriends, or talking about make-up." Vicky's voice was thickening as she spoke. "Can't remember ever sitting on the end of her bed either. Or on her knee, come to think of it."

"I can," Paul supplied helpfully. "Remember sitting on her knee, I mean. Not talking about boyfriends or make-up... but I remember her tucking me in, sitting on my bed, telling me stories."

"Lucky old you," Vicky sneered. "You always were the favourite."

"Yeah!"

"Great!" Vicky sulked. "You needn't be so bloomin' smug about it! Anyway, where is she?"

Paul looked around furtively then leaned across the table conspiratorially.

"She's..." He looked round again. "She's in hiding."

"Look Paul, I've got more to do with my life than sit here watching your infantile games."

"You could always join in. Have some fun."

"Paul..."

"You remember fun?"

"Paul..."

"No, I don't suppose you do. It never was your scene was it, Sis?"

"I wish you'd stop calling me 'Sis'. You know I hate it."

"Sorry, Sis... I mean, Vick."

"And I don't like 'Vick' either."

"Don't you? Oh that's a pity. Quite a nice girl really. She's my sister, you know."

"Right! That's it!" Vicky rose from her seat. "I knew it was a mistake trying to talk with you."

"Aw, sit down, Sis."

Vicky glared at him.

"Okay, Sis... I mean Vicky... Victoria?"

The glare intensified.

"Okay! Okay! I'll try to behave. But you know, you really do take life too seriously."

"And you don't take it seriously enough. Mum's left home. She's God knows where."

Paul raised his hand. "I know too actually."

"Where is she, then?"

"Can't tell you. It's a secret."

"Grow up, Paul," his long-suffering sister sighed.

"Still can't tell you. She doesn't want anybody to know. Especially not you, 'cos you'll tell Dad," he sniffed.

She stood up again. "That's it! I've had enough. I'm really going this time."

Paul shrugged.

"Just tell Mum next time you see her... tell her... tell her..." Her voice broke with frustrated tears.

Paul reached out to her. "Sorry Vicky," he said, with genuine penitence at last. "You always did bring out the worst in me."

"You can say that again... but don't bother," she added hastily as he opened his mouth. "Just stop fooling around and let's talk."

* * *

166

"Vicky sends her love," Paul announced as he bent to kiss his mother's cheek. "She thinks you should stop fooling around and go home."

Kate closed the door on the winter chill and drew him into the welcome of Phyllis's hallway. "Oh she does, does she?"

"Yes. She doesn't think you're being fair to Dad. He's miserable without you."

"Oh good," Kate beamed. "I hoped he would be. Serves him right."

"Tut, tut, Mother! Do I detect a note of malice there?"

"Certainly."

"Thought so. Well, Vicky says…"

"You've been discussing me then?"

"Of course. Vicky called a family conference… or at least, she and I met for coffee to discuss what on earth we were going to do with you."

"And did you decide?"

"Yes. I said we were to leave you alone." Paul shook his head. "She wasn't happy. In fact, she was quite frustrated at what she called my 'lack of co-operation'."

"Poor Vicky. I hope you were nice to her."

"Of course. I am always nice to Vicky."

"Except when you wind her up."

"Well, she makes it such fun." Paul rubbed his hands gleefully as they entered the living room. "Hi, Phyllis! D'you know," he said as he gazed around. "It's like entering a different season, coming in here out of the rain." He took a deep breath. "Lovely. Oh! Hi there." He offered his hand to Naomi, who had risen quietly from one of the sofas.

"This is Naomi, a friend of ours. She's been staying with us for a bit."

"Lucky you," Paul said as he shook her hand.

"Yes," she blushed. "I know."

"I can't blame you really for wanting to stay here," he said to Kate. "Superb décor and good company. I bet they even talk to you in the evening," he added in a mock whisper.

167

Phyllis laughed. "Talking is something we are very good at! But now, if you'll excuse us, Naomi and I have some things to see to, so we'll let *you* do the talking."

"Who's the new one?" Paul asked when the door was safely closed behind Phyllis and Naomi. He pulled a face. "One of your lost causes?"

"Paul!"

"Well, she certainly looks like a lost cause. She's let herself go a bit, has she not?"

"She's been through a hard time."

"It shows. You should get her to do something with her hair… and feed her up a bit."

"We're working on it. D'you know, I never realised what a nasty chauvinist you were."

Paul grinned smugly. "But you love me anyway."

"So why have you come? To torment me?"

"Absolutely. And to tell you that Vicky is demanding to know where you are. She thinks Dad should have this address too."

"Oh, she does, does she? Did you give it to her?"

"Of course not. But I was under severe pressure. Next time I might have to give in. She's threatening torture."

Kate sat down heavily. "Bother! I suppose I'm going to have to let them know. Probably ought to talk to them both."

"Probably. It would certainly take the heat off me."

"And let's face it… that's what matters."

"Absolutely!"

"Okay. I'll give Vicky a phone."

"And Dad?"

"And Dad." She sighed. "I suppose 'all good things must come to an end'."

"You're going home then?" Paul asked hopefully.

"I didn't say that. I said I'd give them a phone, that's all."

Chapter 14

It had been three weeks since Kate had brought her here the second time. Three more weeks of pampering, feeding and sleep. They had even put her into a musty old bedroom. There'd been a lot of whispering and bumping and banging. The man who cleaned the windows and tidied the back garden had been called in to help with clearing some old junk or something out of the room. Finally, Phyllis had shown her into it, apologising for its undecorated state. Naomi hadn't cared about that, had barely noticed that was the case. The room was huge. Bigger, by far, than her whole bedsit, including the grotty old bathroom and kitchen area, And this room even had an en-suite. And *that* was not much smaller than the bedsit! It was incredible!

Physically, she felt much better: the obvious consequences of eating a regular, balanced diet and getting plenty of rest. Which just goes to show that Mother knew what she was talking about!

Naomi closed herself against the pain that shivered through her at the thought of her mother.

Emotionally, she was a wreck, but beginning to cope. She had begun to trust them, begun to believe their motives were okay... weird... but okay. She had returned to worrying about things outside these walls: money, for instance: debt, in particular. The debt she had run up on her Visa and Access cards, store cards, bank overdraft, the loan she'd taken out last year... to try to sort out the credit card debts she had even back then...

The burden was crushing: she had no idea how she was going to pay it off... if she *ever* could pay it off.

And now, she didn't even have a job. Not that *that* had helped. Pete had paid her so little, it barely fed her... didn't feed her once the final demands started arriving. She had been juggling one card against another for months and getting nowhere. The interest was all she was feeding, never the debt. Like a hungry animal, it kept demanding more, growing with each demand, becoming hungrier as it grew. Practically every penny she earned went towards satisfying its greed.

If she could survive a little longer in this crazy house, at least it couldn't hunt her down. She could buy time: time to sort something out, to find a way to keep the proverbial 'wolf' from her door: time to work out what on earth she was going to do with the rest of her life. Just looking around at the comfort and luxury of her surroundings, she could believe anything was possible.

Last night, she had cried for the first time since…

Better not go there.

Better try to forget the rape of the bedsit.

Better just sit tight here for a while.

The bedsit had been Pete's. He paid the rent, kept her there, like dirty washing in a closet, caring nothing for her welfare as long as she was there when he wanted to dress in a different guise. Loving husband, doting father, suave businessman, these were the personas he shed at the door to the basement room. Naomi shuddered to think of the roles he played inside it.

Kate had taken her back once, to collect the rest of her things… for what they were worth.

Kate had gone herself before that: had worked hard, had cleared up the mess, had even scrubbed the lipstick message from the wall, but the room still bore signs of its desecration… and it still smelled, of gas, damp and cat's pee.

Already, hard to believe that this had been her life… here and the office.

She had sent a note to the office, to Pete: a note of Resignation from her job, of Termination of their relationship… with no return address. She wondered at how easy it had been. After all these years, it had been as easy as a short note on plain, white paper, telling him she wanted out… *was* out.

But, as she closed the door of the bedsit, she shivered, thinking that it had been *too* easy, that she would not get away with it. His rage was not hard to imagine, thinking back to the last time she opened this door.

Kate took the key from her hand. "It's over. That part of your life is finished," she said. "Whatever you decide to do, wherever you decide to go, you don't ever need to come back here." She put the key into the envelope in her hand, an envelope addressed to the landlord of the property, an envelope containing a letter terminating her occupancy of the flat and referring him to her employer for settlement of any outstanding rent, etc.

Naomi had been rather pleased with the wording of the letter, proud when Phyllis and Kate had congratulated her on its business-like form. But suddenly, she feared that somehow it would bring trouble, somehow Pete would turn it against her. "Do you think I'm doing the right thing?" she asked Kate.

"I know you are," she replied. "And I'm sure you'll know it too once you're out of this... this..." She looked around at the dingy, stinking stairwell, unlit by window or lamp, her senses assaulted by the sight and smell of the place, words failing her to find a name for it. She led Naomi out into the fresh air.

They hadn't noticed the Grey Face behind the grey net at the ground floor window when they had arrived, nor did they notice it now. They were unaware that the Grey Face had grinned with pleasure at her part in the outplaying of a drama she would unlikely witness but had been paid to ensure. Part of the payment, the bright, colourful, mobile phone, incongruous in her wrinkled, grey hands and recently used to report two visitors to the basement flat.

* * *

Naomi woke up crying.

She was weeping for the loss of her life.

She felt lost in a wilderness of unaccustomed kindness, wanting to find her way home. But where was home? Not in the stinking, damp, Hell-Hole she had lived in for the past three years. She had never been happy there, was only there because Pete installed her there, paid the rent, took her dignity, kept her.

He had promised great things, had told her that her salary was being paid into a high-interest account. She had to leave it there for six months, then they would be able to buy somewhere better... together. Meanwhile, he would keep her, give her enough for food and a few bits and pieces. Gullible. She'd been so gullible. By the time she realised it was all lies, that there was no high-interest account, no salary, no better apartment and no love... only a wife and children... it was too late. He had tightened his hold on her. She was dependent on him, hooked on his ego, held by his lies, his pleading, his threats.

When had she lost her own will? When had she become his slave, his toy, his filth?

She looked around desperately. This place was too clean, too bright. It was everything she was not. She was soiled, degraded. She shouldn't be here. She was suffocating. Air, she needed air.

Naomi burst out of the door and ran onto the pavement.

A walk, she would go for a walk. Find somewhere to hide, somewhere else to lick her wounds, somewhere more comfortable. A refuge perhaps? One of these places for battered wives. She'd found out about one before, one of the times she had tried to run away from him. Where was it? Oh, think, think! Where was it?

She started to walk in the direction of the city centre, her mind bemused still with sleep yet her senses heightened by the panic attack. Her bare feet splashed softly on the wet pavement but there was another sound.

Someone following her.

She'd been dimly aware of him as she'd run down the steps. He'd been standing across the street, watching the door. He must have been. Why else was he standing there?

But now he was walking. Following her.

She crossed the street, turned a corner, quickened her pace.

He was still there. He was gaining on her. She started to run.

Looking around wildly... nowhere to hide.

Each breath painful in chest... fear closing throat... pains shooting through feet, up legs... heart racing...

Run... still following... running too.

Hide... nowhere to hide.

Head spinning... ears singing.

Another corner, cross the street, double back, run...

Need to get back to Kate... Kate...

Tears hampering now... can't see... Where is he? Still following?

Can only hear blood pounding, no footsteps.

The taste of fear. The smell of fear.

A cul-de-sac.

Have to stop. Have to breathe.

'Oh, God, help me,' she begged, turning back, wiping her eyes, searching in the street-lit gloom for his shape.

He wasn't there. She'd lost him, shaken him off.

Leaning against a wall, she tried to let her heart-rate return to normal.

'Thank you, God. Oh, thank you,' she whispered.

But now she had forgotten why she was running away, only knew she needed to go back.

Footsteps again. His footsteps? How had he found her?

She shrank into the shadows. He walked by the end of the cul-de-sac. He was looking for her. She willed herself to wait: wait till his footsteps walked into silence. Then she ran the other way. Unencumbered by coat or shoes: she had not intended to go outside. What was she doing out here in the rain? She ran till she could see the lights of the house. The front door was open. Light spilled out and cascaded down the steps. Someone was there at the door, looking out, looking for her.

"Kate....Oh, Kate," she wept.

"What on earth? Where? We were worried."

"He followed me. He knows I'm here."

"No, Naomi. I'm sure he can't."

"But I saw him." She looked round frantically, searching the empty street outside. Satisfied, she allowed herself to be drawn into the warmth of the hall, closing the door firmly behind her. "I doubled back. I ran. I lost him."

"Good. Good," Kate soothed. "Now come, let me fill the bath for you. You're soaked through and your feet are bleeding."

"But he knows I'm here. You won't open the door to him, will you? Promise you won't open the door to him."

Kate held the shaking hands, stopped their frantic tearing at her collar, poured the soothing oil of her calmness over the trembling girl.

"I promise. I promise. Now come, take these wet things off."

"He can be very charming. Don't let him charm you."

"I won't let him charm me."

"Oh, Kate, I was so frightened."

"I know, I know. But it's all over now. You're safe here."

"But he knows I'm here."

"Nonsense! How could he possibly know? You just *thought* it was him because you were frightened."

"But I *saw* him!"

"You *thought* you saw him. It could have been anyone walking down the street." Kate had been leading her towards the bathroom all the time she'd been talking. While the bath filled, she bundled her in warm towels, helped her sip Phyllis's 'special-brew' hot cocoa and held her closely, crooning reassurances.

They didn't hear his curse as he leant on the car to catch his breath. Nor did they hear him drive away. In fact, by the time they had tucked Naomi safely back in bed, the glow of his discarded cigarette stub was all there was to verify her fear... but they didn't note it.

Chapter 15

"Please, Paul."

"No, Mum. I don't do charity dates!"

"But you're not dating anyone just now. You told me."

"And I'm certainly not dating weirdos!"

"She's not a weirdo! She's just... "

"I know. She's been through a hard time. You told me."

"Well, she has. And now she's terrified to go over the doorstep. She thinks her ex-, ex-whatever he was... she thinks he might be waiting to grab her or something."

"Exactly! Like I said... a weirdo!"

"No! Just a poor frightened girl who needs some help."

"Then get her some help. Get her to a doctor or a psychiatrist or someone."

"We have. She's on medication and she's getting counselling. But now, she needs a friend."

"Great! She's got you... and Phyllis."

"But, Paul."

"No, Mum. Definitely, absolutely, positively NO!"

* * *

"Why on earth have you brought her here?" hissed Vicky in the privacy of the kitchen.

"I didn't know where else to take her," Paul hissed back.

Vicky took the mugs from their hooks and set them on the worktop. "How on earth did Mum talk you into this?" she grinned.

He scratched his head, looking genuinely puzzled. "I've no idea! It just sort of happened. One minute I was vehemently refusing... the next, I was holding open the car door for her."

"Well you shouldn't've brought her here. What about the kids?"

"What about the kids? She's not exactly dangerous or anything. She's hardly got the energy to stand up."

"But she's... strange. She might frighten them."

"Hardly! More like they'll scare the hell out of her."

"Mind your tongue!"

Paul shrugged. "Anyway, I thought maybe you could do something with her hair."

"Come again?"

"I thought you could style it or something. Make her look less gothic."

"Oh you did, did you? And what makes you so sure she's going to want anything done with her hair?"

"Have you seen it?"

Vicky thought of the long, dull brown pony-tail, broken ends frizzing the otherwise lifeless, thin bundle scraped severely back from a lack-lustre, thin face. She shook her head. "It's still up to her... even if I was to agree to do it," she added hastily.

"Thanks, sis," he grinned, kissing her on the cheek as he grabbed a couple of the filled mugs and pushed open the kitchen door.

"Look, Uncle Paul," Callum said. "Naomi and me built a marble run. Watch this!" And he fed a handful of marbles in at the top, squealing with delight as they hurtled down the run, through the obstacles, turning the wheels, spinning the cogs and cascaded into a tub at the bottom.

"Wow!" Paul applauded.

"Isn't it wicked?"

"Absolutely!"

"She's cool," Callum confided in a loud whisper, causing Naomi to blush and look away.

Paul grinned at Vicky. "Sure she is, son," he whispered back.

"I want a marble run," Joshua demanded.

"But this one's for both of you," Naomi said quickly. "Look! If you feed marbles in this other bit," she demonstrated. "They'll run down this way, all the way down, through this wheel, over here, through this and..."

"And it'll be a race," finished Callum.

"Exactly! Now, get your marbles. Ready? On your marbles! Go!"

Paul and Vicky looked at one another in amazement. The pale, dowdy 'weirdo' had been transformed into a pink-faced enthusiast, the boys obviously totally at ease with her.

"You've done this before," Paul remarked.

"Once or twice," she blushed. "It's fun."

"I can see that. Can I play?" he asked the boys.

"Okay. You can help Josh, Naomi's on my side."

"That's not fair," Joshua wailed. "I want Naomi!"

"It's my marble run."

"We'll change at half-time," Naomi, peacemaker, interjected. "Ready?"

* * *

When Phyllis saw the new hairstyle, a sleek bob, the colour enhanced with gentle highlights, the shape framing Naomi's small face, giving her an altogether softer, healthier look, she declared that Naomi must have some new clothes.

"But I have no money."

"I didn't say anything about *buying*."

"How else can I get new clothes? Steal them?"

"I've got some," replied Phyllis. "They'll maybe be a bit baggy, but that's fashionable, isn't it?"

"I wouldn't know," Kate answered. "But..."

"But, with all due respect," Naomi interrupted. "You and I. We're not exactly... well, we're not exactly the same age group or anything. I mean, I don't want to seem ungrateful or anything," she added hastily. "But really!"

"Yes, Phyllis. I don't suppose you often wear jeans and t-shirts," Kate agreed.

"Doesn't mean I don't have any!"

Kate and Naomi exchanged a puzzled frown.

"I really don't think..."

"You really don't *know*. Neither of you do," said Phyllis.

"The plot thickens," grinned Naomi.

"What are you on about, Phyllis?" asked Kate.

Phyllis sighed. "You'll not believe me if I tell you."

"I think she's finally gone."

"Just take it from me. I have clothes that will suit. Perhaps not exactly jeans and t-shirt…"

"Exactly!"

"But suitable. And attractive. And less… less…" She waved her hands about, seeking a description for what was, to her, indescribable. The jeans Naomi was wearing were fashionably old and faded, suitable perhaps for a teenager going to a disco, but hardly appropriate, in Phyllis's view, for a young woman in Naomi's position. Though what exactly her 'position' *was,* even Phyllis would have been hard pressed to say.

"You mean you don't like my t-shirt?" Naomi asked with an innocent smile, holding out the bottom of an enormous baggy garment bearing a 'Save the Whale' logo. "You don't care about the fate of the whales?"

"Stretch that t-shirt any more and you could get one in there with you!"

"Nice one, Phyllis," Kate laughed.

"You look like an orphan."

"I am an orphan."

"You know fine and well what I mean. Oh! Are you, my dear?" Phyllis was immediately contrite. "I didn't know. You're still so young. There's so much we don't know about one another, isn't there?"

"When did you lose your parents?" Kate asked gently.

Naomi shrugged. "A while ago. It doesn't matter."

"But of course it matters."

"Look, I'd rather not talk about it. Okay?"

"Of course, dear," Phyllis said quickly. "But if ever you want to talk…"

"Yeah, yeah. I know. Thanks." She shook her head, the new bob swinging. "But, no thanks!"

"Right," Phyllis rose from her chair. "You two wait here. I'll be right back."

The telephone rang as she walked from the room. "Answer that for me, Kate, there's a dear. It's probably for you anyway. No-one phones me at this hour."

"Hello. 225-0936. Who's speaking please? Hello. Can I help you?" She shrugged and put the phone down. "No-one. Wrong number probably." She looked puzzled. "It did sound as though someone was there though. You know, the sound a mobile phone makes?…"

But Naomi wasn't listening. "What d'you suppose she's up to now?" she asked.

Kate sat down again. "Getting you some new clothes probably."

Naomi looked at her watch. "It's half past nine. Where on earth is she gonna get new clothes at this time of night?"

Kate shrugged. "But I bet she will."

"D'you think she's all right?" Naomi asked after a while.

"Oh, I'm sure she is. She'll just be…"

"No. I mean: d'you think she's All Right… as in All Right… in the head?"

"Of course she is," Kate said defensively. "She may be a bit older, but she's all there, in fact, I'd say she's very much 'All right'."

"But she's weird, don't you think?"

"No."

"I mean, who else do you know would take in people off the streets, people she knows nothing whatever about, feed them, give them a bed… not just any bed, but a bed with completely new bedding, new rugs, new towels, new everything? Now she's talking about new clothes. I mean, what is she on? Or, more to the point, what does she want?"

"I don't think she wants anything. Except perhaps a bit of company."

"You have to admit it's all a bit strange?"

Kate shrugged. "Unusual, perhaps," she admitted grudgingly.

"Weird, if you ask me. I mean, where does she get all the new stuff?"

"Buys it?"

"Why? Why would a woman of, what age is she? Eighty? Eighty-one?"

"Eighty-eight, I think she said."

"Why would a woman of her age have anything in her wardrobe that she thought might interest a thirty-year old woman? Why would she have bought it?"

"Perhaps she likes to keep up with fashion?"

"She dresses like a typical, eighty-year-old, rich, old lady. Hardly fashionable, the Wrinklies' Look!"

"Naomi! That's ageist, classist and ungrateful! Besides, you haven't seen what she's going to offer you yet!"

In the event, Phyllis brought a selection of jumpers, skirts and trousers, all of them new, most of them too big for Naomi but none of them too old-fashioned for her taste. Eventually, she chose a long denim skirt and a periwinkle-blue twinset with bracelet length sleeves, and went away, happily, to try them on, leaving Kate to wrestle with the questions she had raised earlier. Where *did* these things come from? And why *had* Phyllis bought them?

Chapter 16

"Woo her," Paul had said.

Woo her?

How do you 'woo' someone who refuses to come home? Dan had deliberated long and hard about it. Basically, he just wanted her home. He missed her. Not just, as she probably thought, to look after the house and cook his meals. The house was fine and he wasn't starving. No, he missed her just being about the place. He'd even settle for knowing she was out in the damn outhouse! It would be better than not knowing *where* she was. Wondering what she was doing. Who she was doing it with.

There had never been Anyone Else. From the first time he'd seen her, there was no-one else he'd ever wanted. He'd had his chances. From time to time he'd been attracted to Another Woman, sometimes he'd encouraged a bit of flirting, had even gone so far once as to meet someone for lunch. But each time he'd stopped before it went too far, before it got too serious, because, at the end of the day, it was only Kate he wanted.

He ached for her now. He was lonely in a way he'd never been before. When he'd been a lad, growing up, he'd been a loner, but he'd never been lonely. It was different, being alone and being lonely. Then, he'd learned to live with himself, *within* himself. He'd learned to occupy himself, studying, reading, walking; quiet things, things you did alone, things you didn't need company for. But the trouble now was that he'd learned to live *with* someone, with Kate, with her busy-ness, with her banter, even with her silence. He just needed her to be there. Nothing felt the same. Silly things, like her sigh when he turned on the telly... it used to annoy him, but now he would have welcomed it, would like the chance to turn the sigh to a smile. He would turn off the telly, ask her what she'd like to do, make her a cup of tea, ask about her day if she'd been at work.

He'd learned, but had the lesson come too late?

The little book he'd found sat beside his chair. He picked it up and turned it over, careful how he handled it, it was so old, looked so fragile. This had been his tutor. From its gently yellowing pages had poured a steady stream of revelation.

He learned how someone could feel lonely in the midst of a crowd; the feeling of not being seen, not being counted important. He'd never felt that kind of loneliness, because he'd never sought the approval of the crowd.

It made him think about all different kinds of loneliness and he wondered if Kate had been lonely when she sat in her glass house. He'd thought she was shutting him out of her life, but had he shut her out first? Had he ever let her into his? He wasn't one for talking much; maybe he should have tried harder.

He flicked the book open to one of the beautiful illustrations: a sunset. The sun disappearing behind the hills, leaving swathes of glowing colours dressing the sky. It had been painted with feeling and he had a lump in his throat as he looked at it.

He'd always appreciated beauty though he'd never enthused the way Kate did. He could never find the right words to describe feelings, or scenery, or music, or… or anything, it seemed. He sighed. Looking at the watercolour mellowed him, like some music could. Whoever had painted it knew how to express their feelings… and not just through painting. The stories and poems were like peering into the author's soul. So much was revealed, so much explained. And it was catharsis for him. He found himself relating to the expressions, understanding them, making them his own.

And he longed to share it with Kate. To sit in the evenings reading its pages, enjoying its images, soaking in its wisdom; that would surely heal their hurt.

And as he thought of her, he became aware of someone coming in the back door. Kate? His heart leapt in hope.

"Only me!" his neighbour called. "The door was open," she explained breezily.

'In that it wasn't actually locked,' Dan breathed to himself.

"Brought you over some casserole for your dinner. Braised steak and onions," Maggie simpered, putting the dish down on the worktop and lifting its lid to display the contents and release its inviting aroma. "I know it's your favourite," she blushed.

"Look, you really don't need to feed me," Dan objected. "I told you, I'm a very competent cook."

"Ah yes. But no man *really* likes to cook for himself. It's not natural." She looked around the kitchen. "Here, let me peel a few potatoes for you too." She opened the vegetable drawer and selected a few, chattering all the while. "It's not right, leaving you to fend for yourself like this."

"It's not your business, Maggie."

"I know, I know. But I just can't bear to see you look so sad."

"I'm not sad."

"Of course you are. No-one to cook for you... or anything," she added coyly.

"Maggie," Dan said firmly, taking the potato peeler from her hand. "I don't need anyone to cook for me. And I don't need anything else you might care to offer. Thank you for the thought, and the casserole. I will enjoy it, but I'd like you not to do it again. Perhaps you'd like to take the dish you brought last night as you go."

And it was at this point, as he had his arm round her propelling her towards the back door, that Kate came in.

Her eyes took in the scene, the fresh casserole, yesterday's empty one, *her* dishtowel drying Maggie's hands, *her* husband's arm round Maggie's waist. Oh yes. She took it all in.

* * *

"How could he?"

"How do you know he did?"

"She was *there*, in *my* kitchen."

"So?"

"He had his arm round her."

"Mmmm... Not so good."

"She's been cooking for him."

"Best way to get a foot in the door."

"I know where I'd like to put *my* foot! Oh, how could he? With Maggie Webster, of all people!" Kate was pacing round the sitting room. Even its summer warmth had not calmed her, though the soft carpet under her bare feet was doing its best. She kicked angrily at an imagined flaw in its sumptuousness. "Maggie Webster, local lush! I can't believe he let her in the door."

"Perhaps it's not as bad as you think."

"How bad does it need to be? He had his arm round her. She was gazing up at him all fish-eyed."

"Fish-eyed?"

"She's been taking him his dinner every night."

"You don't know that."

"And goodness knows what else she's been doing for him!"

"You certainly don't know *that*."

"That's it! I tried. I was going to do as you wanted."

"This has nothing to do with me," Phyllis protested.

"I was going to hear his side of the story. Let him tell me *why* he went ahead, knocked down my summerhouse when he knew... he *knew*... I would leave him if he did. Well, obviously that didn't bother him. Probably part of his plan." Kate had stopped her pacing. She banged her fist on the back of the sofa. "How long has this been going on? Right under my nose!" she exclaimed.

"Now, Kate, you don't know anything *was* going on. Or *is* going on."

"That's it! I'm not going back. He can keep his rotten old house."

"Don't you think you're being a bit childish about this?"

"She can have him! If she wants him, she can have him and good riddance!"

"You *are* being childish about this. Now sit down, Kate, dear, and I'll make you a nice cup of cocoa."

"I don't want cocoa!" Kate stormed. "I'm not a child! I don't need calmed with... If that's Dan," she said as the phone started to ring. "Tell him I've gone out. You don't know where, and you don't know when I'll be back!" And, true to her word, she stormed out of the room, thrust her feet into her shoes, her arms into her coat and slammed out of the front door.

"Hello, Mrs Thaine speaking. How may I help you? Hello? Hello? Hmm... Nobody there," Phyllis muttered to the empty room as she replaced the receiver.

When Kate returned from her walk... more of a march really... she noticed the man loitering across the road. He looked away quickly when he realised she was examining him. Stubbing out a half-smoked cigarette with the heel of his leather boot, he climbed into his car and drove off. Yet somehow, she just knew he'd been watching the house. Perhaps he'd been there when she'd flung out the door. Perhaps that's why she felt so certain that he'd been hanging around for a while. She shrugged off the creepy feeling it gave her, telling herself she was surely becoming fanciful. Probably adopting poor Naomi's fear.

Phyllis was waiting, a pot of chocolate ready as she walked in the door, pushing the incident from her mind before she had resolved its import.

"Now, Kate," Phyllis greeted her. "I insist you come and sit down. We need to talk this through. Rationally. Besides, if you look like staying here a bit ..."

"I've been thinking about that," Kate interrupted. "I really can't impose on you any longer."

"It's not an imposition."

"I'll need to find a flat or something."

"Nonsense. Why would you want to do that? We can make you perfectly comfortable here. We could..."

"Oh Phyllis, you're so kind. And it's very tempting to stay, but I feel it's not really fair to you. You never have your home to yourself."

"I've had my home to myself for years... too many years. I'm getting old. I like company. I like *your* company. I'm asking you, please, to stay."

"Thank you, Phyllis. In that case, I'd love to stay. The only trouble is, I don't know if I'll ever go back to Dan. It might be for a very long time… till we're both old."

"At least we won't be lonely."

"But we'll have to come to some better arrangement, financially, I mean."

"Well, there is a proposition I'd like to put to you."

"Good," Kate said, settling herself down at last with a steaming cup of chocolate. "This is not one of your 'specials', is it?" she raised her cup.

"No," Phyllis laughed. "No. I need you to be awake for this."

"Oh. Sounds ominous."

"But first. I think we need to talk *rationally* about your situation with Dan. And before you say anything, you have to admit that you have jumped to rather a lot of conclusions. You have no evidence that anything was taking place other than neighbourly kindness."

"Huh!"

"Or that Dan was doing anything more than showing her to the door."

"He should never have let her in."

"You're still angry."

"You bet your life I'm still angry."

"Then perhaps this is not the best time to talk about it after all."

"Agreed. Let's talk about your proposition instead."

"More cocoa?" Phyllis offered.

"The proposition?" Kate prompted.

"Yes. Well. Yes. You see, I need to ask you for help."

"What kind of help?"

It was Phyllis's turn to become restless. She hoisted herself painfully out of her chair and walked over to the high, Adam fireplace. "I'm getting old, you see." She moved the clock on the mantel an inch or two. "Who knows how long I have left."

"I don't like you to talk like this, Phyllis."

"I need to set some things in order."

There was a tap on the door. "Is it all right if I join you?" Naomi asked as she opened it.

"Yes, yes of course, my dear." Phyllis said with evident relief. "Come in. We were just having a nice hot cocoa before bed." She sat down again and started to pour. "Come and join us. I put an extra cup on the tray in case you did." She turned to Kate. "We'll talk again another time."

"Oh, I'm sorry," Naomi said. "Am I interrupting?"

"Not at all," Phyllis replied. "Nothing important. Nothing that can't wait."

* * *

Dan came into the shop. He must have asked at the office to find out which department she'd be in... either that or he'd just searched them all till he found her. He stood quietly now, waiting, watching her as she served a customer. She found herself blushing under his scrutiny but she told herself it was anger that coloured her face.

"Hi, there," he said.

She nodded without looking at him, tidied the counter, looked for the next customer.

"We need to talk," he said.

She shrugged.

He trapped her hand as it fluttered across the counter, tidying already tidy paraphernalia. His touch was gentle but firm. He didn't remove his hand until she was forced to look at him, to see the earnestness in his eyes.

"It's not good here," she managed to get out, her heart quickening at his remembered touch, her blush deepening.

"Where then?"

"Away from here."

"Where?"

"I'll soon be finished. You can walk me to the bus stop."

"I'll take you home. Wherever," he added with a smile.

They walked to the parked car without touching or speaking but she felt his presence as strongly as though he had his arm around her. She had wanted to be angry still, had intended to greet him coldly... but she had missed him.

"So what do we have to talk about?" she asked, as coolly as she could, once they were seated in his car.

"When are you coming home?"

"I don't know that I am," she replied. Not that she believed him guilty of infidelity. Thirty-four years of marriage to a stranger, but a stranger she knew well, told her that he was not unfaithful... taciturn, boorish, selfish... but not unfaithful. Not yet ready to let go of the balloon of anger, still hard and firm inside her chest, she felt it lodged there, resisting the forces that could deflate it. So she chose to punish him in his innocence. "You seem to have made alternative arrangements in my absence," she added icily.

"Come on, Kate. You know that was not as it seemed."

"And how was that?"

"Maggie has been dropping in meals for me."

"So I noticed."

"Uninvited."

"So you say."

"You know I can't stand the woman."

"She was in my kitchen... sorry... *your* kitchen."

"Uninvited."

"Presumably you did invite her in."

"She walked in."

"You opened the door."

Dan sighed. "Can we stop with the adolescent, jealousy bit, Kate? You know there's nothing going on with me and Maggie Webster. You're angry with me about the summerhouse."

"Yes."

"Come on, Kate, you must see that it had to go."

"No it didn't!"

"Let's not rehash that."

"Never mind rehashing, we didn't have that argument... not to a conclusion anyway." Dan had not started the engine, so the condensation curtained the windows, providing privacy and obstructing their view. Kate used her glove to clear an area she pretended to peer out of. "I told you I didn't want it to come down. You said you did. The argument was never resolved. You just went ahead with what you wanted. It was selfish and overbearing and just about sums you up, so, as far as I'm concerned, we've nothing to talk about." They both sat staring straight ahead.

"Is there someone else?" Dan asked.

"Don't be ridiculous!" she snapped back at him.

"Where are you staying then? Who are you with?"

"None of your business."

"Of course it's my business, Kate. You're my wife, damn it!"

"No need for language."

"I have a right to know where you are, who you're with."

"Get yourself a lawyer to find out for you then," she hurled at him.

"Come on, Kate. We don't need to be talking about lawyers. Just come home and let's forget all this nonsense."

Without warning, Kate opened the car door and got out. "If you'll excuse me, I'll go for my bus now," she slammed back at him… and was gone.

* * *

The telephone was ringing as she entered the hall. "No, I don't want to talk about it," she shouted into the receiver, assuming Dan to be the caller. When her tirade was met with silence, she became less strident. "Hello! Hello? Who's there? Oh well," she observed to no-one in particular, "it can't have been anything important or he wouldn't have hung up."

"Who was it?" Phyllis asked as she came into the hall.

"They hung up."

"Again?" Phyllis frowned. "It's getting to be a habit. Are you all right? You look a bit flushed. And you're later home than usual."

"I didn't get the bus. Felt the need of a walk."

"Still angry with Dan then?"

"He came to the shop."

"Good. Did the pair of you sort it all out?"

Kate threw herself into the depths of one of the sofas. "Oh Phyllis, I know there's nothing going on between him and Maggie. At least, I don't think there is."

"Of course there's not."

"It's just that, he still doesn't see he was wrong. He seems to think I owe *him* the apology or something."

"You realise you are both behaving like schoolchildren?"

"Probably," Kate sighed. "But we just can't seem to reach one another."

"One of you will have to swallow your pride."

"Well it won't be me. Not till he apologises properly." She put her head back wearily. "Anyway, Phyllis, how was your day? You look tired," she observed, scrutinising her friend's face carefully. "Are you all right?"

"Yes, yes. I'm fine."

Kate sat forward. "Oh, I remember now. You had something you were going to tell me."

"Nothing important. Anyway, dinner's ready."

"Who was on the phone?" Naomi asked as she joined them in the dining room.

"No-one... or no-one who wanted to speak to me anyway," Kate replied.

"It's him. I'm sure it is!" Naomi declared.

"Who?"

"Pete. My... My..."

"Your ex-boss, ex-boyfriend, ex-whatever?"

"Pete. Yes. I'm sure it's him!"

"Oh, I don't think so," Kate said.

"No. How could it be, my dear?" Phyllis asked.

"I don't know. I just know it is. It's him. Trying to frighten me."

"I'm sure you're wrong. He couldn't possibly get this number, could he, Phyllis?"

"Well, I don't see how. Unless he knew the address, saw the name on the door, looked it up in the book."

"You're in the book?"

"Of course."

"Not unlisted?"

"No. Why should I be?"

"It's him."

"But how would he know the address."

"He followed me, remember."

"No," Kate said carefully. "I remember you *thought* he followed you. But I'm sure you were wrong. Anyway, you were here, you thought he followed you *from* here... not *to* here... if you see what I mean?"

"Yes, dear," Phyllis added. "He would have had to know you were here in the first place, and how could he possibly know that?"

"I don't know. I just know he does. He did. He is. It's him. I'm sure it's him."

"But why? What could he possibly hope to achieve by phoning you here, then not speaking when Kate or I answer?"

"I don't know, but I'm just sure he's up to something."

"But you made it very clear in your letter, dear. We both read it. You said you wanted nothing more to do with him. At work or personally. It was very clear."

Naomi had not touched the food Mary had set on the table. Instead, she was pacing, wringing her hands, pulling at her clothes, hugging her body, bowed by fear and pain.

"Come and sit down, dear," Phyllis soothed. "I'm sure you're wrong about this. Perhaps you'll feel better when you've had something to eat."

"Good grief, woman. Don't you know not everything can be made better with Something To Eat!" Naomi rounded on her. "You and your bloody Cocoa!"

"Naomi! Stop it!" Kate had risen too.

"It's all right, dear."

"No! It's not All Right!" Naomi shouted. "Don't you see that? Nothing's All Right. A Warm Bed and a Cup of Hot Cocoa don't make everything All Right. Life's not like that. But what do you know of Life? You've had it easy. Living here in your fancy mansion, all you could ever want."

"Naomi! That's enough!"

"It's all right, dear."

191

"NO! IT'S NOT ALL RIGHT!" Naomi screamed, head thrown back, eyes closed, hands covering her ears. "He followed me. He knows I'm here."

"Naomi," Kate tried to put her arms round her.

"Don't touch me! I don't know who you two are, or what you want of me, but you're weird. Both of you. You're weird. You scare me."

"We only want to help, dear."

"Why? What's in it for you? Eh, Phyllis, tell me, what's in it for you?"

"Nothing. I don't want anything."

"Then why'd you do it?"

"Do what?"

"Take people in off the streets?"

"Now just a minute…"

"And you. What's in it for you Kate? You've got a husband, poor sod, and kids. What're you doing here with a sad old woman you hardly know?"

"That's enough!"

"Enough? Enough what? Enough truth? Enough questions? You're living here in the lap of luxury and you never ask, 'What's in it for her? What's in it for Dear Old Phyllis?'"

Chapter 17

"I tried, son. I went into her work. I tried to talk to her."

Paul looked around the room: vacuumed, dusted, tidy. All the usual furniture: clock on the mantelpiece, pictures on the wall, ornaments. All just as they'd always been. But no signs of life being lived. Cushions plumped up and carefully placed: no imprint of a body at ease. No newspaper here, no cup or plate there. His father had stopped living in the room.

The kitchen had become his base. It used to be Mum you would meet in the kitchen as you came through the back door. Dad would be here, in front of the telly. This had never been Mum's Room somehow, yet it was her presence that made it Home. Ostensibly, nothing had changed: nothing new, nothing replaced, nothing missing, yet homeliness had walked out with his mother.

"You've got to get her back, Dad."

"So you said, son. But how?"

"I told you."

"'Woo her', I know. But how can I 'woo' her if I don't know where she is, who she's with?"

"She's not with another man."

"I'm not so sure."

"But *I* am, Dad. I'm telling you, there's no-one else."

"How can you be so sure?"

"I am sure. I've been to see her. I know where she's living. And who with."

"Fine. Then why can't you tell me?"

"I don't think she wants you to know."

"So that's that then," Dan shrugged.

"Not necessarily. You can't just give up."

"Look, if your mother doesn't want me to know where she is, then she obviously doesn't want me around, doesn't want to be 'wooed'. Not by me anyway."

"Not necessarily."

Dan picked up the paper.

"She just might not realise that she does."

"Or she might have someone else," muttered Dan.

"I'm telling you, Dad. She does not have someone else."

"So where has she been going every Saturday?" he demanded, throwing aside the paper.

"Walks. She walks."

"Walks?"

"Yes. She joined a walking club."

"Who with? Who does she see there?"

"Give it a rest, Dad. I'm telling you, she isn't seeing anyone else," Paul repeated in exasperation.

"Doesn't mean she wants me," was the sulky response as Dan reached for his paper again.

"Aw, come on, Dad," Paul pleaded, snatching it from him. "You can't give up. You just can't."

Dan shrugged. "I'm open to suggestions, son," he sighed.

"Look, why don't you turn up for the walk on Saturday?"

"Just 'turn up'?"

"Yes. I'll find out from Mum where they're going, when they're meeting, etcetera, then you can just sort of…"

"… turn up?"

"Yes."

Dan relaxed, at last, into his chair. "A walk?" He thought about it for a minute or two while Paul waited, congratulating himself on his good idea.

"Just turn up for the walk? But what if there is someone else?"

"Stop it, Dad! I've told you."

"Well, what if?"

"DAD!"

Dan thought some more. "I suppose I could."

"Go for it, Dad," Paul urged.

"A walk you say?" Another long silence. "A walk. Yes. Might be nice. Might just work." Dan leant back, hands behind his head, eyes closed. The clock ticked out the heartbeats. "Okay!" he decided. "You find out. I'll give it a try."

Paul punched the air. "Yes!" He looked round the sterile room. "It's just *got* to work."

* * *

Naomi had stormed out of the room. She thought about leaving again. But where would she go? Where else would she be safe?

Despite all Kate's assurances, she knew Pete had found her. If she stepped out of the door, she was his.

Her bedroom overlooked the street. Without putting on the light, she crept across its evening shadows and peered out of the window, keeping far enough back to remain unseen. He was there. She could feel it. Out there somewhere, in the dark, watching.

He had too much to lose to walk away.

A shiver ran through her body and she drew her jumper close around her fear.

Weird or not, she needed these people, needed this house. With a cold shudder, she drew back from the menacing darkness outside, ate a large helping of humble pie and went back downstairs to warmth and safety.

"Who is it keeps moving about upstairs?" she asked Phyllis, unable to relinquish her curiosity despite her need for protection.

"Upstairs?" Kate looked puzzled.

"Didn't know there was an upstairs, did you?"

"Of course I knew there was an upstairs! But it's a flat. Someone else lives upstairs."

"Not true, is it Phyllis? While you're out at work, she disappears upstairs with Mary and the odd-job man and they make a hell of a racket moving stuff about or something, I don't know."

"It's none of your business what they do. This is Phyllis's house and she can do what she pleases."

"As long as she's got me caged up here, it *is* my business."

"You're free to leave whenever you wish. You're not a prisoner." Phyllis's voice was quiet but firm.

Naomi pushed her seat back.

"You ask, 'What's in it for me?'" Phyllis stayed her with a hand. "I'll tell you what's in it for me," she said calmly.

"I don't even care," Naomi declared... but she didn't move away.

"I'm an old lady. A lonely one, I admit, but not a sad one. You're right, I have all of life's luxuries around me. Always have had. I wanted to share."

"Big of you," Naomi sulked.

"I tried to share with those I knew, but it was difficult. I think I embarrassed people, giving them presents all the time. Besides, most of them have plenty. There was nothing I could give them that could make a difference."

"You don't have to explain yourself, Phyllis."

"Yes, I think I do, Kate. Naomi is obviously upset. She feels that I've taken advantage of her in some way."

"Hardly!"

Phyllis held her hand up. "Rightly or wrongly, she feels it."

"You've done nothing to harm her. You've cared for her. Given her a home when she needed it."

"But she's not sure of my motives, are you dear?"

"Damn right, I'm not."

"So, perhaps I can try to explain."

"I still don't see why you should."

"No matter. I will."

Kate shrugged, went back to her seat and recommenced picking at the crumbs of cheese and biscuits on her plate.

Naomi sat down at last, her chair still pushed back from the table, her demeanour that of a hedgehog on alert.

"You're right, Naomi. We are strangers. I know very little of you."

"And I know nothing of you!"

"Precisely. So perhaps it's time we did some talking."

"The floor's all yours!"

Phyllis nodded acceptance of the challenge. "As you know, I was a doctor. A good doctor, I believe, but not a brilliant one. I didn't discover a cure for cancer, or lead the field in surgery, or do anything else of great note. I like to think I cared well for my patients, but I doubt if any of them even remember my name now. In short, I've done nothing outstanding, nothing to be remembered for. I've been retired now for more than thirty years. I have no children, no family, no-one to remember that I ever lived."

"But your daughter?"

"I want someone to know who I was. I want to make a difference in someone's life."

"Oh Phyllis. You have already. You've made a huge difference in mine," Kate reached out to her.

"Thank you Kate," Phyllis smiled back at her. "But I haven't really. If you had never met me, you'd still have left Dan, but you'd have gone to your daughter or your son. You haven't *needed* me."

"But..."

"But it's been good. It's been lovely having you stay here. Like having a daughter living at home. But I haven't made a difference. When my husband was alive, I didn't think about these things. I had a satisfying career, a happy marriage. I suppose I took things for granted. We'd always had a lot of money. It was just there. Not something I ever thought about."

"Nice for some."

"Yes. I suppose it was 'nice', Naomi. But then Thomas died. I retired. Suddenly, all that money for one person with moderate needs... well, it didn't seem right any more. I started spending: expensive clothes, luxurious holidays. And, to a point, it was fun while it lasted. But there are only so many places to travel to, only so many adventures to enjoy, especially on your own. I needed to share the pleasures and there was no-one to share them with. Like watching a beautiful sunset. It seems unseen unless there's someone there to witness that you saw it."

Kate was nodding. "I know that feeling. I used to love sitting quietly in my summerhouse but I could have loved it more if Dan had shared it with me: sat and felt the peace, watched the light fading, listened to the garden," she sighed.

"Exactly! So I started asking friends to holiday with me. As my treat, of course. They were puzzled by the offer, wondered what it was about. The 'What's in it for you?' syndrome. Anyway, I didn't really have any friends of the sort who could understand. Thomas and I had been a bit exclusive, I suppose. He wasn't really a sociable man."

"Tell me about it," muttered Kate.

"As I said, I tried giving people expensive presents. But it made strangers suspicious, friends uncomfortable. Poor Mary and her husband get positively embarrassed by all that I try to force on them. It breaks the employer-employee code. A few perks are one thing. Good wages, pension plan, security... that's all acceptable, tokens of high regard, merited, earned. Overdone, it feels all wrong, they no longer cope with it."

"Okay, so far. But what about us? Why are we here? And what's going on upstairs?" Naomi demanded.

"I really don't think that's anything to do with you."

"Actually, Kate, it does have to do with Naomi... and with you, in a way."

"So?"

Phyllis sighed. "So," she said, pushing back her chair, carefully folding her napkin and leaving it on the table. "I think it will be easier to show than to tell."

They followed her into the hall.

* * *

"Okay, Paul. Where is she? I need to know."

"Why?"

"Because I need to know she's all right."

"She's all right."

"She's my Mum too, you know. In fact," Vicky grinned, remembering the teasing phrase she used to torment him with when they were children. "She was my Mum before she was yours!"

"Oh, naah, naah, naah, naah, naah! Tough! I'm not telling you."

"Paul!"

"If she wanted you to know, she'd've told you."

Vicky came towards him menacingly, her index finger outstretched, her face set for torture.

"No!" he groaned. "Please, no tickling. It isn't fair!"

Her advance continued, the finger circling in the air then bending in a tickling motion. "All's fair in love and war!" she said as she lunged at him where he sat on the couch.

He caught her hand. "And which is this, then, Sis? Love or war?"

The seriousness of his tone caught her off guard. Instead of the gibbering wreck of their childhood, her hand was held in the strong grip of a man in control.

"Well? Love or war? Do you want to know where Mum is because you love her, miss her, worry about her? Or," he drew her to sit beside him, "do you want to know so you can have a go at her? Give her the guilt trip? Make her 'pay'?"

"She had no business leaving Dad."

"As I thought. Not love, then, I take it?"

Vicky pushed against him as she pulled away to stand up. "Of course it's love! Just because we love someone, we don't have to like what they do."

"Love the sinner; hate the sin?"

"Exactly!"

"Except, there is no sin."

"She left!"

He shook his head. "No sin."

"She's married. She made vows."

"She's not broken them."

"Yet!"

"Why assume she will?"

Vicky walked over to the window, drawing the curtains closed, shutting out the night. "Why didn't she come to me?" she asked, resting her face against the soft material, her voice soft with tears.

"Oh, Vick!" Paul came to her. "Is that what's eating you up?" He put his arms around her, holding her against him. "Think about it, pal. How could she come here? She couldn't come to me either. She needed to be away... right away."

"She could've had our spare room."

"It wouldn't've worked. You'd be at one another's throat within the first afternoon."

"Not true!"

Paul held her away from him a little and pulled a face.

"Well, I know we don't always see eye to eye, but I do care, Paul. I do love her."

"I know you do, Sis. But she needed time. Needed space. She'll be back."

"You don't know that."

He nodded and winked, tapping the side of his nose. "Trust me!"

Vicky stepped out of his embrace. "What are you up to, little brother? I remember that ridiculous expression. You always wore it when you thought you hade an 'Ace Plan' and your 'Ace Plans' always meant trouble."

"Not this time. You'll see!"

* * *

A walk.

A great idea.

There'd be other people about. She's hardly likely to make a scene in front of everyone.

Dan could see the possibilities. Beautiful scenery, fresh air, get the endorphins going. Yes, this could work. At last, an 'Ace Plan' of Paul's that might just work. Roll on Saturday!

He decided to have an early night. Nothing on the telly anyway. Sleep would shut out the emptiness that echoed through the house.

* * *

There was a lift. Kate had assumed it was just another closet door, but it was a lift, big enough for the three of them, with room to spare.

"I had no idea, Phyllis."

"Cool," Naomi pronounced it.

"Practical," Phyllis replied.

When they stepped out of the lift on the floor above, they were once again in an enormous hall, echoing the one downstairs. This one lacked the fresh décor but was still impressive. It had retained the opulence of the age it represented, a time when it had been a family house, a Wealthy Family house, when guests regularly filled the rooms and their petticoats filled the wide hall.

Here, the old paintings had not been replaced with modern ones: the faces that observed them were those of a time long past, the portraits formal, redolent of a time when the rich had their likeness preserved by a Master. The landscapes were reminiscent of Constable or Turner, might even be their work for all Kate knew. The carpet, faded and a little threadbare, looked as though it had been placed over the dark wood long before Phyllis walked there... and possibly long before her great-grandmother.

"Is this the original carpet? And the paintings? Are these your ancestors?" Kate asked in a voice hushed by the weight of the history around her.

"Some of them," Phyllis nodded. "Because we never lived up here, Thomas and I didn't get around to changing anything. Neither had my parents. So, yes, it probably is more or less as it would have been in the early 19th century."

"Wow!" Naomi breathed. "These paintings. Some of them. They're worth a fortune, Phyllis."

"Yes. Don't you think it's a bit sad that no one has had the pleasure of looking at them for such a long time? I know I do."

"You should get them valued," Naomi suggested. "Pete could..." She stopped herself. "Someone could do that for you." Her voice tailed off. "The insurance..."

"Yes, I know I should. But it's, well, it's just that..."

"You're probably totally under insured."

"I'm sure I am. The trouble is, I can't face someone, a valuator, traipsing through my home, judging me."

"Judging you?"

"You'll see what I mean in a moment." Phyllis took a deep breath and walked across to one of the doorways in the hall. "I wanted to prepare a proper suite for you," she turned to Kate. "This was to be your bedroom," she said quietly. "Only we'll have to clear it for you, because," she opened the door and switched on the light, "as you can see, I use it for storage."

Kate stopped at the threshold of the room. She had to. She couldn't go much further even if she had wanted to. Naomi bumped into her back. The room was filled to capacity with everything imaginable. It was almost possible to make out the shape of a bed and some chairs and other furniture, but it was all buried; buried under an amazing assortment of items, all of them new, many of them still wrapped.

Kate stared. Naomi pushed against her, craning to see round her. Phyllis held her breath, watching Kate.

"But Phyllis, it's...it's Aladdin's cave. I don't understand. What is all this?"

Phyllis bit her lip. "It's hard to explain. I told you I was a foolish old woman," her voice, a watery whisper.

"It's okay. You don't have to explain."

Phyllis looked at her gratefully. "Thank you Kate," she said softly. "But I do." She led her and Naomi into the room, as far as they were able to walk, which wasn't far... a few steps.

"You see," she began. "All of this." She indicated the contents of the room; the stacks and stacks of boxed items on the floor, the bundles of unopened packets on the bed, the pile of rugs against the wall and the many and varied items that covered every surface. "All of these are things I have bought. Things I don't need, things I could never use if I had ten lifetimes," she laughed shakily. "You see," she shrugged her shoulders in a gesture of surrender, "I like shopping."

Kate moved a pile of towels from a nearby chair. She looked round for somewhere to put it. There was nowhere. In all the room, there was hardly an inch of carpet showing and none of the bed or any other surface. She sat down holding the towels, resting her chin on top of the pile.

"I'm sorry, Phyllis. I just need to sit down for a moment." She closed her eyes. When she opened them again, it was all still there. And so was Phyllis, still there, still watching and waiting.

"You're shocked," she stated.

Kate nodded, then shook her head. "Not shocked exactly," she said quietly. "Surprised, perhaps. But I knew you liked shopping." She looked around again. "I just didn't know," she swallowed. "I didn't know how much you liked it." She smiled up at her friend. "But, what the heck, Phyllis? If you can afford all this then so what? What's so shocking? You didn't steal it." She laughed. "You didn't, did you?"

Phyllis shook her head, laughing too.

"Then, where's the problem?"

Phyllis smiled back. "You're a good soul, Kate, thank you, but you don't have to pretend. I know it's pretty shocking. You probably think I'm crazy."

"No, not crazy. A little eccentric, perhaps. But I've always thought that," she grinned.

"And sad, probably?"

Kate looked up at her. "Oh, Phyllis," she said as she rose to give her a hug. "No wonder you hesitated when I asked if I could stay. I really put you on the spot, didn't I? I'm sorry."

"Don't be," Phyllis said, still trying to smile despite the constriction in her throat. "It was time to tell someone about it. I want to sort it all out. I need to get rid of all this. Stop gathering more. It's started to weigh me down. I needed to tell you. I want your help."

"If you had *told* me about all this," Kate indicated the contents of the room with a sweep of her hand. "I just wouldn't have believed you," she said.

"And I thought *I* had a problem!" Naomi breathed.

"And you haven't seen it all yet," Phyllis confessed.

"There's more?"

She nodded. "The noises Naomi's been concerned about. Mary and Joe. That's her husband."

"The odd-job man?"

"And gardener, yes. They've been helping me to clear another of the rooms to be your sitting room," she said to Kate. "And a room up here for you, Naomi, presuming you want to stay."

"And where on earth have you put the things you moved?" Kate asked.

Phyllis shrugged and looked around her. "Some of it's here. Some in another room, along with the stuff we'd already moved from the rooms downstairs. Till we can work out what to do with it all."

"By 'we' do you mean you, Mary and Joe, or…"

Phyllis shook her head. "I mean 'you, me and us'," she supplied, indicating the three of them.

"I was afraid of that," Kate grinned.

"Always supposing that Naomi wants any part of it."

Naomi shrugged. "Depends."

"Oh, my!" Kate scratched her head. "In that case, we're going to need a plan of action." She looked at Phyllis's worried face. "Presuming, of course, that you really do want to do anything at all about it."

Phyllis nodded.

"I mean, you don't have to. This is your house. These are your things. There's no need to do anything."

"But I want to," Phyllis said quietly.

"Well, then."

"You see, I have a plan."

"Great!"

"No," Phyllis said quickly. "It's not what you think. It's not about all the things I've bought… well, not directly. But, I do have a plan. It's something I've been thinking about for a long time, but I'm going to need some help."

Chapter 18

"Let's hear your plan then," Kate asked Paul. He'd phoned just as Phyllis was about to reveal her own.

"It's Paul, for you," Mary said, poking her head round the door. "You could take it next door. There's a phone in there."

"It's to be your sitting room," Phyllis said with a rueful smile.

"Hi, Mum! Only got a minute. Just going out."

Kate looked at her watch. "At this hour?"

"Mum!"

"Sorry! Sorry! Once a Mum..."

"Listen! I've got an Ace Plan."

"Oh, oh! Why does that make the hair on the back of my neck stand up?"

"No. This really is an Ace one. Nothing can go wrong with it."

"Let's hear your plan then."

"How about if I join you on Saturday for your walk?"

"Well..."

"Give us lots of time to talk. Catch up and all that?"

"Yes, but..."

""You don't need to sound quite so keen!"

"Sorry, darling. It's just that, well, I'm kind of in the middle of something here and I'm not sure I'll be going on Saturday."

"Oh!"

"But maybe the next week?"

"Are you sure you couldn't make it this Saturday? It's just that I've kinda made plans."

"Plans? Oops! There go the hairs at the back of my neck again! What kind of plans?"

Paul sighed. "Nothing. Nothing really." She could hear him take a deep breath. "It's okay I can rearrange," disappointment in his voice.

"Rearrange what?"

"My schedule. I can rearrange my schedule," he said in a rush.

"Pa-ul? What are you up to?"

"Nothing! Gotta go, Mum. Love you. Be in touch." And he was gone.

* * *

"Let's hear your plan then," Naomi had moved some of the sheets and duvets and assorted packages from the bed to join those on the floor, in an increasingly precarious mountain. "Here, Phyllis. You look as though you could do with a seat." She flopped down and nodded towards the chair Kate had vacated to answer the phone.

"Thank you."

"You have a plan," Kate reminded her, making a space for herself beside Naomi.

"Well," Phyllis toyed with the fringes of a rug that stood, neatly rolled up, near her hand. "I don't really know how to start."

"The beginning?"

She shook her head slowly. "I don't think there is a beginning, really. Only an end. I'm an old lady now."

"Eighty-eight is not so old."

"I'm an old lady," she repeated. "And I…"

"And not when you are as active as you are. You could live to a hundred."

"Thank you, Kate," Phyllis smiled. "But I think that's unlikely. Oh, I don't intend to pop off for a while yet. Quite a while. But I doubt if I'll live to be a hundred."

"Who knows?"

"Who indeed? But, that's not the point. The point is, I am going to die *sometime*."

"Well, we all are."

"Exactly. But, as I keep trying to say, I am an old lady now." Her look dared Kate to interrupt again. "And it's time I was making arrangements for that eventuality. I have no family."

"Of course you do. What about your daughter? You bought her that lovely cashmere."

"I don't have a daughter. I told you, we didn't have any children."

"But you said it was for…"

"I lied. I don't have a daughter."

"Your sister?"

Phyllis shook her head.

"No sister?"

"No sister."

"Niece?"

"No."

"But…"

"As I said, I have no family at all."

"You must have some. Cousins?"

Phyllis shook her head.

"Second cousins?" Naomi suggested.

Again, a shake.

"Once-removed?"

"If I have any cousins at all, they would be so far 'removed' that I doubt if they'd know of my existence. I certainly don't know of theirs."

Kate sat back in her chair. "But…"

"I was an only child. My mother was an only child. My father's brother was killed in the Great War, unmarried, childless. And so it goes. The same with Thomas. His family line ended with him. There just *is* no-one."

"Goodness."

"Not a very productive family."

"That's amazing."

"Oh, it's probably not so very unusual. Just that it doesn't always signify. There must be many family lines that died out after the two world wars and such tragedies. Normally, no one would notice. Just when there's wealth or property involved."

"I suppose so."

"To get back to the point. I want to make some arrangements."

"Have you talked it over with your lawyer?"

"I have made a will, if that's what you mean?"

"Yes, I suppose it is."

"But I'm not happy with it. I never have been really. It's terribly unsatisfying. I'd like to know that all this," she waved her hands about, embracing all that she owned in the gesture. "Well, I'd like to know what it's going to be used for. I'd like to have a say. Be in control of how it's used."

"And aren't you?"

"Not really. As things stand, I've left everything to various charities, apart, of course, from taking care of Mary and Joe. But, as I say, it's not a satisfactory arrangement. This house would be sold and the proceeds absorbed into the rest of my assets. I've done a lot of thinking and decided that's not what I want."

"I see."

Phyllis leaned forward in her chair. "So I've made a plan."

"A plan?"

"Yes. A plan. And that's where you two come in."

"Right."

"But, before I tell you my plan, let's go down to the sitting room. We'll be more comfortable there, don't you think?"

"I want this house to be used as a sort of private club," Phyllis said as soon as they were comfortably seated.

"What, like a Youth Club?" Naomi asked.

"Sort of. But not exactly."

"Like a Gentlemen's Club?"

"Yes... Only for ladies." Phyllis said enthusiastically.

"A Ladies' Club?" Kate sounded puzzled.

"Yes, well... that kind of thing. What do you think?"

"Well, I think..." Kate looked around at the delightful room. "I think it's a great idea, and can I be a member?"

Phyllis smiled. "That's what I hoped you'd say. But I want you to be more than a member. More a sort of administrator."

"Me? Oh, but I'd be hopeless. What about Mary?"

"I want her to stay on as housekeeper, if she will, but I'd like you to be the one to decide who comes and who goes, if you know what I mean."

"I'm not sure that I do know what you mean." Kate shook her head. "I'm not trying to be difficult, but I really don't understand."

Phyllis sighed. "Oh, it's probably a silly idea anyway."

"I didn't say that. Just tell me what you would want me to do."

"Well," Phyllis sat forward in her seat. "I've not thought it all out yet... and I'd need to check with my lawyer what is and isn't possible, but it's something like this. I would like to set up some kind of trust fund for the upkeep of the house. The money shouldn't be a problem, because it's all in investments already. The running of the house only uses a part of the interest now, so that shouldn't change much. I want the house to be a place where people can come. Ladies. When they need a break from the stresses and strains of day to day living. Family life, work, things like that."

"Like a Refuge?" Naomi asked.

"Yes," Phyllis replied uncertainly. "But not like a home for 'battered wives'. That would need a different set-up, more into the social work area, with specialised staff etc. No, I'm thinking more in the way of a home from home for ladies who just need a break... not somewhere to hide, just somewhere to rest."

"And it would be sort of like a club?"

"Yes."

"Like a health club, but without the gym and the sauna?"

"Exactly. You've got the idea, Naomi," Phyllis said with relief. "A place where you could pursue things that you enjoy... like writing," she nodded in Kate's direction. "Music," she continued. "You won't know, but there's a piano buried under a pile of purchases in one of the rooms. Painting: if someone wanted to, we could set up a little studio in another of the rooms, once we've cleared it. A library: I've a room full of books upstairs." Phyllis looked at them both. She was beginning to relax now, to enjoy laying out the plans that had been forming in her mind for such a long time, making them seem less of a dream, more of a possibility. "The other thing," she paused, wondering if she was going a step too far. "The other thing I thought about. I wondered if it could be a sort of a clinic too?"

"What sort of a clinic?" There was more than a hint of suspicion in Naomi's voice.

"Well, for ladies like me," Phyllis met Naomi's questioning frown. "A clinic with counsellors for ladies with a shopping problem. You know, debt counsellors, medical help."

"Psychiatrists, you mean?"

"Well, yes. I suppose that is what I mean. I have friends..."

"So really, what you're talking about *is* a clinic?" Kate clarified.

"But *more* than a clinic. A place to help the mending process, to back up the advice with practical help. Group therapy. The opportunity to put into practice the things the professionals suggest. Like pursuing a hobby, meeting people, making friends. We could have a Reading Circle, a Writing Circle, whatever... all sorts of clubs meeting here."

"An Art Club."

"A Music Club."

"Whatever. Now, what do you think, girls? Is it a good idea? Could it work?"

"I'd love to think so." Kate looked around herself. "I love this room. The Summer Room. Soothing, healing," Kate mused. "Professional help. A library, music room, surroundings to allow people to express themselves... *find* themselves." She relaxed further into the cushions. "Mmm, but I see your problem."

"The other rooms."

"The other rooms," she agreed. "They'd need cleared."

"And redecorated. I'd want them all, including yours, of course," Phyllis said to Naomi. "I'd want them all to be as special as this room. A Summer *House*."

"Yes."

"So," said Phyllis. "First move is to get rid of all the things I've gathered over the years."

"Precisely."

"Perhaps I should just find some way to give it all away," she sighed.

"Where's your sense of adventure? Besides, giving it away wouldn't be any easier now than it was before. Unless you can think of a really good explanation as to why you have quite so much surplus?"

"Not one that doesn't show me up for the fool I am."

"I didn't say that." Kate said gently.

"You didn't have to. I know it myself."

"Come on, Phyllis. Head up. We'll sort it out."

"Maybe I should give it all to various charities."

"You could. Perhaps some? But would that still not give you the same problem, of embarrassment? Explaining where it all came from?"

"Probably. Or I could say nothing, just give it."

"And leave them wondering."

"And concluding that you're as loopy as we know you are," added Naomi helpfully.

"You've not said much," remarked Kate. "What do you think of the idea?" she asked Naomi.

"Of a club cum clinic? Or of giving as opposed to selling?"

"Either. Both."

"The idea, I like. It could work. The legalities would have to be checked, the practicalities worked out, but yes, I think it's basically a cool idea. Satisfying for you, Phyllis, knowing where your wealth was going after you die. Wicked memorial to you."

"Wicked?" Kate questioned.

"Yeah! As in 'cool'? Wicked!"

"It's not so much the Wealth, it's this House. I love this House. It's been my home all my life. I've been so happy here. I don't want it to become offices or student flats, uncared for, unloved."

"Hence the plan."

"Hence the plan." Phyllis agreed.

"Right. So it's down to practicalities. You need to get rid of a heck of a lot of goodies, but how?" Naomi asked.

"Exactly."

"I think selling them."

"I agree," Kate chipped in. "Apart from the fact that it could prove awkward to donate to a Worthy Cause, I think you might enjoy the selling process. It might help you stop buying. You'd have the thrill of sort of *reverse*-shopping!"

"Okay," Phyllis laughed. "Perhaps you're right." Her laugh faded into a wry grimace. "I have looked up about The Shopping Problem and they do say that I need some kind of project. To re-channel the energy, to change how I get 'the buzz'. So, yes, I can see how that could work. But, how do we go about it?" she asked.

"Open a shop," Naomi suggested.

"Can you do that on a short-term basis? Once my hoard has gone, I don't think I'd want to continue."

"A market stall?" Naomi.

"Car boot sales?" Kate.

"Both?" Both.

"It'd have to be split into 'lots'. Lots of 'lots'!" Naomi suggested.

"How on earth would I do that?"

"And it would have to be several." added Kate.

"Several what?"

"Car boot sales," they answered.

"There's too much for one," Kate said wryly, thinking about the stacks of goods.

"I wouldn't have a clue what to do."

"Don't worry, it's not difficult."

"Have you done this before?"

Kate laughed. "I've been to loads of car-boots, but never as a seller. I usually go to seek out bargains. But I've a pretty good idea of the other side of the counter!"

"I'll be glad when we've managed to get rid of everything."

"Why did you suddenly decide you needed to?" Kate asked.

"It wasn't sudden. It's been bothering me for a long time. What had started as 'liking shopping' had become more of an addiction. I've never liked not being in control, so eventually it began to be a pressure to me."

"But you still do a lot of shopping." Kate was thinking of all the inevitable parcels surrounding Phyllis whenever they met for coffee.

"Yes, but I've really cut down," Phyllis said earnestly. "I used to be much worse!"

Kate swallowed. "Right," she said carefully, wondering just what the scale of the problem was and had she stumbled into something that needed professional help.

"You probably think I need help," Phyllis said shrewdly.

"Well…"

"And you may be right," she admitted. "But you see, because I was a doctor, I have the arrogance to think I can cure myself."

"Perhaps you can help *me* along the way." Naomi's voice was small.

Phyllis squeezed her arm. "Perhaps we can help one another. I need to employ someone to help me sort this lot out." She gestured in the direction of the upper floor. "And I'm lonely. I need a companion. Someone to live in, to be here when I need company, to do things with me, go places, help me enjoy my remaining years. And, before you suggest Kate," she said, holding her hand up to ward off objections. "She has a husband. One she'll no doubt go back to soon. Whether she thinks so or not." She grinned at Kate. "You." She turned back to Naomi. "You need a job and a place to stay."

"But…"

"What do you think? Are you interested in the position? It pays well. Bed and board thrown in. Lots of perks."

"But… I'm sorry. I don't think I've been very nice to know."

"We can do the formal interview if you like."

Naomi shrugged. "I don't know as I'd get the job if you did."

"I'm offering it to you. Come on," Phyllis coaxed. "What have you got to lose? What do you say?"

"Thank you?" Naomi suggested with a smile.

"So, what d'you think, Kate. Will you be my manager? My agent? My advisor?"

"Oh, I'm not…"

"You're not qualified!" Phyllis said it along with her. "I know that. But I happen to think you have the main qualifications necessary. You are kind and patient and you care. What I think I need more than anything is a friend; a friend with those qualities."

"But…"

"You have helped me already. As I said, I used to be a lot worse." Phyllis hoisted herself out of the chair and, beckoning them to follow, led the way into the hall. She walked over to one of the doors at the far end of it and flung it wide.

"Wow!" Naomi said with a whistle.

The cupboard, a large one, was neatly stacked with toilet rolls. Shelf upon shelf of them.

"Toilet rolls. It's full of toilet rolls."

"I've got one like this in the hall downstairs next to poor Mary's kitchen… full of coffee, jars and jars of coffee. And another full of toilet cleaners and toothpaste. In this bedroom," she walked over to another of the doors and opened it too, "there's one full of marmalade and jam. The kitchen pantry is stocked so full of tins, poor Mary can hardly bear to open it. And I don't like tinned food!"

Leading them into the room, she threaded her way through the maze of boxes and parcels neatly stacked everywhere and cleared enough floor space to open one of the wardrobes.

"This one is full of dresses. And that one," she indicated the other wardrobe, "it's full of coats. Then there is another one for skirts and suits, and one for shoes. Do I need to go on?"

Kate shook her head slowly. "No," she croaked. She cleared her throat. "No, I think we get the picture."

"Do you, Kate? I wonder. Do you picture a poor, sad, lonely, rich, old maid?"

Kate shrugged. "Well, I…"

"It's okay," Phyllis said kindly. "That's what I'd think too. But you know, for one thing, it isn't quite true. As you know, I'm not an old maid. I was married for twenty-seven gloriously happy years. But we had no children. That was my only sadness. I would have liked to have had children."

"Oh, Phyllis. I'm…"

"Sorry?" Phyllis supplied. "Don't be sorry for me, Kate. I have had a good life. There's room for a little regret. But I'm not a 'poor soul'," she continued. "I'm not unhappy. Lonely, yes. Sometimes I've been lonely. Very lonely. But not unhappy. Not like Naomi." She took Naomi's hand. "But I'm hoping that will change. Is changing?"

Naomi nodded.

"I've not been unhappy… just stupid. I let something I enjoyed doing take over. I lost control. In modern parlance, I got 'hooked'."

Kate smiled in sympathetic understanding.

"But I'm getting things back in control. I have a plan now, something to concentrate on, something to keep me busy, out of trouble… and hopefully, out of the shops!" she laughed.

Kate looked at her. "You're a very remarkable lady," she managed to whisper.

Phyllis laughed harder. "Hardly remarkable. Just a bit foolish."

"No," Kate shook her head. "No. You're not foolish. I think it takes great courage to face your… your…"

"Foibles? Eccentricities? Craziness? Take your pick. It's all of those."

"Whatever," Kate acceded. "But it takes courage to confront it and try to do something about it. And I love your plan," she said firmly.

"Ditto," Naomi encouraged.

"Good! What do we have to do then?"

"Well," Kate looked around, trying not to look too daunted by the sheer scale of Phyllis's 'eccentricity'. "We're going to need more than the few car-boot sales I thought at first, but, till we sort something else out, I think we should have a go. Make a start." She tried not to let panic creep into her voice. Phyllis needed action, not negative fears. "It's Saturday tomorrow. I think we need to find a car-boot sale, fill the boot of the car with a wide selection of all these things. Not too much of the same thing. Bargain hunters like to think they've found something special. Take them out of their wrappings too.

Nearly new is not so 'suspicious' for them. You don't want anyone thinking they 'fell off the back of a lorry'. Right?"

And she started gathering a few towels and sheets to take to the car.

By the time they had managed to cram into the back of the car as much as they felt was reasonable, the room looked no different.

"This is going to take some time," Kate realised out loud. "We'll *have* to think of some other outlets."

Chapter 19

They had a great day at their first car-boot sale. Phyllis was an enthusiastic and generous saleslady. She seemed to take as much pleasure in giving a bargain as the person who got it... more probably.

"Look, Phyllis. I know the money isn't important to you," Kate remarked at one point. "But I don't think it's a good idea to practically *give* all this away."

"Why not?" Phyllis asked innocently.

"Well, for one thing, people will begin to wonder what's going on. They're used to having to haggle a bit to get their bargains. You're making the fight too easy for them... taking the fun out of their triumph."

"Point taken," submitted Phyllis.

"Anyway, it goes against the grain for me to throw good stuff away. You know what I mean," she cut off Phyllis's objections. "It *feels* like throwing it away. And if you really are serious about some sort of Ladies' Club, you ought to start looking at all this as part of the business plan."

"Okay, you say what the fair price for things should be, and I'll try to behave." Phyllis grinned. She looked like a schoolgirl. Her face glowed, her eyes sparkled. "I'm having so much fun," she added, unnecessarily.

By the end of the day, they were exhausted but happy, having 'learned the ropes' as Phyllis put it.

"Now we can really get organised for next week. Now that we know what to do," Naomi said.

"Yes, but I think we could do with having a think about some other places we can try during the week. Perhaps we can sell some things to one or two of the wee independent shops here and there. Down Leith and places like that," Kate suggested.

So, one day during the following week, blissfully ignorant of any VAT regulations or merchandising licence or any other legalities about their operation, they managed to sell quite a few of the household items to one of the shops on Constitution Street. The owner seemed suspicious of how they came by the merchandise but not too concerned. He was obviously happy with their prices and didn't ask any questions. He even offered to take more of the towels, if they could 'come by them'. They assured him they had plenty more in stock and would bring them tomorrow. A satisfactory deal all round.

"We need to find another outlet," Kate said when they were back at the house. "Somewhere we could sell the rather more expensive items, the cashmere and things like that."

"What do you suggest?"

"I don't know. I can't imagine we could get their true value back."

"But that's not the important thing."

"No... but... I was thinking. You know, the same women who would benefit from your 'club' idea... well, they're the same ones who would really enjoy wearing some of these things, but could normally never afford them."

"So how could we get it to them?"

"I don't know. I'll have to give that a bit more thought."

"Would that not run counter to the point of the clinic, though?" Naomi asked. "Encouraging shopaholics to shop?"

"Good point. Bad idea. We'll have to think of something else."

"Meanwhile, we're doing frightfully well with some of the other things," Phyllis said proudly.

"Yes, especially the household stuff. We've cleared a little space. And there's quite a bit in the 'kitty' now. So what are you going to do with it? I think it would be nice to put it towards decorating the rooms. Sort of putting it back where it was taken from!"

"I like that," Phyllis laughed. "Seems poetic almost. But I know what I want to do with some of it."

"Yes," Kate enquired.

"I want to give you both a share."

"Oh no, I..."

"I know you aren't helping me for a reward."

"That's right we're not. You're already paying me as your Manager, or whatever you want to call it."

"And me as your companion," added Naomi.

"But you've told me I need to be businesslike about the whole thing."

"But we're having fun," Kate objected.

"I want to pay you."

"Besides, you're giving us bed and board at the moment."

"That's just the perks of the job," grinned Phyllis. "Look, I'm quite determined. I want to give you a share."

"What about a small percentage of what we make then?"

"Okay, I can go with that. Fifty percent each?"

"More like ten," Kate spluttered. "The merchandise is all yours. You paid for it."

"Over a very long time, years. The outlay is long forgotten. Forty percent?"

"Twenty."

"Thirty percent each… and I refuse to go any lower," Phyllis declared.

Kate shook her head. "This is ridiculous! I've never heard of anyone having to bargain their bonus down!"

"And you don't have to. Thirty percent. Is it a deal?"

"But we don't want any of it."

"Thirty it is, then."

"Phyllis!"

"Look Kate, I really don't need the money. It's been spent. It's forgotten. What I need now, is the help you're both giving me and the help I'm going to need up ahead. Okay?"

"Okay," Kate capitulated.

Naomi nodded her agreement, too stunned to say anything, her mind busy calculating how much she'd earned in the fun of the day. More than she'd earned in a week with Pete, she knew… with the promise of more to come, plus her wages as Phyllis's companion. The mountain of her debt began to look conquerable.

"Now that that's settled," Phyllis rose from her chair and intimated that Kate and Naomi should follow.

"It's okay," Kate assured Naomi, seeing her hesitation.

Phyllis walked down the hall and into the lift, Naomi and Kate following. The lift smoothly raised them to the floor above and Phyllis led the way down the upstairs hall. She opened a door, stood back, and invited Naomi to view her newly decorated bedroom.

"I had no idea…" she began.

"I know," Phyllis smiled. "We thought we'd surprise you. Joe has been very busy while we've been out and about. I hope you like everything."

"It's gorgeous," Naomi breathed.

"You said you liked bright colours, so we tried to make it modern and bright."

"It's fabulous. I love it."

"Good. Mary can help you bring your things up and you can make yourself at home. And this is 'home' for as long as you want it. You'll be safe here, and you mustn't worry anymore about your old boss. He can't touch you here. Mary would never let him in, and he'd never find this room if he did get past her," Phyllis reassured her. "I said I only lived on the ground floor, and that's true, but the house has three floors, four, if you count the basement."

"That's the kitchen?"

"And Mary and Joe's suite. The other two floors were unoccupied. I thought you'd feel safe up here: more private, more independent."

"Thank you, Phyllis. I don't deserve all this."

"I think you do. And I certainly intend that you should," Phyllis laughed. "There's plenty work to be done to get the rest of this house in order."

"You said there was another floor upstairs?" Kate said thoughtfully.

"That's right."

"More storage?"

"'Fraid so," Phyllis hung her head.

"But also, more potential bedrooms in the bigger plan."

"Well, that's one way to look at it."

"The best way! We have to look at things positively if we're to make it work. Okay," she declared with determined resolution. "Let's get organised with who's doing what."

"Where to start?" breathed Naomi. "We could do with a fork-lift to deal with all this."

"Sorry," mumbled Phyllis.

* * *

"Sorry, Paul. I'm not going to manage this Saturday either. There's so much to do. We need to organise the stall for the Sunday Market. We need to load the van we're hiring and we need to load the car boot again."

"If I helped with that first?"

"I'm not picking the van up till six o'clock Saturday."

"I'll help you load it after the walk."

"Why are you so keen to come with me this week, anyway? Could we not do it another time?"

"But I'm free this week. You know I'm not always. My company is much in demand in some quarters."

"And *I'd* love to have your company. But it really would be difficult this week. It's our first serious go at this Selling Lark."

"But that's not till the Sunday. Promise I'll help. Saturday *and* Sunday. I'll drive the van for you."

"Now that *is* tempting. I've never driven a van before. Wasn't looking forward to it. But..."

"I'll drive it for you any other weekend as well."

"What about all your other engagements? You might not be free another weekend, remember?"

"I'll make sure I am."

"You're very persuasive. But why exactly is it that you've suddenly decided you'd like to walk with me?"

"Not suddenly. I've been fancying it for weeks. Old times sake and all that."

"Right." Kate looked hard at him, suspicion in her frown. "Saturday *and* Sunday?"

Paul nodded.

"And you'll drive the van?"

He nodded again.

"Whenever we need you?"

He held his hand out. "Put it there!"

"It's a deal."

* * *

And so it was that Paul met with the group of walkers on Saturday afternoon, just as Kate drove up to the rendezvous.

"That was silly," she said as she got out of the car. "You could have picked me up. Saved two cars. Should have thought of that."

"Sorry."

"Never mind. Nice to see you, darling."

"Nice to see you too, Mum."

"D'you think you'll be okay in that jacket, love. It's not very thick. Is it waterproof? The forecast's not great, you know."

"Yes, no, no and yes, I think. Good idea. Another jacket. Got one in the car. Back in a mo'.'"

"Don't be long then, Paul. Looks like Martin's ready for off." Her voice trailed after him. "And I'd like to introduce you first," she finished lamely to the space he had left. "Oh well."

She was busy putting her boots on and assumed it was Paul's shadow that fell across her. "Those shoes look okay though," she remarked to his feet. "Good thick soles, plenty of grip I should think. Are they new?"

"Hello, Kate. Mind if I join you?"

Surprised, Kate looked up from the job of tying her laces. "Dan? But... Paul?"

"Paul suddenly found he had another engagement after all," Dan shrugged. "Here, let me help you with that." And he took the laces from her trembling fingers and set about the task.

When the boots were laced, his fingers lingered.

"Thank you, Dan," she said hoarsely.

He patted the boot. "Pleasure," he replied, standing, helping her up from where she sat on the sill of the boot of Phyllis's car.

"Dan..."

"It's just a walk, Kate. No strings. Just a walk," he said gently.

He waited while she stowed her driving shoes and locked the car.

"Everything okay there, Kate? Ready for off?" Martin called over.

Not trusting her voice, Kate signalled her assent with a nod. As they drew closer, she cleared her throat and tested her larynx. "Dan, this is Martin. Martin, my husband, Dan," she croaked.

The men exchanged 'howd'youdos' and handshakes.

"Martin leads the group out," Kate said, her voice getting a little stronger. "Shows us the way."

"Yes, I see," Dan smiled. "I'm looking forward to the walk, Martin."

"Nice to have you with us. Okay everyone?" He turned to address the rest of the company. "If you're all ready, let's get under way. Not too long a walk today since the weather doesn't look too promising. Everyone got waterproofs? Let's go then."

They walked in silence for the first half hour or more then the smile that had been growing in Kate's heart reached out to her lips, her eyes, until it grew to a chuckle. Dan waited patiently as he walked, the smile reaching out to him too, touching him, warming him.

"Just wait till I get hold of our Paul," Kate laughed. "I had no idea he could be so devious."

It was a walk she'd done before, not a difficult one, a gentle, steady climb to a little lochan nestling in the hollow of the surrounding hills, but this time she noticed how green the grass was, how soft the breeze as they neared the water, how tiny white flowers peeped out from the rough grass.

"Eyebright," Dan told her when she bent to examine them. "*Euphrasia officinalis.*" He crouched beside her. "They're pretty aren't they? So delicate, yet so sturdy. Amazing that they can survive up here, in our climate."

"It looks like a little face peeping out at you. Is that why they're called eyebright, d'you think?"

Dan smiled. "Perhaps. That's certainly the more romantic reason. But I think they got their name from the fact that they are used, quite literally, to make your 'eyes bright'."

"Really? That's fascinating," she said as they walked on. "I didn't know you were a wild flower buff."

Dan blushed. "Well, I'm not really. But there are one or two that I can recognise."

"Like this?" Kate pointed out another slightly larger, purple flower.

"*Prunella vulgaris*. Self-heal."

"I'm impressed."

"Thank you," he bowed.

"When did you learn about wild flowers?"

"Oh, a long time ago."

"Before we met?"

"Before we met."

They had started walking again and Kate had to stay close by his side to hear what he was saying.

"I used to walk up here and all around, when I was in my teens. It got me out of the house."

"I didn't know."

He shrugged.

"You never talked about growing up."

He smiled. "Well," he said holding out his arms. "Seems, I did... grow up, I mean. Or is that a matter of opinion?"

"Well..."

"Better not answer that."

"Better not," she grinned back at him.

The ground here was soft and a little marshy and Kate became engrossed in picking her way carefully, trying not to get too muddy. She became aware of a soft chuckling coming from behind her.

"You never did like getting dirty," Dan laughed, as he himself squelched recklessly through the boggy bits.

"Well..." She didn't know how to defend herself. "Well, I don't suppose it matters up here, but..."

"But you still don't like getting dirty."

"Not unnecessarily, no."

He shook his head, smiling at her. "You're absolutely right," he said. "I mean, you'd only have to clean off the mud later."

"Exactly."

He looked down at their boots. "You know, yours don't look much cleaner than mine, do they?"

She laughed. "No. They don't. That's not fair. I've been so careful."

"And I haven't. But then, that's the difference between you and me."

"What? That I'm careful and you're not?" She stopped walking and turned to look at him.

"That unimportant things matter to you. Like…" He made a vague gesture, plucking thoughts out of the air. "Like, whether your boots are a little bit dirty or a lot dirty. Or whether the dinner is piping hot or just hot."

She could feel the heat rising up her back, through her throat, into her voice. "While you, on the other hand, don't think little things matter at all," she retaliated. "Like, whether you walk a little bit of mud into the house or a lot of mud into the house. Or whether you look up from the paper when you eat your piping hot dinner or not."

The silence between them seemed weighted with unspoken hurts, the load too heavy, ready to spill over. Dan reached out his hand and, touching her arm, held back the flow. "I'm sorry, Kate," he whispered. "So very sorry. You deserved better."

His hand still on her arm, he started to walk again, encouraging her forward too, cooling the heat that had risen inside her with the warmth of his words.

"I'm glad you came today," Kate said after a while.

And they walked on in silence. Companionable silence, not the kind that gapes as a chasm to be avoided, but a warm, enfolding one to be embraced.

"Oh look! A kestrel." Dan pointed to the bird hovering some distance away.

"Birds too! I am impressed." Kate shaded her eyes to look where he indicated. "Oh, I've seen them before. I didn't know that's what it was."

"Watch it pounce. There it goes. Some poor mouse or something for dinner today."

"Oh, poor thing."

"Nature's way, I'm afraid," Dan shrugged. "You're just too soft," he added, giving her a friendly push.

"Hey!" She pushed back, laughing up at him.

When they reached the lochan, he pointed out the herons, what excellent fishers they were. He helped her identify the plants and flowers that grew on the marshy ground. He taught her how to make a grass whistle. Things she didn't know he knew.

They had lagged far behind the group, but Dan seemed confident of the path, guiding them round the lochan and across the scrubby heather-clad hillside.

"You really have been here before," she said, impressed by his lack of hesitation as he selected the path to follow.

"Yes."

She waited, but he didn't tell her more. "But it was a long time ago. How have you remembered so well?"

"I always liked it up here. Been quite regularly over the years."

She frowned, searching her memory for a time when he could have been here without her knowledge.

"From work. Sometimes took a longer lunchbreak. Brought the car to places like this to eat my lunch. Somewhere quiet, a bit of fresh air, a bit of exercise, somewhere to think."

She was stunned. "I didn't know."

"No."

"You never said."

He shrugged.

"I didn't know," she repeated.

He took her off the path to examine a deserted nest he had found once before, showing her the intricate weaving of the twigs. "A blackbird probably," he said as he allowed the hawthorn bush to fold around it again. "The nest might get used again in the spring, if the winter is kind."

"Recently?" she asked.

"Coming up here, you mean?"

She nodded.

"When I got the chance."

"I had no idea... you never said."

He shrugged again. "Didn't think you'd be interested."

She bowed her head, filled with the shame of knowing it was true. She had shown little interest in his days, never enquiring how he spent them, imagining him always entombed in his office, never freed of its stuffy environs. That he had had such freedom shocked her because it just never occurred to her that he should need it or want it. How little she knew this man who walked beside her.

"Your boots? I've never seen them before."

"I kept them at the office. And some old trousers, a jacket..."

It was after six o'clock and already getting dusky when they meandered back to the car park, long after everyone else. Martin had waited to see they were safe and waved from his car as he drove off.

"I've had a wonderful day, Kate. Thank you," Dan said as he crouched to help her off with her boots.

"Thank you. I've really enjoyed myself."

"May I come again?"

"I'd like that. Very much." She studied his head as he bent to the task of untying the stiff, wet laces. "You've changed," she said softly.

He didn't look up. "Have I?" he asked, gently easing her feet free.

"Yes. You're..." She searched for the word: *softer? warmer?* "...different," she said.

"Am I?"

"I said so," she sighed, a note of impatience so soon.

"See you next week," he smiled. His task finished, he rose then bent forward to gently kiss her cheek.

As she watched him drive off, she felt vaguely disappointed. But he had said, "Just a walk. No strings." She hadn't wanted to believe him.

Chapter 20

The van! She'd forgotten about picking up the van.

She looked at her watch. Seven fifteen. Too late now. The depot closed at six. Damn!

Oh well, they'd just have to get as much as they could over to the market in the car. Heaven knows how many trips it'll take.

Kate sighed as she pushed open the front door, her apology ready, her contrition tempered by her happiness.

"Hi Kate. Had a nice walk?" Naomi looked livelier than Kate had ever seen her. She was carrying a pile of towels and heading past her to the front door. "Could you open the door again, please, and I'll just take these to the van."

"The van? But I…"

"Hi Mum. Had a good walk?" Paul leant around the boxes he was carrying to peck her on the cheek. "See you in a mo'." And he followed Naomi out the front door.

"What's going on?" Kate asked Phyllis, who came in the door as the other two disappeared out of it.

"Oh, hi Kate. Had a nice walk?"

"Yes! Thank you. I had a lovely walk."

"Good."

"Now will you please tell me what's going on?"

"We're loading the van for tomorrow."

"I can see that. But whose van is it? Where did you get it?"

"The same place we'd booked it. Paul picked it up. He's been such a help."

"Good," Kate smiled. "I'm glad." She looked with concern at Phyllis's pale face. "I hope you're not overdoing it, Phyllis?"

"No, no. They won't let me carry anything. I was just out at the van keeping an eye on it as they went back and forth. They'll lock it this time, come in for a cuppa. Want one?"

"Yes, that'd be nice. You go sit down. I'll put the kettle on."

"Give Mary a shout as you go past the stair door. She's upstairs helping sort everything into 'lots'. I expect she's ready for a cuppa too."

"What about Joe?" Kate called over her shoulder as she went, though she needn't have bothered because Phyllis followed her to the kitchen anyway.

"He's over at the market place, constructing the stall. Apparently they'll let you do most of it the night before," she explained.

"Oh good. That'll make things easier in the morning."

"That's the idea."

"Phyllis." Kate took her friends hand. "I'm sorry I let you down with the van. I forgot the time."

Phyllis smiled and patted Kate's hand in her turn. "You didn't let us down. Your Paul told us you'd be later home than you thought and he offered to pick it up."

"Did he tell you he set me up?"

Phyllis chuckled. "Did it work out okay?"

They were sitting at the kitchen table by now, their hands linked across it. Kate blushed and smiled. "Oh Phyllis. It was lovely. I felt like a young girl on a date. He was so kind and attentive. We had such a good time."

Phyllis squeezed her hand. "I'm so glad."

Kate leant over conspiratorially. "To tell the truth, I felt quite disappointed he didn't try to kiss me."

"So when are you seeing him again?"

"Next week. If that's all right with you. It depends on whether you need me to help here."

"Of course we need you to help here!" Paul exclaimed loudly as he and Naomi tumbled, laughing, into the room. "Where were you anyway?"

"You know where I was, you rat!" Kate replied, punching him playfully in the stomach. "You set me up!"

"Good job one of us has a sense of responsibility," he said, jingling the van keys in front of her.

She grinned, giving him a push as she passed.

"Where are you off to now?" he asked.

"Just to call Mary for her well earned cuppa."

"Better tell her to hurry before Naomi eats all the biscuits," Paul commented.

Caught with her mouth full, Naomi blushed. "Caught in the act! Sorry," she said, reaching for another. "Famished."

"Perhaps I'd better make some toast for the workers, then," Phyllis offered.

"I'll do it," Naomi said, rising and heading for the bread bin.

Kate and Phyllis exchanged a meaningful look, recognising the sign that, at last, Naomi seemed to feel at home.

"And I'll help," Paul added, much to the delight of the older two women.

Some time later, the telephone ringing interrupted their companionable supper. Naomi was nearest but hesitated to pick it up, looking desperately at Kate. "Please... I can't..."

"D'you want me to get that?" Paul asked, reaching towards it, picking it up in obedience to Phyllis's nod. "Hello? Yes, she's right here. It's your neighbour or someone, Phyllis," he said as he handed her the phone.

Phyllis took it and the others moved through towards the sitting room to give her privacy, Kate giving Naomi's shoulders a reassuring hug as they went. She made eye contact with Paul, indicated with an almost imperceptible shake of her head that he should say nothing.

Phyllis followed them through almost immediately. "That was my neighbour from across the road just letting me know that the van window is slightly open. Kind of her, but you have to wonder how she knew it was our van."

"Her curtains have been twitching since I first drew up." Paul walked towards the door again. "Okay. Time I was off anyway. Early start tomorrow girls. Mother, I think you and I should have a talk about this 'date' of yours. You may walk me to the van, while I attend to its security. And I'll say goodnight to the rest of you. See you tomorrow."

"See you tomorrow," Naomi smiled.

"Thank you, Paul. I don't know what we'd have done without your help. You've been great." Phyllis gave him a hug.

"Shall I just hang on to the keys?"

"Yes," Phyllis agreed. "Since you've so kindly agreed to drive the van tomorrow."

"Night everyone."

"Mmm! Quite the hero, aren't you, you rat," Kate teased as they walked towards the van.

"Mum. I need to talk to you." Paul held her arm tightly. His manner had changed, the banter gone, the teasing ignored. "What's going on here?"

"What? With Naomi and the phone?"

"No! With Phyllis and all this stuff!"

"What d'you mean 'going on'?"

"Where did she get it?" He asked as he marched her towards the van.

"What did she tell you?"

"She claims she bought it."

"She did buy it."

They had reached the van now and Paul reached in to wind up the window. He looked into the back of the van, piled high with boxes and packets, sheets and towels. "What? All of it?"

Kate nodded.

"You believe her?"

"Of course. Why? Don't you?"

"I like Phyllis and I had bought the Shopaholic Story. Till I'd been loading the van for a while." He looked up at the house across the street and waved to the curtained window. The curtain moved a little as though someone had suddenly dropped the edge. "She's not the only one showing an interest in proceedings," he nodded towards the movement.

"What do you mean?"

"Your sweet old lady, Phyllis, is under surveillance."

Kate waved her hand towards the twitching curtain. "Oh that's just some lonely old soul with nothing better to do."

"Not her. I mean, Proper Surveillance. As in Official. As in Plain-Clothes Police."

"Oh don't be silly, Paul."

"There is a man. Don't look round. There is a man standing over beside a green BMW. *Don't* look! I told you *not* to look, Mum!"

"Sorry," Kate giggled.

"I'm serious. Mum."

"Sorry." Contrition.

"Like I said, there is a man standing beside a green BMW."

"I'm sorry, Paul. I wouldn't know a BMW from a... from a..." she searched her mind for the name of a car, "... from a Mini!"

Paul sighed. "The make of car is not really the point, Mum. What I'm trying to tell you is that someone has been watching every move we make."

Kate looked around. "Oh I'm sure you're wrong, Paul. Why would anyone want to do that?"

"I don't know. I was hoping you could tell me. He was sitting in his car when Naomi and I made the first run."

"Naomi!" Kate clapped her hand to her mouth. "Oh no. Perhaps it *is* him."

"Who? You've lost me now. Why would a plain-clothes police officer be watching Naomi? Unless he fancies her, of course."

"No. He's not."

"Not what?"

"He's not a policeman. Or at least I don't think he is. Come to think of it, I don't know what he does."

"Who?"

"The plain-clothes policeman."

"I thought you said he wasn't?"

"Wasn't what?"

"MOTHER!" Paul shouted quietly, through clenched teeth. "Getting sense out of you sometimes is like trying to guide ball-bearings down the appropriate hole in one of those puzzles we used to do."

"Fancy you still remembering those puzzles. We used to have hours of fun, didn't we? In the old summerhouse. Do you know, I'd forgotten them. What's more, I haven't thought about the summerhouse all day."

"Good, great! Now can we get back to the point?"

"Which is?"

"Why is Phyllis being watched?"

"No," Kate shook her head. "That's not the point."

"I beg to differ. I don't want either of us mixed up with..."

"No. I mean it's not *Phyllis* who's under surveillance. It's Naomi. She tried to tell us he was following her. We thought she was just imagining it."

"So what's she done?"

"Done? Nothing, as far as I know."

"So why is she under surveillance?"

"Poor Naomi. I wonder what he wants. Why doesn't he just knock on the door and ask to speak to her?"

They had been standing by the van as they talked but now Kate turned to go back to the house.

Paul stopped her. "Why on earth are they watching Naomi?"

"*They*'re not."

"You just said they were."

"Not *they*... *he*. Her ex-whatever he was!"

"Are you sure?"

"I don't know. She seems sure. Did she notice him too while you were loading the van?"

"I don't think so. Once I realised he was watching us, I tried to keep her attention, stop her from looking round. I thought he was watching Phyllis. I didn't want her to get scared if she noticed. I didn't suppose she'd *know* the guy."

"If it *is* him." Kate started walking again. "I'd better see if she's all right. Make sure she didn't see him." She looked round furtively. "Is he still there by the way?"

"Yes," Paul hissed. "He's sitting in his car. He's been watching us. And the house. Mostly the house actually. He's using a mobile phone now."

"The phone!" Kate quickened her pace. "Any bets our phone is ringing?"

It was. As they went in the front door, Phyllis lifted the receiver. "Hello. Phyllis Thaine here. Hello! Hello? Who is this? Look, I don't know what your game... Oh, they've hung up again."

"It's him. I'm sure it is. Quick Paul, look out the window. See if he's still on his phone."

Paul shook his head. "He's put it down. He's driving off."

"What on earth is going on, you two?" Phyllis demanded. "What's with all the cloak and dagger carry on? And I thought you'd gone home, Paul."

"I had, I mean, I was... whatever... " He led Phyllis into the sitting room, Kate following. "Where's Naomi?"

"She went to bed."

"Good."

"Poor dear was tired. She's not used to all this physical activity."

Paul closed the door. "We need to talk. I need to know exactly what's going on."

Chapter 21

"So what should we do?" asked Phyllis. "Do you think we should tell the police?"

"Alert them to our suspicions perhaps, but it would be difficult to prove anything at this stage." Paul shook his head. "Until we know his motive, it's hard to know what best to do. I mean, you say it might be her 'ex'. Maybe they rowed. Perhaps he just wants to talk to her, make up, get back with her."

"Get back *at* her, more like," Kate said. "*She* left *him*, and I don't think he was pleased!"

"No," Phyllis added. "And he's a man with a terrible temper, by all accounts."

"Then we need to protect her," Paul decided. "Until we have evidence of malicious intent, I don't see that we can really involve the police."

"No, perhaps not," Kate agreed. "Though she does seem really scared of him."

"Tomorrow, for instance," Paul stressed. "She must not be left on her own at any time. Here, in the van, at the market, the car boot sale. One of us must be with her at all times."

"Right." Phyllis agreed.

"Phyllis," he directed. "I think you and Mum should go to the car boot sale and I'll go with Naomi to the market. We could take Joe with us for good measure. Between Joe and I, we should be able to protect her from any unwelcome advances."

"Right."

"That's fine with me too," Kate agreed.

"Do you think we should say anything to Naomi?" Phyllis asked.

"Absolutely not!" Paul was emphatic. "From all you tell me and from what I've seen for myself, she's scared enough already."

"True."

"We'll just watch out for her and hopefully she'll not notice anything."

* * *

Sunday dawned cold but dry: the sun a bright, new fire rising majestically, bestowing warmth grudgingly, as befitted the season.

Paul parked the van carefully, taking his time, giving himself opportunity to check around for anyone watching the house. Satisfied that there was not, he locked up and headed for the door.

"There's been a change of plan," Kate announced as she cuddled into his greeting. "Phyllis hasn't managed out of bed this morning. Unusual for her," she said with a worried frown. "Mary says she seems very out of sorts and thinks we should leave her to rest. She's going to call the doctor later, if Phyllis doesn't improve. So the plan can be as it was, except that it looks like I'm on my own at the car-boot."

"No way!" Paul shook his head emphatically. "No-one is going anywhere on their own."

"But you must go with Naomi and I do think you should have Joe with you."

"And Mary's staying here. No. It won't do. You can't do the car-boot yourself, and even if you could," he silenced her objection. "I won't allow it."

Kate didn't argue. She had known herself that she couldn't, shouldn't? do it alone. "But what else can we do?"

"I'm phoning Dad," Paul decided, already punching out the digits on his mobile phone.

"Dad? But…"

He held his hand up in front of her as he turned to speak to Dan.

"What's happening?" asked Naomi, coming into the hall. "Mary says Phyllis isn't up to things. Shall I come with you, d'you think, Kate?"

"No."

"Leave the market to Paul and Joe?"

"No. Paul has another idea."

"That's it. All settled," he announced, putting the mobile in his pocket. "Dad'll be here in half an hour. He'll go with you to the car-boot, Mum, and we'll do the market as planned," he smiled.

"But…"

"No buts, Mum. Sorry. That's what's happening. Has to be," he shrugged. He turned to Naomi. "The van's packed, we're ready. Let's get Joe and we're off."

"But…"

"Hope it all goes well. See you later." He gave Kate a kiss on the cheek and was gone, leaving her standing, clothed in her dismay.

While she waited for Dan, Kate slipped quietly into Phyllis's room after first tapping softly on the door. She had not expected the room to look like a hospital room, but it did. Despite the deep pile carpet, the soft drapes, the flowers and the china ornaments, there was, unmistakably, an air of illness and its accompanying paraphernalia. Perhaps it was the bedside table with its tray of pills and potions, or was it the discretely covered sick-bowl on the table at the other side of the bed? Or was it just the sight of Phyllis lying propped up a little, her eyes closed, her face ashen white.

Kate drew in her breath with a gasp, causing Mary to look up from the chart she was filling in. She beckoned Kate to follow her out of the room.

"I'm sorry, Mrs Morgan. I didn't mean for you to see her like this. She wouldn't want it."

"Mary. What's wrong? I didn't realise. She seemed… I thought she was just a little under the weather."

"I'm sorry, Mrs Morgan. Perhaps you could look in later, when she's awake. I think Mrs Thaine wants to tell you herself."

"Tell me?" Kate stared at her, seeing for the first time Mary's quiet air of competence, like… like a nurse. "Tell me what?" she whispered.

Mary led Kate gently down the hall. "I'm sorry, Mrs Morgan. "Perhaps later."

"Is she?" Her voice failed her. She tried again. "Is she going to be all right?"

Mary smiled the practised smile of the trained nurse. "Excuse me, Mrs Morgan. I really must go back in to her. Perhaps she'll be able to explain everything herself later on. This afternoon, perhaps?"

What's happening? What's going on? Phyllis. Dear Phyllis, what's wrong?

Kate wanted to shout after Mary, wanted to demand to be told what was wrong with her friend, but she knew instinctively that it would be useless. Mary had no intention of telling her anything without Phyllis's permission, and it didn't look as though that would be forthcoming just at the moment.

Instead she sank down into the nearest chair and sat motionless, waiting for the doorbell to ring, waiting for Dan.

"What is it, Kate? What's wrong? You look awful," he said almost as soon as she had opened the door.

"I don't know," she said quietly. "Something terrible, but I don't know what."

Dan drew her to him. "What?"

"It's Phyllis. Something wrong with Phyllis, but I don't know what."

"Phyllis?"

"She's ill."

"Who's ill?"

"Phyllis. My friend. This is her house." She leant into his embrace. "Oh Dan, I'm scared. I'm afraid for Phyllis. She looks so dreadfully pale and so... I don't know. So ill, just *so* ill."

"Have you called a doctor?"

"Mary seems to have it all under control."

"Mary?"

"Her housekeeper. Or, at least, that's what I thought she was. I'm beginning to wonder now. I think she might be a nurse. I think Phyllis must have known she was ill for quite a while."

"But you didn't?"

"No. I had no idea. Either she's been a very good actress, or whatever it is has been in remission or something."

"Look Kate, I'm sorry your friend is ill," he said gently, "but I don't know what you want me to do or why I'm here."

"Paul. It was Paul's idea," she sighed. "He thought you could help me with the car-boot sale."

Dan drew back a little and looked at her with complete bafflement. "Car-boot sale?"

She smiled up at him. "Come into the sitting room and I'll explain what's been happening," she said, leading him by the hand.

He whistled softly as he looked around him. "This is a stunning place."

"Beautiful, isn't it?"

"Beautiful," he repeated, taking in the long sofas, the soft chairs, the sumptuous colours, everything: the glorious ambiance of the whole room. "Stunning!"

By the time Kate had tried to explain about Phyllis, their friendship, the house, the vast store of new purchases, the market stall, the car-boot sale, Dan was looking decidedly confused. She started again, more slowly, trying to fill in the gaps she had left, trying to help him see the picture, build the jigsaw of her life here with Phyllis over the past few months, but, at best, she guessed he only saw the hazy outline. It was clear he was grappling with the concept of two people building such a close friendship in such a short time, given the differences in their ages, circumstances and backgrounds.

More than an hour had passed: she had done her best to help him understand. Now she needed to go to her friend. She left him sitting in thoughtful silence while she went to see if Phyllis was awake.

For Dan, friendship was something he had never mastered, not through lack of interest or lack of feeling, but because of his shyness. He didn't allow himself to need what he felt he could never have.

He could, however, understand why she loved the house, this room, its peacefulness, its sunshine, how she had found solace here for the desecration of her summerhouse. His regret was like a deep ache in his chest.

It wasn't just a beautiful room, it was a room filled with life and memories, he felt sure. There were many ornaments and pictures, but they were not just the random choosing of a dedicated shopper. There was a theme, a melody, in them. The African paintings tied in with some gilt-framed photographs of dusty, smiling children waving happily from their heat-parched homeland, holding up little hand-made trinkets... the same carved and woven mementoes placed carefully on the shelves beside their facsimiles. Other photographs: records of remembered occasions, remembered people. Books, not just for show but well thumbed, their treasures often visited. Flowers, everywhere flowers, lovingly arranged, displayed, not in matching, chic containers, but in such an assortment of posy bowls and vases only gathered through years of happy times. Even the furniture whispered, not only of elegance but also of love: each piece carefully chosen and placed to best advantage, not only for appearance but also for comfort. The sumptuousness of it all was enhanced by the obvious signs of contented occupancy. A room in which to relax. A room in which to dream. A summer room.

"Oh, Kate," he whispered. "I'm so sorry. So very sorry."

At last, the full weight of her loss crushed him. He had thought of it only as an ugly, old outhouse, but now he knew he had destroyed her house of dreams.

Her furniture may not have had the class and luxury of this, but it was no less lovingly gathered. He had thought the rugs old and threadbare, suddenly he understood they were richly woven with memories for Kate. Memories he had refused to share.

No matter the cost, whether money or effort, only a room furnished with love could feel so warm and welcoming.

Now he understood.

When Kate rejoined him, she found him sitting on one of the sofas, his eyes closed, his head pillowed by the deep cushions. She thought at first he was asleep, but, becoming aware of her presence, he looked up and she caught a glimpse of his misery.

"Are you alright, Dan?"

"Me? Yes, of course I am," he replied, rising wearily to his feet. "What about your friend?"

"Phyllis? Mary says she's okay, but I didn't go in to see her again. She's still sleeping." Kate was pulling on her coat as she spoke. "I'll look in when we get back," she added. "If you're sure you're all right," she frowned. "We'd better get going. All the best positions will be already taken as it is. If we want to sell anything today, we'd best get a move on."

"Ready when you are," Dan assured her with a smile. "Though I have to tell you I've never been to a car-boot sale in my life and haven't a clue what to do."

But he was a good learner. He was soon bargaining like a 'pro', refusing to undervalue their wares, but making the sales anyway. To Kate's astonishment, she found he had 'the gift of the gab'. He drew customers to their pitch with an almost constant flow of patter, enticing them to part with their money happily, teasing them into paying what he considered a fair price for their purchase.

"I didn't know you could talk like that," she exclaimed at one point.

"*I* didn't know I could talk like that," he grinned back at her.

"You look as though you're really enjoying yourself."

"In my element!"

"Incredible!"

And to her, it really was incredible. That this taciturn husband of thirty-odd years could suddenly become positively garrulous was amazing. Watching him closely as he performed, she realised it was just that... a performance. He was playing a part. For today, he was a market trader, and a good one at that. With no trouble at all, he was getting through the bundles of assorted goods that had been loaded into the car the night before. And he was enjoying it.

"You should have been an actor," she told him during one of their quiet spells.

"Always did fancy a shot at it," he replied.

Kate shook her head in disbelief. Yet another thing she didn't know about him. "Really?" she asked. "Did you?"

"At school. Fancied joining the drama club."

"And did you?"

Dan laughed. "With my Dad? He'd've broken my neck before he'd let me be a 'Nancy-boy'."

"But actors aren't all 'Nancy-boys'."

"I'd like to've heard how you'd convince my old man of that! He had no time for the 'arty-farty' stuff, as he called it."

"Pity. You'd've been good at it."

Dan shrugged. "No matter," he said. "I'm enjoying myself now."

And then Kate realised. That's the way Dan is. The way he's always been. He has this philosophy in life: if you can't have what you want, learn to want what you have. Contentment, she supposed you'd call it. She'd thought in the past that he was unambitious, but, on reflection, realised that he had done very well in the field he had chosen, had quietly got on with his job and risen through the grades to head his department. He'd done it quietly, without fanfare, but he had done it. It may, or may not, have been the profession of his choice, she didn't know any more, but, on finding himself in it, he'd been content. It was a quality to be admired and she hadn't cared to notice it before.

Her blush was one of shame at her own long-standing lack of sensitivity mixed with a rush of tenderness toward him and, when he smiled into her eyes, she could feel its warmth intensify.

"I'm glad you're enjoying yourself," she said, her voice husky with emotion. "And I'm glad Paul phoned you today."

"Me too," he smiled back at her.

By the end of the day, when they all met up back at the house, the venture was voted a huge success.

"But we'll need to do this every week for years if we're to move all that stuff," wailed Naomi. "There's masses more upstairs. We've hardly touched it."

"But it's a start," Kate argued. "Once we've sorted out a few vanloads for charity etcetera, it'll…"

"It'll still be only the tip of the mountain!"

"Iceberg." Paul corrected her gently. "'The tip of the iceberg,' is the saying."

"Whatever. All I know is, we'll be exhausted if we have to do this every week for the rest of our lives. It's not just going to melt away," she added with a grin at Paul.

"No, but I am, if I don't get a cold drink soon. It's thirsty work in the marketplace. Anyone for a beer?"

Kate followed him out to the kitchen. "I'll help him find some," she excused herself.

"Well," she asked when the door was closed behind them. "Anything to report?"

"Nothing. All quiet on the western front. And you?"

"No trouble. Nothing."

"Good. Perhaps he's too busy on Sundays. Maybe he goes to church," Paul suggested.

"Unlikely. He seems a nasty piece of work."

"So? Doesn't mean he doesn't put on his best 'bib and tucker' for the family outing to church every week. There's no shortage of rogues in that gallery."

"True. And you may be right," Kate agreed. "According to Naomi, he enjoys playing happy families when it suits him."

"We'll just have to watch out for her during the week then, especially the evenings. I assume he works during the day?"

"Yes. He was her boss. Though I don't know what he does. Some kind of office I gather."

"Right. Then Dad and I'll just have to become frequent visitors here at night. Hope you'll not mind too much," he teased, as the blush crept across her cheeks.

Chapter 22

"I know what he wants!" Naomi sank down onto the floor. "I know what he wants."

She had been safely ensconced in her room upstairs for weeks now, but had only just begun to believe she really was safe: the night sweats had stopped, the bad dreams were fading, she had been eating better, sleeping better, feeling better than she had in years. She was even having fun: laughing in a way she had forgotten she could.

They had found a great outlet for most of the huge array of goods that Phyllis had accumulated: one of these places that sold off fire-damaged or over-stocked items: a sort of 'clearing house'. It was a shop in George Street, one that she had often walked past, had even been lured into, on occasion, by the promise of a bargain. It tended not to cater for her taste, as a rule: the stock was seldom well displayed; the shop was too dimly lit and stuffy, and the goods were frequently sub-standard. If nothing else, she needed her purchases to be upmarket or at least to appear to be: 'cheap and nasty', a label she feared.

When Paul, for it was he who had suggested the venue, had met her and Kate outside the shop, he had an air of smug triumph. "Look where I've found," he crowed. "*The* outlet!"

"Oh well done, Paul," Kate smiled. "Yes, that's perfect. Let's go in and find out who we have to see about stocking it, etc."

Naomi hadn't liked the place but recognised that it probably was ideal for their purposes. It turned out better than she'd hoped because she hadn't reckoned on Kate's capability and charm. Before the place was rented, it had been given a thorough clean, the lighting was adjusted, the layout properly planned and the manager eating out of Kate's hand. By the time it was opened for business, *their* business, the merchandise was temptingly displayed, the salespeople recruited and trained by Kate and the whole ambiance of the shop altered. It had 'morphed' into somewhere any shopper would feel comfortable seeking a bargain. And business was booming.

They had emptied several of the rooms in the house, had sold a huge amount of the hoard and were using the proceeds to decorate and set up the rooms ready to fulfil their various roles.

They had gathered books from every corner of the house and brought them together to form a very respectable library. Phyllis had most of the 'classics': poetry, plays and prose, as well as a fair selection of modern literature: Shakespeare, Austin, Keats and Chaucer rubbing spines with Grisham, Shreve and Eco. They even had a non-fiction section. Joe and Dan had turned out to be very competent joiners and had shelved every wall in the room. Decorated in soft shades of green, the furnishings whispering comfort and tranquillity: a perfect reading room. The plan was for this room to serve, not only as the library, but also the venue for weekly meetings of the Writers' Circle and the Book Club which they hoped to set up.

Another room was almost ready to serve as a music room, its clutter gone, revealing the usual, beautiful dark mahogany, but, this time, not just the floor. The doors and skirting were the original dark wood along with the panelling. Paintings: classical muses, family portraits and old-fashioned landscapes adorned the walls giving the room a graceful, sombre atmosphere which Phyllis felt would compliment the wonderful, old grand piano they had unearthed. It was a large room and the high ceiling added to its fine acoustics.

A piano tuner was summoned and the piano was ready for service.

Phyllis was certain there was an old violin hidden in its case somewhere. "It belonged to Thomas, you know. But I've no idea where it was put away. He hadn't played it since he was a boy, you see." But they hadn't come across it yet. There were still rooms to be cleared, so Phyllis felt confident it would "turn up" along with a couple of music stands she "seemed to remember" were also there, "and possibly a flute or some such thing. My father had one at one time or another," she added.

The music room would grow as the work progressed, it seemed.

Phyllis was feeling much better now and, refusing adamantly to discuss her illness, though looking a little frail and tired, she presided over the proceedings with great enthusiasm and obvious pleasure as her dreams became reality.

She had approached one of her friends who had been a psychiatrist and persuaded her that part-time clinic work was just what she needed to keep her busy and happy in her retirement. Once Dr Rosemary Leach saw the transformation that was overtaking the old house, and the more wonderful one that was overtaking her dear friend, she very much wanted to be a part of the plan. Having chosen a room, she was now busy choosing the colour scheme and furnishings to make her clinic a warm and welcoming place.

"Phyllis, I can hardly thank you enough for this opportunity," she had sighed. "Time has begun to hang a little heavily since Edward passed. Somehow travelling without him is just not the same and I'd been wondering what I was going to do with myself till it was time to join him. And I don't imagine that'll be soon," she laughed, "since I'm a hale and hearty sixty-eight, still a young woman really."

Phyllis had chosen well, for Rosemary had worked for many years with Obsessive Compulsive Disorders, which is what she explained the Shopping Problem to be. "Oniomania is the technical term, or CSD, Compulsive Shopping Disorder. It's becoming very prevalent these days. It will be good to be able to help again, feel useful." She looked around at the bustle of activity in the house. "This will be a good place for patients to come," she nodded. "A happy place; a place of healing."

Phyllis smiled her pleasure. "That's what I thought too," she agreed.

"Have you anyone in mind to give debt counselling? There are some excellent services available. Places like the CCCS, the Consumer Credit Counselling Service. It's a charitable organisation, very good, but there are others too."

"Then I'll leave that up to you," Phyllis assured her. "You can either recommend someone we could ask to come here to work with us, or you can send patients to them. Whatever you think best.

"Mmm! Let me think about that one and get back to you."

And so it went...

The plan was taking wings and beginning to fly.

Naomi came forward as Rosemary's first patient. All the bustle and activity had been good for her: her problems overshadowed by fulfilling, hard work. Overshadowed, but not resolved.

Rosemary helped her to work out a plan. She cut up all her credit cards and contacted their sources to change her address and start repaying the mountain of debt that she had accrued. A 'must', according to Rosemary.

"You need to take back control. If I were you, it would be a very long time before I applied for new ones. They make it too easy to overspend. If you must, then you could keep one; for *real* emergencies. But it would be better if you could do without at this stage."

So Naomi cut them all into tiny pieces, enjoying the surge of power she felt as she did so. Kate helped her make quite a party of the event, encouraging her not to be content with just cutting them in half.

"Make a ceremony of it," she suggested. "It's like they say about eating chocolate: be in the moment. Savour it. Make it more satisfying."

So Naomi concentrated hard as she snipped. Thought about the liberation it would bring. "No more mounting bills. No more debt. No more silly spending," she chanted.

"The minute she walked in the joint," Kate sang.

"Boom, boom!" Naomi provided the percussion, the cuttings falling from her lap.

"I could tell she was a girl of distinction, a real big spender."

"Good looking," Naomi preened, "and *so* refined." She smoothed her hands over her hips as she oozed across the room. "Wouldn't you like to know what's going on in her mind?" She turned. "So let me get straight to the point."

"Boom, boom," Kate took over.

"Oops!" said Naomi, her foot slipping on the pieces of plastic strewn around the floor. She bent down and scooped up handfuls of them. "I'm singing in the rain," she sang, throwing the bits in the air, letting them shower down around her, in her hair, on her shoulders, just wherever they landed. "Just singing in the rain."

Kate was laughing, scooping up the plastic as it landed and throwing it again.

"What a glorious feeling," Naomi suddenly stopped. "I'm happy again," she said, almost quizzically. "I am," she repeated. "I'm happy again. I'm actually happy, Kate!"

"Oh, Naomi."

"I'm singing." The plastic shower was in the air again. "Just singing in the rain," Naomi sang at the top of her voice. "Do-de-do-do, do-de-do-de-do-do!" She shuffled through the puddles on the floor.

When Phyllis arrived to find out what all the noise was about, she found them in a happy, laughing heap on the couch.

"My goodness," she smiled. "That was rather a boisterous rendition of 'Singing in the Rain', was it not? What *are* you two up to?"

"I had no idea it could be so much fun, putting your life in order," giggled Naomi.

"And I had no idea that anyone outside Shirley Bassey knew the words to 'Big Spender'!" Kate said with a laugh.

"Oh, my dad, he was a fan."

Because she had been working for Phyllis and earning so well, she had been able to pay quite a substantial amount to each account, making the debt more conquerable.

And Naomi felt happy for the first time in her adult life.

But now she knew what Pete wanted!

At last, she felt secure enough to unpack the few belongings she and Kate had rescued from her old bed-sit. Some of them she consigned straight to the bucket: they were too much part of her past, her unhappy past. The few clothes she felt worth keeping she shook out from the hold-all they had been stuffed into and it was as she was hanging them up that, there in the pocket of one of her jackets...

"I know what he wants," she whispered.

Peter Cartwright had been seen hanging around outside the house again, but every time Dan or Joe or Paul tried to tackle him about why he was stalking Naomi, he would jump in his car and drive off as they approached, the cigarette end he threw from the window the only sign he'd been there.

He kept phoning too: they were all certain it was him. Naomi never answered but invariably, when the caller hung up without speaking, they'd look out the window and, sure enough, he'd be putting his mobile phone back in his pocket.

"I'm going to change my number, go ex-directory," announced Phyllis. And that ended the harassment of the silent calls, but, still, he kept showing up outside.

"What on earth does he want?" Kate asked.

"I don't know," Naomi had cried. "I just don't know. Unless he just wants to frighten me."

"Well he's certainly managing that," Phyllis muttered. "We have to find a way to put a stop to him."

"Where does he live," Paul asked. "I'll go round there and sort him out."

Kate pleaded with her to tell them who he was, what he could possibly want, but Naomi couldn't bring herself to give them any information about him. She didn't know whether she was more afraid of confronting him herself or of what would happen if one of the others managed to hunt him down. She knew the harm he was capable of causing. So she stubbornly refused to tell them his full name, where he worked or where he lived.

Phyllis decided that it was time to involve the police, report him as a stalker, possibly a violent one, but Naomi begged her not to. "He hasn't done anything yet. Perhaps he won't," she reasoned. "I don't think I could stand the questioning, the explanations about who he is, why I left him, what he might do."

Paul felt that he could track him down without too much trouble, but Naomi begged him not to try. "He'll give up soon.

I've nothing he could possibly want. He'll get fed up eventually with this game he's playing. Probably thinks he's some kind of Private Eye, or on some surveillance exercise or something. Pete likes to role-play," she said with a shiver.

So they all did nothing and waited. Waited and watched. Watched that Naomi was never alone or vulnerable.

But now she knew what he wanted.

Chapter 23

At last, the work was done.

The rooms had been de-cluttered. They had worked extremely hard and the Clinic was up and running, the Ladies' Club in operation. Kate had contacted various friends she thought might be interested in the Club side of things and was rewarded with several new members including Liz, the wife of Dan's colleague, who she had spoken to at Dan's leaving dinner. Although she had recovered well from her operation, Liz was eager to have somewhere she could go to relax, take up new hobbies, meet new friends.

"Sometimes I can feel a bit isolated, a bit depressed. My 'get-up-and-go' seems to have 'got-up-and-gone'. I'd love to have a try at learning the piano. You did say there was one at the club?" she phoned to ask.

"Yes, there is." Kate assured her. "And we've organised a piano tutor. I'll send you out the information, times, cost, etc. Then we can organise that for you. And, of course, the piano will be available to you for practice. We can work out the best times for you once the lessons are booked."

"Oh, I'm really getting quite excited about all this! What did you say the name of the Club was?"

"Ah, we're having a spot of difficulty deciding that. What we thought we could do, is get everyone to put forward some suggestions that Phyllis could think about. See if there's any of them she'd like."

"Right. I'll get my thinking cap on, then. The other thing I was thinking about: you used to go walking. Do you still belong to that walking club?"

"Yes, I do. Though I've been so busy, I haven't had much chance to do a lot of walking just lately."

"Derek and I were just saying the other night that we could both do with a bit of exercise. We keep promising ourselves that we'll go for regular walks, but we never do. I wondered if joining the club might help. Give us a bit of motivation to get up off our backsides of a Saturday. You know what it's like. If Derek had his way, we'd just sit in front of the telly watching sport all day."

Oh, yes, Kate knew 'what it's like' all right. She remembered how much she had hated Saturday afternoons before... before...

And it was as she was about to say as much to Liz that she realised... that *was* before. Things had changed. Dan didn't watch sport on Saturday afternoons now. He was usually here at Phyllis's, helping with the work, loading and unloading the van they had decided they needed to buy, fitting shelves, painting walls and woodwork, scrubbing and polishing. He seemed to be here a lot... and not just on Saturdays. In fact, now she came to think of it, he still seemed to be here a lot even though the work was more or less finished. In fact, now she came to think of it, she realised she *enjoyed* the fact that he was around so much.

It just seemed so natural that they should work together, whether painting, scrubbing or transporting merchandise: it was never *said*, never *planned*. They just seemed to end up doing things together.

After her conversation with Liz ended, Kate sat there, in the little office Phyllis had insisted she must have, with the phone still in her hand.

She was enjoying Dan's company! Now, who'd have thought it? She was *glad* he was around so much. She actually missed him if he didn't pop by most days. It had crept up on her. She'd been so busy getting everything done that she hadn't stopped to think about who she was doing it with.

And they'd talked. They'd talked more in the last few weeks and months than they probably had in years. In all their married life even.

Kate leant back, the buzzing telephone unnoticed in her hand. They were getting to know one another! After all these years, they were getting to know one another.

She started to laugh. At first it was just a soft, chuckling sound, but soon it grew to a full, joyful belly laugh. "I've fallen in love with my husband," she laughed. "I do believe I've fallen in love with my husband!"

At last, she put the phone back in its cradle, without noticing that she had been holding it.

"Where's Dad?" she asked Paul when he came by to pick Naomi up. They were going to the pictures. It seemed that Kate and Dan were not the only ones getting to know one another.

"Dad? Haven't a clue?" Paul shrugged. "Is Naomi ready, d'you know?"

"It' just... it's just... he hasn't been in for a day or two. I was just wondering if he's all right."

"Probably busy," Paul flung over his shoulder as he went upstairs to find Naomi.

"Busy? But..."

But Paul had gone, too busy himself to note the dismay on his mother's face.

"It's been a week since Dan was here," she complained to Phyllis a few days later.

"I wonder what your Dad's up to," she said casually to Vicky the next week. "It's been a while since I saw him. Is everything all right?" she added equally casually.

Vicky shrugged. "Seems fine. Why don't you phone him and ask?"

"Oh no! It doesn't matter. It's just that I wondered."

She *did* wonder. And it *did* matter. Yet, somehow, she couldn't bring herself to phone.

Maybe *she* had fallen in love with *him*; but maybe *he* hadn't fallen in love with *her*. Maybe he had sensed what was happening to her and had backed off, not wanting it for him. Maybe it was too little, too late. Maybe he was glad the work was finished and he had no reason to be here, in her company. Oh, maybe, maybe, maybe...

Frustration flooded over Kate in a tide of self-pity. Tears stung her eyes and steamed up her reading glasses.

No matter how hard she tried, she couldn't go back to where she'd been: the anger and resentment she had felt towards him over the summerhouse could not be summoned to her rescue. No matter how hard she tried, she couldn't forget the touch of his hand on hers as he helped her into the car, his hand brushing her neck as he helped her on with her coat, his smile, his laugh, everything... everything about him!

Throwing her pen onto the desk in frustration, she pushed back her chair and, snatching her coat from its hook in the cupboard, she practically ran out of the house, tears blinding her.

"This is stupid," she said out loud. "I'm not a teenager! I'm a grown woman. He's my husband. What is *happening* to me?"

She didn't notice Pete standing across the road.

Naomi had heard Kate slam the door, heard her crying as she did it. From the window, she saw her running along the pavement. Grabbing her own coat, she ran after her. When she reached the corner, she stopped for a moment to see which way Kate had run.

"Ka..." Her shout was strangled in her throat before it could be heard, strangled by the hand that caught her round the neck, any chance of being re-uttered stifled by another hand across her mouth.

In her haste she hadn't been careful. After all this time, she'd been lulled into a false sense of security.

He punched her in the kidneys, his other hand tightening round her throat.

"Where is it, Naomi?" he hissed in her ear, his hand stopping her breath.

She shook her head the little she was able, her body writhing from the pain in her back, tried to kick him, tried to pull his hands away. But he was too strong.

He punched her again, laughing, pressing her back against him, pushing her throat, making her head go back, back until she thought her neck must break. Then he bent his head and kissed her savagely, his tongue invading her mouth, making her gag. He was pretending that they were having a lover's scuffle for the benefit of anyone who was watching. The hand he had used to punch her he now thrust inside her coat, gripping her breast fiercely, causing a wave of pain that weakened her further.

"Where is it?" he asked again, turning his hand, twisting her flesh.

She was going limp as consciousness seeped from her.

"Where is it?" his lips so close, making her ear his megaphone.

He had dragged her backwards and they were almost at his car. "Get in!" he ordered, when he'd got the door opened.

Barely breathing, barely conscious, Naomi tried one last feeble resistance.

"Get in, I said!" and he threw her into the car.

But he had to walk round to the driver's side to get in himself. He had miscalculated Naomi's strength, not just her physical strength, she had little enough of that left, but her new-found strength of will. She'd always cowed under his bullying before. He used to have her in his power. She used to obey him, her fear making her suppliant.

Not any more.

As fast as he was, she was faster. With a huge effort of will, she lunged across the car, pushing down the lock and holding it with one hand while she leant on the horn with the other.

He punched the window impotently, cursing her loudly, but his vile words were drowned out by the Mayday call of the car's horn.

It was as Pete moved to open the rear door that Joe came running down the steps of the house, a saucepan brandished in his hand. He'd been helping Mary to prepare the dinner when he'd been summoned by the urgency of the noise. He shouted now, first to Mary, who'd followed him to the door, "Call the police!" then to Peter, "Leave her alone!"

Kate had also heard the noise of the car horn and it brought her to her senses. In an instant, she realised what had happened. Her intuition told her what her tears had hidden. He had been waiting. Waiting for just such an opportunity as this.

She ran back and arrived at the car door just as Peter tried to open it. He flung her out of the way but she clung onto his arm, stopping him from getting the door opened. He raised his hand, about to punch her, when the saucepan hit him across the ear. Howling in pain, he turned in time to see Joe raise it again, ready for a second strike.

Like most bullies, Peter Cartwright was also a coward. Faced with the promise of further pain, he chose to run. Hampered by the blood running down the side of his face, he stumbled a few steps, bumping off the railings of the house opposite before making his escape along the road.

Joe started out in pursuit, but was stopped by Naomi's cry as she tumbled out of the car.

"No," she screamed. "Let him go!"

Stunned, Joe hesitated for a moment too long and Peter disappeared round the corner and was gone. Joe guessed he, being a much older man, would not be as fit. Even though Peter was hurt, he would not catch him. He lowered the saucepan and turned to help Naomi into the house.

"Ach! Ye should've let me tak anither swing at 'im!" he declared. "He surely had it comin'!"

"Come on Naomi," Kate said gently, taking her arm to help her up the stairs. "Joe, forget him just now and take her other arm. She's hurt. Mary, ask Phyllis to come down to the clinic, we'll take her in there. Phyllis had better take a look at her. See what damage that man has done! And then," she said to Naomi, "I think it's time you told us exactly what this is all about, don't you?"

Chapter 24

"I know what he wants," Naomi said quietly.

She was sitting cosied up on one of Phyllis's big sofas, pillows supporting her all around, a rug tucked over her and a mug of Phyllis's favourite remedy in her hands.

They had taken her to the A&E at the Royal Infirmary, just to make sure Pete hadn't damaged her kidneys with his vicious punches.

"Just badly bruised," the doctor had diagnosed after consulting the scan results. "Plenty rest and lots of fluids," his prescription.

"Okay, so what does he want?" Kate asked.

"I found a floppy disc in my jacket pocket. I'd forgotten I'd done it."

"Done what? I don't understand."

"I'd downloaded some information from the computer at work. I'd forgotten."

"And that's what he wants?" Phyllis asked.

"That's what he was probably looking for at the flat." Naomi shuddered, remembering the chaos he had left when he had searched her bed-sit, the anger he had vented when he didn't find what he wanted. "And that'll be what he wants now," she added.

"Then why doesn't he just knock at the door and ask for it?" Phyllis wanted to know.

"Yes, why all the cloak and dagger stuff? The months of stalking? The assault? Was that really necessary?" Kate asked.

"Because he knows I'll not just hand it over to him."

"Why not? Perhaps if you had done so when you found it, you could've saved yourself a lot of fear and a lot of pain," Phyllis said, nodding towards her huddled figure.

"Because I need it."

"Need it?"

"For protection."

"Well, it doesn't seem to have protected you so far!" Phyllis pointed out.

"Not exactly that kind of protection."

"What kind then?"

"Just believe me. I need it."

"Look! I'm sorry, Naomi, if we seem to be bullying you..."

Naomi snorted. "If you want to know about bullying," she mumbled.

Kate moved over to sit on the edge of the sofa, resting her hand gently on Naomi's legs. "We don't want to upset you. We only want to help. And it seems to me that you're going to have to explain to the police what it is Pete wanted from you when he attacked you."

"I really wish you hadn't called in the police, you know?"

"Well, we did," Phyllis retorted. "We want to make sure nothing like this happens again. He should, at least, face charges of assault with menace. And stalking. And the nuisance phone calls."

"But I don't want to press charges."

The police had been very understanding when they had arrived on the scene earlier. They had taken a statement from Kate and one from Joe, but Naomi had been too upset at the time and they had agreed that the first priority was to get her to the hospital. They planned to come back for her statement later.

"But you *must* press charges," Phyllis declared. "That's possibly them now," she said when they heard the doorbell. "And they'll want to know what happened. If you don't identify him and press charges, he'll get off scot-free."

"Don't you want him punished for what he did to you? Not just earlier on, but *all* that he's done to you?" Kate asked.

Naomi closed her eyes.

She looked very small and very vulnerable.

It was not the police at the door, but Dan and Paul. Phyllis had phoned them while the others were at the hospital.

Naomi opened her eyes in response to their concerned greetings, but then closed them again as they filled with tears. She turned her head into the pillow and wept silently, her body curling up like a wounded animal's.

Kate had taken the unheeded mug of chocolate from Naomi's hands and moved from her position on the sofa when the men entered the room, and now she was replaced by Paul. He took Naomi's hand in his and gently bent to kiss her wet cheek, murmuring tender condolences in her ear.

She sobbed the more.

They all looked at one another, not knowing how to help her in this raw grief.

They couldn't know that their very presence made it worse. Made it all worse. Conscious of them gathered round her, sensing their genuine warmth and sympathy, their love, even: it was too much. Any memory of such tenderness was very dim and very distant. She felt unworthy. *If they knew. If they knew the truth: what she really was, what she'd done.*

Her sobs grew louder, they racked her frail body: huge gulping sobs, piteous wails.

Paul drew back a little, realising that his compassion was causing more pain. He looked helplessly at Kate. "What should I do?" he whispered.

"Leave her a minute, son," she replied. "And you, Dan," she smiled sadly.

"I'll go too," Phyllis whispered. "Perhaps, if it's just you?"

Kate nodded.

When they'd all tiptoed out of the room, soundlessly closing the door behind them, Kate sat down again and put her arms round the bundle of misery that was Naomi. "There, there," she cooed, as she had so often soothed her children, rocking her gently as she had rocked them in their distress. But this was no childhood mishap needing a mother's cuddle. Kate knew instinctively that this was something deep and dreadful, something needing a lot more than a cuddle to make it better. She shivered with apprehension of what was to come.

"You poor, poor girl," she whispered as she stroked her hair, letting her cry, making no move to encourage her to stop, knowing that the tears would dry up eventually. More important first to let the grief out: it had been stored up too long.

So they stayed that way for a long time: Kate soothing and rocking, Naomi keening and weeping. And, sure enough, gradually the sounds changed: the keening became a whimper, the weeping slowed to occasional sobs.

"Oh, Kate," Naomi whispered hoarsely after a while. "Oh, Kate. If you knew... if you knew."

"Then why don't you tell me," she encouraged.

"I can't... I can't!" The wailing started up again. "It's too awful." she gulped.

"No, it's not. Whatever it is, it can't be that awful."

"You don't know me. You know nothing about me."

"Tell me then. I'm listening. I'm listening," she repeated, lifting Naomi's head to look into her pain. "I'm listening."

"I'm not nice. I'm not a nice person." She looked at Kate, waited for a reaction, but there was none. Kate sat patiently, her expression soft with gentle concern.

"I've done some... some awful things."

Kate waited.

"My mother." Tears began to roll down Naomi's cheeks. "My mother died." She faltered and fell silent again.

"Yes, you said you were an orphan, I remember," Kate tried to help her along.

But Naomi shook her head. "Not true. Not an orphan. Just my mother. Just my mother died."

"Oh, okay. That's okay. Do you want to tell me about it?"

Naomi looked forlornly into Kate's eyes. "It was... it was my fault," she gasped out, the sobs strangling the words in her throat. "I didn't mean for it to happen. I didn't mean it."

"Oh, you poor thing, you poor, poor thing. Tell me about it. Please, can you tell me about it?"

So, between sobs and tears, Naomi managed to tell her story. It would be wrong to say that it 'poured out'. That would infer a constant flow. Rather, it was pushed and cajoled out in fits and starts until Naomi lay back exhausted.

She had grown up in a small town near Edinburgh, the oldest of three, the other two being boys and younger than her by quite a few years. She was always her father's favourite, arousing a fierce jealousy in her mother. Nothing Naomi did was good enough, nothing she said was right, as far as her mother was concerned.

"I wasn't really a bad kid," she told Kate. "But she brought out the worst in me. After she'd yell at me for nothing, I'd go off and do something naughty. As if to make the row worth it, or something. I'd put on her favourite lipstick and pull faces at myself in her mirror. Or I'd put on her favourite scarf or her necklace and pretend to be her, only I'd deliberately trip over, or bump into things. 'Oh, silly me,' I'd mimic. 'What a fool I am!" Then she'd catch me saying nasty things to my reflection in her mirror. Pretending I was saying them to her. She could hardly wait for Dad to get home so that she could tell on me, get me into trouble with him." She smiled a little. "Only he wouldn't really be cross and he'd wink at me as he told me off. 'You're too soft,' she'd tell him. 'She'll be the death of me, that girl!' she'd say."

It was a while till Naomi could compose herself then to continue with her story, mumbling through her sobs about 'gifts of prophecy'.

"When I got older, I'd go off to the shops after we'd had a row. I'd buy something. Anything really. Usually something bright, really gaudy, to wear. 'Cheap and nasty!' my mother took delight in informing me. 'Won't last ten minutes!' she'd say. But I didn't care... or, I pretended not to care. I didn't need them to last. I just wanted something cheery, something new. And, she was right, they were cheap. They had to be. I had no money, to speak of." She shook her head and laughed, a hard, dry little laugh. "Huh! Rosemary would have a field day with all of this, wouldn't she?"

"Well, it is rather classic, I suppose, isn't it?" Kate had to agree.

"Anyway," Naomi took a deep breath. "This is where we come to the hard part of the story," she sighed. "One day, we'd had this terrible row. I can't even remember what it was about. Something trivial, probably. But, anyway, I stormed out and went shopping up the town. I came back with this silly, floaty sort of…" She pulled a face, her nose scrunched up in distaste. "Sort of …*creation*. A dress. Very flimsy, summery. Nothing much of it really. I'd chosen it deliberately 'cos I knew it'd make her furious. I knew Dad would love it because it was all frilly and feminine, and that would only make her hate it more."

Naomi turned her head into the pillow.

Kate waited.

"Anyway," Naomi continued, pulling herself up, summoning her strength. "I put it on and said I was going out. 'Not dressed like that, you're not!' Mother said. She said I looked like a wee tart. 'Look at it,' she said, lifting one of the frills at the shoulder. 'Cheap and nasty!' and she tried to rip off the frill. She often did that. Ripped up what I bought. Said she was showing me how rubbishy they were. Anyway, I tried to pull away, to stop her destroying my dress. Only... only..."

Naomi looked at Kate, desperate horror in her eyes. "Only, she was right. The dress was cheap and nasty. It ripped in her hand. The frill ripped clean off and, because I was pulling away... and... and... Oh! God help me! I was pushing her away. She lost her balance and she fell... she fell..." Naomi put her hands over her face. "She fell all the way down the stairs. I saw it as though it was in slow motion. Her eyes staring at me, her mouth open, screaming my name... over and over... over and over I see it... she fell down the stairs. Oh, Kate... *she fell down the stairs!* She had the silly frill in her hand, still holding it, clutching it as though it might stop her falling. She hit her head on the banister. The angle was bad. It broke her neck."

Naomi's voice was flat, her eyes were dry. She looked at Kate numbly. "Broke her neck," she repeated, shaking her head, holding it, wishing she could shake out the memory, the picture, clear and fresh, of her mother lying at the foot of the stairs, her head twisted, bent at a strange angle, her mouth twisted too, in a strange grimace, the frill of material lying across her throat like a scarf.

"But she didn't die," Naomi continued. "Not then. Not right away. She lay in a semi-coma for fifteen months. A vegetable.

Unable to do anything for herself. Her eyes were open, just staring... accusing... for fifteen months."

"Oh, Naomi! How awful! How dreadful for you, for all of you."

"And it was my fault!"

"No! No! You mustn't think that! It was an accident!"

Naomi turned her head as though realising suddenly that Kate was still there. "An accident? Yes, that's what the police, the doctor, everyone said. But I knew. I knew it was my fault."

"No," Kate shook her head vehemently. "No! You mustn't say that. It *was* an accident. You didn't mean it to happen. It was as much your mother's fault. More."

"My two little brothers were motherless. They were only ten and twelve. And it was my fault. I watched them cry, knowing that I had brought their grief. And my father. He hardly knew how to go on. He was lost. He'd adored her. She'd loved him too. They'd been so happy." Her voice started to break and she stopped for a moment.

"I went to the hospital every day at first, begging her forgiveness, but she just stared. Stared at me with hatred in her eyes. She knew... *I* knew... it was my fault."

"Your father?"

"My father didn't say as much, but he knew. He knew. He tried to pretend he thought it was just an accident, but deep down, he blamed me. I know he did."

"No, Naomi. I'm sure you're wrong about that."

"The day after her funeral, I was upset."

"I'm not surprised."

"I made a mess of the meal. Chicken. It was chicken. I didn't cook it enough. When Dad cut into it, the pink juices seeped out. He threw down his knife and fork. 'What the matter with you?' he shouted. 'Was it not enough that you killed your mother? Are you trying to kill me too?'"

"Was it not enough that you killed your mother?" Naomi whispered. *"You killed your mother."*

"Then I knew. I knew for sure, he blamed me. He'd lost *her*, and he blamed *me*." Naomi sat perfectly still. Her calmness was eerie after the earlier storm of grief.

There was nothing Kate could say.

They sat in silence for a long time. Kate tried to put her arms round Naomi again, but Naomi didn't want it, drew away.

"I ran away after that," she said eventually. "I came to Edinburgh, lived in a hostel till I got a job. That's when I met Pete. He was my boss. I didn't know he was married. It didn't matter at first. He was just being kind. Listened while I told him what had happened with Mum and everything. Found me somewhere to stay. Offered to help with the rent till I 'got on my feet'. Only, he started coming round to the bedsit. Evenings. He'd appear at the door, flushed, out of breath as if he'd been running. Said he'd been out jogging, thought he'd pop in, see how I was doing. Only, he wasn't dressed for jogging. Wrong shoes, wrong gear. Didn't think much of it at the time. Anyway, he started coming regularly, brought chocolates, bottles of wine, flowers. My Dad didn't agree much with 'alcoholic beverages', as he called them, so I wasn't used to it. It was easy to get me drunk and then to... to..."

"I didn't know he was taking a video. I was too drunk. It was awful. He tried to show it to me another time, thought I'd be excited by it," she shivered. "It was disgusting. I was disgusted, tried to throw him out. 'Whose bedsit? You want me to leave *whose* bedsit?' he said. 'I pay your rent, and don't you forget it! You'll do what *I* want,' he said. 'And I'm not ready to go anywhere yet.' He... he made me... He made me do... things..."

At last, the tears came again, and Kate was glad to see them. She held Naomi in her arms, told her that was enough, she didn't need to tell her the details. She had told her enough. Enough to know that Peter Cartwright had seduced her and abused her.

"He told me that he'd send the video to my Dad. He'd got his address. He said it was ready, in an envelope. He'd send it if I didn't do what he wanted, if tried to leave him. My Dad... my Dad... he'd..." She shook her head. "He'd be so ashamed," she sobbed. "I'd shamed him already. It would be too much. I didn't want him to see... to see..."

"Of course you didn't."

"I couldn't let him. I couldn't let him send it."

"No! No, of course you couldn't."

"So I was trapped."

"The computer disc?"

"Yes, I've got that. It's the only way I could be sure he wouldn't send it. When he wanted to be cruel, he'd say he would send it anyway."

"But you've got the disc."

Naomi nodded. "After a while I began to realise that everything at work didn't add up, the books and that. I found out that he was cheating the VAT, income tax, even the customers. Any way he could cheat, he did cheat. Then I found out he was married. He was even cheating his wife. I felt angry and humiliated. So I downloaded all the information I could. More than enough to get him convicted of fraud."

"Your protection?"

"Exactly. I guessed that, if he knew I had all that evidence against him, he wouldn't send the video to my father. I didn't have to be his slave, or whatever I was, any more. But it doesn't work like that," she sighed. "It wasn't easy to break off with him. He kept coming to the flat. Sometimes he'd even be kind again. Bring me flowers. I was lonely, desperate for attention, any attention. He still had power over me and he knew it."

"Oh, Naomi."

"And I was still frightened that he'd send the tape," she sighed.

"No wonder you were ill."

"I couldn't sleep, couldn't eat. Didn't have money for food anyway Especially with the shopping..."

"The shopping?"

"It was the same thing as with my mother, happening all over again. Every time we had a row, I'd go shopping!" she spread her hands. "I couldn't help myself. I couldn't control it. Even when I had no money, no credit." She looked up at Kate. "So there, you have it. The whole sorry, sordid story."

She had been sitting, curled up on the sofa all this time, and now, she turned her face away from Kate, too ashamed to look at her, too tired even to cry.

Chapter 25

"I can't believe you didn't press charges!" Paul shook his head.

"Naomi had her reasons," Kate defended.

"Peter Cartwright is a menace and should be locked up!" Paul was not to be mollified. "I can't think of any reason..."

"Peter Cartwright? Peter Cartwright. Now, why does that ring a bell?" Dan rubbed his forehead. "Peter Cartwright. I've seen that name somewhere. Written down. Recently." He walked across the room, seeking inspiration in the carpet. "Got it!" He turned round, triumphant. "Peter Cartwright 'Auctioneer and Valuator'! That's who he is!"

Naomi's nervous jump at his exclamation, proved him to be right.

"I didn't get that good a look at him when he was skulking about outside, but I knew there was something familiar about him! I was in his office once. A while back, but I remember! Well!"

"Do you remember where his office is, Dad?" Paul asked.

"Yes, yes I do. It was in Rose Street."

Naomi turned to Paul. "What are you going to do?" Alarm sounded strident in her voice.

"I'm going to sort the s..."

"Paul!" Kate warned.

Paul looked at his mother, shaking his head, but acknowledging her warning just the same. He modified his language. "I'm going to sort the 'nice gentleman out'!" he said sweetly.

"No! Please! You don't understand," Naomi begged.

"It might be best if you left things alone just now, Paul. Naomi knows this man. She knows what he's capable of."

"I'm not afraid of him," Paul asserted, pulling himself up to his full height, pulling his broad shoulders back.

"That's not what I mean. Naomi knows what he's capable of doing to hurt *her*... not you. No-one is questioning the fact that, in a fair fight, you'd marmalise the poor man."

"We can protect Naomi."

"Oh, yes? Like we protected her earlier on?"

Paul dropped his shoulders. "Mmm," he grumbled.

"Anyway, that's not the kind of harm I was referring to."

Naomi started up in alarm again. "Please Kate!"

"It's okay," she reassured. "Don't worry, pet. I would never betray a confidence. I was just going to say, the man is capable of doing harm in other ways than physically."

"So, we're just going to let him get away with assault and battery? And the rest?"

"For the moment, until Naomi decides what to do."

Dan had been standing, looking out of the window, remembering the scenes of utter chaos in Peter Cartwright's office the day he was there. He turned to Naomi now and asked, "Do you, by any chance have something belonging to him?"

"No," she replied shakily.

"Something he wants though, yes?"

She nodded.

"Something he wants very badly?"

She nodded again.

"But you don't want to give it to him?"

Naomi shook her head.

"Something that could hurt him?"

"What is this?" Paul asked, still petulant that his plan had been vetoed and now he didn't know what was going on. "'Twenty Questions' or something?"

"Oh, stop badgering the girl, both of you," Kate bustled in between them and Naomi. "Naomi needs a bit of space and time to work out what she needs to do, don't you, pet?"

So they all backed off, Dan and Paul saying their goodbyes and assuring her that they'd pop in the next day, see if she needed them at all, and Kate helping her up to her bedroom for the night.

Phyllis had gone to bed hours ago. The excitement had proved too much for her and she was exhausted. But, before she went, she had left instructions for Naomi to be administered her 'prescription' hot cocoa to help her sleep.

"She's going to make a junkie out of me, you know," Naomi muttered, but was glad of the comforting drink nonetheless.

"Well you didn't take much of the one she gave you earlier and it's a very mild sedative. I think you'll be all right," Kate smiled. "Just knock through if you need me," she added, indicting her own bedroom, through the wall from Naomi's.

When Naomi awoke the next morning, she had slept well and felt much better.

"I know what I have to do," she announced to Kate over breakfast in the kitchen. "I'm going home."

"Home? D'you mean?"

"I mean 'home'. I'm going home to my Dad."

Kate was a mother. She knew how it felt to have grown children who left home. Albeit her children left without acrimony and she still saw them regularly, still, she knew the pain of losing your children to adulthood, to independence. She could only imagine the pain of losing a child who had left without saying 'goodbye', who you didn't see again for years, or hear from or even know where they were. Her eyes misted over, her voice was husky when she spoke. "Oh Naomi, I think that's a wonderful idea!"

Naomi smiled. "I thought you'd like that." She closed her eyes. "I know it won't be easy. He might not want me back."

"Oh, he will," Kate said with the assurance of parenthood.

"He might not forgive me."

"He will. He probably regrets so much the things he said. Wishes he could take it all back."

"Maybe, maybe not. But I have to try. I have to try to make things right with him. And, and I miss him," Naomi sobbed. "And the boys. I miss them so much."

Kate walked round the table, put her arms round Naomi. "You poor, poor thing. I'm sure you do. It's been a long time."

"I didn't let myself miss them, didn't let myself think about them," Naomi sniffed. "But, now that I've decided to go home. Oh, Kate," she cried. "I miss them so much. I want to go home," she wailed. "I just want to go home. And I want my Mum to be there. I just want my Mum." And she cried then as if her heart was breaking. All the grief that Naomi had stored up for years, the grief her guilt had prohibited her from indulging, all the pain and grief of losing her mother, spilled out now in a torrent of tears and shuddering sobs.

She cried for her mother, wanting her, needing her, finding it strange, even as she did so, that she should want her so much when their relationship had never been a congenial one. There was no nostalgia for a mother's cuddles because there was no memory of cuddles: her mother held back from such shows of tenderness, claiming they would make the children 'soft'. Yet, still, Naomi cried for her mother, yearning for her as she had probably yearned for her all her life. When her mother was alive there was always the chance, the hope, that there would be a way to win her approval, her praise, her affection. Now that she was dead, the hope died too. There would be no approval, no praise, no affection. Only the silent accusation in staring eyes. Naomi's heart ached to close those eyes with kisses, to soften the face of her accuser. And so she cried for her mother and what could never be.

There were tears for her father too: tears of longing and tears of apprehension. She longed to win back his favour, to bask in the warmth of his love, but she was afraid that he would still be bitter, still need to hold her from him in resentment. But she wanted him desperately, wanted to see him, to feel his arms round her, his hand stroking her hair, his gruff voice telling her he forgave her, he loved her.

Now that she had opened the door behind which she had dammed up all her familial feelings, they burst out in a torrent and there was no way to hold them back. All that she had denied herself for so long could be denied no longer. She could only ride the tidal wave of emotion that engulfed her and pray that she wouldn't drown.

All Kate could do was hold her and let her cry... and cry along with her.

"Going home?" Paul repeated foolishly when they told him later that day. "But I thought *this* was your home now. You seemed happy here."

"And I am happy here. But it isn't my home," Naomi said gently. "This has been a wonderful place to be," she turned to Phyllis. "And I can't thank you enough for taking me in," she smiled. "For rescuing me, Phyllis. You have given me so much help. To get better, to put my life in order. And now," she drew herself up. "I feel I can make it home and set things right there too."

She told Kate she intended to tell her father as much as she felt he could cope with about her life over the past few years. She would tell him about Peter, how he'd gotten her drunk, taken advantage of her, taken a film. She'd explain he'd been using it as blackmail all this time, that she wanted to be free of him, so she would intercept the package if it ever came. She'd make her father promise not to open any video-sized envelopes that were delivered, let her destroy the tape, unseen. Naomi felt sure he'd agree to do that. Kate knew he would.

Naomi had given her statement to the police, and had given them the computer disc. They had agreed that the evidence on it was very damning. Peter was probably facing charges as they sat here in Phyllis's kitchen, drinking a last cuppa together. They all hoped so.

"So will we see you again?" Paul sulked.

Naomi shrugged. "Probably. I hope that Phyllis will let me attend the clinic for a while yet."

"Of course!"

"And possibly a few of the clubs? I was enjoying the Book Club. I'd even read the book for next month's meeting."

"Then, certainly you must come," laughed Phyllis. "We'll need your input. I found that a hard one!"

"But what about me?" Paul whined.

"I thought you believed in personal freedom?" Kate asked. "An independent spirit?"

"I do, but…"

"Oh, Paul. Of course I'll see you," Naomi blushed. "I'll see you around the house here, if you happen to be around when I come."

They all laughed at Paul's discomfort.

"She's not going to the other side of the moon, Paul," Kate reminded him. "She'll only be ten or fifteen miles out of Edinburgh."

"S'pose so," he shrugged, beginning to recover his equanimity. "It just was all a bit of a surprise really. I didn't know you *had* a home to go back to!"

"No, Paul," Naomi said quietly. "Neither did I."

Chapter 26

After Naomi's taxi pulled away... for she insisted she would get a taxi, "I need to do this on my own," she'd said... the others looked at one another, a sense of loss settling on them.

"I'll really miss her," Phyllis said as she turned from the door. "It's all been a bit sudden."

"Yes," Kate agreed. "I think we'll all miss her. She had become one of the 'gang', hadn't she?"

"I just hope she knows what she's doing," Paul grumbled.

"Well, I know what I'm doing," Phyllis said with a yawn. "I'm going to lie down for a bit. There's been a lot of excitement around here the past few days, what with one thing and another. Too much for an old lady like me," she joked, patting Kate's arm as she passed her.

"Good idea," Kate replied absently.

Paul prepared to drift off to do whatever he decided to do with himself. In truth, he was a little lost, and more than a little put out that Naomi had gone. He'd been enjoying her company, had begun to think of her as his current girlfriend. He wasn't used to being 'ditched', as he thought of it. Usually he was the one who ended relationships. But he hadn't been ready to end this one. As far as he was concerned, it was just getting started.

Kate had tried to reassure him, telling him, that once Naomi had reconciled with her family and had time to decide what she wanted to do, she may well decide that she still wanted to work for Phyllis in one capacity or another. Probably not as Phyllis's companion, because she may not want to live away from home again for a while, but Phyllis agreed she had plenty of ways in which she'd love to employ Naomi. "Don't fret," she coaxed him, "you're mother's right. Naomi'll be back."

The clinic was busy and Rosemary felt the need of a receptionist of some sort. Kate had been performing that duty, but, really, she had enough to do with all the other administrative tasks she had: running all the various clubs took a bit of organising, and they still leased the clearance shop, which she supervised.

There was certainly a place for Naomi, if she chose to fill it.

Kate had handed in her notice at 'Harrison's' when they started the whole venture. The management had been sorry to let her go, but gave her no gold watch for her services. After all, she was 'only a part-timer, a 'floater' at that!' She left with no presentation and no regrets. Life was busy and rich and she was enjoying its challenges.

There was one disappointment, however, and that was that her re-developing relationship with Dan seemed to have petered out, and she didn't understand why. They seemed to be getting on so well, getting to know one another after all these years as intimate strangers. She thought he loved her, she knew she had fallen in love with him all over again, but this time far more profoundly than she ever had as a teenager. This time, she knew him better, appreciated him more, understood him, or...

Had she misread him? Was the new-found closeness they'd shared been no more than friendship? Could he really live without her? She'd been away from home for several months: did he not need her any more? As her yearning for him increased, had he none for her? Despite all her earlier protestations, she had begun to dream of their future together. *Together.*

Apart from today, and yesterday, she hadn't seen him in weeks. He hadn't been around, had made no contact, no phone call.

Yesterday, he had gone without so much as a 'Goodbye!' Certainly, she had been occupied with Naomi, but there hadn't been so much as a special glance her way, only a nod to everyone in general.

Today, he had been here for a short while, here to support Naomi, to show his concern for Naomi, to offer her a lift, but he hadn't stayed long. When Paul went, so did Dan.

Kate had hoped he'd stay, that they could talk. When Phyllis went off to lie down, she had intended to offer him a cuppa in the kitchen thinking she could find out what he felt, why he was staying away. But he'd brushed her cheek lightly with his lips as he said 'Bye!' A friendly kiss, nothing more, and made his getaway along with Paul.

It was while she was sitting in the office, toying with her consolation cup of coffee, feeling sorry for herself, that Joe burst in.

"I think ye'd better come, Mrs Morgan."

Phyllis had taken ill again, seriously ill. Mary had called the doctor, but she wasn't sure he would get here in time.

"I think she's having a really bad attack."

"What kind of attack?" Kate asked Joe, as they ran to Phyllis's room.

"I think it's a heart attack, a bad un this time."

"Mary?"

Mary rose from the seat beside Phyllis's bed. "I'm sorry, Mrs Morgan, I thought you'd want to see her. But... but," Mary started to sob. "I think it's too late. She's gone." She kissed the hand she'd been holding and laid it gently by Phyllis's side.

"Gone? What d'you mean gone?" Kate cried out. "She can't have 'gone', I spoke to her not more than an hour ago. She was fine. A bit tired but..."

But Phyllis had 'gone'. She had suffered a massive heart attack and it had all been over before Joe had reached the office door.

At least she hadn't been alone. Mary had been there, waiting to see if she needed anything before she settled for the nap she'd said she needed. The events of the last few days had tired her and she admitted that she wasn't feeling too well. After Mary had helped her into bed, she had taken her hand and kissed it, "You're a good friend, Mary, and a good nurse. Thank you!"

"And then she just seemed to go to sleep," Mary sobbed. "Except that her breathing suddenly stopped and I knew she'd gone." She lay her head on the bed beside Phyllis and wept, until Joe gently coaxed her up and into his arms.

Apparently, Kate learned from the doctor, Phyllis had a congenital heart disease and her already weakened heart had been affected by the regular recurrences of malaria she had suffered since her return from a lengthy trip to Africa.

"She never said."

"No, she wouldn't. A brave soul, and a private one."

"I knew she was ill. Knew there was some underlying problem. But I didn't realise," Kate's voice broke.

"She didn't want anyone to know," Mary declared. "Just Joe and me. We looked after her."

"And very well too, Mary. But there was nothing you could have done in the end," the doctor reassured her. "The attack was too strong this time. She had no chance." He handed Kate the death certificate he had written and Mary saw him out.

So clinical, in the end. No histrionics, no wailing and gnashing of teeth. Just the calm services of a calm man. Kate supposed the doctor dealt with death all the time.

But *she* didn't.

She wanted to scream. It wasn't fair! It wasn't right! That Phyllis should die so suddenly. That only hours ago she could be talking to her, laughing about Paul's obvious peevishness that Naomi had chosen her father over him, laughing at his childish chagrin, 'the selfishness of youth,' Phyllis had called it, though really, Paul hardly qualified for the 'youth' label any more.

How could she possibly die so suddenly? There had been no warning, no chance to say 'Goodbye!' Worse, no chance to say 'Thank you!'

Kate was shivering, hugging her cardigan round her shaking body. When did it turn so cold?

Oh bad form, Phyllis! This is bad form.

And only yesterday... *yesterday*... they'd sat and talked. They'd sat right there in Phylliss' gorgeous sitting room, and talked about her and Dan, where it was all going... or not going. And Phyllis didn't say a word about feeling ill, or tired. Just let Kate go on and on about Dan.

Maybe if I'd not been so self-absorbed, maybe I'd have seen she wasn't well.

All I cared about was how I felt about Dan. Instead of 'Dan, Dan, Dan.' I should have been looking after Phyllis.

"Oh, Phyllis, I didn't think I'd feel like this," she'd told her. "It's a physical pain," she said, pressing her hand to her chest.

"I really, really miss him coming round. I don't know what's happened, why he's stopped coming. Did he say anything to you?"

Phyllis shook her head. "Nothing. Maybe he's busy."

"But busy doing what?"

"*I* don't know. Why don't you phone him?"

"I can't!"

"Why not?"

"I just can't. I don't want him to think I'm desperate."

"Aren't you?"

They laughed together. *Yesterday! They laughed together only yesterday!*

"Oh Phyllis, I feel so silly. So out of control. I've never wanted anyone or anything so much. When he's near me, I just want to touch him, to feel him touch me. When he's not near, I ache to be with him. I want him so much it hurts. My own husband. And it seems I can't have him."

I, I, I, me, me, me...

"I don't know what to do. I just don't know what to do."

"Oh, you'll know when the time comes," Phyllis nodded wisely.

You'll know when the time comes.

It was one of the things Phyllis often said, *'You'll know when the time comes.'* But what did it mean? It always sounded so wise when Phyllis said it, but, suddenly, it didn't seem to make much sense to Kate. But, then, nothing made much sense right now.

Phyllis was dead.

Just like that.

Phyllis was dead.

Kate let the tears fall.

It felt so strange trying to organise a funeral for someone you hardly knew.

Kate had *thought* she knew Phyllis, but now she realised she only knew such a tiny part of her. Only what Phyllis had chosen to reveal. Phyllis was eighty-eight years old when she died, and Kate had known her for less than one. Eighty-eight years Phyllis had summed up in a very few sentences. She had never liked talking about herself. But, surely, in eighty-eight years there must have been so much *to* talk about. So many interesting places she'd been. Africa, for one. Yet she never told them about it. So many fascinating people she must have met. There was a photograph in the sitting room of Phyllis with an African witch doctor. Surely there was a story there worth the recounting? And what of other adventures she'd had?

Phyllis had chosen not to talk of herself, yet hers was surely a life worth recording? And now it was too late. All the stories died with her. Her history was lost forever.

Kate knew, with hindsight, that she should have drawn Phyllis out, talked less about herself, pushed Phyllis a little until she shared the treasures of eighty-eight years.

Regret is such a useless, impotent thing. It flows through the mind like slush running through a gutter: too slow to clear away the debris that clings to the sides, saturating the rubbish then freezing it in its swollen, distorted shape.

All the good times she'd had with Phyllis were being pushed to the edges of her mind, swollen and distorted out of shape by the regret they hadn't been different; they hadn't been spent examining Phyllis's life instead of her own. And what of her own? Would anyone remember her with tenderness, wish they had known her better? Is a life really lived if no one remembers its details? Does it become like a dream which, upon waking, can never quite be recalled? Or does having children mean that something of your life is preserved through them? When the seeds of a dying flower fall to the earth and grow again in their season, does anything of the original remain?

The loss of Phyllis was a double blow to Kate. She'd lost the friend she knew and the opportunity of discovering the woman she'd been.

Kate resolved to search for a diary, a notebook, letters, anything that could disclose the life that had been lived, anything that could prevent it from fading into obscurity as though it were no more than the imaginings of the night.

Meantime, she was left with the dilemma of the funeral: she didn't know who to contact, who to invite, who should take the service, who should come back afterwards for refreshments.

Thankfully, Mary came to her aid: she produced a list of instructions from Phyllis herself. Nothing had been left to chance. Phyllis had arranged her own funeral months and months in advance. Not only had she arranged who should be told, who should be there, who should take the service, she had even chosen her own coffin. She hadn't wanted a lot of fuss: a pompous ceremony by a pompous minister; a dreary service in a dreary crematorium or a sad goodbye round a cold hole in the ground. She wanted to be remembered by her friends in the place she loved to be.

They had a small, warm memorial service in the sitting room. No coffin present: she'd requested that her remains be dealt with at the crematorium while her friends gathered at the house. "It's only dust, after all," she'd written. And no dark clothes: she'd asked that they all dress in bright colours to 'send her off'. Flowers were not only allowed, but requested: lots and lots of flowers. But no lilies: it was the only flower Phyllis didn't like. She claimed they were sad flowers and she didn't want 'unnecessary sadness' around her. "There is enough sadness in life without putting it in vases," she told Mary once, when she had inadvertently bought lilies for one of the vases in the hall.

There was no sermon, no minister, but each friend shared a special memory of Phyllis, a memory they'd made together. "Preferably something funny," she'd asked.

So, as funerals went, it went well: unusual, but not dreary or overly sad.

Of course there *was* sadness. Everyone's lives had been enriched by their contact with Phyllis. Everyone would miss her dearly.

Kate gathered the stories of Phyllis's life, hoarding them in her memory for future perusal, craving a fuller picture. Not a word that was spoken that day fell as an unheeded crumb, but all were swept up by her eager, listening ear and saved to assuage her hunger. She shamelessly scavenged details from former colleagues and long-standing friends. *'What was she like as a doctor?': 'What was she like as a young woman?': 'What was she like as a friend?' : 'Did you know her as a married woman?': 'Was she happy?': 'Was she beautiful?'*

She added stories of her own, memories of her too-short time living here, in Phyllis's sunshine.

But, the more she added to the picture, the more she knew it was, at best, an impression rather than a likeness. As Kate looked around at everyone who had gathered to pay their respects to Phyllis, she wondered how long it would be until none of them remembered the sound of her voice or the feel of her skin. They all had their sadness and they all had their life.

Naomi came. She was ready to blame herself for causing Phyllis to have her heart attack. "It was too much for her. The nuisance phone calls, the stalking, the attack."

"Even if that was what hastened it... and it wasn't! That was hardly your fault," Kate reasoned. "Mary said she had already lived a lot longer than the doctors had predicted. Anyway, she loved you, loved having you around."

"But, if I hadn't been here."

"Please, Naomi, don't even go there. It's a nonsense and it would break Phyllis's heart to hear you talk like that. She did so much to help you. Not for you to add her death to your guilt list!"

"So, how was your dad?" Paul asked her.

"Oh, he was pleased to see me. We're kind of tip-toeing around one another right now, but, it's early days. We're going to be fine, I think. I've managed not to go shopping, at any rate," she added shyly.

"Good, good," he smiled at her. "D'you think, perhaps we could catch a movie together sometime? Or something?"

"Yeh, sure. Why not? Give me a ring later in the week."

"Yeh, yeh, of course." Paul sounded a little crestfallen.

"Give me time to settle a bit?"

"Oh, yeh! Sure," he nodded.

And Dan was there.

It wasn't really the time for tackling him on why he'd backed off, so Kate tried instead to avoid him. It wasn't difficult because there were plenty of people to talk to, plenty of plates to hand round. By the time everyone was leaving, she had managed to share only the briefest of conversations with him: expression of their mutual grief and condolence.

"I'm so sorry, Kate."

"Yes, it was a terrible shock."

"She was quite a lady."

"That's exactly what she was: a Lady. A real Lady. The kindest, wisest lady I've ever known," Kate said huskily.

"I'm so sorry."

But Kate had moved on to speak to Dr Leach.

"Had Phyllis decided on a name for the clinic?" Rosemary asked.

"No, but I thought we might call it 'The Phyllis Thaine Memorial Clinic'. What do you think?"

"Well, it's not very punchy, but it does say what we want it to be. A memorial to a special lady."

"Exactly!"

"To 'The Phyllis Thaine Memorial Clinic', then!" Rosemary raised her glass.

Chapter 27

The words echoed through her mind.

You'll know what to do when the time comes.

She laid back on the wet grass, the letter still in her hand, its pages stirring in the breeze; memories stirring in her mind, memories warmer than the breeze, shifting and changing like the grey clouds constantly changing shape overhead.

I told you, 'You'll know what to do when the time comes.'

Choices.

Suddenly, after all the stagnant years, there were choices.

But it wasn't sudden. She had worked her way to some of these choices. Phyllis had helped her. Over weeks and months, Phyllis had shown her the way.

Dear Phyllis. Kate smiled. She always smiled when she thought of Phyllis. Phyllis had been good for her.

She sat up, hugging her legs, already stiffening from the damp and cold, knowing she should get moving, but to walk on would be to move toward a decision and she could no more make the decision than catch the wind.

So she folded the letter and tucked it into her pocket and sat in a huddle on the hillside wondering at what point her life had been shaken out of the humdrum and brought to this hiatus.

It was Saturday, only a week after Phyllis's funeral, when Kate found the letter, addressed to herself, in Phyllis's desk. She didn't open it at first but decided to go for a walk. Not with the Club, but on her own, anywhere, anywhere she could be alone with only the sunshine and the cold wind to witness the grief that threatened to overwhelm her.

So, she had come here, to this cold, windy hillside, to read her precious letter.

Phyllis had known she was dying and had made her plans. Her will provided for all those she cared about. A Trust Fund had been set up for the clinic and it should run smoothly, financially, for the foreseeable future. She was offering Kate the post of President, Managing Director, whatever the Top-Dog would be called. She could continue to live in the clinic, if she chose, but, in her letter, Phyllis threw down the gauntlet: could she rebuild her marriage, putting the clinic in second place to her husband.

To do that, Kate knew she would have to show her hand. She'd have to let Dan know how she felt. Pride and fear made the decision impossible.

*Okay, Phyllis! Seems to me, the time has come... and you're wrong! I **don't** know what to do.*

Eventually, the damp, the cold and the approaching evening, won the day: she *had* to move, without the decision made.

As she was walking back to her car, she saw that Dan was waiting beside it, bathed in the warm glow of a glorious sunset; waiting for her, and her heart seemed to skip a beat. A flush spread across her cheeks, bringing warmth to them.

"Mary thought I'd find you here," he smiled. He opened the door of his car. "Here, jump in a minute, you look cold. I kept the engine running when I saw you coming."

"Have you been waiting long?" she asked as she settled gratefully into the warmth.

"No, just a half hour or so. Saw the car, knew you'd have to come soon." He nodded towards the warm blush in the sky. "And I knew you couldn't last too long in this cold. Not if you weren't walking all the time."

"How did you guess I wouldn't be? Walking all the time?"

"Mary told me you had a letter to read."

"Ah, yes, the letter."

"Are you okay?"

Kate shrugged. "Sort of," she said. "Phyllis has given me a lot to think about. Decisions to make; difficult, life-changing decisions."

"And have you made them?"

She shook her head. "No. I sat up there for what seemed like hours and I'm no nearer than when I first read the letter. One of Phyllis's favourite sayings was, 'You'll know what to do when the time comes.' Well, I don't!"

"Maybe that's because the time hasn't 'come' yet."

"How d'you mean?"

"Maybe you haven't got all the information you need to help you make the decision."

"Like?"

"Like, Kate," he put the car in gear. "Will you come somewhere with me for a bit? I could show you easier than tell you. Before the light's completely gone?"

"O-kay."

"It's all right. Nothing to be afraid of." And he drove out of the carpark.

"Where are you taking me?"

"Home, Kate. I'm taking you home."

Chapter 28

Stupidly, Kate thought Dan meant to drive her back to Phyllis's house. "It's okay," she told him. "I've got the car."

"I'll bring you back," he said. "You can pick it up later."

"But that's silly," she started to say that she would only have to come back to go back, when she realised that he didn't mean Phyllis's house. Of course, he didn't mean Phyllis's house. He wouldn't call that 'home': it wasn't *his* home. But, what really stopped her, was the sudden realisation that it wasn't *her* home either. It was *Phyllis's* home, of that she was certain. It would always be Phyllis's house, even now that she was gone.

They were having a sign made for the wall outside: 'The Phyllis Thaine Memorial Clinic'.

Could it ever be her home? Certainly, it was where she lived, just now, at any rate, but... was it *home*?

She still hadn't puzzled it out when they turned the corner and pulled up outside the house they had shared for twenty-eight years. *Home?* She wasn't sure of that either.

Dan shut off the engine and turned to look at her. "You've been very quiet," he remarked softly.

Kate nodded silently. "I'm confused," she admitted at last, her voice low and quiet. "You said you were taking me home and I just realised that I don't know where 'home' is any more."

Dan looked down at the keys in his hand. "I know, Kate, and I think that's my fault. No, I *know* that's my fault." He looked up at her. "Kate, I'm *so* sorry. I should never have done what I did. I should never have knocked down the summerhouse. It was unforgivable of me. You'll never know how much I regret it." The keys in his hand jingled as he grasped them tighter. "I want so much to make it up to you," he continued. "And there's only one way I think I can do that... or try to anyway." He started to get out of the car. "There's something I want to show you."

He led her round the side of the house, to go in the back door, as they had been in the habit of doing for the past twenty-eight years. But, as they turned the corner, she stopped, her hands flying up to her mouth. "Oh!" she exclaimed. "Oh, my goodness! Dan?"

"As you see, I've been kinda busy the past wee while. I hope... I hope it's all right?"

"All right?" Kate replied. "I don't know what to say."

"Just tell me that you like it," Dan suggested, pleading in his voice, his hands clasped before his face.

"It's beautiful," Kate said, shaking her head in disbelief, walking over to the brand new conservatory attached to the back of the house. "Did you build this yourself?"

Dan nodded proudly. "Twenty or so years late," he said. "But not too late, I hope?" he asked, his voice deepening with emotion. "I'm so sorry, Kate. I know it can't make up for the loss of your old summerhouse. That was *yours* and I shouldn't have touched it. But I thought... I hoped... that this might be *ours*. I thought perhaps we could furnish it together? Fill it with new dreams? Make it a special place for us to share?"

"Oh, Dan," she cried. "I thought you didn't want me any more. You'd stopped coming round."

"The work over there was finished," he said. "I had work to do here."

"I can see that," she agreed.

"It's not the old summerhouse. I know that. And I knew that there was no point in trying to rebuild it like it was."

Kate laughed. "It wouldn't be easy, that's for sure."

"I thought we could start again. I thought that if it was attached to the house it would be warmer. The central heating: I've put in extra radiators."

Kate looked at him. *"You* have? D'you mean *you* did it? Or you got someone in to do it?"

Dan sighed. "Oh ye of little faith. Yes. I mean *I* did it. Well, with a little help from Paul, and the kids."

"Paul? And the kids? They were in on this?"

"Of course."

"And Vicky?"

"Of course."

"The horrors! I saw Vicky and the boys just three days ago. They didn't say a word. Or any of the other times I've seen them over the past however many weeks you've been doing this! I can't believe them!"

"Look, are we just going to stand out here, discussing this?" Dan opened the conservatory door. "Or, maybe we can go in and get warm?" He stepped aside to let Kate go in before him.

She paused on the threshold and looked around herself in the last of the glowing twilight. The rest of the garden was tidy in a scrubbed sort of way. There was no trace of the old summerhouse: the debris was gone and the ground tidied and raked.

The new conservatory stood proudly against the house, its wooden frame newly varnished, the glass panes recently buffed till they shone.

Dan saw where her gaze settled. "I could have gone for a PVC frame but I thought you'd prefer the wood."

Kate nodded.

"It's more work, more upkeep."

"More natural, more 'us'."

"Exactly!"

It was a large structure, taking up the whole length of the back of the house. Where the back door used to be, there was now an archway into the kitchen.

"Easy access." Dan explained.

The sides were glass all round, rising up to the glass roof sloping back to the wall.

"Vicky thinks it'll need blinds, or voile curtaining or something for the sunnier days. I thought we'd think about that together, see what we feel after we've gotten used to it."

Kate stepped inside. It was warm. Now that the door was closed behind her, the gentle warmth spread round her like the joy that was rising in her heart as she looked at the shelf that ran all round the whole room, at about waist-height. All her potted plants were there. All of them rescued and looking well. She turned to Dan. "They seem to have thrived under your care."

"Beginner's luck," he shrugged.

"Thank you, Dan," she whispered. "For all of this," she embraced the whole scene with the graceful sweep of her arm.

"There's nothing much in it yet," he mumbled, clearing his throat. "I thought you might like to find some furniture. I thought maybe I could come with you? You could teach me how to spot the bargains."

Kate nodded. "I'd like that," she said. "Oh, my treasure chest!" she exclaimed, "You kept my treasure chest!" and she bent to touch its gorgeous waxed surface. "Oh, I'm so glad you kept my treasure chest."

"Actually," he coughed. "I found a new treasure to go inside it," he said proudly, opening the heavy, oak lid and reaching inside.

Kate waited, curious to see what he had found, what he would consider a 'treasure'.

He took out the old book he had rescued from the hole in the wall of the summerhouse. It was still in its fragile wrapping and he offered it proudly to Kate.

"Oh, Dan," she started to cry. "Oh, Dan."

"Beautiful, isn't it?" He watched as she gently unwrapped the silk from around it and, almost reverently, opened the book. "Wait till you read it," he said, as she stroked the old, browned pages. "It's... it's..." his voice failed him. "I can't explain. It touched me so deeply. As though it was written for *me*."

"Maybe it was, Dan."

"I found it in the brickwork when I knocked down the old summerhouse."

She nodded.

"It must be incredibly old," he continued. "I tried to find out when the summerhouse was built, when it appeared in the deeds, who built it, who could have hidden it." He shrugged. "But I had no luck tracing its ownership through the house records. You know, who owned the house before us, before them, and so on and so forth. But I couldn't come up with anything that made any sense."

Kate shook her head, hugging the book to her, tears running down her face.

"We always did guess the summerhouse couldn't have had planning permission. D'you know, I hadn't noticed before, but it's not actually on the deeds of the house!"

"It doesn't matter, Dan," she said, sitting on the old oak chest, caressing the book, obviously pleased with it.

"I know. I know," he agreed. He looked pleased to see her pleasure in his find. "I tried to get it valued," he said, pointing to the book. "That's when I met that Cartwright fellow, incidentally... but that's another story." He watched her gently turn the pages. "Silly, really, because it's one of those things you could never put a value on. Should never try to put a value on."

"But you said it was a treasure," Kate said through her tears.

"To me, yes. It's just so special, Kate. Obviously written by a woman."

Kate nodded.

He was puzzled that she should agree so readily without the chance to read it. But, then, Kate always had been intuitive about these sort of things. "Obviously by a very sad, a very sensitive woman," he added.

She nodded again.

"I *felt* it. It just... well, it just touched me. Like I said, it's like it was written for me. Like I was *meant* to find it."

Kate shook her head," No," she said. "It was written for me."

"You'd already found it?" Understanding dawned on Dan's face, disappointment too. "You already knew about it, didn't you?"

"I should do," said Kate. "I wrote it!"

Chapter 29

It had been years ago, when she first started going out to the old summerhouse, even before she had scraped the windows and scrubbed it out, but she had already started looking in second-hand shops for furniture and pots and bits and pieces... that's when she found the book.

It had been buried in among a stack of children's toys, bedfellow to broken dolls and Lego bricks. The basket had drawn her because there was an old model bus sticking up from the general muddle: she thought Paul would like it.

When she bent to examine it further, the corner of the book caught her eye so she dug it out too, recognising straight away that it was something rather special. Although it had been neglected and mishandled, it had survived in surprisingly good condition.

The woman behind the counter was less discerning and gave it to her for a few coins; she could no longer remember how many.

For a while, she just enjoyed touching it, running her fingers over the faded gold leaf, looking at the old, yellowed pages, smelling its antiquity: it would be hard to buy a notebook of that quality nowadays or even back when she found it. Eventually, she decided that she would use it as a sort of journal: a book of thoughts and memories, drawings, poems and the children's stories that they loved her to tell them. This would be the perfect place to record such intimacies. It would be a private thing, for her own eyes only.

In an old-fashioned newsagent, tucked away in Morningside, she joyously came across what she wanted: a dusty old bottle of brown ink. It may not have started out brown, but time had caused the pigments to fade, and it was a fine, pale brown colour now, and just what she felt would complement the yellowed pages.

Once, when she was in school, she had won an essay prize, a fountain pen, and she rummaged in the drawers of her dressing table at home till she found it, still in its presentation box, unused.

Now she had all the tools she needed to build a vessel of dreams.

And that's what she had done.

Over many sad, lonely evenings, her even copperplate flowed across the pages and the stories, poems and pictures that had so moved Dan were the outpourings from the deep springs of her heart.

"You wrote it?" Dan repeated, his voice husky with emotion.

She looked up at him, her eyes sparkling with tears. "I thought it was lost, gone with the rubble."

"It caught my eye. The scarf," he said, pointing to the flimsy material. "It caught my eye, the colour of it."

The scarf, she found in an antique clothes shop in the Grassmarket. Like Dan, the rich colour had caught her eye. Because it was pure silk, she had paid more than a few coins for it, but was glad to have found it.

"You called it a treasure?"

Dan nodded. "It's how I think of it. As soon as I lay eyes on it, I knew it was something valuable. I still do," he smiled.

"Thank you so much for keeping it safe."

"I'm more glad than ever that I did." He shuddered. "I would hate to have missed it, to have thrown it out."

They were still in the conservatory, Kate sitting on her beloved oak chest, Dan standing, leaning against the door-frame because there was no other furniture. "So, what do you think?" he asked, looking round the empty room. "Could we furnish this together? I thought we could bring some things back from Africa, bring sunshine into it."

"Africa?" she spluttered. "What d'you mean Africa?"

"I thought you might like to visit some of the places Phyllis had been. Find a little of her over there, perhaps?"

"She certainly had a love of Africa."

"I thought we could go there on our honeymoon."

"Honeymoon?"

"Yes, we never did have a proper one. Or, you could go to Africa yourself?" he teased.

"No," she blushed. "I think I'd rather honeymoon with you."

"Well, that's settled then! And we can bring back whatever you want. Whatever would help to make this house your home again."

A fresh wave of emotion swept over Kate. "Oh, Dan," she sighed. "It isn't souvenirs from Africa, or anywhere else that makes a house a home."

"I just thought, Phyllis..."

"Oh, forget Phyllis," she started to say, then quickly, "No, I didn't mean that. I just meant..."

"You seem to like Phyllis's house so much. You seem at home there."

"I love the house. Who wouldn't? And I loved Phyllis. But it isn't *home*. Home is where, well, it's where you *fit*, you feel *right, comfortable*. It's where you love to *be*, and where you feel loved."

Dan knelt in front of her. "Kate Morgan, will you marry me?"

"Get up, you idiot! I did that thirty-five years ago!"

"Yes, but I never did ask you properly, and maybe it's a bit late, but I've been wanting for the longest time to put that right."

Kate gently touched his face. "Oh, Dan. I thought I'd lost you. I thought you'd changed your mind about me, didn't want me to come home."

He sat beside her, confident of the solid oak chest, confident in his love for her. "Kate, Kate. I've never stopped wanting you. Since the first time I set eyes on you. It's like with the book," he explained, touching it where it lay on her lap. "I knew *you* were special too, something to be treasured but I," he searched for the right words. "I just seemed to forget *how* to treasure you. Somewhere, among all the bricks and mortar of family life, I seemed to lose what was important, hide away the feelings I should have expressed. But I never stopped loving you," he assured her, taking her face in his hands. "Just didn't know how to show you."

And, in those few sentences, he spoke more of love than he had in the thirty-five years they'd shared a marriage, twenty-eight years of it living in this house.

And *that's* what made it home.

End

Christine Campbell

Christine Campbell

www.ingramcontent.com/pod-product-compliance
Lightning Source LLC
Chambersburg PA
CBHW030959260626
47169CB00002B/610